Multnomah County Library

Books are due on the latest date stamped below.
Fines are 10¢ per day for adult materials; 5¢ per OR
day for juvenile materials.

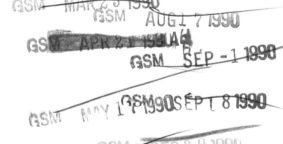

DROPSHOT

Tor books by Jack M. Bickham

Ariel
Day Seven
Dropshot
Miracle Worker
The Regensburg Legacy
Tiebreaker

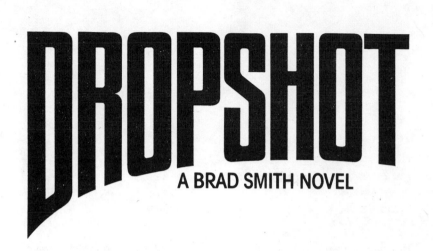

DROPSHOT

A BRAD SMITH NOVEL

JACK M. BICKHAM

TOR®

A TOM DOHERTY ASSOCIATES BOOK
NEW YORK

Popular Library

DROPSHOT

Copyright © 1990 by Jack M. Bickham

A Tor Book
Published by Tom Doherty Associates, Inc.
49 West 24th Street
New York, N.Y. 10010

Library of Congress Cataloging-in-Publication Data

Bickham, Jack M.
    Dropshot / by Jack M. Bickham.—1st ed.
        p.   cm.
    "A Tor book"—T.p. verso.
    ISBN 0-312-93228-6: $17.95
    I. Title.
PS3552.I3D76 1990
813'.54—dc20   89-39880
                                                              CIP

Printed in the United States of America

First edition: January 1990

0 9 8 7 6 5 4 3 2 1

DROPSHOT

one

Al Hesser's letter arrived early on a beautiful October day in Dallas, the kind of day that makes you forgive the ugly sky-anvil days of spring and the endless dusty furnace of summer: a day perfectly cobalt clear, with the temperature at seventy and only the faintest breeze out of the south. Only a crazy man could fail to rejoice on such a day.

Unfortunately, it was the autumn I was pretty crazy.

AL HESSER'S COURT COLLEGE
The Emerald Resort
Isle of St. Maarten
October 2

Dear Brad,

The world-famous Al Hesser's Court College is expanding! And our growth means a FANTASTIC opportunity for you, as a tennis professional, to share in our good luck and enjoy a FREE, NO OBLIGATION vacation!

During October and November—before the big tourist season begins on this tropical paradise in the Lesser Antilles—I'm inviting many of my old pals from our professional tennis playing days to come to The Emerald and have fun in the sun! Best of all, this vacation holiday package, worth more than $3,000 a week at going rates, WILL COST YOU NOTHING!!

What's the deal? It's simple, Brad. When you and other great players show up at my Court College, it makes for good publicity—and more. People see that my operation is TRULY THE FINEST AND WORLD CLASS. They rush to sign up for one of my courses here. Those that come in while you're here will hope to maybe visit with you, maybe even be so lucky as to rally with you and other net greats.

I want YOU, Brad, with me here at my famed Al Hesser's Court College, one or two weeks. No charge to you except your airfare down, and I guarantee you'll have a blast, pahdnuh! CALL AND SAY WHEN YOU'LL ARRIVE!

Al Hesser

It was one of those computer-generated form letters, the kind that inserts your name once or twice to make you think Al typed it himself. If I knew Al, he had probably sent out fifty of them.

It sounded like Al: loud braggadocian, arrogant and outrageous. Sportscasting had had its Howard Cosell, basketball had its Dick Vitale, and tennis had Al Hesser.

Al was not entirely a bad sort, and once he had been a solid second-rank player on the world circuit. His entrepreneurship was definitely world class. His wildly promoted "Court College" tennis camps—first at Hilton Head and now also on St. Maarten—had grown hugely, leaving pioneers like Vic Braden in the dust.

At the best of times I would have ignored Al's offer. In my mind I had three file drawers: *do now*, *do later*, and *too hard*. Putting up with Al would always have been filed as too hard. This fall, just about everything was in that category.

I tossed the letter onto the file cabinet beside my

leather-working bench in the extra bedroom of my condominium and thought no more about it. Then.

Two days later, on Friday, a member-in-good-standing of our tennis club in Richardson came in early to practice for a weekend business tournament in Fort Worth. During warm-ups, his $400 Italian racket inexplicably shattered at the neck. Panic. Without his much-loved racket, my member knew he would disgrace himself in Fort Worth.

"I've got to find a duplicate!" he moaned.

"I'll check," I said. I figured the nearest duplicate was in Rome.

Miracle of miracles, on the fourth telephone call I located the exact same racket at the Netmasters Club in South Dallas. I drove there, checked it out, told the Netmasters pro shop manager to string it at sixty, and said I would wait around.

Standing outside the shop, I smoked a cigarette and bleakly watched a couple of middle-aged hackers having a great time on the nearest of a dozen immaculate, sun-flooded Tartan Turf courts.

If I hadn't been half-crazy with grief, I would have enjoyed this moment. I love watching hackers play when they're doing it for fun, and they don't take themselves too seriously.

There's a powerful beauty in world-class tennis that makes you blink your eyes, sometimes, trying to believe it. But from that class down—through the ranks of grim, posturing, kill-'em pretenders—there's nothing much fun to watch again until you get to the people who simply love tennis and in their enthusiasm and ebullience—and lack of skill or coaching—play a game so innocent and filled with human imperfection and wonderful accidents that it again becomes a joy to behold.

The two gents on court number one were in this class. Watching them, I was aware of the sadness in me, a realization that even moments like this meant nothing to me anymore. And I mourned this, too, this loss resulting from loss.

Try, goddammit! I told myself angrily. So I watched.

The player nearest me, on my right, was perhaps sixty, a shade under six feet tall, a little overweight, only a fringe of faded kinky hair remaining on top of his dark brown skull. He had broad, friendly features and was playing with a $60 Prince. His red shorts, white T-shirt bulging over a slight potbelly, and Converse shoes were off-the-shelf, unpretentious.

His game was unpretentious, too. He had a moderately big, flat serve off an awkward western forehand grip, but he moved around the court like a submarine maneuvering in deep water. As I watched, he trundled crosscourt after a backhand, netted it, and bent backward at the waist, hands to his eyes. "Oh, no!" he cried. Then his big homely grin shone. "Nice shot, Ted!"

"Lucky!" his friend Ted called graciously from the backline. He was shorter, perhaps 5-8, whip-slender, deeply tanned, with a full head of bushy gray hair and a goatee. I guessed his age at mid-fifties. His togs were as ordinary as the bigger man's, and he was the better player, with smoother legs and a passable forehand. He walked to the net and put his elderly Dunlop Maxply on the netcord. "We better stop, Jerry, or we'll be worn out before those guys get here."

Jerry nodded thankfully, and the two of them came my way, heading for the Coke machine beside me.

"Hi there," the one called Jerry said to me. He had a rich, chocolate voice. "Great day, isn't it?"

"Beautiful," I said, moving aside so he could feed quarters into the machine.

His friend Ted patted his own chest with a gesture of immense satisfaction. "Tell you what. They couldn't have picked a better week for this tournament."

"Tournament?" I said.

4

Ted looked me over, taking in my dirty cutoffs, scuffed Adidas, and faded blue T-shirt. I hadn't shaved this morning and had been working on the club swimming pool filter when my member broke his favorite racket, so I had residual grease on my hands. There was no snobbery in Brer Ted's once-over, but he was clearly putting me in the outsider category.

"Not a member?" he asked, putting it as delicately as possible.

"No, I work at another club."

Jerry handed his friend a Coke and glanced at me. "Want one?"

"No thanks."

He tugged on the fliptop and drank thirstily. "Big tournament," he rumbled with heavy irony. "*Big* tournament!"

Ted filled me in: "Open deal. Twenty bucks apiece to get in it. Goes to the Cancer Society."

Jerry chimed in, "They said it's open to everybody, but they pair you with guys your own class." He rolled his eyes. "I hope so, man."

"It's for a good cause, anyway," I observed, starting to turn away.

Ted's eyes got sad. "Yep. I lost my wife to cancer two years ago."

I turned back to him, but didn't say anything.

There are times like that when you want to say you *notice*. I've never known how to say it in a way that will make sense. We walk around, making our social noises, and occasionally someone opens the shutters over his eyes and we see the same desolation we have felt. We want to tell them we see that glimpse, that we share something crucial. But it always seems to come out wrong, and everyone ends up being embarrassed, or mystified. And so we don't try to say it.

So I just went back into the pro shop, leaving them there with their Cokes.

Inside, Bernie was just finishing with the racket that cost a lot more than the first car I had ever owned, and while watching him tie off and trim, I looked out through the dark windows and saw that my new friends' opponents had arrived: two young guys, college age, six-footers, uniformly tanned and blond and coiffed, wearing expensive tennis whites and carrying several rackets each in leather cases. Even through the glass you could smell the condescending arrogance. My guys stood chatting friendily with them while cases were opened, $300 weapons taken out and ponged against heels of palms to test string tension.

"Here you go," Bernie said, handing over the racket.

I paid him and we visited a couple of minutes. Then I waited through a telephone call to say so long, and watched the match that had started outside the glass on the nearest court.

My poor guys were getting slaughtered. The first smiles of fun and enthusiasm had already faded from their faces. As I watched, big Jerry served a fireball and lumbered netward, but the opposing jock in a headband handled it easily, returning it to Jerry's feet. Jerry awkwardly got it back, almost falling down, and Headband brought his racket up from the pavement in a huge loop. The ball sailed over Jerry's head, a vicious topspin lob, and hit near the baseline for a clean winner.

Jerry hustled back to retrieve the ball, and the two kids smirked at each other.

By the time Bernie got off the phone and I got my receipt and said goodbye, the slaughter outside had become a massacre. Both my guys had been broken at love, and unless I had missed something they had yet to win a point. Headband was fond of dink shots and lobs, and had poor Jerry soaked with sweat and visibly struggling to get in enough oxygen after repeated, futile attempts to chase down shots tantalizingly just out of reach. Ted, my smaller guy, was poaching a lot at the net, trying to help, but

Headband was toying with him, going behind him every time.

As I left the shop, the other young player, a handsome kid with an ocean of freckles, started to serve. He tossed the ball and came over the top beautifully, blasting a comet to the deepest corner for a clear ace.

Poor Jerry, who hadn't had time to so much as make a twitch after it, called out, "Great serve!" But the cheer was phony, forced. He had come out expecting to have some fun, and maybe help friend Ted contribute to a good cause. They weren't having any fun. They were getting humiliated. As I paused in the shade to watch a couple more points, the young studs began hitting soft ones just out of reach to enhance the enjoyable humiliation.

They had that look about them—that glossy, super-cool, condescending air of contempt that I despise more than most things in this world. It crossed my mind that it would be pleasant to get either of them oncourt, and destroy him.

But it was none of my business. The world was full of assholes. I started to walk away.

"Back, Jerry!"

The yell from Ted made me turn back. The little tableau was frozen in time.

Jerry was at the net, with Ted back—a losing position for a doubles team in the first place. Worse, the moment was frozen because Ted evidently had scooped up a desperation get, a high, lazy lob that was going to clear the net by only a foot or two. So there it was: the ball just at the top of its trajectory, Headband moving back a step with murderous eyes raised to the target, Jerry standing there in front of him, just across the net, his Prince at chest level, gamely waiting to try to volley it back.

I saw it coming. But Jerry didn't.

The ball descended. Headband wound up for an overhead blast.

He could have put it away anywhere on the court. He aimed right at Jerry. *Wham!*

I didn't see the ball, and of course Jerry didn't either. It hit him squarely in the face, staggering him back two steps. He put a dazed hand to his mouth, and suddenly there was bright red everywhere.

"Partner!" Ted cried, hurrying forward to where Jerry was staring numbly at his blood-covered hand and wrist.

Freckles and Headband came to the net. Their eyes met for part of a second, and they almost started laughing. Headband instead did the sportsmanlike thing. He vaulted the net in a single bound, like Superman. "Gosh, man!" he cried. "I'm sorry about that! I thought you would get out of the way!"

I strolled back nearer the court. Ted got a towel and Jerry tried to stanch the bleeding, meanwhile assuring the studs that he knew the blow hadn't been intentional, it was his fault for not dodging, great shot, et cetera. They did a good job of pretending remorse and concern. Ted was sheet-white and trembling.

The bleeding didn't seem to want to slow down. Seething, I went oncourt and offered to take a look.

"It's split clear through, Jerry, my friend. You need some stitches."

Jerry nodded. He was still a little dazed. "My doctor isn't far."

"I'll drive you," Ted said.

"No, you stay and play some more, man. You *paid* to play."

"I don't—"

"It's not that big a deal, man. Stay. Find you another partner." And Jerry lumbered off, holding the towel to his mouth.

"Well," Freckles said with a good imitation of sadness, "I guess that's the match."

"But," Headband offered gallantly, "if you can

8

scrounge up a partner, we have the court for an hour. We can still have some fun."

Ted looked around forlornly at the pretty people on other courts. "I don't belong here," he said sadly. He meant the statement in more ways than one.

Headband looked at me, taking in the scuffed tennis shoes, dirty cutoffs, stubble beard. "How about you?"

"What?" I said. I was so angry I didn't trust myself. For months I had been almost out of control. Seeing big, dumb Jerry creamed for no reason had set off something violent in me.

"I'm talking to you," Headband said, just managing to control the mirthful twitch at the corner of his mouth. "Do you play?"

All right, asshole, fine. "Yes. I play a little."

"Play with the old guy here, then."

"I—"

"Hell. Come on. You can use one of my spare rackets. We'll take it easy on you."

I looked at Ted. "What think, my friend?"

His forehead wrinkled with misery, but he was trapped and he knew it. "Well—"

Headband bounded to his racket case and came back with a composite. "Here you go." It was his cheapest racket.

Ted moved close. "I guess my heart just isn't in this anymore."

"You want to stop?"

"No." He blinked sorrowfully, a spanked puppy. "They want to play some more. I hate to disappoint them."

"Right," I said. "We wouldn't want to disappoint them."

We lined up. They let me serve without warm-ups. I hit the first one just right and had the satisfaction of seeing Headband's eyes change when the yellow blur went past his frantic, outstretched backhand. I eased up slightly on Freckles in the add court and he got it back, and I caught the

9

volley coming in and hit it down the alley for another winner. Then I aced Headband again and after the next serve went over behind Ted to get an alley return and lob it to the far corner, and then catch the short return lob and blast it between them for a winner. I reminded myself to take it easier, the bulky knee brace I usually wore to play was miles from here.

"Hey!" Ted panted. His expression had begun to change. There was a grin starting in there somewhere. "Hey! You're pretty good!"

"Lucky bounces, Ted." I tossed Freckles a ball.

The expression in their eyes across the net gave me a sickish pleasure. Suddenly they weren't having quite so much fun. Nobody to humiliate, all of a sudden. *Who is this bum?* they were thinking.

My intent—with the anger welling out of my own half-crazy grief—was to play them the entire hour, every miserable second of it, and punish them. I had not been able to do anything about that airplane. I had not been able to move the mountain. I had not been able to kiss her cold lips and breathe life back into them. I had not been able to abide my existence since then. *This* stupid, shitty little bit of wrongness I could do something about. And I intended to make them eat it until they dropped, or the court time ran out.

But on Freckles's second serve, with me at the net, Headband facing me, Ted managed to get the serve back and Freckles tried to lob over my head for a winner. It was a little short, and without premeditation my craziness took over.

I could have hit it anywhere. But there he was—just as Jerry had faced him earlier. I timed it right.

Headband screamed and went to his knees, and then over onto his back, legs bent up in agony. He clutched at his groin—just where my forehand drive had hit him at a speed of about ninety miles per hour.

10

"Oh, God!" he cried, writing. "Oh, *Jesus!* Oh! I'm *dying!*"

"Gosh, man!" I said. "I'm sorry about that! I thought you would get out of the way!"

Freckles, kneeling beside his pal, looked up at me. His eyes showed he had gotten it.

I put my arm over shocked Ted's shoulder. "Thanks for the game, my friend. I hear a swimming pool filter calling me."

I went to the car and drove back north on the Central Expressway, thinking how stupid I had just been. Noble Brad Smith, knight of the tennis court and swimming pool filter, striking a blow for justice and the American way. What would my beautiful lady shrink think about *this?*

Maybe I wouldn't tell her. Maybe I wouldn't see her again. I was almost as sick of her as I was of myself. Nothing was going to get me unstuck anyway. A man was supposed to get on with things, have some courage. But I was getting nowhere.

I got back to the club in Richardson and walked into the pro shop, and there he stood.

"Brad," he said, smiling, walking over to shake hands.

"Collie," I said, "what the hell do *you* want?"

Collie Davis held out a sheet of paper. I saw that it was a duplicate of the Al Hesser letter I had received earlier in the week.

"Did you get one of these?" he asked.

two

In simpler times, Collie Davis had been the man who sometimes provided contact for me. Maybe you would have called him my case officer.

I should explain.

In the years when my nerves were good and my reflexes hadn't been over thirty, and professional tournament tennis was my life, the tour had taken me all over the world. Once, quite a while ago, before a French Open, Collie had bought me a drink in a cafe off the Place Vendome and revealed that whoever he worked for knew just about as much about me as I did. Who he worked for, as it developed, was the Central Intelligence Agency. What he wanted, as it developed, was for me to pick up an envelope from a locker attendant during the tournament and deliver it to him through an intermediary.

I had been in Vietnam and had had some friends killed, which tends to make you think in black and white rather than in all the shades of gray so dear to the intellectuals. Whatever our side did might not be all good, as I saw it, but it was infinitely better than what the other people were up to. You may, if you are smarter than I am, figure I was shallow and over-idealistic. Think what you want. I agreed.

Over the next handful of years my tennis career went great, and I was lucky enough to win most of the big ones. Most of the time I was a tennis player, nothing more. But on a few other occasions I was contacted by Collie, or someone like him, and I did some other things. My tennis career provided, as they say, perfect cover.

It was no big deal. Once or twice it got very slightly dangerous, but not much. Mostly it was routine, which is to say, done right. While recovering from a knee injury one time, I even got the benefit of some intensified training in Virginia, the kind the real guys get.

That was long ago. Collie worked stateside now, and sometimes we saw each other. Ordinarily I was happy to see him.

"Just a matter of information," he said that night when we met in the Steak & Ale.

"Did I get a letter from Al Hesser? Yes."

"Do you plan to go?"

"Of course not."

"What are your reasons?"

"For not going down there?"

"Yes. It's a free vacation. You must have good reasons for not going."

"Yes, Collie, I have three. One, Al Hesser is an asshole. Two, Al Hesser is an asshole. Three, Al Hesser is—"

"You might do us a service if you were to accept."

"Forget it," I told him.

He flushed with irritation. "You haven't heard what I have to say yet."

"Collie, whatever you say, the answer is no."

"Why did you agree to meet me tonight if you won't even hear me out?"

"Number one," I told him, "I wanted you out of the club. Number two, you offered dinner, on you. Which means on the Company. I don't recall ever turning down a chance at a free meal courtesy of my good friends in Virginia."

"Bitterness doesn't become you, friend."

"If you don't like it, Collie, take a walk."

He started to reply hotly, but then seemed to think better of it. He frowned at the menu in silence. A pulse thumped in his neck.

In the almost two years since I had seen him, Collie Davis had aged considerably. His hair was almost all gray now, and he was thinner. Too thin. I remembered when he had been young and full of grins and optimism. Even two years ago, when he came to me with the proposition that changed my life—first making it a dream and then turning it into a hell of loss—he had had a quiet enthusiasm. That was gone now. He was middle-aged.

It was wrong and unfair to blame him for anything. But I did. I blamed *everybody*.

Two years ago they had needed someone with tennis credentials to go to Belgrade and help them get Yugoslavia's rising court star, Danisa Lechova, out of the country—help her defect to the U.S. They could get me invited to the celebrity portion of the new Belgrade International Tournament, and provide writing assignments from two of the best tennis magazines. As a club pro in Richardson, a part-time tennis journalist, and a tournament player with his future all behind him, I was a natural for the part. I had accepted readily enough. Collie Davis had not had to twist my arm.

He had not forced me to go and meet Danisa and fall in love with her.

He hadn't caused her airplane to hit that mountain almost a year ago, either.

He had even sent me a sympathy card, a dollar one.

"Look," I said after the first drinks were on the table and we had ordered the steaks. "I didn't mean to take your head off. I'm just not good for anything right now."

His eyes sagged. "It's a very simple request, Brad."

I watched him and fought an irrational impulse to hit him—this man who had always been decent, and a friend.

"All we want you to do," he told me, "is go down there, have a good time, and . . . sort of keep your eyes open for us."

"Watching for what?"

"Just . . . being alert."

"No."

"Maybe you would think it over."

"No. I am doing just fine right here in Richardson, Texas, pal, teaching a few students and maintaining the pool equipment and messing with my new hobby of leather-working. Did you know I have taken up leather-working? My shrink told me to find some new hobby to interest me in my spare time. You cut leather and you learn to punch and roll it and you make belts and such. It is supposed to be good therapy."

"Brad, Jesus Christ."

Without any warning, I had tears in my eyes. I felt like a total fool. "Consider the matter closed."

His face twisted. "I'm sorry, man."

"Don't give me any of your goddamn sympathy! I don't need it!"

The dinner didn't go too well after that. We talked about other things. Collie did not mention Al Hesser, or the letter, again. At 10:15 we stood in front of the restaurant.

"You won't reconsider the possibility?" he asked.

"No."

"Okay." He held out his hand.

We shook, and then he walked away from me, a too-slender man, getting bald, alone in the dark. I wrapped my self-pity around me like a nice warm afghan, and went home.

"Brad?" the voice said on the telephone early one afternoon the following week. "This is Pat Reilly."

15

"Good lord," I said. "Serve to the backhand and I'll poach."

His chuckle sounded warm, the old Pat. "How goes it, my friend?"

"Okay," I lied. "Where are you?"

"DFW Airport. I don't leave until morning. Can we get together?"

"I can be out there in an hour."

"I don't want to put you out."

"You're not putting anybody out. It's my day off."

"I can rent a car and meet you somewhere."

I hesitated, looking at the eight-by-ten picture of Danisa on the bookcase beside the telephone. What I was supposed to do now was tell Pat that driving out there was no imposition, that I would love to have him spend the night at my condo, and I could drive him back to DFW in time for his flight in the morning. That was what I was supposed to do, and what I would have done ordinarily.

As much as I loved Pat Reilly, however, having a house guest was another of those things in the *too hard* file. I could put up a good front for an hour or two, maybe. I didn't want anyone around overnight.

I told him, "Let me come pick you up and help you find a motel. Then we'll attack a Texas-sized steak someplace."

He sounded pleased by the offer. I showered, shaved, changed into clean cotton slacks and sleeveless shirt, and backed the Bronco out of the garage into the fiery Texas afternoon sun.

Trying to stay out of the way of the Mercedes and BMWs playing Indy 500 on the LBJ Expressway, I tooled along toward the airport at a sedate sixty miles per hour. Traffic was light at the mid-afternoon hour, and there were no problems. The blinding sun glittered off north Dallas's explosion of new business buildings: amber glass spires and blue porcelain blocks and mirror-dazzling concavities and great faceless monoliths, and here and there the tumbled immensity of a dirt-colored stone shopping mall or apart-

16

ment complex, and I registered some of the names without really thinking about them: Unisys; TRW; Panasonic; Honda; IBM; Delta; Phillips; AT&T; Texaco; Ford; Tandy; Saks; Southwest; Icom; RCA; Technics; Mobil; Delco; Hitachi. The Dallas megapolis had continued to mushroom even as dreams crumbled in other Texas metroplexes such as Houston. At some magic point, a city reached a density— of people and money and power—that made it keep growing despite its problems, its own fiscal gravity sucking in new investment and construction like a black hole pulls in matter by virtue of its density. Dallas, for good or ill, had reached that point. There were new roads, new complexes, new massive buildings, entire new cities everywhere. Half of what I drove through looked like it had been dumped down whole yesterday.

I had seen it before—all except the part that really had been built yesterday—and I let memories flood in as I drove to pick up Pat Reilly.

A former all-American at Stanford, Pat had been in the top one hundred in the professional tennis world for a long time. He had won few majors, but was always competitive and won the French once, and twice made the finals at old Forest Hills.

Comparatively short and squatty in stature, he moved the court well and had an adequate serve. As he slowed down in later years, he played sort of like Harold Solomon did, sending up moonballs to harass younger attacking opponents and to give himself time to get back to midline for the next shot. As a singles player he was good, but as a doubles player he was great, with fantastic intuition and a marvelous sense of the angles, and that was where I came in: we were partners on the pro circuit for six years.

It was Bud Collins, I think, who first called us Mutt and Jeff at Wimbledon. Pat didn't like it much, but as with most things he laughed it off and went right on scurrying after balls no one in his right mind would have tried for, sending up those infuriating lobs, and fighting his guts out beside me against guys who should have beaten our tails off. I had a cabinet full of trophies in my condominium bedroom to prove that sometimes we clicked. One year we even won the Davis Cup doubles, and that, since it was for the country, meant most of all.

More important than the titles was the friendship.

It may be that there have been doubles teams composed of people who didn't like each other, but I am not aware of them. Doubles is to tennis what bridge is to cards: the partnership is everything, and to do really well at it, the two members have to learn to anticipate, understand, sometimes sacrifice for each other. Oncourt and off, Pat and I had been close for a long time.

It had been a year since I had seen him this time. Before the thing that had happened to Danisa. Pat had been working at a California club and playing in some celebrity tournaments. There had been a couple of letters from him that I had never gotten around to answering. I felt bad about that. Unfailingly cheerful, unpredictable, and as honest as the day is long, Pat Reilly was one of the few people on earth I really would have gone to the wall for.

I wondered what brought him overnight to Dallas.

Driving through the acres of parking lots at DFW, I followed the Delta terminal signs and approached the glass-walled exit area. I spotted Pat well off, long before I could get the Bronco through the crazy-angled cars and vans picking up other passengers. Short, bareheaded in the fierce sun, with a lumpy canvas bag slung over his shoulder, he was wearing a loud Hawaiian shirt, white duck pants, and deck shoes. As I got nearer, he spotted me and his grin shone like a lighthouse. Dodging agilely between impatient vans and buses, he hotfooted his way to meet me halfway.

Jerking the door open, he tossed his bag over the seat into the back and climbed inside, slamming the door behind him. "Holy whillikers! Turn up the air-conditioning, boy! My pants zipper is melting!"

"Your pants zipper was always melting," I observed

18

mildly, working my way back into the through lane and drawing an angry honk from a motel van driver.

"You can say that again." Pat chuckled. He banged me on the shoulder. "How you been, old bean?"

"Fair to middling." I fell easily back into the old kind of talk. "What brings you to our fair climes?"

"Well, I'm on the way to the Netherlands Antilles, my man, where I'm going to suck up to celebrities and use up every bit of free hospitality I can get out of obnoxious Al Hesser."

"You got a letter too, then."

"Yowsah, yowsah. Didn't you?"

"Yes. But I pitched it."

"That's what I thought you'd do, my man. And that's why I'm here. To change your mind and get you to come with me. Think of it! Fun in the sun! All to the—"

"Hold it, Pat," I cut in.

He stared at me. "Uh-haw?"

"Did anybody put you up to this?" I asked.

He looked blank. "What the hell do you mean?"

I backed off immediately. "Nothing." My first thought had been that Collie Davis had been in touch with him—wanted Pat to work on me to go to St. Maarten with him. But—while I thought I had had some hints—I had absolutely no certain knowledge that Pat had ever done anything whatsoever for the CIA. It was something you didn't discuss. And maybe he hadn't—maybe his visit was just as innocent as it appeared.

"So how did you get off work to go down there?" I asked.

"Let us," he suggested somberly, "find a place to imbibe. And we can discuss it, as they say, at length."

In the dim, cool recesses of a bar at the Holiday Inn, Pat swizzle-sticked his Harvey Wallbanger and reminisced about a tournament once where we were down 4–6, 4–6, 6–3, 0–5 and 15–30, and got charged up when my backhand down the line kicked up chalk in the corner, and we came all the way back to win the thing, 7–5, 7–5, in five hours and fifteen minutes. I leaned back and turned my spritzer around and around in its tiny pool of sweat and waited for him to get back to business.

After forty minutes, he did.

"You look peaked," he told me. Then, without waiting for a reply, he added, "What you need, my man, is a change of scenery."

"And you think St. Maarten is it?"

"Of cawse. I'm headed there now. Why don't you get a leave of absence from your snooty club here and come down there with me and hang out for a while at a *real* snooty place? Change of pace will be good for you. Sunshine will do wonders."

I glanced at my watch. "My timepiece says October, Pat. Fall is the best time in Dallas, and it's real sunny, too."

He reached out and caught my wrist, staring at my heavily worked black leather watchband. "Wow! Is that a piece of work!"

"Thanks."

"Thanks?"

"Made it myself."

"You're shitting me!"

"Back a few months ago . . . when I was *really* pretty crazy, my psychologist—"

"You're seeing a psychologist?" he asked, incredulous.

It stung and stirred my anger. "It doesn't make me a pussy."

"Oh, no!" He rubbed his eyes, embarrassed by his slip, and trying to recover. "I didn't mean that, man! I just meant . . . I guess I figured you were the kind of guy that would never . . . uh . . . want to admit he might need some of that kind of help . . . uh . . . and I think I am rapidly inserting my foot deeper into my mouth, here—"

"When Danisa died, I went off the deep end," I told him. "One night I had the revolver in my hand and was down to thinking about whether to do it in the bathroom or the garage, for the least mess. Then something clicked in my head and I decided maybe I didn't want to be that kind of a quitter. Which is when I asked around and found this doctor, and among the things she did was convince me to scrounge up a new hobby to take up some of my alone time. Which is where the leather-working came in. It's kind of neat. I'm not doing as much of it as I was, but maybe I'm not quite as crazy, either. Although there are days. And now let's change the subject."

Pat studied me soberly, his sheepdog eyes filled with love. Then he sort of shook himself. "Yowsah. Back to St. Maarten. Picture it, my man: a lush resort on the Dutch side of the island, not far from Philipsburg. Palm trees, gorgeoso irrigated championship golf course, casinos out the kazoo, sixty-four championship courts, the moonlight over ancient tropical hills, the Love Boat steaming in in all its communion-white splendor, lovelies of all ages and persuasions—the persuasions being yes, hell yes, oh my God yes, and your place or mine—"

"And shilling for Al Hesser."

Pat grimaced. "Well, nothing is perfect."

"I'm not interested."

"Wish you were."

"How did *you* get off long enough to take up Al's offer?"

Pat's lazy, pasted-on grin became a shadow of itself. "It is not a fun tale, my friend."

"Want to tell?"

He sighed. "It seems there was a little ladies' tournament. Members and guests. One of the local queen bees, name of Davona Redwine, to be precise, decided she didn't like the seed position I gave her when I drew up the brackets. So, good rich lawyer wife that she was, she came by and talked to me about fixing the seeds so she could cruise into the semis, as would befit her sense of her own importance and prowess. I said no. I mean, my man, I was

21

diplomatic and everything! I thought that was it. Was that it? Wrong.

"A night or two later, the lady appears at the door of my humble bachelor abode and suggests that she has been ravenously lusting after my moist, plump body for ever so long, and she is here to take the edge off what she knows is a mutual burning desire."

Pat removed the swizzle stick and downed a fourth of the Wallbanger. "You got any cigarettes?"

"I quit."

"Again? Shit." He signaled to the mini-clad waitress. "Darling, will you take this five dollars and buy me a pack of Winstons and keep the change, please? Thank you. You're sweet." He watched her move away with the elegant swish of twenty-year-old hips. "Holy mackul, Andy. If she was of age, or if I wasn't a hundred years old—"

"You were saying."

"Yeah. Well, I told the lady she was married. She said she hadn't thought that would hold me back. I told her I was quaint that way . . . had been ever since Sandy put the horns on me with that doctor, and forcibly changed my previously ultra-liberal attitude toward adultery and such like."

He sighed again. "To make a long gross story only gross, Mrs. Redwine did not take kindly to being turned out on her elegant ass in a midnight thundershower. She came by the next day and kindly asked me—again—to readjust the brackets. Once more, sir, in my earnest nobility, I declined with tact. So the gorgeous Mrs. Redwine sullenly goes out and plays the match as scheduled, and gets her pretty butt waxed by a fifty-two-year-old lady with a killer moonball and the patience to scurry around endlessly, getting everything back.

"The next afternoon I got summoned to the manager's office, where I was confronted with a letter from said loser Mrs. Redwine, alleging continual sexual harassment and a recent tender of certain illegal drugs, namely cocaine and grass, if only she would surrender her pristine body to my vile manipulations. Said letter said I had drugs previously mentioned in my personal locker at the club. The manager, kindly and fair gentleman that he is, had immediately broken my locker open, where he found a small stash of both aforementioned illegal commodities."

"Oh, Christ," I said. "A plant?"

"Of cawse—and thank you for the vote of confidence. But when I attempted to point out the possibility of a plant—that virtually anyone could have slipped said incriminating evidence through the vent slots in the top of the locker door—my manager was unconvinced. In a blue-balled panic would be a better description of his mental state. He said Mrs. Redwine was very influential, and it would be his ass if he didn't pacify her, and we all shared an interest in keeping the good name of the club unsullied, and I could resign quietly—Mrs. Redwine was not a vindictive person and was mortified about the whole ugly mess—or I could argue, and his duty as a patriotic citizen would be to turn me over to the narcs, and when it got out my career would be ruined either by the publicity or Mrs. Redwine's husband, who, when he heard about my dastardly deeds, would very likely try to cut off my balls with his very own Jack Armstrong scalpel kit, not to mention legally."

Pat stopped and looked into the vast distance of the dark blue windows with eyes that had no life in them. "So I bugged out."

The girl came back with his cigarettes. She had brought Camels. He didn't point out the mistake. She went away. He watched her all the way across the room with a bemused fascination. "Funny. Girls look so *nice*. But sometimes the stuff they do . . ."

I said, "Pat, hell. I'm sorry."

He shrugged and looked around inside for the smile, found it, and pasted it back on somewhat crooked and pallid after its brief storage. "No sweat. That was six months ago. Since then I've had another job with a country club in

Indiana. But it has two kinds of future—little and none—so when I got Hesser's letter, I jumped at it. I can use the vacation. Maybe Al might even want to put me on staff. Maybe I'll meet somebody else down there that will want to hire me. Maybe I'll seduce a wealthy matron and spend the rest of my days working on her backhand and lubing her wheelchair."

"You're right," I told him after another pause. "The change will be good for you."

"The change would be good for you too, buddy. I know what you've been through."

"Yes. Thanks. But I'm not going anywhere."

"You sure?" Suddenly he looked forlorn. "It would be a lot more fun with you there."

"Pat, I just can't face Al Hesser's kind of operation right now."

"He'd promote us, my man. World champion doubles team, all that stuff. Maybe you *need* to get away—help yourself forget."

"No, Pat. Sorry."

He lit one cigarette off another. His hand trembled. I wondered what other bad things had happened to him in recent months. I didn't ask.

Finally he said, "Okey dokey. I wanted to ask, anyhow."

We changed the subject. Got reminiscing about old tournaments, old matches, friends we missed. It felt good. During it, in a part of the back of my mind, I had a picture of Danisa here with us, her hair loose on her shoulders, her ample tanned hands gesturing to tell a story of her own, and the gleam of her happy laughter. It seemed like she was always nearby, but never, of course, here anymore. The feeling could make me feel alone even with somebody like Pat right across the table.

In the morning I picked him up at the motel and took him back to the airport. We got out at the curb to shake hands. He looked so sad and lonesome that on impulse I took off my watch and popped out the little metal studs and handed him my bench-made leather band.

He looked down at it in his palm. The sun gleamed dully off its richly ornate surface, deeply cut-in and embossed diamond and oval patterns interlaced to form a dense, masculine block O on either side at the widest point. It was by far the best piece of work I had done, unique and really damned good, and part of me. So I wanted him to have it.

"What for?" he asked quietly, meeting my eyes.

"You'd better put it on your watch. It's too small for a jockstrap."

He was really touched. He almost clouded up with emotion. Then he caught himself. He shoved the watchband into his pocket. "Asshole," he growled, and hugged me.

I gruffly pushed him away and then leaned against my Bronco, watching him go through the automatic doors into the terminal. He turned back from inside and gave me a jaunty final wave. I grinned and turned away, and when I looked again from inside the truck, he was gone.

It felt more lonely driving home. I wished now I had pumped him more about whatever bad things had been happening in his life that he had not chosen to volunteer.

In not asking—or perhaps in refusing to go to St. Maarten with him—I had the vague and nasty feeling that I had seriously failed him.

three

Elsewhere

Boulder, Colorado

Winter was coming early in the central Rockies, and with a vengeance.

A Pacific cold front had boomed down through Washington and Utah, and now laid dense, low clouds, thick with howling snow, over Colorado. The temperature this morning was 16 degrees Fahrenheit. The radio said that was going to be the high. *"Get out the tire chains and the snow shovels, friends! They're predicting ten inches of snow by nightfall!"*

Pulling the fur collar of his bomber jacket tighter around his neck, Mannie Hawthorne popped the door of his Acura sedan and got out to hurry across the parking lot against a gale that felt like it was filled with needles. The world already seemed wrapped in gauze, and the mountains had vanished in obscurity. Hawthorne opened the front door of Boulder TechnoSys and ducked inside with a sense of relief—and foreboding.

The front lobby of one of the nation's premiere high-tech research laboratories was small, in keeping with its small but elite work force, and gleamingly contemporary, as befitted a company on the cutting edge of applied computer research. The girl at the curving walnut reception desk gave Hawthorne a blinding smile and a sheaf of telephone message memos. Hawthorne glanced through them as he walked back into the rear section of the long, low facility, heading for his own lab. He saw no new problems among them. Not that he needed any.

Hawthorne was thirty-seven years old, a short and chunky man with unkempt red hair, bifocals, a passion for expensive casual clothes, and a mind for engineering that had been pronounced genius level in college, above average at age thirty, and "very hard worker—adequate" in his latest TechnoSys personnel evaluation report. People universally liked him. He was easy-going with others, hard-driving on himself, a perfectionist who could always be counted upon to give one hundred and ten percent on any assigned project. Secretly he was eaten by his own growing sense that somehow he had fallen short of his promise. No one knew about this pain. He was unfailingly cheerful and a good sport, always in the office football pool, and the first to know the bookmaker odds on all the games next weekend. His gambling, considered innocent, was an office joke. His divorce two years earlier had come at least in part because his gambling was far more serious than most people suspected. In this year of our Lord he owed, in back alimony and Las Vegas IOUs, almost enough money to make a minimum down payment on one of the Cray Supercomputers in the back room. But no one at the lab knew that, either.

At the security door in the rear of the building, Hawthorne paused to check out his lapel ID tag, stick it into the slot of the TV surveillance system entry box, and get a green light. Clipping the ID tag to his shirt collar, he walked on past the guard desk, where a thickset, uniformed man of indeterminate middle age was pouring himself fresh coffee from a red Thermos.

"Morning, Dr. Hawthorne! Fine day, isn't it?"

"Burt, you can get away with saying stuff like that. You're wearing a gun!"

Guard Burt chuckled, his ample tummy jiggling under the too-tight uniform shirt. "Take up skiing. You'll appreciate snowfall like this."

"We may *all* have to take up skiing to get home tonight!"

"Well, have a good day anyhow, Doctor."

"Thanks, Burt. You too."

There were several research lab areas beyond the perimeter security system. Hawthorne walked past three of them, exchanging greetings with a couple of colleagues. He entered Room 24 on the right, going into a spotless white laboratory dominated by a single gleaming white trestle table, some forty-six feet in length, along which were spaced about twenty small metal computer component cabinets in various states of assembly and testing. Two other scientists, a man and a woman, were already in the lab, beginning to power up and calibrate the racks of test equipment and programming computers that filled the back wall.

"Hey, Mannie, good morning!"

"Morning, Richard. Morning, Virginia."

"Good morning, Mannie. Did you bring your snowshoes?"

"Might need 'em!"

"Want to start an office pool on how much we have on the ground by midnight?"

"Sure! A buck a guess?"

"Why not?"

"All *right!*"

Hawthorne went to the personnel lockers on the left side of the room, hung away his jacket and cap, touched a comb through his mop of red hair, and slipped his arms into the freshly laundered white lab smock that was replaced every night by the custodial crew. His nerves tightened as he walked over to join his colleagues at the trestle table. But he had begun to get used to the painful tension; he had made his decision and he was going to go through with it because it was his only way out, and there was no turning back. He had already gone too far.

"How did the night bunch do?" he asked, peering over the line of precision chassis and cabinets on the table.

"Damned good," Richard Perdue told him. The lank, perpetually blue-stubbled physicist pointed. "We'll be ready to close up this fifteen today and send them on back to shipping. We'll have the ROMs ready to go in the others, and as soon as the subassembly EPROMS are in, and we check out the motherboard interlock controllers, we can start buttoning this bunch up, too."

"At this rate," Hawthorne murmured, glancing at a checklist report on a white plastic clipboard, "we'll have every B1-B in the country operating at treetop level by next spring."

"And then," Virginia Jurgensen said cheerfully, "they'll start breaking them, and we can start repairing them again." She was a handsome young woman, a PhD from MIT with the face of a young Hepburn and the body of a Margaux Hemingway. "Fix 'em and break 'em. Fix 'em and break 'em."

"Don't knock it," Perdue said mildly. "It puts bread on the table."

"Well, yes," Virginia agreed dubiously. "And it does happen to fit right into the best automatic terrain-scan autopilot system in the world, too. But other than *that*, what good can you think to say about it?"

Hawthorne put his hands reverently on the gleaming stainless steel lid of one of the TSAS-1 subassemblies. The box was featureless except for a dozen small holes on one end, where fittings could be inserted, and three flush-mounted LED indicators on the top near the front right corner. Each $525,000 unit was packed with the equivalent of 1.23 billion discrete electronic components. And somewhere in the heart of the jungle was a superconductive wafer more powerful than any ever described in the literature of world cybernetics.

"I guess," he said in answer to Virginia Jurgensen's question, "you could always take the guts out of the thing and use the case for a lunchbox."

They grinned at the feeble joke. More of their colleagues came in. Everyone got to work. Hawthorne worked diligently. In the back of his mind, the intricacies—and perils—of his plan kept turning over and over, prismatic, shining with a starlike glow of fear.

Soon, he thought dully. *What have we overlooked? What can I have missed? How can it go wrong?*

It had to work. He had to get away with it. The plan had to be perfect. For treason, the maximum penalty was death.

In the afternoon the snow slacked off, and the storm was not as bad as had been predicted. That night Hawthorne drove slowly toward his college-area apartment complex, the headlights of his Acura lighting a world of silvery white. He stopped on the way at a convenience store, and dialed the memorized number as he did twice each week.

"Darling," she said, her voice warm as maple syrup. "How lovely to hear from you."

"All seems to be well," Hawthorne said, his words indistinct because his mouth was so dry.

"That's wonderful, luv. Next weekend, we must get together and talk family."

"Yes," Hawthorne managed. They were putting on the pressure. They would not let him delay much longer. Any chance of backing out was long since gone.

"Oh, and darling?" she added warmly, as if amused by some delicious private joke. "You'll find a little gift in the mail tonight. I want to be *sure* you start taking advantage of it immediately."

"A gift?" Hawthorne echoed blankly.

She broke the connection.

Hawthorne drove home.

In his apartment mailbox he had two pieces of junk mail and his electric bill. She had finally made a mistake; there was nothing special for him here.

He idly ripped open one of the pieces of junk mail and felt the beginning of a baffled tingling of surprise. It was not junk at all.

There was a note in her handwriting attached to the card and brochure:

Hi,
I know you'll start using this right away, since it's your new and consuming passion.

The brochure was for a plush indoor tennis facility not far away, and the card was for a membership in his name.

He had no idea what it meant.

four

Mid-October brought unseasonably hot weather and a note from Pat Reilly:

Hey my man,

It's great down here. Al is the same old bunghole but his place is FABULOUS, gawd, he must be a millionaire. He's less than half full, too, so if you want to change your mind, come on down.

You know how I love to scuba. It is the greatest down here. I can teach you.

One of these rich guys noticed my watchband you gave me the other day and said it was gorgeoso work and said he'd give me $200 for it. I told him forget it, the guy that made it was so dumb he would rather fart around Big D than play in the sun.

You can still change your mind.

Pat

DROPSHOT

As the month went on, thunderstorms rolled in and a tornado tore up some trailer homes near Plano. I taught my students at the club, saw my psychologist, resumed my distant seasonal concern about the Dallas Cowboys, and spent an inordinate amount of time at home alone, tooling a new leather watchband for myself.

The new band wasn't as nice as the one I had given Pat. The leather itself lacked the unique patina of the old one, and my handwork didn't turn out quite as well.

Pat's second letter arrived a few days before Halloween:

Dear Brad,

There is some really weird shit going on down here. I tried to call you twice but couldn't track you down. This is not a joke, buddy, and it is not a trick.

I don't want to put down more because you never know who might open your letter, especially in this deal. I will call you from a safe phone Sunday afternoon the 2nd and for Christ sake BE THERE, this is serious and I mean it.

Just in case, I have got a bank box in Philipsburg and put your name down with mine. Here is the signature card you need to sign and mail back in right away, and your key stuck to the back.

It is just in case because there is a real heavyweight down here and maybe I already know more than they'd like if they realized what I've noticed already. Maybe nothing will come of this. I HOPE.

Love n kisses
Mutt (or is it Jeff)

It was a strange kind of communiqué, and not at all like Pat. I searched between the lines for a joke, and couldn't find one. There, in the envelope with the sheet of paper

33

covered with his near-illegible scrawl, was the bank box signature authorization card, with a heavy bank-type key taped to the back.

Any established procedures for contacting Collie Davis had long since rusted into the ground, and it took three days for him to return the messages I left for him hither and yon. When he got me on the line, he sounded brisk and irritated.

"What is it?" he asked.

"Pat Reilly."

"The man who used to be your doubles partner? What about him?"

"Collie, does he now or has he ever worked for our stock company?"

There was a brief pause. I could almost hear the wheels turning. Finally—

"No."

My teeth gritted. I had forgotten Rule 1: Never ask a question expecting a straight answer. I told Collie, "Pat's on St. Maarten. I got a strange note from him. I'm worried about him."

Another pause, even longer. Then: "I expect to be near your town next week. Suppose we have lunch."

It was not satisfactory, but it was the best I was going to get. I made sure Collie had both my club and home phone numbers and said I would wait to hear.

I signed the key card and mailed it back to St. Maarten.

Pat did not call on Sunday.

On Monday the small item in the sports section of *USA Today* hit me with a shock of nausea:

NET PRO REILLY DEAD

MIAMI—Word reached here Sunday of the weekend death of veteran tennis professional Pat Reilly, Fresno, Ca., former doubles champion of the French and U.S. Opens.

DROPSHOT

Police on St. Maarten said Reilly's body was found on a beach near The Emerald Resort. An expert scuba diver, Reilly apparently drowned while diving off the coast.

Reilly, 41, was vacationing at Al Hesser's Court College and Emerald Resort nearby.

I read the item twice, standing at the clubhouse counter. Then I narrowly made it to the men's room in time before breakfast came up.

First Danisa. And now Pat.

Collie had been among those who had warned me, after I got Danisa safely out of Yugoslavia and into this country, that my dawning, amazing relationship with her could not last. She was almost twenty years younger, beautiful, filled with zest for life and laughter, sure to be the greatest women's tennis player in the world within a year. I had been to the top, but some guys named Borg and McEnroe had shown me long ago that I could no longer compete at the highest levels. I had bad knees, and my hair was not as thick on top as it once had been, and I had already known unacceptable losses.

But God, I loved her. The way she played tennis, moving like a golden shadow oncourt, getting everything, never awkward or hurried, in control, always waiting for the chance to unleash that stunning forehand drive that could root the opposing player in her tracks. I loved everything about her: her face and hair and eyes and sweet-slim body filled with graceful strength, and the way she laughed and spoke and looked at me, and murmured when I held her.

And for those few months it was unbelievable.

Until she and two lesser tour players chartered the small business jet to take them from Chicago to the next tournament site in Seattle, and something—never determined—went wrong. The pictures on CBS Evening News showed parched Montana mountainside brush still

35

smoldering, a blackened three-hundred-yard scar in the lodgepole pines, a ruptured, fire-blackened mass of metal, the rescue workers picking their way gingerly among orange body bags and little sheets of orange plastic covering other things. The picture is never going to be flushed from my memory.

How I got through the early days following that, I have no way of knowing.

Now, somehow, the shock of Pat Reilly's death rubberbanded me right back to that horror and grief. I felt like my lungs would not take in air. I had loved old Pat, too.

And there was an added dimension. As terrible as Danisa's death had been, I had never thought that I was in any possible way responsible for it.

But Pat had wanted me to go with him. Had asked for help. And I had stuck in my wallow of self-pity, ignoring all the signs. So he was dead now, and this time I *was* responsible.

"Brad," Collie Davis said, shaking his head, "that's just bullshit."

"Somebody killed him," I insisted. I was hanging onto my emotions with the tenacity of a rock-climber, but could hear the way my voice shook. "Pat was a *world-class* scuba diver, Collie. He was a certified instructor! He made extra money that way in California."

Collie sat morose in my condo living room easy chair, his canvas shoes propped on the ottoman, swirling his scotch-rocks. "Everybody makes mistakes."

"It was not a mistake."

His eyes swiveled to mine with iceberg intensity. "Is this conclusion based on evidence you haven't shared with me?"

"No," I lied.

"Then I don't know what I can tell you, Brad. You say he sent you a note that said there was something strange going on down there. You say there were no details, no hints. You say you threw the letter away. You say there's no other evidence. What is it you want from me?"

"Was he working for your people?"

"Of course not."

"And if he was, you wouldn't admit it."

"Of course not."

I turned for a moment and looked at the picture of Danisa in the frame on the table beside me. The photo had been taken at the Italian, in her match with Martina. She was moving to her right in full stride, long legs fully extended, golden hair swinging in her patent ponytail, her eyes intent on the approaching ball, her arm coming back, her whole body cocking to unleash a forehand. *Oh, Danisa.*

I looked back at Collie. "Just a few weeks ago you suggested that it might be beneficial for me to go down there."

He looked tightly controlled, wary. "Yes. But that was then."

"I'm ready to go."

"No."

"I *am* going."

"No."

"Why?"

"The situation has changed. We . . . might have thought there was something to be observed in that area. But new information has developed. We were mistaken. There is no need. Other priorities have emerged."

"Pat Reilly was probably the best friend I had in the world. I'm going down there. I'm going to accept Al Hesser's invitation. I've got to see for myself."

Collie put the heavy tumbler of scotch on the table with a sharp *clack.* "Even if there was something, situations change. Even if we were looking into something in that area—I'm speaking hypothetically now—you are no longer the person who might be of value in such an operation."

"Why?" I shot at him again.

He studied me with those mercury eyes. "All right. You asked. Your activities and attitudes in recent months have just undergone a complete reevaluation and new psychological profile. You are not considered stable enough to take part in any operation at this time."

"Are those the same shrinks who made me come back to Langley four fucking times in 1977 to take new lie detector tests because the psychopathic bastard running the machine made my flesh crawl with his creepy talk about all jocks being latent homosexuals?"

"You know damned well what happened to that moron. And you also know I think the same thing you do about their polygraph mania. I'm not responsible for that."

"Right! You act like you're not responsible for anything! But Pat Reilly is dead and you don't even have the decency to verify for me that he was probably doing something for Kinkaid and his bunch, and then when I get set to go down there and do *what you asked me to do less than a month ago,* you expect me to shut up and sit tight because you say so."

Collie's lips got white, but he hung on. "You have no idea what you're talking about. Your emotions are raw meat. All you can accomplish by going down there is getting yourself killed the same as he did. Use your head for a change!"

"I didn't ever say we could debate it, Collie. Old-fashioned, archaic gent that I am, I merely felt compelled to advise you of what I am going to do whether you or anybody else likes it or not."

"You always were a loose cannon. You're clearly in no shape to go anywhere or do anything. You're over-reacting—"

"You've been informed, Collie. You can leave now."

"Brad. Leave things to the professionals."

"Is that what you told Pat before you sent him down there?"

"Lighten up!"

"No. *You* lighten up. I've discharged my obligation to you by informing you. I'm leaving Saturday."

"You're proving what I just told you."

"What?"

"You're in no shape to go anywhere."

"Fine."

His head snapped up. *"Fine?"*

I didn't answer him. I got up and went to my bar table and poured another drink, dimly aware that I had had too much already.

"You," he said to my back, "must—not—go."

"I'm going."

"So you can commit suicide?"

"So I can find out what happened to Pat, and maybe finish what he started."

"You won't leave it up to us? You won't listen to reason?"

"I don't care about any of that."

His face had gotten very red. "You don't care about anything, do you?"

"If I don't, it's my business."

He stood, spilling magazines off the ottoman in front of his chair. "I'm really sick of you."

"Then leave."

He didn't budge. "I know how badly you're hurting. I know how much you loved Danisa. But I'm totally fed up with this Christly pitiful martyr act of yours."

"Then—"

"Shut up, goddammit! It was okay, as long as you just wanted to slink around Dallas and feel sorry for yourself. But now you want to drag the whole world into the pit with you, screw something up that you don't know anything about—"

"You don't know *anything* about the way I feel," I told him, my own anger out now. "What I do—"

"I don't?" he broke in bitterly. "I *don't?"*

"You don't."

39

His eyes changed, and suddenly I was looking into a gigantic room as cold as the arctic night. He said huskily, "You loved someone and you lost her. At least it wasn't your fault."

"Spare me the lecture."

He made a slashing hand gesture that would have fractured a two-by-four. "Five years ago I met a lady—I use the term loosely—and stumbled into bed with her. It went on a year, me hiding and lying to my wife and telling myself no problem. I mean, nobody knows, nobody gets hurt, right? The lady kept saying she loved me. Finally I started to believe her. I left Trudy and she divorced me."

I started to say something, but the hell was open in his eyes and the words tumbled out, totally unlike him, a dam broken.

"The minute I was really available, the lady in question suddenly couldn't feel the same about me anymore. I had been an escape hatch for her, see, in her own marriage. She could use me as an excuse not to commit to her husband, and her husband as an excuse not to have to commit to me. But suddenly there I was, the dumbfuck, *really available.* So she gave me the 'let's be friends' speech, and then she dumped my ass. I left my marriage for all the wrong reasons. Trudy won't have me back. I've got nobody, and every morning I wake up and face the fact that I almost destroyed the only woman who ever really loved me, that I was a dumbfuck, that I was taken in by a whore's tricks, that I got exactly what was coming to me."

Shocked, I was silent. He studied me with a look so unlike any I had ever seen on him that he was in this instant a stranger.

He said, his voice dripping acid, "You know what you do when you've destroyed a family for an illusion and been used like a dildo and realize too late what you threw away, and the pain you inflicted for *nothing?*"

"Collie—"

40

"You just go on with your business. Hey. You wait awhile and you try it with another woman, and you find out that you can't get it up anymore. You say, 'Well, this is probably guilt or fear or something, and I won't worry about it.' You worry. Which makes it worse. So, dumbfuck that you are, you just press on."

"Collie—"

"Then you come talk to a guy you used to respect—a man who's done good work for you in the past, and you like—and he's lost someone he loved a whole lot, but *it was not his fault*. At least he's got that. And you try to talk sense to him, and he tells you you have no way of knowing how he hurts. And he doesn't know what hurt is, man. He—"

Collie stopped. His chest spasmed like he was unable to get air. I could only stare.

He heaved a breath and regained partial control. "You go ahead," he said with brutal sarcasm. "You go right ahead thinking you're the only person who ever had a loss, and you've got a corner on the misery market, and you just go on down to St. Maarten and get yourself killed."

His voice fell to a raspy whisper. "So long, buddy."

Before I could respond, he walked out. I stood there numb, listening to the ugly cough of his rental car's engine and the squeal of tires. Then it was quiet.

It shook me badly, and forced me to take a long, hard look at myself. There was a lot in the inventory I didn't like.

But with Pat they had taken one of mine. I was responsible. I could never do a thing about Danisa. About Pat, maybe there was something I could do.

Collie had been right in telling me what a self-indulgent idiot I had been. He had been wrong if he had thought he could deter me. Nothing was ever going to expunge this guilt except *going there*, checking out that bank deposit box, seeing some things for myself.

I picked up my plane tickets the next morning. Two

days later, carrying my racket cases, I boarded an early flight at DFW.

The same afternoon, I climbed aboard my connecting flight in Miami, and we blasted out of the Florida smog, turning onto an ocean heading southeast, destination St. Maarten.

five

Elsewhere

Langley, Virginia

"Damn," J. C. Kinkaid said.

He had just poured strong, bitter black coffee out of his plaid Thermos into his office mug, spilling one small drop on his desk blotter. He meticulously opened the middle right-hand drawer of his desk, extracted one pale blue Kleenex from the box nestled there, and dabbed at the spot.

"Want some?" he asked the man facing him across his desk.

"I prefer to live," Tom Dwight told him.

Kinkaid was thirty-seven, a slender man of medium height and build, with wide-set eyes the color of asphalt and brown hair, cut close, going to gray. He wore an immaculate dark suit of the kind bought at one of those places with plain pipe racks. His shirt was white, his tie dark blue, his general impression totally ordinary. His office, ten-by-ten with buff-colored metal walls and two straight chairs, was equally unremarkable. Nothing about him or his office hinted at the special nature of his administrative assignment inside the Central Intelligence Agency. His name wasn't even on the door. Standard procedure.

"We have a new problem," he told his colleague.

"Well, I figured that," Dwight replied. Slightly older, with pale hair and sallow complexion, he wore the same kind of totally boring business clothing as his supervisor and had the same kind of build: lank and of no interest unless you happened to give his arm a companionable squeeze—and encountered what felt like steel cables under the skin. He added, "It's Wednesday. We always get neat new catastrophes on Wednesday."

Kinkaid removed an onionskin TWX from under the desk blotter. "The Junta is getting ready to make a move in Guatemala City. We don't know exactly when and we don't know exactly how."

Dwight's eyebrows knit. "Swell."

"We're to get as many additional people in there as fast as we can, and in no case later than tomorrow at 0800."

"Where the hell are they going to come from!"

"Where some of them come from is not our problem. What *is* our problem is that orders have already gone out to Lasher, Maxwell, Trepps, and Kennedy."

Dwight's head snapped forward. *"All four?"*

"And we may be asked to find one additional."

"And how, if I may ask, are we supposed to operate without a single case officer functional in Haiti? And holy shit! Without Lasher and Trepps on St. Maarten, what happens to *that* surveillance?"

Kinkaid's face was stony. "St. Maarten gets shut down for the time being."

"We can't shut down there!"

"We *are* shut down there."

"Goddammit—"

"I've already argued about it. The reports were rescreened this weekend. You take out one sighting that was quite possibly an accident—meaningless—and a couple of half-baked speculations, and we've got no proof of *anything* on St. Maarten."

"But," Dwight said miserably, "we don't know that. We haven't been watching long enough. Maybe it's nothing. But we agreed to check it out. Then we lost Pat Reilly. That was no goddamn accident and we both know it. Now—"

"Now," Kinkaid said with the kind of frosty self-control that helped one maintain sanity sometimes, "it's on the back burner. Period."

Dwight leaned back. He thought about it. "Maybe I'll have some of that battery acid out of your Thermos after all."

Kinkaid got busy with the Thermos and a white Styrofoam cup. "Meanwhile, I have some more glorious news sure to make your day. Collie Davis reports Brad Smith is going down there."

"Down to Guatemala City?"

"Down to St. Maarten, you jerk."

Dwight put elbows on knees and held his head. "I forgot. He was our first choice. Well . . . fine! But I thought we had agreed after looking at the psych profile again that we were better off without him, and his first refusal was probably a good thing. What changed our mind? What changed *his* mind?"

Kinkaid handed over the white cup and its ebony contents. "Nothing changed our mind. What changed his mind was Reilly's death. Now he's got it in his head that if he had gone, Pat wouldn't have, and Pat would still be alive, et cetera."

"Oh, shit! You mean he's going on his own?"

"A rolling cannon gathers no moss."

"Can't we stop him?"

"Do you remember Belgrade?"

"We can't stop him."

"And we won't," Kinkaid pointed out, "have anybody else on the island anyway, even if we wanted to try to stop Smith. Not after this afternoon. Our guys are going to Guatemala City for we don't know how long."

"Then what happens to Smith?"

Kinkaid leaned back, and the frost in his eyes had deepened to the color of liquid oxygen. "We didn't send him."

"He gets no information? No help of any kind?"

"We have no hard facts anyway."

"You don't really think it's all innocent fun and games down there!"

"Doesn't matter what I think. We deal with reality here, and real guns in Guatemala take precedence over pipe dreams on St. Maarten."

"But what," Dwight persisted doggedly, "is our official position about his visit?"

"There is no official position."

"Do you think this is the right way to handle it?"

"Not really."

"If our suspicions are correct, does he have a prayer down there?"

"Not really."

"Do we tell him *anything*?"

"No."

"He can get in some really deep shit."

"That's his problem. Collie told him to butt out. Now, as far as we're concerned, he doesn't exist."

Dwight sipped his coffee, grimaced, and sighed. "And before long maybe he won't."

Boulder, Colorado

Rubbing his chilled hands together to warm them, Mannie Hawthorne walked across the breadth of Boulder TechnoSys Room 24 to join Virginia Jurgensen, who was already standing at the long, immaculate worktable with a twelve-foot printout of computer statistics spooled around her on the tile floor. She was frowning, obviously puzzled and displeased.

Hawthorne was happy to see that. It must mean things were going according to plan.

"Good morning, Virginia!" he said cheerfully. "You're in early."

She glanced up at him. "Hi, Mannie. It looks like we've struck a really heavy discrepancy here."

"Oh?" Hawthorne was careful to look both concerned and innocent. "Nothing we can't handle, certainly?"

She handed him the top end of the printout. "The night crew ran the ROM install diagnostics and motherboard vector interrupt analysis program on all sixteen units that were ready last night."

"Good! Right on schedule!"

Virginia Jurgensen's pretty eyebrows arched with worry. "Look at the data."

Hawthorne studied the columns of digits. "These can't be right!"

"Unfortunately, they are. The whole sequence was run three times."

"But what can be wrong! My gosh! We've never had data collisions like this! Look here! The entire data transfer and compiler circuit doesn't seem to be getting anything out of the backside of the second layer of the 24864!"

"And," Virginia Jurgensen added, pulling the sheet higher to point to data columns on the ninth page, "we've got nothing but garble downstream in the coprocesser."

Hawthorne rolled his eyes toward the acoustic ceiling. "How many units malfunctioned this way? More than one?"

"All twenty-four!"

"All twenty-four! Oh, no!" He hoped he wasn't pouring it on too heavy. "This is a disaster!"

"I already talked to Richard, and to Dr. Pellton. They're on their way in. We have a staff conference set for nine o'clock. In the meantime, they suggest rechecking the data."

Hawthorne had anticipated this. "Before we do that, I think I ought to run some tests on the mainframe. It's conceivable that we got some kind of voltage spike or temperature variation that trashed a section of the program."

His colleague nodded. "That's exactly what Dr. Pellton suggested."

"Fine. I'll start on that right away."

"How long will it take?"

"Not more than an hour."

Virginia Jurgensen looked dubious. "That's a very big program. But you're the expert. You wrote a lot of it. If you say you can do it in an hour, I'll just hope you're right."

"Leave it to me," Hawthorne said, making his face worried again.

Pleased with himself, he left Room 24 at once and hurried down the hall to Room 26. Here, in a constant artificial chill, the lab's supercomputers worked their magic.

Except for the control stations and screens along the left-hand wall, there was little an outsider could observe . . . except that some awesome technology was in here. The two Cray machines stood at the left, pairs of flat black panels almost reaching the acoustic ceiling tiles, featureless, as stark and mysterious as anything a science fiction writer could have imagined. To the right, on its own heavy, hydraulic-damped pedestal, was the new pentagonal machine from Canada. No one was in sight at the keyboards on the left. Even the printers and most of the screens were in the adjoining room.

Hawthorne went to the glass door separating the rooms and signaled the technicians on duty that he needed a hand.

Two of them, CalTech PhDs, came out and followed his verbal orders. The TSAS-1 test program was reloaded, and everything checked normal by Hawthorne's own memory-bank programs. Using an artificial intelligence routine, they then had the computer run its own internal diagnostics, in effect giving itself a physical, and then it ran programs of its own devising to further check out the TSAS-1 data.

"Dr. Hawthorne," one of the CalTech boys said with a frown fifty-five minutes later, "the program is perfect. And so is the computer."

Hawthorne sighed and sat down at a keyboard, tapping a dozen macro command keys that sent orders to dump the test programs and restore the computer to normal operation. "Hand me those printouts, will you, Stan? I've got a meeting to attend in five minutes."

The meeting was grim as a funeral. Seven persons besides Hawthorne attended, the best brains in the company.

The diagnosis: failure of a microscopic electronic component or pathway somewhere in the deepest guts of the half-million-dollar radar operation units.

Problem: there had never been a general systems failure—affecting several tested machines at once—in the history of the program. It was almost impossible to guess where to start searching out the failure.

Certainty: a start had to be made at once, and given the highest priority. Given the astronomical overhead of the lab, to fall more than a week behind on delivery to the Department of Defense could spell ruin.

Theory: since all twenty-four units had failed in an identical way, it appeared highly likely that some component installed in all had come into the building defective. Earlier units had not had such a failure, and the three on the newest and least-complete end of the assembly-test bench were not far enough along to be checked.

Plan: no further assembly on new units. Testing of the defective TSAS-1 subassemblies would begin at the furthest possible point downstream in the data flow, and they would check out each module component in isolation from the rest of the system, working backward until the failed component was located and could be replaced.

Dr. H. I. Pellton, founder and presiding genius of Boulder TechnoSys, looked somberly up and down the conference table, pausing momentarily on the face of each of them. They sometimes called him "the old man." He was thirty-two.

"I don't have to tell any of you how serious this is," he said. "Let's get after it. Let's kill gremlins."

Hawthorne left the meeting looking as worried as the others, perhaps more so.

He was not very worried about getting caught in this stage of the operation. The subtle change he had introduced into the testing software to create this kind of reported abnormality was hidden under two hundred thousand complex operations that were absolutely correct, unassailable. A team of programmers could work weeks and not discover what he had done—the exquisite scramble he had created to make the program run perfectly— and always report puzzling defects in perfectly good test units.

So this stage was going fine.

It was the next stage where the most danger lay.

Or the one after that.

But—Hawthorne reminded himself—he had absolutely no choice. And—he tried to convince himself—it was not so serious a theft after all, really, was it? How could anyone really be *sure* that the superconducting wafer at the heart of the subassemblies—the sacred, secret 24864— really was so uniquely valuable?

Perhaps, after all, he was not planning to steal anything very important anyway.

DROPSHOT

It was a long hard day. Hawthorne was dragging when he left the lab. Nevertheless, an hour later, he was on one of his new club's indoor tennis courts with his instructor, flailing away at forehand drives and pretending to be enormously interested in keeping his eye on the ball, getting the racket back in plenty of time, etc., etc., etc.

six

When you fly over islands in the Antilles chain, you understand why primitive inhabitants had in their limited vocabulary a dozen words for "blue." There are that many shades and more. I suppose the depths and currents do it.

As the 727 made a lowering ocean turn on approach to St. Maarten, I was treated to most of the shadings. The island—lumpy gray-green mountains, the astonishing inland harbor, the low-lying clutter of Philipsburg—was rimmed by beaches aglow with the amber-white brightness of late-afternoon sunlight. The water was yellow-pale near the beach, shading unevenly into areas of gray, robin's-egg, dappled cobalt, turquoise, sapphire, indigo, and the cyan of the deeps. All our mindless dumping and fouling have not yet destroyed the ocean, although we are working hard at it and seem to be making steady progress.

The pilot of our 727 cranked out all his slats and flaps, and then the gear went down with a distant whine and three closely spaced reassuring thuds. *Gear down and locked. Three green lights.*

Some approaches are relatively routine, but I knew the crew up front was paying serious attention right now. The approach at St. Maarten is over water because there's a mountain at the other end of the lone concrete runway. They say there's still one big Boeing out there in the water off the approach end, which is what will surely happen if you approach too low. But you certainly don't want to be too high, either, because the runway is none too long and it isn't considered good form to prang it on and break your airplane or skid off the far end into the brush and the little resort cabins strewn along the parallel beach back there.

I had flown into St. Maarten a few years earlier in a Piper Arrow, which provided none of the problems of the hulking 727. Even in the Arrow I had been extra careful. Of course my nerves had been a little tight anyway, after flying over from San Juan: a single-engine land aircraft always runs just a little rough over water or at night, when you don't know where the hell you would put it down in an emergency.

Our plane sank lower, the nose rising as the pilot bled off airspeed, and then the engine note deepened as some extra power was put on so that we were coming in over the beach carrying lots of RPMs in reserve. There was the briefest flash of beach beneath our wings—some pretty female flesh down there—then some wind-whipped brownish vegetation and a few rocks and a dirt road, and the wheels hammered onto the end of the paved surface and the pilot started reversing thrust.

"Whew!" the woman in the middle seat beside me breathed.

I turned to her. We had talked earlier in the flight, she trying to make conversation. She was thirtyish, already tanned, with sun-touched blond hair and pretty green eyes and silver earrings adangle, wearing an off-white canvas shift, no sleeves, and canvas flats. She was not beautiful but she was very pretty in a slightly boyish sort of way, the kind of girl who had been a cheerleader once, or perhaps a member of the girls' basketball team and a champion in debate. She seemed nice.

"Safe and sound," I told her.

Her eyes were big and round. "I felt like that was close!"

"It's all okay now."

"You've been here before?" she asked, stuffing magazines and things back into her carryall.

"Once or twice. I'm no regular."

She kept looking at me, her pretty eyes frankly but cautiously interested. "I keep thinking I know you from somewhere."

"I don't think so."

The plane turned and taxied back toward the terminal. People squirmed in their seats and stowed things in purses. The flight was over and my flight companion frowned nervously, uncertain and evidently feeling pressure. She had tried pretty hard to start a friendship, and I hadn't cooperated. Now her time was running out and she hadn't quite given up, but she wasn't sure how to proceed.

"Look," she said. "I was supposed to come with a friend, but she had an emergency at the last minute and I had to come on by myself. Maybe you and I will run into each other during our stay." She stuck out a graceful, capable hand with no rings, no nail polish, and a small collection of pretty thin bracelets attached. "My name is Beth Miles."

I took her hand, which was strong and warm. "Brad Smith."

She smiled hesitantly. "You're sure we haven't met?"

"We haven't."

"Are you staying long, Brad?" She spoke a little too briskly, brightly, showing the pressure. The lady did not flirt well, but she was dead game. "I'm here two weeks," she added.

"I don't know yet," I told her. The plane braked to a halt and the crew-alert chime sounded. People started springing out of their seats to unload the overheads. "Whoops. I guess we'd better get moving."

Her face fell a little. "Oh," she said. "Yes." She stood

and moved into the aisle, frowning as she pulled down a little blue overnight case. Poor Beth Miles, I thought. She finally got up her nerve to seek out a holiday adventure, and she picked a loser.

Don't feel bad, Beth Miles. You had bad luck this time. You picked a man who doesn't have anything to offer anyone right now. But you're a nice-looking lady. With any luck you'll have a friend soon, and an adventure if you want one.

Meanwhile I had other things to think about. We deplaned down an old-fashioned staircase on wheels, then straggled across the tarmac toward the cyclone-fenced terminal. The terminal looked like the old ones you used to see in Oklahoma City, Mansfield, Ohio, or—way back—even Kansas City: a utilitarian two-story building with tall windows facing the ramp, and an ugly, utilitarian shed structure stuck on the side. The sun was low in the sky, but the air felt like a wet overcoat.

We went into the terminal, which was dim and crowded and even hotter. I found a car rental desk and waited my turn and was told I could have a Ford Cortina, but not until tomorrow. I signed up for it. Beth, in line beside me, got the same bad news from the other clerk.

Next door, in the concrete-floored, garage-type building, workers brought in the baggage on flatbed carts behind a tractor. Uniformed cops stood around. Nobody challenged me as I picked up the bag.

I went outside to look for a cab and had my last glimpse of Beth Miles climbing into a VW taxi—flounce of pretty hair, glint of sunlight on bare brown arm, and long, nicely turned bare leg. It stirred the slightest murmur of physical interest in me, and maybe a nudge of regret.

It had occurred to me on the way down that I was feeling anticipation, a certain pleasant nervous tension, that had been absent for a long time. That, and the feelings in me now, made me realize that maybe I was on the way back, maybe sometime I would feel good again.

I walked over to a waiting cab, an ancient Chevrolet BelAir with huge chrome bumpers and tail fins. The driver, brown-skinned, wearing khakis and a loud shirt, peered unsmilingly out at me.

"Can you take me to the Mary Mary?"

"Eight dollars, sor."

It was a ripoff, but I didn't want to walk it. I got in.

We trundled off the pull-in area in front of the terminal and did a U-turn, heading down the length of the airport property past a couple of elderly tin hangars and older parked airplanes. At the end of the airport property the road turned to the right to follow the beach, but we turned left onto a dirt road that circled the airport. We rumbled along slowly, heaving over ruts and through water-filled sink-holes, through head-high brush. The road became a single lane and some of the mudholes became big enough to swallow a Sherman tank. Flies and grasshoppers swarmed. The inside of the car was a furnace. I saw a big lizard scurry through the yellow grass.

It was familiar, although I hadn't been here in almost four years. The big resorts and casinos are scattered along the beach on the inland side of the airport. The lone runway, with its jet noise, pinches too close to the beach on one side to make for pleasant accommodations although the beach itself is better. So tiny resorts—ramshackle house-size inns and collections of A-frames—have proliferated along the dirt road among the private cottages, some elaborate and some little more than beach shacks. The development when I was last here had been random and disorganized, with undeveloped brush giving most of the places a feeling of wild isolation. I was glad to see, as we jounced through a moon-crater mudhole, that things hadn't changed much.

The driver eyed me in the rearview mirror. "You are alone here, sor?"

"Yes."

"Allow me to suggest. A pleasant driver can be of assist for lonely gentleman. I live here all my life, know the places.

One can be lonely, can be good for a lady to walk along the beach, see your place, stop in for friendly reasons, eh?"

"Thanks. I'll keep it in mind."

"I can give you telephone number."

"I think this is my place coming up here."

He pulled off the rumpled dirt into a grassy parking area beside a tin A-frame office shed and a peeling blue-and-yellow wood sign reading MARY MARY—*Your Paradise*. A couple of chickens strolled around, pecking in the dirt. I got out and put my bag down with the chickens and handed a ten through the window.

"Maybe I wait, sor? I don't see nobody."

"Thanks, I'll be fine."

"About that telephone number I can give—"

"No, thanks."

He shrugged philosophically and trundled the old car out of the weeds, leaving me alone. I went up to the door of the A-frame office. A window air conditioner chuffed. Inside were bare wood floor, battered desk, funeral home calendar, candy bar and Coke machines, and an ancient Admiral TV set. From somewhere in the back came a brown-skinned woman in a muumuu kind of dress that would have nicely accommodated Ringling Bros.

She gave me a solid gold grin. "Hey, mon, what's going on?"

I showed her my reservation paper. She had me fill out a registration card and stamped my Amex number onto a bill with the only modern piece of equipment in sight. I fed the Coke and candy machines. Then she led me outside and along a weed-choked gravel pathway into the head-high weeds and neglected plants. She said I was lucky because it was off-season and I had a very nice cabin all to myself, and it was a quiet time, it rained some in the evenings and night, but the days were just fine, the best time of year in her opinion, the other people staying here right now were nice, and if I wanted anything just let her know.

There were nine small A-frames strung along the

beach, only fifty feet or so from the water and about that far apart, with palm trees and untended brush in between them, giving each some sense of isolation. My hostess left me at number 6.

The cabin was a single room about twelve-by-twelve with beds under the low parts of the roof on both sides, a writing desk, two folding chairs, a small dresser and mirror and an undercounter refrigerator in what the brochure had called a kitchenette corner. Behind the kitchenette corner was a door into a tiny, tomblike bathroom, basin and stool and shower stall. I checked the shower and ascertained that there was no hot water. A trip outside showed that there never was: the supply came straight out of the ground and through the wall of the cabin without the formality of a hot-water tank.

The surf washed gently onto the beach in front, providing a continuous, pleasant rhythm. A trio of secretary-types, just old enough to have Rubenesque thighs, strolled past in their brightly colored swimsuits and pretended not to peer inside at me. I closed the slat curtain on the front screen window. There wasn't any glass. Around the sides, under the low eaves, the cabin had screening close to the ground.

Al Hesser's resort would have been considerably more plush. But my decision had been to stay here and look in on Al's operation, checking it out, but not accepting his kindly hospitality. I thought I was functioning reasonably well, but I was not up to being paraded around for the paying customers in exchange for a fancy room. This way, too, my real intent would be far less apparent.

By the time I had unpacked and gasped through an arctic shower, it was almost dark. I stood outside in my shorts and T-shirt and smoked a cigarette and watched the stars come out. On my last stay here, I remembered, there had been a place just up the beach a mile or so that sold pretty decent sandwiches and beer. I walked up that way, barefooted in the warm sand, and found a wire fence around the place and a *for sale* sign. I walked back in starry blackness, wading in the warm shallow wavelets, watching tiny firestorms of phosphorescence break around my ankles with each incoming surge. It was all very pretty and very peaceful and very nice, just like it had been one night on a beach in Vietnam when about forty of us had been drinking beer, and after the VC attack thirty of us went home in body bags.

I had not been ready for the VC attack, of course, but that was nothing new because I was not ready for anything about Vietnam. I did not even have a good reason for going, except they told me to. A lot of people told me I was stupid to go, and said I should move somewhere nearer and less hostile, like Canada. I knew just enough to doubt the wisdom of the war, but I had this naive feeling about being an American, and owing.

My memories of that time are still jumbled. The war was rotten, but it was a magic time back home. People said my generation was going to change a lot of things that needed changing, and for a while I bought it.

I remember a day, for example, in the An Loa valley when we were listening to Radio Vietnam and it was playing Peter, Paul and Mary, "Blowing in the Wind," and we found one of our guys who had vanished in a firefight three days earlier. He had been tortured with pointed sticks and he had lived a long time before they finally killed him, and Peter, Paul and Mary were singing on the battery radio about how long must the cannonballs roar, and I thought, *What is this? The world is an insane asylum.* I wanted very badly to believe in peace, but it's hard to be a pacifist when your friends are being tortured and killed, and you walk around feeling like somebody may have painted a bull's-eye on your back.

Of course a lot of that changed when somebody in Washington gave secret orders—I am still convinced somebody did do that—and the Guard killed a few people at Kent State, and it was over, the fashionable idealism died. *Good!* a lot of people said. Maybe so, maybe not. There are things about those terrible times that I still miss. I think I prefer misguided radical idealism to the smug, installment-loan complacency that passes for patriotism today. But then I have always been odd.

I stopped thinking about Vietnam as I neared my A-frame. There was a sliver of moon. For a few seconds I had a sharp, clear, intense picture of Danisa standing there in front of the cabin, waiting for me. She was in her bikini and she had a towel over her shoulder and she was waving, and we were going to swim and then yelp and yuff together in the icy shower, and then pile under the sheets to get warm, and her body would be like marble until she gasped.

With an effort I quit thinking about that, too.

Inside the A-frame, I found the power had failed. There was a candle. I lit it and got a melting candy bar and a tepid Coke out of the now-warm refrigerator. Candlelight supper, yum yum. Down the beach, a half-dozen men and women had built a little fire in the sand and I could hear their laughter. I didn't go down.

It occurred to me that this would have been such an adventure with Danisa. I thought a little more about how it could have been with her here, but then I managed to get her out of my mind again.

I brushed my teeth, ignoring mental pictures of the creatures that might be in the water that came out of the slightly rusty spigot. I even had a sip of the water, feeling adventurous. Then I turned in, and in the night I paid for my bravado.

Before dawn a squall came through with deafening thunder and fiercely brilliant lightning, the wind driving big breakers onto my beach. I awoke and looked out through the screening and saw, in the lightning flashes, a lizard the size of a breadbox ambling along through the mud. He went under my cabin. I went back to sleep.

seven

The car-rental people had not lied. My proprietress, all gold-inlaid cheer, hammered on my door at 8 A.M. Thursday to report that the car had been delivered, and I had to take the agency's driver back to the airport. I staggered out and did that. The night's storm had passed and the day was sunny and still and already hot. The Cortina had no air conditioner. I was sticky with sweat by the time I got back to the A-frame.

A little after 9, after sorting myself out, I left Mary Mary again and drove around the end of the airport property to the narrow two-lane asphalt locally referred to as "the highway," and made my way into Philipsburg.

It's the kind of town you find on some of the islands, a former trading village stuck somewhere between old-world Spanish and modern-day small town. Puddles were starting to dry in the narrow streets. Moist wind blew in off the bay, cracking the Dutch flag in the tiny downtown park. Faded awnings flapped over dilapidated storefronts. Black people, locals, stared down from mildly rococo second-story balconies. A few brightly dressed tourists, lugging cameras and shopping bags, mingled with dark, bone-skinny locals in one-piece dresses and worn-out cotton pants. There were a lot of wide-brimmed straw hats and an unbelievable number of cars parked everyplace there was to park one. By luck and persistence I found a spot for the Cortina and then found the police station, a small Moorish building not far from the park.

Inside, I identified myself to the officious little sergeant at the desk as a personal friend of the late Pat Reilly. The sergeant tried to brush me off but I refused to brush, and he went away to an inside office and came back with a portly, middle-aged man wearing captain's insignia on his faded uniform.

"You are a friend of the deceased?" the captain asked, his eyes frisking me.

"He and I were tennis partners for several years on the professional circuit. I saw him only a short time ago. His death was a great shock to me. I need to learn more about the circumstances of his death . . . that way, I might come to terms with it better."

The captain's expression contained all the sympathy of a traffic cop. "I see. And your name . . . ?"

"Brad Smith. I—"

He lit up. "Brad *Smeeth?* The Brad Smeeth of the championship at London and the United States?" He clapped his palm to his forehead. "But yes! I recognize you now!" He seized my arm. "Sergeant! This is the famous Brad Smeeth, the great tennis player, and a former partner in the doubles of our poor drowning victim, Señor Reilly! Señor Smeeth! Please to come this way with me, into my office! Sergeant! Please to bring the file on the poor departed Señor Reilly!"

The office was an eight-by-ten room with cracked plaster walls, water-stained plank ceiling, fly-specked windows looking out onto an alley, and a calendar showing a man and a woman drinking rum at a cafe table. The captain busily pulled a straight chair up to face his battered, olive-drab metal desk and enthusiastically pumped my hand. "Allow me the introduction of myself. I am Captain A. A.

Suarez, and I am the officer on duty at this time. Sit down, Señor Smeeth, please! Make of yourself comfortable. I am a great fan of tennis. I have saw you play many times in years gone past. I remember you and the poor Señor Reilly in the doubles championship in the French Open many, many years ago! Sit! Please!" He hurried around his desk and plumped down, facing me. "Tell me what I can tell you!"

"For one thing, Captain, if Pat's body has not been claimed, I want to make arrangements for its shipment back to the United States. He was a military veteran. The government of the United States provides burial—"

"Ah, Señor Smeeth, the body has already been claim. His dear sister was here in this very office only yesterday and made all the arrangements."

"His sister," I repeated carefully.

"*Si.* The body was ship yesterday night on a flight to Miami, with arrangements for taking of it to California. Miss Reilly, she said there would be a . . . ah . . . I cannot remember the word . . . it is when there is a burning of the remains—"

"Cremation."

"Yes! Cremation. That is correct. The poor Miss Reilly was very sad, as we all are."

We were interrupted by the sergeant coming in with a somewhat dog-eared brown file folder. Captain Suarez took the folder, shooed the sergeant out with an impatient gesture, and briefly flipped through some of the many pages inside. He kept nodding affirmatively.

Finally he handed the folder across the desk to me. "This is the complete report, Señor Smeeth. As a friend of the poor departed and a great former tennis player, you are given my permission to examine its contents in the entirety. The entirety!"

With a feeling like I was reading someone's personal diary, I opened the folder and examined its contents. It was very complete, remarkably well done for a small-town police force. Evidently the captain had recognized from the start that Pat was someone of some importance, and he had supervised what appeared to be a thorough investigation.

The first report told how Pat's body had been found facedown in shallow water on a beach about two miles from The Emerald Resort, which was also the site of Al Hesser's Court College. The local people who made the discovery were identified, and attached papers gave considerable information on who they were and what they did for a living. They were locals and they appeared unremarkable.

The coroner's report showed that Pat had died of asphyxiation or drowning. There was a small amount of salt water in his lungs which might or might not have been sufficient to drown him. Except for some minor abrasions on his hands and wrists, evidently caused after the body washed onto rocks scattered along the beach, there were no marks on him. He had been dead about eight hours, which fixed his time of death as between 9 P.M. and midnight the previous night.

The scuba gear had been subjected to rigorous examination. Everything was in good order. The gauges on both air bottles showed dead empty, a reading verified by testing them. If Pat had been diving off the point where his body had been found, he had been working in less than twenty feet of water, and in an area noted for its many colorful tropical fish occupying underground rock formations.

There were reports from investigators who had traced the scuba equipment. Pat had rented the gear—top-quality stuff—from an outfit across the island on the French side in the town of Marigot. He had rented it for a week with an option for a second week, and had already been back once since renting it to get the bottles recharged. Copies of the records on the company's recharging were in the folder and looked perfect. Pat had left the dealer's with four fifty-pound aluminum bottles, all freshly recharged, less than forty-eight hours before his death.

The conclusions section of the report said two tanks filled to capacity were found in Pat's room at The Emerald.

The investigator speculated that either Pat mixed up his near-depleted bottles with the fully charged ones, or ran into a regulator malfunction underwater when switching supplies. It looked like he had spit the regulator. His holster that was supposed to contain a small cannister of emergency air was empty, leading to further speculation that the quick-release had opened and he had lost the backup.

A series of tragic coincidences, the report suggested.

I looked up at last to the captain, who had brought us both bottles of a rancid-tasting orange drink out of the hallway machine. "This is very complete, Captain."

He preened. "We pride ourselves on good work. I myself have been to the FBI school in your country."

"I find it hard to believe that a man of Pat's experience and expertise could have had this kind of bad luck."

The smile clouded over with worry. "*Sí*. I have myself a worry of that kind. But, Señor Smeeth, there is no other explanation."

"How do you think it could have happened?"

He shrugged dubiously. "It was perhaps late. Earlier, as the investigation reports tell you, our poor Señor Reilly was at a party at the Al Hesser school. One witness there told me Señor Reilly had several drinks, gin. It is my belief that poor Señor Reilly then made the decision to have a brief dive for trying to observe marine life by night. As the report says, he carried an underwater light of high intensity. It is my belief that something of the equipment failed, he found his emergency supply lost, and there was no way out."

"As the report says, all coincidence?"

Captain Suarez sighed. "There are some slight undertows in the area. There was later a strong sea running. It is even of possible that your friend had entered one of the many small but beautiful rock grottos which lie on the sea floor in the area. Then, when his system alarm warned him, he could not back out of the rocks with a sufficient swiftness, and the tragedy occurred."

I put the folder back on the desk. "Captain, you have been most helpful and I thank you."

"Señor Smeeth, for a great former champion such as yourself, bearing such a sadness, it is my duty and honor."

"Just one more question. Did Miss Reilly—Pat's sister—provide you with a forwarding address?"

"*Sí*, but of course. I have it here." He scowled through other papers on his desk. "Ah, yes. Here it is. Miss Reilly is in the process of moving. She said any further correspondence can be temporary addressed to her in care of General Delivery, Los Angeles, California."

I shook hands with him. "I can't thank you enough."

Outside on the street again, I lit a cigarette and took the smoke deep. It tasted bitter, but not as bitter as my thoughts.

Pat had shown me once how he checked his equipment. He would have been extraordinarily careful, diving without a buddy—which I knew he seldom did. He had once gotten me far in over *my* depth, intellectually, in explaining how the new underwater digital instrumentation worked in informing the diver of everything from tank pressure to surface interval.

I simply did not believe that a certified diver of Pat's ability and experience could get himself into a situation where so many things could go wrong in sequence, without a way out. And the drinking explanation left me cold. I had never seen Pat drunk. I had never seen him drink gin. He was a vodka man—concoctions like the Harvey Wall-bangers he had had with me in the Dallas lounge so recently. The autopsy report had not listed alcohol in his blood.

I took a walk and found the bank where I had mailed my signature card. I half expected to learn that darling sis had found and rifled the box. But she had missed this. The bank official was courteous and attentive, and after examining my identification and comparing my signature with the one on the card I had mailed back, he escorted me personally into the vault area where he matched his key with mine, opened the steel door on the small deposit box, and discreetly withdrew.

Fifteen minutes later I was back in the Cortina, fighting the jammed traffic on the narrow streets to get out of town and headed back in the general direction of the airport. The contents of the box were stuffed in my pants pockets, and I had no idea what any of them meant.

I needed some time to think about them.

Just like I needed some time to ponder the fact that a loving sister Reilly had rushed in with great speed to claim Pat's body and ship it away somewhere. For cremation.

There might be things about Pat Reilly I had never known. But I knew about his family. He had no sisters. And no brothers either, for that matter.

The Emerald was one of the newer resorts on the Dutch side of St. Maarten, but not far from some of the more established ones. I drove past the edge of a golf course so lush its green looked artificial, its wealthy patrons perched in red and yellow golf carts under palm trees or standing on elevated greens beside little artificial lakes with artificial fountains. The water was a tipoff to the money here; despite periodic storms, good water was at such a premium that ships came regularly from Curacao, their cargo drinking water; even if the fountains and little lakes weren't drinkable, they were conspicuous consumption, in spades.

Past the golf course I came to a chest-high stone wall running alongside the road, and then a massive stone archway with a wrought iron gate. The stone-and-bronze sign said I was welcome to The Emerald Resort, home of Al Hesser's Court College. I turned in.

After driving slowly through acres of manicured lawn studded with flower gardens and palm trees, I reached a squat, blue glass casino building and, beyond a mile of parking lot, a curving, three-story resort hotel done in gleaming steel and pale green glass that looked a little like the mother ship in *Close Encounters*. A futuristic sign identified The Emerald Resort, and small bronze signs along the driveway pointed beyond the mother ship to tall shrubs with low white metal roofs just showing over the top: *Tennis Facility.*

My intent was to look around a bit, being as inconspicuous as possible. If I was recognized it was okay. I couldn't expect to be incognito around a tennis resort. For this trip, however, the idea was to get the lay of the land and then retreat to the Mary Mary and give some heavy thought to the contents of Pat's bank box.

I had not taken the small, heavy metal box out of its slide-hole until the bank officer was well out of the vault area. Then I had opened it with anticipation and maybe a touch of dread. Even now I didn't understand what I had found, but it was not what I had anticipated.

There were four items in the bottom of the box: a three-by-five filing card, a sheet of tablet paper with a drawing on it, a newspaper clipping, and a heavy, rather large brass key of the type sometimes used in hotels or resorts. But it had no number on it.

The filing card had a single line printed in Pat's hand. It read:

ACCESS CODE—FIRSERVE.

I had no idea what that meant.

The tablet paper was a rough but legible drawing of the blueprint of a house, a large one. It showed a two-story entrance, a sprawl of large downstairs rooms, a huge patio or deck area and pool surrounded by gardens, and upstairs enough unidentified rooms to impersonate a small hotel. One of the rooms had several rough circles drawn around it. Written below the floor-plan drawing were the numbers 6-7-4-7. I had no idea what those meant, either.

The clipping was of a grainy newspaper photograph taken, the caption said, at Al Hesser's tennis school. It showed Al with some students, he grinning and posturing as he demonstrated a backhand. In the small group watching were several other students, a beautiful, dark-haired younger woman wearing a sundress and heels, and close to her—Pat had drawn a hasty penciled circle around them—two thickset, unsmiling men who looked about as in place at a tennis school as they would have been in church.

Pat had considered this stuff crucially important. Maybe he had died because of it. Somebody had gone to all the trouble of sending in an imposter sister to claim his body and get it out of there before anyone else could run a second-look autopsy. It was a minor miracle that they hadn't also found out about the bank deposit box and sent her over there to get this evidence, too. So I had been lucky.

The only problem: I did not understand the evidence.

It was going to take some thinking. Possibly I could come up with some observations of my own that would provide a clue.

Leaving the rented Cortina in the vast resort lot between a Cadillac Seville and a Mercedes 450SL, I walked along a beautifully bricked sidewalk flanked by bougainvillea and geraniums and came after a while to another walk which led around the vast building to the north. The sound of tennis balls being whacked came distantly, and I homed in on it.

Walking around the end of a tall hedge beyond the building, I came out on a little grassy area sloping down to the tennis facility. High cyclone fencing enclosed dozens of courts arrayed beside one another in all the space available between my vantage point and what, far at the other end, looked like a gully construction area and scrub-infested hill that went straight up on the far side. A sign proclaimed it Al Hesser's Court College.

On most of the far courts, individual lessons were in progress. Well to the other end, white-clad instructors were working with groups. Nearer, other teachers coached individuals hitting back at ball machines. On two courts, intermediate players rallied while an instructor stood to the side, running videotape equipment to record their moves. I had never seen so many teaching pros in my life.

A few of the courts closest to me were vacant, but in the nearest court, close by the long, low pro shop building on my right, there was a match going on.

The players were both youngish, the one on my right perhaps sixteen, built like a budding Boris Becker and with the same coloring. His opponent on my left was shorter, dark-haired, and whip-slender. They were hammering it back and forth at each other the way juniors will do, and they even had a man in the umpire's chair, watching intently from under his umbrella.

As I strolled nearer, slipping inside the fence gate and walking toward the shade of the pro shop, the big blond kid double-faulted. He was red-faced, sweating heavily, gritting his teeth, and stomping around with a serious case of bad manners. He said something nasty-sounding to the ball boy, then prepared to serve from the deuce side.

I lit a cigarette and watched, getting my bearings.

The blond Boris Becker type slammed a ferocious first serve deep to his opponent's backhand. The kid over there stabbed at it and got it looping back. Boris blasted one deep in the corner and charged the net. The slender boy in the far court glided back and threw up a gorgeous topspin lob. Friend Boris saw his mistake and put on the brakes, racing back.

He paid a dear physical price to get to it. I saw the wild, angry look in his eyes, the facial grimace, and heard his grunting effort. He had to come almost as far back as I was standing, but he got there and blasted back an angry forehand, deep, a very long shot.

At the other end, the kid wound up like he was going to blast one back of his own, but at the last instant he dropped his racket and cutely undercut the ball, a perfect little dropshop from the baseline that just tweaked over the net and dropped squarely on the line on the ad-court side.

Boris stared like an elk that had just been shot in the gut.

The man up in the chair nodded good. The slender kid grinned from ear to ear and came around the net.

Boris rushed the umpire. "That ball was out!" he screamed.

The man in the chair, a school instructor, judging by his immaculate tennis whites and Hesser school armband, leaned forward solicitously. "The ball was good, on the line."

Boris went crazy. *Wham!* His racket hit the green-coated concrete, shattering. "You're crazy! That ball was out six inches! I demand a let, goddammit! I *demand* it!"

The umpire climbed wearily down out of the chair and started toward me and the pro shop. Boris, ignoring his slim opponent's proffered handshake, ranted after him, spouting as foul a stream of obscenities as I have ever heard.

The umpire was a sun-baked man of about fifty, perhaps five feet, nine inches tall, perhaps 160 pounds soaking wet. His face showed he didn't like the bombardment of verbal abuse.

Boris—well over six feet tall, and probably weighing 205—grabbed him by the arm and spun him around. *"Listen* to me, you goddam stupid son of a bitch!"

"Billy," the older man said with a pleading tone in his voice, "don't make a scene, son, okay? The ball was good. I called it—"

So it wasn't Boris, but Billy.

Billy: "You bastard, if you don't reverse that call, you're going to be out of work inside fifteen minutes!"

"Billy—"

"I own you, Thornton, and you'd better do what I say!"

Thornton pulled away and hurried past me on the way to the pro shop, his face twisted in equal parts pain and rage. Billy spouted some more filth and charged after him. I happened to be in his path and he bumped into me.

"Get out of my way, you dumb shit!" he yelled, and pushed me.

My temper went, and by reflex I pushed back. The big kid's momentum was such that my push carried him sideways into the next step and he went down heavily, tangling his legs up, and hit on his rear end with a satisfying thump.

He looked up at me with total shock and outrage. "You *pushed* me!"

"So I did," I admitted quietly.

"You asshole! Don't you know who I *am*?" He started to scramble up as if he was going to come at me in earnest this time.

"Sonny boy, don't do it," I told him.

The umpire had retreated into the pro shop. Our little altercation had gained some attention, and I was dimly aware of a small clot of men hurrying toward us from the far courts. Billy boy got to his feet and looked down at himself and saw that I had bloodied his little knee. He turned to the approaching men like a picked-on first-grader.

"Dad!" he bawled. "This prick tried to beat me up!"

I turned to face the short, dumpy-looking man out in front of the others. He wore tennis whites, and he was all-too familiar.

"What's this all about?" he growled, looking me up and down. "Who the hell—?" He stopped then, and recognition dawned with surprise on his wide, flat face. "*Brad?* Brad Smith?"

So much for quiet reconnaissance. I stuck out my hand. "Hello, Al."

We spend much of our lives trying to be rational. We argue for our point of view. We logically defend our actions. We seek theory, we look for connections. We analyze ourselves and try to make sense of ourselves and others and life. We try very hard to be "cerebral," which is to say *sane*.

The truth of the matter may be different. It could be that

there is wisdom built into the gene structure which defies all rational analysis: it is simply there, *us*. And it may also be that the furry chill on the back of the neck, the sudden soft-hot rush in the loins, or the inner, defensive puckering of the threatened animal inside us are just as legitimate— just as rational below the level of conscious rationality— and infinitely more reliable—than all our dusty logic, all our gut-mistrusting abstractionism. We live in the cortex and proudly try to ignore the brainstem, but the brainstem and limbic system have a wisdom of their own which we try to ignore at our peril.

In the moment I shook hands with Al Hesser, it was the primitive, sensing part of me that picked up all the signals.

Al had changed. Not for the better.

I don't simply mean he had gotten older. It had been five years and I expected that. He was somehow fundamentally different—shrunken and desperate and *diminished*. The impression hit me hard.

He looked much the same. Certainly he was the same short, squat, homely man he had always been. His red-and-white tennis togs clung to him like sausage skin, and the fringe of hair remaining around his skull was still densely curly and black. He had the same thick pelt of body hair, the kind that made you remember our closeness to monkeys, and his broad face was lighted by the same quick, bright, close-set eyes that always looked wary, suspicious.

The sense of shrunkenness came a little from the sagging skin and musculature of his neck, perhaps. It was an old man's chicken neck. And his legs had started to go bony below the knee so that he looked perched on spindly stilts, with shoes too big stuck on the ends. But the impact of the change in him came from inside of him and hit inside of me, brainstem level: he was *cornered*. Once, hunting, I saw men chop open a hollow fallen tree to get at a fox. When the poor damned thing came out of there—in the instant before my courageous outdoorsmen shot him to pieces so they could get a cheap rush—his eyes had been like this.

Out from under Al Hesser's loud togs and swagger of arrogance leaked the fetid odor of rot and defeat. And I was startled by it.

"What are you doing here?" Al demanded. He looked at the blond kid. "What happened here, Billy?"

Billy, his lower lip trembling, pointed at me. "I was having a little talk with Andy about my match with Lipner, and this guy came over and started pushing me around for no reason at all."

Al grimaced. Of the three men with him, one was obviously another teaching pro, thin and sun-baked and court-attired. The other two men were older, wearing cotton slacks and short-sleeved shirts, and both stood over six feet, with bulky bodies and thick necks and eyes like ball bearings. *The guys in the photo in Pat's deposit box.*

The brown one took a half step forward. "You get off on beating up kids, buddy?"

"Ricardo," Al said nervously, "just—"

"I'll handle this, sir. I don't like people that beat up on kids."

"The kid," I pointed out, "is six-three, and he outweighs me at least twenty-five pounds."

Ricardo had the stolid, implacable bullshit tone of a cop. "You're looking for trouble, is that it?"

Billy had left his shattered racket oncourt. I strolled over to it and picked it up, casually carrying it back. "Look what he did."

"There are plenty of rackets, smart guy!"

I was only half paying attention to friend Ricardo. In my limited experience, tough guys who talk a long time before starting the action are not the ones you have to watch out for. Ricardo looked formidable, but he talked too much to greatly worry me. His associate, the other thickset man, had never said a word; his intelligent eyes watched me intently, weighing and sizing me, and I knew he understood exactly why I had gone over and picked up the racket. I did not think anyone would start anything nasty here on the courts in front of all the high-paying guests. But if I was wrong, the broken racket was considerably better than no weapon at all.

Al Hesser moved between us. "You can go, Ricardo. You too, L. K. I'll handle this. Jeff, you can get back to your lesson. And Jeff?" he added as the three men started to move away, "be sure you change the cassette in the camera and mark the old one for a group-look at four o'clock."

Jeff went on back toward the far courts, and the bodyguard-types walked over to stand silent, menacingly, in the shade of the pro shop building. I marked them in my mind. The one called L. K. worried me, but it was Ricardo who was the type who might take it upon himself to check in with me later on his own if he dimly determined that his status as an Al Hesser protector would be enhanced by bashing me about a little.

Al turned back to me with those pained eyes. "What are you doing here, Brad? Did you really knock Billy around? *Why?*"

"Billy lost a match a minute ago," I said. "He started doing a McEnroe on your man in the chair. He was just escalating from yelling to shoving when I happened to get in the way. He pushed. I pushed back. Sorry."

Billy whined, "It was none of his business, Dad. I got a terrible call—"

"Billy," Al said, "how many times have I got to ask you: don't throw your weight around, son. It's not good for the club."

"What do I care about the fugging club?"

Al's tone became wheedling. "Billy, *please.* Give me a break."

"You never take my side! You let people pick on me!"

"Billy. Son. Let's forget this. Can we do that, please? As a favor to your old dad!"

"What about my match? Andy made me look like a fool with his crummy calls! What are you going to do to him?"

"Billy, you're a real talent. But you've got a responsibili-

ty to act mature out there. Surely one little match—you can
forget it, right, son?" Al patted the hulk's arm. "Okay, son?"

It was a weak speech, and Billy exploited it: "You
always try to tell me what to do. Some of these staff guys are
jealous. They pick on me. Just because I'm big for my age is
no reason why I should get picked on. Now are you going to
have this guy arrested, or what?"

"Billy," Al pleaded, "just go shower down, all right?
We'll talk this out, Brad and I. I'm sure he's sorry if he
hurt you." He turned beseeching eyes to me. "Aren't you,
Brad?"

I met the kid's look. "If I did anything to you that was
not provoked, Billy, please accept my apology."

Childish—dangerous—rage smoked in his eyes for a
moment. He swung back toward Al. "You never give a shit
about *me*. You always brush me off."

"Billy—!"

"Oh, suck me, old man! Just suck me!" Billy rammed
into the clubhouse and slammed the door with a sound like
a gunshot.

Al Hesser heaved a heavy sigh and shook his head.
"Oh, boy, oh, boy. He's got spirit, that kid, huh?"

"I guess."

"He gets a little out of control sometimes, but he's a
good kid basically. He's just got a lot of spirit. And good
God, what am I supposed to do? Crush him? Set all kinds of
rules? He's insecure enough. He would just take it as
rejection. I mean, it's my fault."

"What's your fault?"

"His *insecurities*. His *frustrations*. I mean, my God, Brad,
I was a famous tennis player! Now I'm known the world
over for my fabulous tennis instruction techniques, and my
first book will be out soon. Imagine the poor kid, trying to
live up to a father like me!"

"I guess," I said, "he definitely could be a happier
young man if you were more of a failure."

"That's right! That's exactly right! And kids need their

freedom. You don't get anywhere trying to control them all the time. My God. He would hate me."

I just nodded.

"Let's forget it, okay?" Al asked. "What brings you here, man? Hey! I didn't get a card back from you, but you decided to take me up on my invitation, right? That's great! Hey, that's spectacular! Hey! Billy Jean is here for a few days, and Karyn is scheduled to get here anytime now. And I got Jimmy Connors here right now, and Pat Cash, and hey, Lendl might come, I haven't heard from him back yet. I mean, is that great or what?" Al put a sweaty hand on my arm. "How long can you stay? This is fabulous!"

"Al, I appreciate the invitation, and I'd like to spend some time around here. But I've made plans to stay at a beachfront place, a place where I stayed once before a long time ago."

"What the hell would you do *that* for?"

"Personal reasons."

He stared at me, his piggy eyes puzzled. Then he slowly beamed. "Oh, wait a minute . . . I get it . . . I think I get it!" He leered. "A personal deal, right?"

"Well—"

He lowered his voice so that it had an itchy insinuation in it: "Not traveling alone, eh? Not too anxious about the general public—or some damned photographer—taking pictures of you and the lady, eh? Because she might be married to somebody else, something like that, maybe, Brad baby? Eh?"

"Al, you always were too sharp for me."

He giggled, a high-pitched, girlish sound that startled me. "You just come around as much as you can, right? And your secret is safe with old Al, right?"

"Thanks, Al."

"Hey, lemme show you around."

"Won't your customers here be needing you?"

"Them? Scroom."

"What?"

Jack M. Bickham

"If they don't like it, scroom!"

"Oh."

"Say, you heard about poor old Pat Reilly, I guess?"

"Yes, a little."

"He was a great guy. I loved the guy. I'm really feeling sad."

"Yes. Me too, Al." Then I added, "I guess you never know when fate—or somebody out there—is after you . . . when your luck is just about to change and go sour."

The fear, like a quick rat, scurried behind his eyes. "I've got protection. I mean, I'm a celebrity. I need it, so I got it."

"Of course," I said, "who would want anything from a couple of old guys like you and me anyway, right?"

He thought about it. The rat went back into the dark somewhere and a crafty weasel looked out. "Sure. Right. Hey! Let me show you around this joint. It's the greatest in the world. Of course what would you expect, coming from Al Hesser, right, buddy boy? Come on!"

"Al, I deeply appreciate the hospitality."

He grabbed sweatily at my arm again. "C'mon, baby! Are you gonna be impressed? You're gonna be blown away!"

I went with him up the backside of the courts, strolling up toward the dirt cliff at the far end. When we got there, I was able to look into the gully and see the construction. A local crew—a half-dozen men and two bulldozers—were moving earth around down there.

"Six more courts," Al told me. "Three clay—and I mean world-class clay, old buddy, and three grass. It's costing me a fortune, but it will be worth it. I'll get people like Steffi and Ivan and Martina down here. Did I tell you Ivan might be coming already? I mean, is that first class or what? Hey! You see the way we got automatic cameras on all the courts? We tape everything, man. We play stuff back for classes and individual students, and I get some great footage sometimes for my syndicated cable television show. Have you seen it? It's great. Dynamite!"

DROPSHOT

We started back toward the distant pro shop and instruction building at the far end, near where I had first entered. We passed a court where an instructor was working with two thirtyish men who looked like they might be business executives on vacation. Both students were tall, mature, good-looking. One was sandy-haired, with blue-blockers, and the other was gray-haired with—

When I saw it, the shock very nearly dropped me to my knees.

There was no mistake.

I was twenty feet from the gray-haired man. But my vision caught it and it was like a zoom shot in film—I couldn't see anything else *but* that one item.

Maybe I made an involuntary sound.

Al looked back at me. "You get a pain or something, pal?"

Christ, get hold of yourself. I took a slow, shuddering breath. "I drank some of the local water. I think I ingested some local bugs that don't agree with me."

Al guffawed and hammered me on the back. "Drink more bourbon, baby! It kills them microbes deader than you were in that last set at Wimbledon against Borg!"

I managed some kind of dutiful chuckle. My gut was turned inside out, all right, but it had nothing to do with the drinking water. My shock was profound.

Almost at the point of being unable to function at all, I got myself together enough to walk on with Al Hesser. Behind me, the gray-haired man was still listening intently to his instructor, and I knew that now nothing here—for me—was ever going to be the same again.

eight

Al Hesser's Court College was not yet as famous as Vic Braden's tennis schools, but it was getting there. When Vic branched out his psychology method coaching and high-tech analysis into other sports and even business, it was Al Hesser who was just getting started on pure tennis instruction. Al took the best of Vic's approach and added a little John Newcombe, and then put in his own gimmicks: more cameras, computerized analysis, VCRs, slow-mo playbacks and biofeedback equipment; a lodgings-instruction package deal with a famous resort at Hilton Head, and then with The Emerald here on St. Maarten; a ratio of one coach for every six students, with all the coaches youthful and attractive; graded programmatic instruction sets that charted progress numerically on a computer screen; little tournaments at least once every week at all levels of play, with prizes for hacker and semi-pro alike; take-home VCR instruction tape packages; his cable TV show; direct mail, and soon a set of books.

Even filled with the icy sludge of my shock, I was impressed as I walked around with Al on a slow, braggado-cian tour. This place had everything. For a hacker or intermediate club player wanting to *beat* somebody next

80

time, it was Oz. Assuming you had enough money to pay for it all.

Al took me past a small, pearlescent swimming pool in which about a dozen swimsuited players of various ages were standing in nipple-high water, slowly repeating and repeating the full-body motions of a backhand ground stroke. They all had steel or aluminum rackets with some kind of thick nylon rope stringing. A coach at the head of the pool called cadence over an electronic bullhorn, and three other pretty assistants walked along the pool edges, calling out cheerful corrections and encouragement.

"You can't move too fast underwater," Al told me. "You practice your strokes with the water resistance, and every flaw is magnified. And you sure got to transfer your weight properly on that backhand, boy, or you can't get that water racket through before tomorrow!"

"I never saw this kind of drill before."

"That's because I invented it, baby." He thupped his thumb into his chest. "Me. Al Hesser."

He showed me all the rest of it: the indoor gym and classrooms, the video equipment and hard-disk computers that could be interfaced with the VCR material for interactive quizzes on tactics or computer games testing split-second decisions on angles and shot selection, the showers, lockers, sauna, whirlpool, and clubroom prominently featuring trophy cases crammed with memorabilia and cups and platters from Al's own playing days.

He stopped along the way now and then to talk to staff or students. I wished to hell we would encounter the gray-haired student, but we didn't. To the people we did encounter, Al introduced me with enthusiasm. However worried he might be about the things behind his eyes, he had always been a man who rubbed up against celebrity and power like a lonesome cat.

He couldn't resist the needle, either. Another vintage Hesser trademark.

"This is the guy, sweetheart, who went into a fifth-set tiebreaker with Borg at Wimbledon!" he told a startlingly endowed blond instructor. "I tell you what, Andrea, if this guy here hadn't flubbed the easiest crosscourt volley in the history of tennis, he could have been Wimbledon champion two years in a row! Imagine it! All he had was this dinky dropshot and he flubbed it! Incredible!"

"Hey, Al, thanks for reminding me."

Andrea gave me a smiling appraisal from head to foot. Her cyan eyes issued possible invitations. "I bet you're still awfully good. You look like you're in wonderful shape. Do you ever play with women?"

"Baby," Al yelled, stroking her sweet, strong back, "he's the best. Listen. I personally can provide you with a list from memory of at least three hundred women he's shacked up with. On the tour we used to call him Mr. Stroke, and the press thought we were talking about his game!"

The lady's eyes died and she excused herself. I didn't care, but I gave Al the obligatory thank-you-very-much.

"Think nothing of it, baby!" he crowed. "You know how I enjoy making stuff up for the fun of it!"

He asked me to stay the afternoon. I declined, but said I might come back later.

"Well, hey. Come back anytime. Hey. Come back tonight. I'm having a party at my house." He pointed toward palm trees and shrubbery. "It's just over there beyond the cabana. Backs up to the sixteenth fairway. Gorgeous." He leered. "Lots of pussy. Nine o'clock. All right?"

"Okay, Al. Fine."

"Great! We can talk about how maybe you can make some extra bucks while you're on the island, too, what say?"

"Al, you're a prince."

"Right! Here Prince! Here Prince! See you tonight, pal! It will be the greatest party you ever saw!" And he turned and swaggered off, master of all he surveyed; short, chunky man in the latest and most expensive tennis togs, with a bald spot, old-man legs, and that rat behind his eyes, moving around in the dark, restless, hungry, alone.

Back in my car, heading for the A-frame, I reflected on Al's talent for exaggeration, and wondered how much he must be in debt for the trappings he needed to support his hyperbole.

It had to be a lot.

I had done my homework on Al Hesser. Unlike most of the tennis stars of today, he did not come out of a pampered background, or one that saw parents sacrifice everything in hopes of creating a superstar to fulfill their frustrated dreams. He was born in New Jersey and attended public schools there. His father worked in a factory and his mother was what we called, in those simpler days, a housewife. He was the oldest of five children.

Al had told an interviewer long ago that his father was a drunk who liked beating him up. This was said long before Al began creating a mythology for himself, and I believed it. Al was in trouble with the law in high school—drinking problems, a stolen car—and might have ended up in jail for a long time if a parish priest hadn't taken an interest in him after watching him play paddleball in a YMCA. The priest got Al interested in tennis. Al did not have the physique for it, but something about the game turned him on, and he got through both high school and then Florida State on the basis of his skill oncourt.

Al had been married either four or five times. The clip file at the *Dallas Morning News* was unclear. He was seldom a tournament winner but he was usually in the top sixteen. In his day, he played every tournament, large or small, and gave clinics in between times. He was a killer card player, and had been known to make extra money by doing some of the old Bobby Riggs tricks—playing three club players at once for $100, or playing left-handed, or putting four chairs on his side of the court and taking somebody on that way.

83

He made some wise investments. Or crooked ones. Nobody had heard much from him for a while when he started his Court College on Hilton Head with a beautiful, high-dollar facility and a ton of publicity.

The school here on St. Maarten was very new. It—and the resort—had to have cost millions. His talk about the party convinced me he was running with a high-dollar social crowd, as always. The kid from a crummy factory neighborhood in Hackensack proving he was better than any of them.

During our tour I had noted the new computer equipment, still boxed up, in a corner of a spare office. Then there were the new courts under construction. So Al was probably drawing good business now, but he was expanding. I knew how that worked. You plowed everything back in and took on new debts because you had read somewhere that good businesses either kept growing or tried only to hold the line—which meant inevitable shrinkage toward eventual failure. Grow or die. Al would believe that line of reasoning.

So maybe financial fears were one of the things feeding that rat behind his eyes. He might be overextended enough to be in fear of losing it all. Which for a man like Al would be a fate worse than death. But I thought there had to be more. Much more.

The glimpse of the man with gray hair had told me that.

I got back to Mary Mary and parked the rental car in the front dirt lot, then walked the twisted gravel path to my A-frame. Wind off the inlet tossed the palm trees and high brush. The bougainvillea looked like fire in the hot sun. A lizard scurried, and hand-sized sandcrabs strolled around everywhere, their grotesque eyestalks gawking. I thought of Danisa and what she would have thought of this place. She would have laughed and she would have put on the tiny lime-colored bikini and splashed out into the gentle surf, and I would have sat in the deck chair and watched her with the attentive concern of an indulgent elderly gent who happened to adore her. And then she would have come back out of the water, laughing and teasing, sweet-salty, and we would have made love again.

But none of that was going to happen, ever. And I had to stop thinking about it.

What I had to think about was the stuff Pat had left me in the bank box.

Pat, to whom I had given my wonderful hand-cut and ornamented and finished leather watchband, the finest one I had done, my work, and unique.

The watchband that the gray-haired man had been wearing with his Omega.

nine

Just after sunset, with the western sea still defined dark against an obscurely defined area of pale yellow-red, one of the cruise boats departed Philipsburg and headed out to deep water, crossing not far beyond the mouth of my bay. The ship was white and ablaze with lights from end to end. It looked romantic. I imagined I heard music over the steady pulse of the breakers on the shore. Stars came out, vivid, within arm's reach, and the breeze breathed warm.

By car, following the road, it was perhaps three miles to The Emerald. I had calculated that it was not more than a third of that if you walked the beach to the point, then cut across the dark expanse of the golf course. I did that, carrying my shoes and socks until I was out of the sand and on the dense fairway grass beyond the road. I cut across another fairway, the edge of a drainage sluice below an elevated green, everything deep and dense dark except where the starlight and sliver of moon provided the palest shadow-light, and approached Al's house from the back.

I heard the music and voices from hundreds of yards away. There were other houses back among the trees on the west side of the course, but there wasn't much doubt which was Al's, and where the party was. He had a small combo playing on a huge deck around the pool, Japanese lanterns strung from the trees, more lights ablaze inside the giant glass-and-cantilever house. I walked in through some shrubs and into the back of the garden bordering the deck, and joined.

Be here, Gray-Hair.

A few of the guests were wearing cocktail dresses, dinner jackets. Most were dressed more as I was, in slacks and shirt or sundresses, with a scattering of shorts. They were of all ages but most looked in good shape, courtesy of a common passion for tennis or else the kind of clinical conditioning that money can buy. Money was the common denominator. Everybody here had it, or pretended so.

My man wearing my watchband—dead Pat's watchband—was nowhere to be seen.

No one was swimming. Little floating candle platforms discouraged that. On the far side of the pool I found the bar and allowed myself a rum collins. I talked with a banker and his wife from Nashville and a couple who ran hamburger drive-ins in Oklahoma and a young couple from Indiana who told me how production standards had declined on the BMW and how outraged Daddy was about that. Pretty people of all ages talked and laughed and crashed about, changing partners, and boredom had almost reached the terminal stage when Al found me.

"Hey, baby!" he bawled, pushing through the crowd with a tall brunette on his arm. "You came after all!" He shook hands while turning to the people around us. "Hey, everybody! Did you know this is Brad Smith, the famous Brad Smith, champion at the U.S. Open, Wimbledon, the French, and gawd knows where-all?"

While he was saying this, the lady on his arm gave me the full battery of her coffee-colored eyes. A few of the people around us moved closer with interest, murmuring pleasantries, but they might have been on Mars. The lady was stunning. I had only an instant to register beautiful dark hair, those eyes, a wide pink mouth, creamy shoulders bared by a lavender cocktail dress, a tiny waist with extraordinary goodies above and below it. Her eyes made small electrical shocks in my nervous system. She was quite simply one of the most beautiful women I had ever seen.

"Hell's bells, I'm forgetting my manners." Al grimaced, squeezing her lovely bare arm. "Mia, this is the superstar I was telling you about. Brad, this is my wife, Mia."

We shook hands. She had a strong grasp. The way she held herself, and her expression, made for an aura of self-possession and a kind of detached amusement at the world. Uncertainty about herself was a feeling Mia Hesser had never experienced.

"Al has told me so much about you, Brad," she told me.

"And some of it even good." Al chuckled.

Mia's eyes had never left my face. "I understand you plan to be around for a week or two."

"That's the plan at the moment."

"Good." She caressed the word with her tongue like it was a Hershey bar. "We can get better acquainted."

"I'll tell you what," Al cracked, "Brad is one of those guys that the better you get to know him, the more you know you got to watch out for him."

"Is that so?" she asked me, her eyes warm and ironic. "Are you a dangerous man, then, Brad?"

"This man," Al said, "is so dangerous he ought to carry a sign on his back. Let me tell you what he did in Melbourne a few years back when we were over there for the Australian—" He launched into the story and his wife and I stood there, listening, smiling at the right places, but the communication that was really hitting home to me was not from him, and it was not verbal.

I wondered if she sent these messages to every man she met. For Al's sake I hoped not, but I sensed that she was the kind of woman who liked to test, and sometimes tease, and perhaps . . . sometimes . . . even experiment. She was wearing a small necklace that supported a very large sapphire pendant. The giant diamond on her left hand struck blue fire from the garden lanterns, and the stones encircling her watchband kept cadence with dozens of smaller fires. She was perhaps five feet, eight, elegantly slim-waisted and long-legged, possibly thirty-five although the surgeons these days can take off a dozen years sometimes, and Mia Hesser was clearly the kind of lady who would avail herself of every help.

"You finding everything you need?" Al asked me, having finished his story.

"Doing fine," I told him.

He glanced toward the house. "Well, more people coming, so I got to greet them. Give them a thrill. You know. Hang around. Mingle. Lots of nice people. We'll talk later."

Mia subjected me to her eyes again. They were smoky rich. "It's been a pleasure, Brad. We'll see each other again." And she went off with him, lush hips swaying.

I moved around. Still no man with the gray hair and watchband. I had been too shocked this afternoon to register much else about him. If possible, I wanted to strike up an acquaintance, or at least get his name. He might not know it, but we would have another appointment sometime later, after I had gotten some other things sorted out.

There was nothing at Al's party that was not fairly close to first class. Patio party bars for large numbers tend to offer things like Gilbeys and Echo Spring. These bartenders were hustling labels like Boodles and Tanqueray, Jack Daniels black and Canadian Club, Johnny Walker and Smirnoff: perhaps not the very finest, but close. The combo was professional, older musicians who could actually read notes. The trays of food included caviar, great slabs of smoked salmon, and what looked like heaps of crab and lobster meat.

I was checking out the salmon when one of the people standing nearby moved closer and said, "Hey, aren't you Brad Smith?"

I turned to see a slightly overweight, sunburned young

89

man in a seersucker suit. He looked like a decent sort. "Guilty," I told him.

He grinned and stuck out his hand. "Great! I'm Don Abercrombie." He tugged a pleasant, pretty blonde up beside him. "This is my wife, Wanda. Hey, guys," he called to another couple at the table, "come here a sec!"

Wanda was not only pretty in her vivid sundress, but slightly turned-on and roguish, with gorgeous eyes. She said something I didn't catch as I turned to meet their friends, Ed and Marcie Palmer. The Palmers were about the same age; they had the lean look of joggers.

"This is great!" Abercrombie chuckled. "Al Hesser said there would be more celebrities here late this week! Hey, I saw an old tape not long ago. It showed you beating Connors at Los Angeles way back. You were great, man."

"Don," wife Wanda purred with a wicked smile, "don't tell the man he *was* great. I bet he still is."

Ed Palmer interjected, "How long are you here for, Brad?"

I hedged. We stood and talked a few minutes. They were nice people. From Kansas City. Both men were bankers. Wanda Abercrombie was a RN and Marcie was a counselor, she didn't specify what kind.

"Maybe we can swat a few," Palmer suggested carefully.

"Might be," I said.

They were loath to break it up. We agreed we would see each other again. It was possible they could provide useful information, but this wasn't the right place to pump them. We split up.

I went into the house. When I walked through open patio doors to enter, I was greeted with an outrush of refrigerated air. Al had the air-conditioning on full-blast, open house or no.

The house was contemporary, sleek, with high walls alive with the color of good—not necessarily fashionable—

contemporary oils and acrylics. A $20,000 stereo was play-
ing at low volume in what might be called a den, a room
forty feet square with two-story beamed ceiling and walls of
gray limestone that must have been hauled in three thousand miles over water.

It answered one minor question for me. It was the
house of Pat's hand-drawn floor plan.

I was strolling on around, learning the layout and
making mental comparisons with Pat's sketch, when Mia
Hesser found me in the broad flagstone foyer near the
suspended circular staircase. She was alone this time, and
seemed pleased about it.

"Brad," she said, with that way she had of making the
word a caress of pleasure. "Are you finding everything?"

"I think so, Mia, yes."

She linked her arm through mine, establishing a
warmth of touch that started at our shoulders and descended through the hips. It was an intimate, conspiratorial
closeness. "Darling, you don't sound very sure. You must
know you're a very important guest for us. Anything you
see here is yours. All you have to do is ask."

I disengaged myself gently. "Thanks, but I'm just fine."

The smile, brimming with cozy suggestions, held. "Oh,
dear. I hope I haven't embarrassed you."

"No," I said, playing dumb. "Why should I feel embarrassed?"

"No reason at all," she replied blithely. She pointed to
the curved stone benches flanking the lower steps of the
staircase. "Come. Sit with me a minute. I want to talk with
you."

I joined her. The music was distant here, and the
staircase screened us from nearby rooms. There were guests
less than ten feet away, but behind the staircase wall we
seemed quite alone. Close beside me, Mia Hesser's perfume
nudged at my senses. Opium. Her complexion was flawless,
the skin of her shoulders and arms and exposed upper

globes of her breasts the most perfect tan. There was a faint
psychic rot about her, a distant odor of degeneracy, equal
parts danger and fascination. I knew I didn't like her, and at
the same time she stirred in me a primitive sexual response
that had nothing to do with cognition. *If you don't try me out,
won't you always wonder?*

"You won't change your mind and stay at The Emerald?" she asked with a pretty little hint of a pout.

"No, Mia, I really can't."

"Oh, dear. Well, at least you must promise to use the
club. And you must take a little cruise with us on the
Tiebreaker."

"And the *Tiebreaker* would be . . . ?"

"A little yacht we picked up at a very good price. I'm
afraid we don't know a lot about operating it yet, but we
have a nice captain and small crew who are on the payroll
and ready to take us out at any time."

"It must be expensive, having a crew on payroll at all
times."

"Ted is worth every penny. I've always said, if you have
a problem . . . no matter what it might be . . . it can be
cured by finding just the right man."

"Al's schools must be doing very well indeed."

She gestured, light exploding off the huge diamond
ring. "I never trouble myself about details. I warned Al
before we married last year that I have *very* expensive tastes,
and I simply will not abide feeling neglected or deprived.
What I want, I *will* have." She turned the full battery of
those eyes on me with a quick intensity that caught me
off-guard. "You strike me as a man who would understand
that. A man who knows what he wants, and takes it." She
waited, expectant.

I didn't say anything.

She asked, "Have I misjudged you?"

I put my hand over my mouth and yawned. "I think I
must have a touch of jetlag. I'm suddenly feeling worn out."

"You must get your rest," she told me. "And then I want to tell you some other things you must do. You must take me to the beach tomorrow. You must be very entertaining and very gallant. You must be clever and witty, and after our morning at the beach and a lovely lunch at a place I know over on the French side, you must bring me safely home so you can put in an appearance at the tennis school and trouble all the wives."

I had to grin at her. It took a certain kind of class to be this transparently outrageous. "I'm afraid to take you to the beach."

She made her eyes big with surprise. "*Avec moi?* Why?"

"What if I get burned?"

Laughter danced in her eyes. "You won't get burned, darling. I promise. I plan to take very good care of you."

I stood. "What will your husband think?"

"Why should he know? — Look. There's an outcropping exactly one mile beyond the curve in the highway out front, here. A little lookout place with trees. Quite lovely, a wonderful view. I'll drive into that park at nine-thirty tomorrow morning. I'll have wine and a snack and my bikini on under my sundress. We can be at a pretty private beach ten minutes later. What are you driving?"

"I have a rented Ford—"

"Ugh! Look for my candy-red Jaguar. We'll take that. All right?"

Mia Hesser was going to be difficult to handle. I wanted the stress of a flirtation with her about like a head cold. She was fascinating, electric; but I just didn't need the complication, or the irritated certainty that I was breaking the boredom of her rich, pampered existence by giving her a new test of her irresistibility. But possibly she was my key into all sorts of information.

I told her, "Nine-thirty sounds fine."

"Good!"

She linked arms with me again as we left the staircase

seats and started across the foyer to rejoin the party. I was ready to get out of the place.

As we crossed the foyer, however, my eyes caught sight of a familiar figure just outside the lodgelike room on the deck. It was the man with gray hair.

The shock of seeing him again went through me like high voltage. I had to fight to maintain my composure.

He was almost my height, perhaps thirty-seven or thirty-eight, with fine features that somehow struck me as British. He was wearing dark slacks and a white dinner jacket, and smoking a pipe. He had bright eyes, either green or blue, and he was talking with the Abercrombies and the Palmers, the people I had met earlier.

"Mia," I said casually, "who is that man out there?"

She followed my gaze. "Who? The man in the plaid?"

"No. In the white dinner jacket."

She looked puzzled. "Why, darling, I don't know. Is he someone famous and wonderful, do you suppose?"

I shrugged. "I thought I had seen him somewhere, is all."

"I have no idea. Why, look! William! William?"

The person to whom she was calling had just entered the foyer from the other direction. It was Billy Hesser, hair wet-slick from a shower, and wearing ragged cutoffs and a T-shirt with a hole in the front.

Mia hastily unlinked from me. "William! Come say hello to our guest, Mr. Brad Smith!"

Billy, looking none to happy about it, walked loose-jointedly over to join us. He was sunburned and the tip of his nose was peeling for not the first time. He looked like he wished he were somewhere else.

"I didn't know who you were this afternoon," he said, shaking hands.

"That makes us even," I told him.

"I was just so damned mad at that idiot, calling that shot—"

"Honey," Mia purred, moving close beside him to stroke his arm. "Let's not talk tennis at the party, all right, sweetheart?"

Billy Hesser flushed slightly as he looked down at her. She smiled up at him like a fond and trusting lover. It lasted less than a second, and told me something about a teenage kid with a man's body and a stepmother who had never met an attractive man she didn't play the seduction game with. I wondered if either of them knew exactly what was going on, and to what kind of disaster it could lead.

Beyond them, the man with gray hair vanished from my view through the window.

I said I had been on the way out, but was glad to have seen Billy under more pleasant circumstances. He said he hoped we could rally a little together in the next day or two. I said that sounded fine. I left him and the lady who was anything but his mother, and sifted my way outdoors again.

The Abercrombies and Palmers had vanished. I spotted my man far across the pool, on the farthest end of the garden deck. Just as I found him, he walked through some of the high, screening shrubbery at the back of the lot, evidently heading out onto the golf course.

I had no choice but to follow. I went around the other side of the pool and slipped through the garden and shrubbery as quickly as I could without appearing to be up to anything.

It was cooler on the vastness of the golf course, and after the bright lights in the house it seemed almost pitch-black. I looked around for my man, but didn't see him. Bitter disappointment filled me. He had gotten away a second time.

Breathing deep, I paused to light a cigarette and decided the hell with it, I would just go on back to Mary Mary. I set out.

Walking down the fairway, I felt my eyes begin to adjust to the dim light from the sky. I approached the place where the elevated green stood higher in the dimness, with trees scattered along to the right, and a dropoff of some kind beyond the green. I tossed my cigarette end into the grass and then on second thought decided to pick it up and toss it in the creek or somewhere where it would not litter.

Just as I bent over, the bullet went about six inches behind my head.

ten

In a far simpler time of my life, I listened to sound effects on radio shows and Republic's Roy Rogers epics, and thought the sound of a passing bullet sounded something like the twang of a bent handsaw blade. That sound effect is a reasonable approximation of the ripping crack you may hear sometimes hunting, when a sportsman's bullet passes far off, followed by the report. But among the more unpleasant lessons I learned in Vietnam was that a nearby bullet doesn't sound that way at all.

Older weapons, most of the .38s and .45s, fire their heavy slugs on a subsonic trajectory, about 850 feet per second. If you're unfortunate enough to be quite close to their path, you hear a nasty crackling sound that makes the hairs stand up on the back of your neck. Newer weapons, from the Makarov to the Walther P-38, have much higher muzzle velocities, and the ear-snapping sound of their 9 mm. presence is sharper. More than the sound, though, is the hot, ear-popping burst of pressure you feel on your skin and inside your skull.

What I heard—and felt—as I strolled onto the greenside knoll beside a yawning dark sandtrap was the *snap-pap!* of the bullet going over my head, close, popping

97

my skin. Then, almost simultaneously, a soft *pffutt!* like the cork coming out of a bottle of champagne, and the sound of the action working on the weapon. Off to my right, on the far side of the trap, in the dark of the trees.

I didn't have time to analyze or think about it. Old reflexes took over. I went headfirst over the lip of the trap and hit hard in deep, soft sand, half burying my face in it. As I hit, I thought I heard a second *thoop!*

A good silencer doesn't totally silence a handgun. But it can cut the sound remarkably. What's left, if the silencer hasn't been shot out, is the cork-popping sound I had heard from the darkest shadows.

There's an old expression about shooting fish in a rain barrel. Sprawled on the pale sand in the bottom of the cavernous trap, I knew what the fish might feel like. I scrambled wildly across the breadth of the sand depression, every nerve screaming, expecting to get it in the back any second. I didn't know what I was doing, exactly, but one thing I would *not* do was stay in the barrel and wait for my friend with gray hair—who obviously must have seen me coming away from the party after him.

I rolled out of the shallow side of the trap and onto the froghair around the green. There was some stuff like pampas grass along the back edge. I got to my feet, staying low, and rushed through it into deeper black. The back side of the elevated green sloped sharply downward from here, into the drainage sluice I had skirted on the way over. Here it was more a ditch or small ravine, bordered by rough trees and brush. Penalize the shot over the green. But it didn't look like a penalty to me. I charged down the incline and rushed into the black.

The ground instantly vanished beneath my feet and I plunged forward out of control. Fell about four feet and hit with a hell of a splashing noise on chest and thighs in slick mud, knobby rocks, and maybe four inches of tepid drain water. Some quiet "escape" I was making. No time for self-recriminations or even embarrassment, though.

DROPSHOT

Couldn't be doing too badly, I was still alive. Clawing my way out of the drainage ditch, I scrambled into the dense brush on its far side.

Creepers tore at my face and upper torso. Thorny things ripped across the right side of my face, catching the corner of my eye with bright, hot pain. Some kind of animal made a rasping squeak of alarm and tore off in front of me, vacating the premises for this huge idiot bumbling into places he didn't belong. I felt the hot blood on my face from the thorns as I got shakily to my feet again, hunched over, and tried to pick my way more quietly.

The damned vegetation was dry and it was almost impenetrable. I couldn't move without making noise that sounded to me like a tank going through. I paused a moment, gasping as quietly as possible for air, and listened hard.

Behind me and to my right, near the green slope I had just vacated, somebody was moving. I could hear his heavy breathing. I crouched and looked around as best I could in the faint light.

The drainage ditch ran from beyond the downslope of the green to my position behind it, then curved back toward a place near the far end of the series of traps guarding the green on the west side. By straining my eyes I could make out the faint gray of the grass there, and a tiny glint of water where the ditch became merely a slight depression running on between the green and the adjacent raised tee.

My whole "jungle" of shelter was no more than ten feet thick at its widest point. In either direction from where I had entered it, it quickly narrowed and had been trimmed back to become mowed short rough.

My friend with the gun suddenly hove into view atop the rise behind the green. My skin rose up in goose bumps. Even with the additional acuity that shocked fear can bring, the most I could make out was a shadow. But it was a familiar shadow. I couldn't see the gray hair or the white dinner jacket, but I knew they were there.

The shadow stood there, swaying. I could see its heavy breathing, and the outline of the automatic in the right hand.

He was standing still, listening for me. Waiting for my next mistake. He probably knew the territory, and from where he stood he could see the whole breadth of my pitiful hiding place. I thought I knew how he was going to proceed. I sank lower, extending my mud-clammy legs so they wouldn't cramp.

Five or six eternities later, he started doing what I had anticipated. He moved slowly down the hill behind the green, approaching the point in the thicket where I had first dived in. He had figured out that I couldn't run without his seeing me, knew I was still in here. And he was coming for me.

I had had time to calm down a fraction and make my own plan, which I liked about as much as smallpox. As he came slowly down the incline, I crawled very, very slowly and cautiously out of the brush and into the tall grass bordering it below the backside of the trap. He was on my right now, and a clump of the high brush blocked his view of me for the moment. I gathered my legs under me and took five low, quick steps forward, getting behind the shaggy lip of the trap.

Keeping on the move, I crawled around the low periphery of the trap, circling him. I had partly flanked him and could now either run for it or try to come up on him from his back side. Neither option looked good. If I tried to move away from hiding, he could get me at a good distance. A man who killed someone like Pat Reilly, then collected the valuable watchband like a souvenir out of a gumball machine, was not going to worry about missing and hitting an innocent bystander. But my trying to counterattack looked pretty dismal, too.

A short-handled rake, stuck in the sand on the edge of the trap to use in smoothing divots, decided me. *Okay, asshole. Maybe I rake your face with this.*

DROPSHOT

Hanging onto the rake with my right hand, I finished my tortured circuit of the trap and crept up onto the edge of the green. The incline was across a curved corner of the green a dozen feet ahead of me, and I didn't see my assailant. Bent well over, I slipped forward, rake handle slippery in my sweaty grasp. My heart was going about a thousand strokes a minute and I couldn't breathe. I had to get behind him and risk it all on one swing. My mind made a crazy joke. *Just like a hole in one, ha ha.*

Still crouching, I reached the edge of the green and was able to see down the slope toward the thicket. Every pore in my body prickled.

There he was, maybe twelve feet below me, standing very still, peering intently into the dense black of the thicket in front of him. His right arm hung at his side and I could just make out the shape of the pistol, elongated by the silencer.

People who make their living by arguing the power of ESP and most other such phenomena strike me as either fools or frauds. I just don't believe in many forms of magic. But we've all had the experience of getting an odd sensation in a crowd, turning, and catching someone staring at us. There are primitive defense systems that work and don't require a theory involving spacemen or ancient channelers to explain them. I knew I couldn't stand on the green, looking at this guy, for another instant before he would sense my presence.

I thought I had a very good chance.

Started down the slope, hurrying it.

Two steps, three. Four. And I was right on top of him, and had the rake handle raised and could already feel the way it was going to feel, coming down on top of his skull.

He started to turn. He was going to be too late. I stepped into the swing and started to bring the rake handle down.

Then—and only then—I saw the quick-moving shadow to my right. *Oh, Christ, there were two of them.*

The surprise swerved my blow and I missed the gray-haired man entirely in my desperate attempt to avoid the rush of the second. But it was too late. I had been so fixed on the man in front of me that I hadn't even suspected the other one, standing in the deep shadows of the trees behind the green. With a loud grunt and exhalation of whiskey-breath he hit me in the middle like a linebacker coming across on an illegal crackback. We went down in a painful heap, him on top, and I got stiffened fingers into his face, which I had no time or light to make out, and then we rolled and for a split second I almost got free, but then the other one was on top of me too and I saw the blow coming—either the gun or something like a blackjack—and I couldn't get my head out of the way in time.

The blow exploded onto the side of my skull. I started to think, *Stupid, now you've had it.* But I didn't get time to finish the thought before a darker kind of night closed in.

eleven

Nashville, Tennessee

At 9 A.M. Friday morning, in the Pie Wagon, a side-street coffeeshop a few blocks from the *Tennesseean* and *Banner* Building, Collie Davis met a contact man named VanDam.

"Brad Smith has arrived on St. Maarten," VanDam, a sallow man of fifty, told Davis.

Davis put down his coffee cup. "Shit. I thought so."

VanDam picked at a cinnamon roll he obviously did not plan to eat. He was bloodless, ordinary, worn-looking, like a Willie Loman who had spent far too many years on the road. "You asked about support for him."

"After the other thing happened, I figure he'll end up in a box unless we provide support."

"The thinking at the home office is that we have no proof the other matter was anything but the accident it appeared to be."

Collie Davis flushed with anger. "If we hadn't been looking the wrong way and let that woman get the body out of there—"

"The thinking at the home office is that that's not sufficient proof of foul play."

"What do they *need*? A smoking gun?"

103

"The thinking is that many other explanations could exist for the sequence of events. Other assignments have taken priority for the present. There was no indication on St. Maarten that any significant activity was imminent—if indeed there is sufficient evidence to suspect that any significant activity might be anticipated at all."

"That," Davis said through tight teeth, "is the kind of thinking I would expect out of those bureaucrats. Don't they *ever* get bored with having their head up their ass?"

"The thinking—"

"George, just save it. Just can it. Just shove it."

VanDam stared, emotionless as a whore, into his coffee cup. "Your concern is understood. However, the man was not asked to go there. Recent developments make clear that a man of his limited training and experience is not qualified for an assignment there. Therefore, no contact or assistance is contemplated."

"So," Davis gritted, "we asked him to go and he said no. Then he changed his mind and said yes, but now we don't know him anymore."

"The thinking at the home office is that an operative can be assigned if developments appear to warrant."

"And how the *hell* is the home office going to know if 'developments warrant' *when we don't have anybody left on the island?*"

VanDam looked up. His eyes were bleak. "My friend, that is a very interesting question."

Boulder, Colorado

Mannie Hawthorne walked out of his apartment into a snowy morning: fine, dry flakes that would not accumulate, but misted the bitter winter sky and instantly chilled his face.

Reaching the complex's parking lot, he immediately

spotted the man sitting in a brown Chevrolet sedan parked next to his Acura. They were always there on the appointed day. They were never late.

Hawthorne went to the passenger side of the brown car. The burly man in a heavy overcoat reached across the seat to pop the door-lock button and let him in.

It was warm inside the Chevrolet, and the driver had been smoking a cigar. Hawthorne's eyes immediately began to sting. He reached into the inside pocket of his bomber jacket and took out the envelope and put it on the seat between himself and the driver.

The driver, as he did every month, picked up the envelope, opened it (it was never to be sealed for pickup), and deftly—with a maddening indifference—riffled the $100 bills inside. Then he licked the flap of the envelope with his heavy, liverish tongue, ran thick fingers over the seal, and put the envelope in an attaché case close beside him.

He handed Hawthorne a small card on which had been typed the date and the amount of the payback. "You're faithful," he said. "Prompt. That's good. Keep being that way and we won't have no trouble."

"Have I ever been late?" Hawthorne flung back in frustrated anger.

"Not since that first month. Keep it up. We don't like trouble no more than you do. Like the man says: 'This hurts me more than it does you.'"

Hawthorne was so filled with frustration and fear that he did not trust himself to say any more. He would not forget the visit to his apartment, the things they did, the time in the hospital. If he lived a thousand years, the memory—and the terror—would remain.

He got out of the Chevrolet's cigar stench, unlocked his own car alongside, and got in again. The man in the Chevrolet started his engine, backed out, and drove sedately away.

Hawthorne's mind writhed. *Why did I ever let myself get*

in so deep? Why didn't I see it coming? What made me think I could sign those tickets and win it all back?

When, in God's name, am I ever going to have them all paid back, and out of my life?

All right, calm down, he counseled himself, driving out of the apartment lot and turning in the direction of the lab. When this is over you'll have enough to make lump payment. And it will be over.

Not so much longer now. A few days, to complete the switch. Then she will tell me how I am to get the wafer into the right hands, and receive my final payment. Then I can pay the Syndicate and I won't have to fear anyone anymore.

All I have to do is carry this off perfectly, to make sure I leave no clues and can never be caught.

Driving toward the mountain valley road, he tried not to think about how he had traded his terror of the gamblers for the terror he felt in this betrayal of his lab and his country—or of how the fear of mob retribution which now haunted his nights would be eliminated only at the cost of a new fear—of discovery, arrest by the government, even death.

It was far too late to think about any of those things.

Hawthorne reached the lab a little early, as he always did. He went to Room 24. Virginia Jurgensen was there ahead of him, along with another technician named Meisen.

Hands still jammed in his jacket pockets, Hawthorne went over to them at the assembly and test table. All the units had their covers removed, and coaxial umbilicals snaked into them from roll-up test consoles.

"What progress?" Hawthorne asked.

"None," Meisen said hollowly.

"It isn't in the pin-out board and it isn't in the ROM-BIOS," Virginia Jurgensen amplified.

"Oh, lord," Hawthorne groaned. "That means we work

through the weekend, right? Oh, well, that's okay. You know, when we get this darned thing straightened out, I'm going to have a lot of accrued leave and a lot of compensatory time coming. I'm going to get out of this awful early winter weather for a week or two and go to a tennis clinic down south someplace, and not even *think* computer the whole time I'm there!"

Virginia Jurgensen gave him a wintry smile. "You've really gotten into this tennis, haven't you?"

"Hey, it beats skiing. It's not nearly as likely that you'll break a leg!"

Meisen's forehead wrinkled in perplexity. "I didn't know you even liked tennis."

"Well," Hawthorne lied, "I played years ago, and not long ago I decided I simply *must* try to get into better physical condition, and there's this tennis club not far from me, so I joined. And I've been having a blast ever since. I get over there every chance I get."

"I hope," Virginia Jurgensen told him, "you hadn't planned to get over there tonight. They've already authorized six hours' overtime for each of us, and the authorization is open-ended."

"Gosh! I guess things don't look good for a quick find and fix, then."

"We haven't found a trace of anything yet that would cause all these units to fail."

Hawthorne sighed as if mightily disappointed. In truth, of course, he would have been stunned if they had reported progress in detecting the problem. His scenario did not call for the critical "discovery" until considerably later in the checkout process . . . not until late tomorrow night, or even Sunday. And then, for him, came the most dangerous, nerve-wracking part. . . .

He went to his locker and prepared to get to work. The fear scurried around inside, but he ignored it. He had had a college classmate who kept a huge snake—a boa constrictor

107

—in his dormitory room. Hawthorne had even gotten used to the damned snake, almost. The fear and worry were like the snake. You could learn to ignore them most of the time, too.

South Bend, Indiana

The early winter storm had swept south of Indiana, hitting hard at Kentucky and Tennessee before losing most of its punch, and the Notre Dame campus was chill, but with only a light, misting rain that had abated by 10:30 A.M.

An honored adjunct professor of English, whose KGB code name was Sylvester, left his office building and strolled onto the campus, heavily bundled up against the chill. No picture or other identifying information on him existed in any investigative file in the United States, although his presence—as a shadowy figure of violence—had been known for a decade. There were men in Washington who would literally have given their lives to identify him. But he had been too good for all of them.

Outside his office hall, Sylvester met a professor who was visiting another department on campus. They shook hands warmly and exclaimed about the weather and agreed to have coffee together. They crossed a sidewalk and started around an oval path in the general direction of the Rockne Memorial, exchanging their verbal bona fides.

"The call surprised me," Sylvester admitted as they strolled, their breath making little clouds of steam.

"The situation on St. Maarten has become complex," his associate told him. "My instructions are to provide you with information to be relayed to Sylvester."

Sylvester nodded, carrying on the deception that kept his true identity a secret from even trusted fellow agents. "I have the route by which I can contact Sylvester."

"This information is of the highest priority."

"I can pass the information to the next link tomorrow morning at the latest," Sylvester told him.

"Good. Here is the message. Number one. Large numbers of temporary reassignments have been made by the CIA. Identified case officers on St. Maarten have departed at this time. Number two. The former agent known as Brad Smith—the tennis player and journalist involved in the Partek case—has appeared on the island. Number three. Related activities on our behalf are on schedule. Number four. Sylvester's instructions are to proceed to St. Maarten at once. He is to register under his cover identification—whatever that may be—at The Emerald Resort. Number Five. He is to observe Smith and related activities. He may be required to take action to assure noninterference by Smith or others in our activities there."

Sylvester nodded and took a thin cigar from his inside pocket, lighting it with his old Zippo. He knew enough to guess or imagine many details of the assignment.

The news that Brad Smith was involved in this was also mildly startling. Sylvester had imagined Smith could never again be utilized by the CIA in any capacity.

Two years earlier, Sylvester's assignment had been to track down and eliminate one of his nation's top agents in the United States. That man, Dominic Partek, had managed to elude Sylvester in Montana, and had almost escaped him again in the Hudson River Valley of New York. While Sylvester had been searching for him, this man Brad Smith—a bumbling amateur—had succeeded in circumventing all the odds and getting the young tennis star Danisa Lechova out of Yugoslavia, where she could no longer be used as a hostage to prevent her brother's possible defection to the West. Except for a lucky telephone tip out of New York City, Sylvester might never have located Partek in hiding—might not have been able to eliminate him scant

109

hours before the FBI and CIA agents descended on his room to take him into protective custody.

Even at that, Sylvester remembered with chagrin, Partek had managed to leave an audio cassette. It had named a dozen of the KGB's top operatives and sympathizers in the U.S., and detailed the operation of a ring at the brink of breaking into America's best-kept Star Wars research. So Sylvester had done his job, but he had not been quick enough fully to avert disaster.

It rankled. It was Sylvester's only failure during his ten years in America. His anger still bubbled, and this miserable amateur, Brad Smith, was at the heart of the anger.

Smith, Sylvester thought, would be only one of his problems, and perhaps not the most important. Once more they might be using Smith as a decoy. The KGB knew Smith's identity full well, and the CIA knew that they knew. It seemed unlikely that he had been sent as more than a diversionary trick. There might be other CIA operatives on the scene, unidentified and far more dangerous. Sylvester would have to proceed with even more than his usual cunning.

But he would watch Smith. There was no doubt of that. He almost hoped Smith *was* operational again. Sylvester felt he owed the American something. It would be a pleasure to pay him back for the partial failure with Partek, and the Lechova girl.

He said, "Sylvester is certain to ask me about equipment."

"You are to provide Sylvester with sufficient identification to allow him to claim an air express shipment of books which will be sent to The Emerald Resort addressed to the name on this card."

"I see." Sylvester took the card with a fictitious name printed on it. "I will comply with instructions and pass the message verbatim," he told his associate.

"I envy him," the other man said with a chill smile. "To get away from this gathering winter!"

DROPSHOT

"Our weather here surely will improve," Sylvester replied. "It's time for Indian Summer, and I will enjoy that. I always do."

"I envy you your position here," the other man said. "Prestige and the academic life. As a scholar of Latvian literature, you have made a niche for yourself that is enviable. How I wish my own academic credentials were as strong! Ah, for a quiet, secure life like yours!"

"It is good here," Sylvester said. "And look, my friend. It is a favorable portent. The sun is breaking through."

As the two men paused and stood together, the sun peered through misty holes in the low gray clouds. It beamed across the tree-shrouded campus, lighting the sedate red brick buildings, gleaming against the high, burnished curvatures of the beloved Golden Dome.

twelve

Mia Hesser, nearly nude in a tiny red bikini, rolled indolently onto her right side, raising herself on her elbow to batter me with those eyes. "So shall we open the wine, darling?"

"Let's wait awhile," I suggested, turning on my beach towel to face her.

"We mustn't stay out in this sun too long." She looked me up and down, taking in the sun-baked dark of my legs and arms and the dough-colored pallor of my torso. "You really will burn."

"I'll watch it."

She reached across the small space between us to touch my chest with a lazy, crimson-tipped hand. "Let me rub some of my oil on you. You'll like it. I will too. You really do have a nice body."

If my head hadn't been impersonating a dropforge press, I might have had trouble restraining a smile. Subtlety was not one of the weapons in Mrs. Hesser's arsenal. Instead, I yawned. "Maybe later."

"Darling, are you saying the answer is *no*?"

"No, I'm saying maybe later."

She sat up, pouting just a little, and took a tan plastic

bottle from her beachbag and began anointing her long, beautiful legs.

We were on the private beach perhaps a mile from The Emerald Resort and her husband's tennis school. There was no one else on the beach here, perhaps because you had to know how to climb down to it as we had just done. Great rust-colored boulders, fallen from the wooded cliffs behind us, blocked easy walking-in along the sand from both directions. This section was invisible from the narrow dirt road far above us.

Except for my crashing headache, it was a perfect day. Pretty little breakers came in gray-blue, rolled onto the pale sand, and broke into foam. We had climbed down from the hidden parking place beside the road, put out the beach towels, and had taken a brief dip. After that plash of cool ocean, which had slightly cleared my throbbing skull and made Mia's microscopic bikini even more devastating, we had stretched out on our towels and lay quiet a few minutes, listening to the whisper of the water and the cries of the seagulls, watching a distant pelican dive for his breakfast.

It had not taken Mia long to turn the conversation to how comfortable she felt with me, how much fun she hoped we were going to have together. To which I had said nothing. She had then suggested opening the wine, and now seemed mildly put out about my unresponsiveness.

The last thing I wanted was to alienate her. I needed information from her, and she could be a valuable if unwitting ally. So I touched the small bandage on the side of my skull. "Mia, I shook up a lot of brain tissue when I took that nasty fall at my cabin last night. I'm not functioning a hundred percent." Then, knowing it was the kind of remark she would like, I added, "If it had been anyone else but you waiting for me, I think I would have stood them up."

Her lips curled with pleasure. "Oh, you're sweet!"

Which postponed the perhaps inevitable time when the answer would have to be finally and clearly and definitively no—at which point I knew I would cease to exist for her.

I watched her oil herself. She pretended she did not know I was watching her performance.

I had been dismally sure last night, when the second man appeared and somebody cracked me on the side of the head, that I was a dead man. I didn't know anything at all for a long time, although today I thought I could remember two male voices arguing over me at some point. I know I was rolled over, searched, dragged a little way, and tossed roughly down. Then a lot of time went black and then slowly I awoke, distant pain first, then funny dreams or hallucinations, then a more general hurt, the awareness of cold skin, wetness around me, lassitude, a pulse crashing through my brain, disorientation, and then—much faster—dark that was not quite dark because my eyes were open, some moving black stuff that was bushes and weeds, starlight overhead, and, when I spasmodically tried to sit up, a rush of vertigo that knocked me down again.

The second time I took it slower.

Amazingly, I was not only alive but generally no worse for the wear. My head hurt badly. I felt confused. My vision kept trying to go double or triple. When I stood, I almost went down again from the dizziness.

But I was not far from the spot where I had tried my stupid attack on the man with gray hair. Just downhill, tossed over the edge of the drainage ditch again. Pockets turned inside out, but nothing missing, my wallet and keys and some change on the grass beside me, and not even the cash taken out of the wallet.

At the moment I was not capable of coming up with a theory as to why I was still among the living. I had followed the man who was wearing my watchband, the one I had given to Pat. Maybe he had been going to meet the other person, or maybe the other one was at the party, too, and saw both of us leave, and followed the follower. And maybe the gunshot had been meant to blow my head off, and maybe it had been meant only to scare me off. But I couldn't get any further than that because my brains felt scrambled. I knew I was alive, not much else.

My watch had said past 4 A.M. I had to get off the golf course and get some help. Walking like a drunk, I found my way across the rest of the golf course and back to the Mary Mary. Repeated pounding on the office A-frame finally turned out the landlady with all the gold teeth. She was grumpy, to say the least, but when she got a good look at the blood-covered side of my face and shoulder, and heard how I had fallen in some rocks out on *her* stretch of beach, she was overwhelmed by either the milk of human compassion or fear of a lawsuit. I reported I was too dizzy to drive and didn't know where to find a doctor. She said she would take me to a doctor, and did, to the emergency room of the little hospital in Philipsburg. A sleepy, amiable local physician put four or five stitches in the side of my head, took a negative X-ray, gave me an envelope of Percodan pills, and suggested that I might want to report back if I started upchucking or hallucinating. The stitches, he said, were to come out in five days.

After that, my landlady drove me back home. I assured her I was not litiginous. She seemed more relaxed after I explained what that meant.

Dawn would be on St. Maarten soon, but I had to sleep. I thought about the flimsy front door and how easy it would be to cut through any of the wallscreens of my A-frame. With my head doing one of the loud parts of the *1812*, I dug a few empty Lipton iced tea cans out of my trash. Spacing them on both sides of the door and down the side walls, I rigged a makeshift burglar alarm.

I lay down on my cot and listened to the roaring in my head and was almost instantly asleep. Forty minutes later one of my cans toppled. I came out of bed like a shot. I don't know who was more scared, me or the juvenile gray rat who had just squeezed under the corner of a screen, looking for a snack. I grabbed my deodorant spray off the dresser and got close enough to shoot him with some of it before he escaped the way he had come. My nerves were too jangled to sleep soundly after that, but I sort of dozed for another hour, past dawn.

I staggered out about eight o'clock. A stiffening breeze off the bay drove two-foot breakers onto the beach. Nobody was out. I took a cold shower, keeping my throbbing skull and small bandage out of the water, and then added to my collection of Lipton iced tea empties for the burglar alarm system. Standing out in front, I watched a small storm cloud pass to the west, and with it went the wind. I allowed myself a cigarette and tried to think straight. Failing that, I remembered and decided to keep the appointment with Mia.

Who at this point in my ruminations finished anointing her body and glanced at me with an inviting smile. "Sure you don't want any of this?" She held up the lotion bottle.

"Thanks, no."

She flopped back down on her towel, turning on her side to face me again, and made a production of gently touching herself here and there, examining tiny bands of pale flesh revealed at the edges of the bikini. "I have to be careful about the sun today, too. This new suit is smaller than any of my others. But it's cute, don't you think?"

"Very cute."

With every pretense of innocence, she raised her left knee, opening herself to me. "Oh, dear," she murmured in mock dismay. She touched the juncture of inner thighs where curly dark pubic hairs peeked out around the tiny central band of the bikini. "I'm going to have to shave a bit closer, too." Her eyes swept up to mine. "I think I'm embarrassed."

I yawned.

She closed her legs and reached into the ice chest for the wine. "Tell me about Danisa."

It caught me by surprise, and hurt. "There's nothing to tell."

"I know you were married to her and she was lovely

and wonderful, and she died tragically. Here, darling, will you please open this bottle? Thank you. I always break a nail and then I'm in a snit for a week. Do you still miss her? Are you still grieving?"

"Yes and yes."

"It was long ago, Brad."

I poured wine into the glasses. She hadn't brought plastic, but Waterford. I said, "Could we talk about something else?"

"But, Brad, you can't live in the past, darling. You need to get involved again. Even if it seems like the last thing in the world you want to do."

I was really uncomfortable and almost angry with this. "You may be right, Mia. Maybe the time is closer than I think. But for right now, for Christ's sake can we please just drop it?"

Her eyes swept down. "Yes. I'm sorry." Her gaze came up again, that up-from-under look. "What shall we talk about?"

"Let's talk about Al."

"Oh, God! Nothing more exciting than *that?*"

"Hey. He is your husband."

"Yes, and I dearly love him, the sweetheart. But he is *so* involved with the tennis program, and always rearranging investments, trying new ways to make money—not that I sneer at making money, you understand—but he just doesn't ever find enough time to *play!*"

"Running all his programs has to be a big, big job."

"He works at it nearly all the time!"

"But surely it's all paying off. He must be worth millions by now."

She sniffed and looked sullenly over the top of her wine glass at the ocean. "On paper, I suppose."

I chuckled. "Where else are fortunes except on paper? The poor guy can't carry a Brink's truck of cash around with him all day!"

"He couldn't fill up a kiddycar!" she shot back at me.

117

Jack M. Bickham

"What?"

I had touched a nerve and she was hot about it. "Cash flow. Cash flow. That's all I ever hear about. What's the good of being the wife of a millionaire if he *never has any money?*"

This was interesting. I started to pry further, but her glare stopped me. I had pushed it as far as possible for now. "Hey, Mia, I'm sorry I brought up a sore point." I reached across and lightly squeezed her arm.

The effect of my casual touch was extraordinary. There was a gasping intake of air, a tiny convulsion across all the curvatures and swellings and indentations and long, glistening surfaces of her body. Her eyes opened wide, the dark pupils instantly dilating as she stared at me. Electricity leaped. Her wine glass went to the sand on her other side, spilling.

"Brad." It was a sound from deep below her throat. Incendiary, she moved across the little band of sand that separated us.

I would like to report I was more controlled and more noble or something. The lady caught me by surprise with her fervor, clinging ankle to shoulder, flesh on flesh, arms straining around me, fingernails digging my back, her open mouth plucking and pleading desperately at my face, and then her mouth found mine, and eagerly her tongue went to work. And I went slightly bonkers for a minute or two.

She was expert. She was also starved for it. I responded to her, stroking the long, straining lushness of her bare back, and she began to murmur, and swung a heavy, oil-slippery leg over my hips, and as her tongue thrust frantically to the back of my mouth, there began convulsive pressings and tightenings of those formidable hips, that hard hungry pelvis.

"Oh, baby," she moaned against my throat. "Do me. Do me. Do me now." Her fingers snaked across my belly.

118

I tried to come up for air. She fought to control me, demanding. I broke from her with a really harsh physical effort and rolled entirely off my beach towel onto the hot sand on the far side from her.

Her eyes were flame-filled and mostly out of control. "What is it? Don't worry about anything. Do you—has it been a long time for you? Don't worry. I can make it all right—" She reached for my crotch.

I avoided her grasp. "It isn't that."

"*What*, then?"

I touched the bandage on my head. "I'm sorry. I'm about half sick."

She made a little mouing sound. "I'm so sorry, darling. I'm so dumb!" She gasped for air and tried to reestablish some control, some irony. She even managed an arch, insinuating smile. "Isn't that funny? No man ever told me he had a headache before."

"Maybe, but I—"

"But you won't have it forever. And don't you already see how fantastic we're going to be together?"

This would not do. I stood. "There's the other obvious problem."

Still recovering, she watched me. "What?"

"You're a married woman."

"Surely *that* isn't going to stop you!"

"I'm a pretty quaint guy."

"Are you just teasing me?"

"No, Mia."

"Then are you sure you didn't knock all the sense out of your head when you took that fall last night?"

I didn't trust myself to answer her.

After a minute or so, she scrambled to her feet and dusted sand off her legs and arms. "I'm going to take one more short dip, and then I have to be going." She turned and ran gracefully to the water's edge and plunged in.

119

I stayed where I was and watched her, a woman too voluptuous to look like a fashion model, thank God, but stunning. She surfaced after her brief dive and played in the hip-deep breakers, kicking in the surf and collecting a fragment of driftwood floating in. No nymph, this lady. More like the sirens of mythology who were capable of luring any man to his destruction.

When she came back to me, shaking her magnificent hair and toweling herself down, she was quieter. "Gotta go, darling."

"Okay, Mia."

"Don't look so sad, sweetheart. There will be other times for us. I promise you that."

We didn't talk much during the climb back to the road and the short drive back to where my Cortina was parked.

As I was about to get out of her Jaguar she leaned quickly across the shifter console and caught an arm around my neck and gave me a blazing kiss, her tongue thrusting hard and deep.

"So you won't forget me," she flashed as I got out.

I was a little shaken. "Thanks for the buggyride."

"Soon, darling. *Soon.*"

"So long."

Tossing her hair, she gunned the luxury car out of the shade, fishtailing it onto the highway under heavy, reckless acceleration. Even the finest cars do not appreciate that kind of abuse. But Al—good old Al—could be counted on to fix anything she broke. Maybe sometimes he even tried to fix her broken people.

My headache had reached mountainous proportions, but I didn't have forever. I climbed into the baking-hot Cortina and drove around the island to the French side, only a few miles across lumpy, useless hill terrain. Marigot, the French town, was considerably smaller than Philipsburg, but with balconied buildings and a hillside chapel that reminded me of parts of New Orleans. Skull thumping, I walked down to the quay where an ancient wooden destroyer of the French fleet was tied up. The marine shop that dealt in boat rentals, tours, and diving equipment was nearby.

The bone-skinny Brit behind the counter looked beyond strong emotion in his faded khaki pants and oil-streaked yellow St. Maarten T-shirt, but he lost his temper immediately. "I've spoken about the matter as often as I intend to, Mr. Smith!"

"Take it easy. The man was a close friend of mine—"

"Forget it, mate! I went through this with the Marigot police. I went through it again with the man from Philipsburg. Then, when the Americans came by, I told *them* all about it! We operate a clean shop here, a professional place. We sell and rent only top-quality equipment and we *maintain* it. The man made a mistake and there's an end to it. Now excuse me, I have a charter boat to get ready."

I walked back up the hill toward the corner cafe with a balcony overlooking the postage-stamp park. I had gotten nothing, but he had told me enough for me to know that somebody from Langley had had the same ideas and checked it out ahead of me. The conclusion was clear: there was nothing to be learned from the scuba gear Pat had used, or the condition it was found in after his death. If they had found anything incriminating, I wouldn't be walking around here like the Lone Ranger.

I climbed to the balcony of the cafe and ordered iced tea and sat by the railing for a while, thinking things over as well as my headache would allow. Below, an occasional French sailor, a few natives, and a handful of tourists strolled the hot, shaded streets. The French tricolor hung limp from its staff in the park. The sun was brilliant on the hillside to my right, where the chapel was, the slope ablaze with brilliant red and lavender flowers I could not identify.

Danisa would have known what the flowers were. I imagined her across the table from me, how it might have been. Then I caught myself and tried to think of other things, and into my mind came the hot, musky odor of Mia Hesser, and the taste of her tongue in my mouth.

My head hurt worse. I gave up and went back to my car.

At the Mary Mary I took more pain pills and drank another can of my stock of Lipton iced tea, and then threw up. I needed to think and I needed to *move*. But I felt truly terrible, and knew just enough to realize that if I babied myself a little now, I might recover faster in the long run.

Rationality won. I closed myself up in the A-frame and stretched out on the bed and waited to see if I had kept down enough painkillers to do me any good. It got hot inside and the sweat rolled. I slept.

thirteen

The next morning I felt considerably better.

Saturday was a big day at Al Hesser's establishment. When I arrived a little after 10 A.M., two of The Emerald's courtesy vans were disgorging newly landed customers. Most of the new patrons were thirtyish and slender and carrying tennis rackets. There were also some middle-aged arrivals milling around, and near the entry I had to walk around a stack of luggage and two book boxes evidently awaiting the arrival of a Prof. Somebody-or-other and more new registrants who hadn't gotten in yet. A sign near the door said something called "The Al Hesser Free-for-All" was in progress.

Going out to the courts, I saw what was going on. All the courts were filled. There was a tournament bracket board, filled with grease-penciled names, on the side of the instructional building. There were tennis players all over the place: playing matches, warming up on the backboards beyond the fence, standing around as spectators, lined up at the soft drink stands, filling the four-row bleachers on the south side, milling around in the pro shop.

"Hey, Brad! I heard you were in town!"

I turned and found Billie Jean, in tennis gear and ready

to play, grinning up at me. "Hey, old lady. Want to play some mixed doubles?"

"Give me a hug first, you jerk."

We hugged. She looked great, and seemed as glad to see me as I was to see her. Billie Jean did much of her championship playing before the days of the big publicity, the big bucks for women. Maybe there wouldn't be big bucks for the women players if it hadn't been for this lady. She had seen it all, and there had never been a player with a bigger heart. She was just damned special.

"How long are you here for?" she asked.

"A week, maybe two."

"Then we *will* get in some doubles." The imp came into her eyes. "You still got any serve left?"

"Well, I can get it over the net about half the time."

She laughed. "Okay, great. My knees only give out about half the time when I try to go to the net, so we ought to make a perfect team."

"Do you think we can get a sponsor?"

"Sure! Maybe the AARP."

"I hear they have a real pretty patch."

She shouldered her rackets. "I'm giving an exhibition. Gotta get out there."

"Later."

She went outside into the scorching sun, and I fed coins into the cigarette machine. I know, I know, I had quit again. But I had found an excuse this morning, as I had most mornings in the last year. Today it was the residual headache.

Seeing no other familiar faces nearby, I wandered back outside and strolled around. The man with gray hair was not in evidence.

It did not surprise me. Because I was still among the living, I had to figure the attack Thursday night was to get me off his tail. I also had to figure that I would be dead if he had needed to stay around. He and his pal had spotted me following him and they had put me out of commission for a while. I had been warned and he had been given time and now it was safe to assume that he was either long gone or in hiding.

I had missed my best chance.

But there were other chances. There was the chance afforded by the contents of Pat Reilly's deposit box. If I could just figure them out.

The shock of seeing that watchband on the stranger's wrist was still with me, fresh and raw. Pat would not have sold the band. It had been taken off his dead wrist. Then, in his colossal arrogance or unawareness of the band's uniqueness, Gray-Hair put it on his own watch and wore it.

Which—unless there had been the most bizarre coincidence—made it clear that Gray-Hair had killed Pat. Knowing this made Pat's death more real to me. And more ugly. Perhaps I had missed my chance to confront him quickly, and have this done with one way or another. And now he was going to be very, very hard to find again. But I had the other clues Pat had left me, and I had the time, and I was going to get to the bottom of things here. And to hell with what Collie Davis or his boss-bureaucrats thought about it.

I sat in the bleachers and smoked and watched some of the matches. Some were fun and some, because the participants thought they were pros, weren't. After an hour or two, there was a break in the pairings and the last morning match came to a conclusion. One of the assistant pros dragged some video and sound gear onto a center court. Then Al Hesser came out, resplendent in his tennis whites, carrying a racket and a cordless microphone.

He strolled to the middle court and waved to the crowd, his famous half-crazy grin shining. He spoke into the mike and his voice blasted out of loudspeakers placed on poles around the periphery of the courts: "Hey, people! Welcome to the Free-for-All! Hey, babies, are you having a good time?"

Everybody laughed and applauded. Al took a comic bow.

Then he went into his routine.

"You know," he boomed over the PA system, jiggling to the sidelines to pick up a pretty white Head composite, "we've seen a lot of good tennis here already this morning. Now, I know a lot of you are thinking, 'I could beat any of these bums.'" He paused and leered. "Right? *Right?*" It got the desired laugh.

"I just want to tell you one little thing about playing tennis," Al went on, strolling toward the end of the court nearest the fencing and the bleachers. "And that's a secret, boys and girls. All of us want one thing when we go onto the court." He lowered his voice so the whisper echoed with a mock-conspiratorial tone. "We want to *kill* the opposition."

Over the renewed laughter, he announced, "Now if I could just get a beginner out here to demonstrate something with me . . . lemme see . . . we need a real hacker . . ." He looked into the shadows of the pro shop, a spot where we couldn't see from the bleachers. "How about you, young man? Yes, you! Come on! Don't be bashful!"

A familiar figure in white tennis togs, with red and blue trim, ambled out of the shadows. The people in the stands gasped, laughed, and then applauded. It was Jimmy Connors.

Al signaled Connors to his side. "Now, son," he said, going on with the gag, "you came to Al Hesser's Court College hoping to learn something about the game, isn't that right?"

"Yessir," Connors said, playing his part. "I was hoping so."

"Okay, son. Now I want you to get down there at the other end of the court and send me some courtesy serves, and I'll give you a tip. Okey dokey?"

"Yessir, that would be just wonderful, sir."

Connors trotted to the other end. While he went, Al kept up a constant string of patter about killing the opposition. "We all want to hit that big winner, right? We all want *pace* on the ball, right? We want to blast the other guy off the pavement, right? Okay! Sonny, do you think you can hit me some short courtesy serves?"

Connors nodded and made a funny production of bouncing a ball, aiming at it, and getting it over the net to Al. Al dumped it. "Now when you get a short ball, people, that's what you've been waiting for, right? That's the promised land of tennis, right? The short ball!" He gestured to heaven. " 'Oh, thank you, God, for this short ball, I am going to kill him with this shot!' "

He faced the net. "Hit me another one as soon as you can get yourself organized over there, son. —Now the problem with the short ball is that you've got to get it back over the net, right? And you've got to keep it in, right? And you've got to *kill* it or you'll have wasted the opportunity, right? So here's what often happens."

Connors hit him a short ball. Al made a clownish, exaggerated forehand preparation and then hit down on the ball, blasting it into the net. He immediately dropped his racket, fell to his knees, and put both hands to the sides of his head in anguish. People laughed.

Al hopped up and danced around with the microphone. "So you were all set to kill it, but it killed *you* instead! What went wrong? What went wrong?"

Several voices called unintelligibly from the bleachers.

"That's right!" Al yelled back excitedly, hopping around. "I hit *down* on the ball. I tried to hit a forehand and an overhead at the same time and I got an overhand forehead or a foreever handhead or something! What did I forget?"

Again there were some scattered, unintelligible voices.

"That's right! That's right! I forgot that *to make the ball have overspin, you've got to hit up!*" He signaled Connors to give him another one. "Here it comes! Oh boy oh boy oh boy, I remember, I remember, I gotta hit *UP!*"

With the "up," he blasted a moonball clear over the

back fence. This time the laughter was louder in the stands, and Al fell onto his back and twitched like a man having a seizure.

It was corny, but it was cute. Al Hesser had taken Vic Braden's spiel and turned it into a vaudeville show. He was so transparent, such a ham, and so outrageous that he was good at it. And he was making perfectly true and valid points about basic tennis along with the act.

You had to admire the approach. So many people took their tennis *so* seriously, when all they had to do was loosen up and have a really good time. Thank God for players who want to improve their game; they help keep bread on the table for has-beens like me who now spend much of our time as teaching pros. And everybody should be as good as they can be, in whatever it is. But the game needed some clowns like Al; they taught just as effectively as anyone else and reminded people that it is, after all, a game. And *it's supposed to be fun.*

Whatever else I thought of Al, I had to give him credit for this.

After his spiel was over, he played a few easy points with Jimmy, and they had some more laughs. Naturally Al "won." Jimmy walked off, shaking his head as if in shock, and then came through the court gate to mix with people in the bleachers. The stands began to empty out, and the PA announced resumption of the tourney at 1:30 P.M.

I went below, said hello to Jimmy, and strolled to the far end of the complex to check on progress on the new courts down there. A tremendous amount of fill dirt had been trucked in, packed, and leveled. The drain tiles were in place. It looked like the next step would be the gravel drainage base. I did some mental arithmetic and figured these courts were costing Al something like $260,000.

I walked back the way I had come. The playing courts

were temporarily vacant, and only a handful of people remained in the stands. The place had cleared out fast for cocktails and lunch at The Emerald. As I neared the little tunnel between the pro shop and the training shed, I heard Al's voice. It came from the tunnel, and he sounded mad as hell.

I got closer and the words fit together to make sense.

Al: *"Look, goddammit, don't give me this shit! You've always been paid before, we've just got a little temporary cash flow problem. You just deliver those soft drinks and hot dogs, goddammit, and don't hassle me!"*

I walked by the mouth of the tunnel. Al was standing in there with a delivery driver, his vending truck parked beyond them outside the tunnel, the back doors open on cases of soft drinks and boxes of junkfood.

They didn't see me and I walked on.

Mia, I thought, hadn't been lying when she hinted about possible financial problems. Al had to be making tons of money, but he was spending more. The growth-or-die syndrome.

It was obvious, too, that he was spending wildly on his social life, and on Mia. She would be about as cheap to keep as a nuclear aircraft carrier.

And Mia was hardly the kind to make it easier for him. I had known a few like her. They attracted, ornamented, used, and then discarded men like last year's wardrobe. It was clear poor Al was crazy about her, was dazzled by her, needed her to prop up his ego—*(Hey, look at me, look at what I've got!)*. The pressure had to be terrible; a woman like Mia had all the loyalty of a leech.

And the first time he denied her something . . . or suggested they go slowly on expenditure . . . she would take a walk. Al could never handle something like that. She was precious to him. Part of his carefully crafted prestige habitat.

129

No wonder Al was desperate behind his facade.

I strolled across the gardens toward The Emerald.

"Brad?" a woman's voice called behind me. "Brad Smith? Is that you?"

I turned. Hurrying up the brick walk after me was a tall, pretty blonde whose tennis whites showed off exceptionally good legs. She was smiling brilliantly, as if really happy to see me, and for an instant I drew a blank and then I saw who it was.

"Hi!" she said, catching me. Putting her racket under her arm, she extended a happy hand. "Remember me? The scaredy cat on the plane?"

"Beth," I remembered, taking her hand. "Beth Miles."

"You're a lot better with names and faces than I am, obviously! My God, when I said I thought I had seen you somewhere before, I didn't realize you were *the* Brad Smith."

I grinned at her. "Somebody told you."

"About twenty people pointed you out to me!"

She was slightly sunburned, happy, relaxed and happy, vividly more alive than the woman I had sat beside on the airplane just a couple of days ago.

"I heard you're staying here, too," she told me.

"Wrong. I'm over at a little beach shack place. It's called the Mary Mary."

She used her racket to shade pretty eyes from the sun. "How come not here? Am I asking dumb questions again?"

"Not at all. I like it over there, is all." I hesitated. She was really cute as hell. "Look. Have you had lunch?"

"No, and I certainly hope you're asking for a reason."

I took her arm, which was smooth and hot from the sun. "Let's find a sandwich or something."

We went in. Everything was packed because everyone wanted to eat at the same time. Mia Hesser passed by and saw Beth and me at the far end of the cafeteria line, and glided over to collect us.

"Darling, just go through that way and you'll find a small private dining room. Your name is on the special guest list." She swiveled coffee eyes to Beth. "Who is your little friend?"

"Beth Miles, your hostess, Mia Hesser."

"Hi," Beth said with a smile. "You have a wonderful place here!"

"I'm pleased you approve, dear," Mia said icily. "It's so encouraging to know that even the economy-class guests are enjoying their little stay." She turned and stalked off.

Beth scrunched her face up. "Ouch!"

"She's a real sweetheart," I observed. "Come on."

She held back. "Where?"

"Didn't you hear what she said? Into the other dining room."

"I can't go in there!"

"The bloody damned hell you can't. Come on."

She hung back and I tugged her along by the hand. Some people stared and it was sort of fun. I got the impression she kept hanging back because it forced me to hang onto her hand that way.

Inside the smaller dining room we found only a handful of people, including Jimmy, Billie Jean, and Pat Cash at a table with several of the resident teaching pros. They waved and—dimly aware that I was showing off a little—I walked Beth over there and introduced her to everyone. She looked stunned.

"Hey, join us," Jimmy suggested.

"Wish we could, but we have a lot of catching up to do," I told him. "We're old pals."

Beth was two shades pinker with excitement when we sat down at our own table across the room. "'Old pals' indeed!"

"Well, *I'm* old. Maybe I should have said, 'We're an old pal and a young pal.'"

She fanned her face with her hand. "Not so young here. I think maybe I'm having a hot flash. And *you're* certainly more chipper than you were on the airplane."

"Yeah. Well, the weather agrees with me."

"Did you hurt your head?"

"Nothing serious. A little accident. So you're staying here?"

"Yes." And she started to tell me all about it.

It was, to my astonishment, fun. She was flustered and happy and excited, and she talked a blue streak. We had lunch and she kept right on babbling. She said she had played tennis since she was a child, and had been number 2 on the UCLA women's team as a senior. "I wasn't really good enough to turn pro, so I went on to law school, and then some years passed, and I got married . . . and *that* didn't last very long . . . and then I got into the make-money trap. Then someone I was seeing . . . for quite a long time . . . died, and I kind of went into a funk. But now I'm better and I came down here to try to get my tennis game back into shape, and this old bod, too." She practiced law now in Sacramento, doing a lot of work that related to the California legislature. I got a few hints that she was a considerably more important and effective lawyer than she let on. She had a brother who taught engineering in Chicago and a sister who was a writer. She was having a fine time here and she loved St. Maarten.

Her questions to me were open, curious, and quietly persistent. I lied a lot. She knew all about Danisa and I found myself talking about all that, with no lies in that part. In about an hour I got to know more about her—and she about me—than I would have thought possible. I really liked her.

"Maybe we can play a few games," she suggested.

"Well, sure," I said. "I'm not very good anymore."

She looked me up and down with dancing amusement. "I'll take it easy on you."

"Then fine."

"Are you staying around this afternoon?"

"Not long."

We walked outside together. She asked casually, "Is your beach nice over there at the Mary Mary?"

"Not bad at all. Not as pretty as the one down below here, though."

"I haven't done much beachcombing yet."

I let that one pass. We stopped on the walk in the garden. She shaded her eyes with her hand this time. "Well," she said.

I had the most astounding impulse to take her into my arms. She was just so cute and vibrant and totally feminine. But the impulse came and went swiftly, because you just don't do things like that, right? It could mean *anything*, a gesture like that. Even the awakening of feelings long since given up for dead.

So all I did was reach out and squeeze her shoulder, like the awkward oaf I can be sometimes.

"See you later, Beth."

She walked away with a lilt in her stride. I watched her go, enjoying it, and then turned back to reenter the resort and passively snoop around.

Sports pages carry a lot of pictures, and there is TV. If you achieve something in a sport such as tennis, a lot of people of all ages learn your face. So I might have been recognized by a few people anywhere.

Here, however, almost everyone was involved in tennis as a hobby. So—as Beth's comment about people pointing me out had indicated—my recognition factor went up by a factor of perhaps twenty. People recognized me and wanted to talk.

I spent more than an hour wandering around, and a lot of people drifted by for conversation.

I did not ask a lot of questions. No sense calling attention to the fact that I was keenly curious about how things were run around here, and what if anything I might glean to give me hints about what could have fatally aroused Pat Reilly's attention. People volunteered information: who they were, what they did, where they were from. I met people from Ohio, Indiana, New York, South Carolina, Kansas, California, Utah, other places. Al Hesser drew them nationally, and they seemed universally enthusiastic about his humor-based methods of teaching.

Unfortunately, all of them seemed to be just what they claimed to be. Unfortunately, too, nobody volunteered anything that might point to illegal or sinister things going on around here. If there was something not kosher about Al Hesser's Court College, I was not smart enough to bring out any hints about it.

It looked like nothing was going to come easy, and I was going to have to keep on digging.

fourteen

Sunday morning, early, a big charter jet landed on the runway less than two hundred yards behind my A-frame. The roar of the reversing engines blasted through the trees and brush to rattle me out of bed. It was just dawn, a clear sky promising another hot day.

The early wakeup didn't irritate me. I felt almost back to normal today, with only a minor residual headache and the slightest feeling of disorientation that came and went. I had spent late Saturday impersonating a hermit and had come to some decisions about my next steps.

I endured another cold shower and shave and was still padding around with a towel around my middle when somebody's footsteps crunched in the gravel and dirt outside. Next came the rap on my door that started changing my schedule for the day.

Peering out through a corner of the screen, I checked.

Standing outside was the Emerald goon named Ricardo who hadn't liked it when I pushed poor little Billy Hesser down. He looked freshly scrubbed and sleepy in his white canvas pants and shoes and loud madras shirt, with a wide-brimmed straw hat shading his dark face.

Oh, swell, I thought, opening up. "Morning!"

Jack M. Bickham

Ricardo didn't smile. Maybe he couldn't. "Mr. Hesser
wants to see you."

"Fine. I'll be over in about an hour."

He blinked. "No. Now."

"Do you think, Ricardo, maybe I have time to put on
my pants?"

"Hurry."

"What's the rush?"

"Mr. Hesser says it's important."

"Okay. You go on back and tell Al I'll be over in thirty
minutes."

"No. I take you back with me. Now."

What a wonderful, subtle guy. Curiosity overcame my
natural inclination to be difficult. I put on some clothes
while Ricardo stood outside, staring at the morning waves in
a good impersonation of those heads on Easter Island.

He had come over in a bright green delivery van with
The Emerald's logo painted on both sides. He drove the
wallowing dirt road in stolid silence, looking neither left nor
right.

I gave it a try: "What's it all about, Ricardo?"

"Huh?"

"Why does Al need to talk to me so early?"

"Dunno."

"Great little tournament yesterday. Good participa-
tion."

No answer.

"Where's your sidekick, L. K.?"

A shrug.

"Do you guys have duties other than protecting Al and
his family, Ricardo?"

"Security."

"You mean, like making sure no one steals things in the
resort?"

"Like make sure nobody does anything they shoul'n't."

"Like . . . ?"

"Like," he repeated with dogged grimness, "nothing they shoul'n't. Causing trouble. Being a problem."

"Man, that's a big job. That covers a lot of territory."

Nothing.

"What do you do," I asked, "if you catch somebody being a problem?"

"Make them stop. Make them leave."

"Do many people give you trouble?"

He made a snorting noise through his big nose. "Couple tried." Then he became positively lyrical: "Guy kept getting drunk. Tried to put some moves on Mrs. Hesser. Boss asked him to leave. He wanted to argue. I broke his elbows. He left."

"It sounds like a great job, Ricardo. Do you have many problems like that?"

"People snooping sometimes."

"Snooping? Snooping into what? What do you mean?"

Ricardo's face sort of twitched. He seemed to realize he was having a conversation. He shrugged and turned on the radio.

So much for pumping good old Ricardo. I hung onto the passenger assist handle over the door on my side and tried to keep my brains from being rattled out through the right ear.

It had been a good thing to play hermit late yesterday. Some second-wave after-effects of the clubbing I had taken on the golf course helped persuade me. But I also needed some time alone to sort things out.

Gray-Hair was gone. Or hiding so deep I could never find him again. That rankled.

His disappearance, however, did not mean I was similarly in the clear: he had seen me, and so had the man who jumped me from behind. They had chosen not to kill me then for reasons of their own—probably because they didn't have instructions on the matter, but possibly because they now had all the advantage: they could keep an eye on me, while I was back at square zero without a clue concerning anyone.

I had blown a golden opportunity.

Pat was still dead, and if there had been any doubts in my mind that he had stumbled upon something, and had been murdered for it, such doubts were long gone. Something was wrong at the Al Hesser resort. Nobody was going to help me find out what it was. I wanted more than ever to find out what it was.

All I had were scattered hints that added up to nothing, and the contents of the bank deposit box.

Locked in my A-frame, I went back over those, trying to see something I had missed. Trying to make them add up to something meaningful.

The review had not been a lot of help.

The rough pencil sketch of a floor plan was obviously of Al Hesser's villa. Maybe the large brass key was to the front door. The numbers Pat had written under his drawing of an upstairs room—6-7-4-7—meant nothing to me. The scrawl on the filing card about an access code had to have something to do with a computer program or something like CompuServe, but guessing that much didn't help me at all.

The newspaper photo showed Ricardo and L. K. with Al and Mia, but if Pat had meant to indicate more than that I ought to watch out for the two goons, I didn't get that, either.

I had decided I could use up about another half day, spooking around and acting stupid and trying to pick up something through observation. If that didn't work—I didn't think it would—then I could either try more drastic measures or pack up and go home.

I wasn't going home. Which left drastic measures. Which meant getting upstairs in Al's house somehow and checking out the room with the numbers written under it on the floor plan.

We reached The Emerald. At this early time of day there were only a few fanatics on the courts. Ricardo drove me back through the bougainvilleas to the house and parked beside the Hessers' Jaguar, Mercedes, Taurus station wagon, and S-10 in the deep, still-cool morning shade of the palm trees.

We walked through the front garden toward the house. Al, wearing boxer shorts and rubber shower thongs and smoking a cigarette, padded out to meet us. "Hey, Brad, thanks for coming over so early, pal. That's all, Ricardo. I'll call you on the handi-talkie when Mr. Smith is ready to go back. What say we go around to the deck, old buddy? The maid's got some coffee and a snack out there."

We walked around. It was still, almost spooky. Early sun slanted over the long cantilevered roof and made sparkles in the immaculate blue-white pool. A round red-wood table was set for two. The "snack," arrayed on a hotel-style heated sideboard, consisted of coffee, juice, papaya, bananas and oranges, scrambled eggs, bacon, toast, muffins, waffles, butter, syrup, sugar and cream.

Al took coffee. I took juice.

"Eat up, man. Don't be bashful. Shit."

I said I would take it a course at a time and sat down. A bird sang. A breath of wind stirred the palms and rippled the pool. Al finished his Marlboro and tossed the butt across the decking, where it rolled and stopped and sent up a thin little smoke plume.

"Sorry to get you out so early, pal."

"No problem, Al. I enjoyed talking with Ricardo. He's a real charmer."

"Yeah, I know. He and L. K. cost me a fortune. Everything costs me a fortune. But you got to have security when you're a celebrity, right?"

"Right."

"So this is the deal. First, I want you to play an exhibition doubles match at noon. You and me against Jimmy and my kid Billy. What say?"

I hesitated. He added, "I'll make it worth your while, if that's what's the problem."

"No, Al, I was just thinking it might not have been necessary to send Ricardo over at the crack of dawn to ask me this."

He lit another cigarette. He was burning them like firecrackers. I noticed his hands shook. That furtive rat was back in there again, nervous, scurrying around, trying to stay in the dark. "Okay, okay, there are a couple of other things I want to discuss with you, too. First things first. Will you play the match? Look. Mia says to invite you on a little two-hour cruise we're going to take tonight. We'll leave the dock downtown at dusk. Just you and us and about fifteen other celebrities. We'll have a blast, man. What do you say? Yes?"

"Al, I'm really sorry, but I've made other plans."

He grimaced. "Mia will crap. She likes you a whole bunch."

"I hate to have to miss it."

He puffed smoke, fidgeted, watched a colorful sparrow of some kind land and hop around the far end of the deck, then regathered himself. He leered. "That secret married lady again, huh? Huh?"

"Al—"

"All right, all right! Forget I asked! Listen, baby, about the match. You'll play, right? Am I right?"

"Sure. I'd be thrilled."

"Fantastic! Okay! Now we're getting somewhere! Have some breakfast. It's free, eat up."

"Let's just put the lids on the stuff. I'm sure Mia and Billy will be hungry when they get up later."

"Scroom. There's plenty for Billy, and Mia won't be out of the rack before ten. Now listen, pal. This other thing I want to talk to you about. I know you were always careful with your money. I know you probably got a bundle in coffee cans in your backyard, right? Am I right? Ha! Sure I am! And you do this tennis mag writing stuff, they probably pay pretty well, too. Okay. What I want to tell you in strictest

140

confidence is, if you want to make an investment that is sure to bring you in twenty to twenty-five percent profit return in the first year alone, I've got the deal for you." He eyed me expectantly, eyes bulging slightly with the synthetic excitement he always generated.

"What's the deal, Al?"

He waved his arm. "This."

"This?"

"The Emerald. The famed Al Hesser's Court College, Inc." He leaned over and put a thick, hairy hand on my knee. "Brad. Baby. This is something you don't want to miss out on, and I'm letting very, very few people in on it. You can invest in this whole operation, the works! You can have a piece of the action!"

This was interesting. Behind the exuberance was even more desperation than I had earlier noted. I said, "I don't have much liquid capital right now, Al."

"Christ, don't tell me about cash flow problems! Man, I am the king of cash flow problems! Do you know how much it costs to put in a new clay court? God! But seriously, Brad, I want to give you this opportunity. What I'm doing is letting a very small percentage of my personal stock go out to people I really know and really like, people I can trust, pros and celebrities like yourself. I want you to know you can get in on this. If you want, I can have one of my lawyers explain the whole deal to you later in the day. The only thing is, Brad, this opportunity is not going to be out there for the taking very long. I mean, this is a now-or-never deal, baby. I just wanted you to be aware of it."

"Al," I said carefully, "I'll certainly give it some thought. But what kind of price are you setting on your stock? I really don't have the kind of money you probably think I do. My playing days came before the big boom in prize money—"

"Fifty thousand," Al broke in jerkily. "Fifty. I can let you in for fifty. Hell, that's chickenfeed, right? I mean, it's

141

not like you're doing me a favor! But I need it *now*. I can't screw around. I'm right on the brink of everything turning around and me making millions, baby, and you can be part of it. But you've got to move. You've got to give me a break. Man, you don't *know* how the money flows out in a deal like this. You think everything is fine, and then, wham! you need bucks *now*. I—"

He stopped. He looked stricken, and he saw how much he had revealed.

He looked down at his hands. "Or," he added hoarsely, "forget it, man. I don't care. In or out. I'm just offering you a chance because I like you, that's all."

He changed the subject after that. Started telling old tournament stories. He kidded me about the WCT in 1975, when old Moody Coliseum at SMU was rocking, and Arthur Ashe took me out on the way to the championship in perhaps the hardest match I've ever played. It took me a long time to get over that one.

After a while, Al's son Billy came out. The tall, handsomely muscled boy wore wrinkled white gym shorts and nothing else, was barefooted. He was rumple-haired and still half-asleep. He grunted responses to the desperately cheerful remarks Al directed his way, and filled a plate with enough eggs, bacon, and waffles to feed a division. Then he poured syrup over everything and sat down opposite me at the table and began wolfing it down.

"Billy's going back to school next semester," Al told me proudly. "He laid out this semester but he's smart as a whip. He can finish his senior year in one semester, right, son?"

"Sure, Dad," Billy muttered around a mouthful of syrupy egg.

"Then a summer's fun and off to a West Coast school," Al went on. "We don't know which one yet, we haven't decided. We're hoping for a tennis scholarship, right, Billy boy?"

"*Uuurmph*," Billy said around waffles.

"Not that we can't afford it," Al added quickly. "Hell, my son can go anyplace he wants. Cost is no object."

A soft female voice said behind us, "The cost is no object to what, dear?"

We turned. Contrary to Al's expectations, Mia was up early. She came out through a sliding glass doorway off one side of the decking, her hair loose on her shoulders. She was wearing a white shortie nightgown and white satin mules with very high heels. The sun glinted briefly on an ankle bracelet.

"Holy shit, Mia!" Al squealed. "We got company!"

She moved across the deck and bent to kiss the bald top of his head. "I know that, darling. That's why I got up. Don't stare at me like that. I'm wearing panties, see? Good morning, Billy. Good morning, Brad." She bent over Billy and hugged him, handsome pendulous breasts almost falling out of the nightgown and rubbing heavily against him. Billy kept his head down as if he was ignoring her. He was not ignoring her. His face got bright pink.

"Christ, go get a robe on!" Al yelled at her.

"Oh, pooh," Mia said, and sinuously went over to pour orange juice.

Al stared at her. His face worked. An artery jumped in his forehead. You could see his temper go. He jumped up, knocking his coffee cup and saucer off the table to shatter on the pavement. Mia started to turn in alarm. He grabbed her by the arm, spinning her on around, almost knocking her down.

"*Dad—!*" Billy cried.

But Al had his scantily clad wife pulled painfully against him, his nose an inch from her startled face like a half-crazy baseball manager yelling at an umpire. He was tomato-faced, out-of-control angry. "Goddammit! Get some fucking clothes on! It's indecent, in front of Brad and my own goddam *son!*"

Mia tried to pull away. "Let me go, you son of a bitch!"

Billy got to his feet. His expression was somewhere

143

between shock and fear. "Dad, you're hurting her! Stop it, before I—"

Al released Mia to wheel on his son. "Before you *what?*"

Billy stopped cold. His throat worked. A dribble of saliva went down his chin. Kid-man, torn, not knowing if he was supposed to obey his father or defend the woman who had just wiggled her breasts against him. "Just—don't hurt her, Dad . . . okay?"

Mia flounced toward the sliding glass doors. "What bullshit! What male supremacy crap! I come out to have a nice visit and you act like Count Dracula! *Jesus!*" The glass door slammed shut behind her like a gunshot.

Al stood transfixed, all his color gone, the light going out of him. Billy stared at him a minute, as if dazed. Then the kid turned and strode into the house by the other doors, the main ones off the back.

"Billy!" Al called sharply.

Billy kept going, and went out of sight.

Al stared again. Then he seemed to remember me. He turned. By what incredible effort of will I could only imagine, he heaved a deep breath and shrugged, then reached for a fresh coffee cup. When he poured, the dark liquid went all over the place. He pretended that didn't happen, either, and came back to the table and sat down again beside me.

"Sorry about that," he said unevenly.

"Happens in the best of families," I said.

"Scroom," he said, and reached unsteadily for another cigarette.

By noon, when we started our guest doubles match before nearly filled bleachers, you would have thought nothing had happened. Billy grinned and acted properly boyish when Al introduced him, reaching up to put a fatherly arm around his shoulders. Mia sat in the front row of the stands, gorgeous in a yellow sundress, her face shaded by a dramatic straw hat, and smiled and applauded every good point. It was my first chance to try out my new Donnay ceramic racket, strung at sixty-five pounds and using the fifteen-gram handle weights. The Kevlar made it feel nice, but Connors and the kid put Al and me away in relaxed straight sets, 6–3, 6–2. In the milling-around afterward, I saw Mia giving her husband a fond hug, and Billy standing back away from them, watching them with eyes that burned.

I found Beth Miles again right after getting out of the showers and returning to the resort's garden area. She gave me a smile that would have lit north Dallas.

"You didn't see what I won yesterday afternoon," she said, rummaging in her big straw bag. She came up with a pretty little silver cup, very plain, the size and shape of a small water glass.

"Great!" I said.

"Read it!"

On the side it said

Flight Champion
BETH MILES
Al Hesser's Court College

"That's tremendous," I said. "Congratulations."

Still rosy with pleasure, she tucked the trophy back in her bag. "I ought to let you think I was all that great."

"What do you mean?"

"Everyone in the tournament got one."

"I still bet you were great."

"I'll buy your lunch."

"Best deal I ever heard." I took her arm and we went inside.

It was typical of Al Hesser, somehow, that every participant in his makeshift tournament won a trophy. It struck me as pathetic that the cups were all heavily silver-plated, and more than one jewelry engraver had to have worked overtime at special rates to get all the entrants' names in place in a few hours. The cups had to have cost Al at least $90 apiece. When he couldn't pay a delivery man and was reduced to scrambling on the edge of humiliation trying to get old tennis associates to provide him with some working capital, he had spent $10,000 on trophies that were meaningless—nothing more than nice, amusing gestures.

I didn't think I would ever understand everything going on with him, especially right now.

With Beth sitting across the table from me, however, I put some of that out of my mind. We talked about her job and my club in Richardson and what was going to happen in the NFL and why somebody had just paid twenty-three million dollars for a painting that resembled a green ostrich in a very high wind.

We were finishing the last glasses of iced tea when she pulled something else out of her bag. "Al Hesser told me you had a very good friend who died in a diving accident here recently."

I didn't know why the thought of Al gossiping to her about me was so irritating. "Al talks a lot, but this time he was right."

"Pat Reilly? Once your doubles partner?"

"Yes."

She held the sheet of paper in her lap, and her expression was drawn, solemn, worried. "Is that why you're really here? To try to find out more about how he died?"

I just didn't feel like lying to her. "Yes. But I'd like it not to get around."

She nodded, somber. "I picked this up in the lobby. I think it's where your friend rented his gear. I thought it might interest you."

The sheet of paper she handed across the table was from Marigot SuperMarine, the place I had visited. I saw that the sheet advertised diving services and specified equipment. It said the outfit had 400 eighty-pound bottles and 200 fifty-pound bottles constantly charged and ready for use. It advertised "state of the art" equipment—Orca

DROPSHOT

Edge dive computers, Spare Air backup air systems, Sherwood buoyancy compensators, U.S. Divers NEDU Class A Conshelf SE2 regulators.

Beth offered diffidently, "A boy in the lobby saw me looking this over, and volunteered that it really *is* top-grade equipment."

I folded the sheet and put it in my pocket. "Thanks."

She looked into her lap. "I meddled."

"No problem."

"I'm sorry, Brad. I didn't mean to step in where I had no business."

I grinned at her. "Will you shut up, please, and do anything you have to do before you can go to town with me to hunt for souvenirs?"

Her eyes widened with pleasure. "You mean it?"

"Come on."

It was a spontaneous idea. It had been a long time since I had wanted to spend an afternoon with a woman. But Beth Miles was special. I already knew that.

We had fun, and hit most of the shops in Philipsburg. Beth bought two brass trinkets that, when we turned them over, said they had been made in Korea, and I bought a conch shell from a native fisherman-diver on the road. It was very late in the afternoon when I dropped her back at The Emerald. She hugged me. I caught her and kissed her lightly, quickly, on the mouth. Friendly kiss, signifying nothing. Her sharp intake of breath, and sudden brief dig of fingers into my arm, signified otherwise.

I told her I would be back to watch the evening training videos with her.

That was a lie.

Dusk neared. That was when Al and Mia and their cozy entourage of celebrities would be pulling out of Philipsburg aboard the *Tiebreaker* for their little evening cruise. I stood in front of my cabin and watched for their lights, but didn't see them. Like a sly burglar, the memory of Danisa slipped up on me. Without warning, I felt devastated. What the hell was

I doing here? What difference could I make? How could I think I was interested in Beth Miles or anyone—or anything —else?

After a while the worst of it passed. As darkness spread around my A-frame, I put on navy slacks and turtleneck, pocketed the big brass key that might or might not gain me entry to the Hesser villa, and headed out across the golf course.

fifteen

Elsewhere

Guatemala City

The setting sun was hot on Rick Fletcher's back as he walked into the entrance of the old Guatemala Biltmore and crossed the lobby to the restaurant. The room, festooned with tropical plants and looking out onto a garden dense with vegetation, was nearly deserted. Few things discouraged the tourist trade, Fletcher thought, like gunfire in the night and armored vehicles tooling up and down the boulevards.

The waitress escorted Fletcher to a table near the windows. He ordered a tequila sunrise and waited, taking a few inventory report documents out of his blue nylon briefcase and spreading them on the tabletop.

Guatarez arrived ten minutes later, a short, dark-skinned man in rumpled slacks and a loud cotton shirt, sweating profusely. The sheaf of catalogue materials and sample brochures under his fat arm would have stopped a low-velocity bullet.

"I am sorry to say," the Guatemalan told Fletcher for the benefit of the hovering waitress, "our reorders are down badly this week."

"We'll have to notify the home office and try to move up the special rebate period," Fletcher replied.

The waitress took Guatarez's order for iced tea and went away.

"Now," Fletcher said, handing his agent a paper and pretending to point out an item on its face. "How are things going, my friend?"

"It is not good in my family," Guatarez said morosely. He was a perpetually sad little man. "My wife has lost her job. Her brother has written to say he plans to leave Chichicastenango and come here to the city. He plans to live with us! How can I support my wife's family as well as my own?"

"He has no prospect of a job?" Fletcher asked sympathetically.

Guatarez launched into a sad discussion of the job market in Guatemala City, where more than a hundred thousand illiterate Indians flooded in every year in hopes of a better life, only to find no work and—instead— life in a cardboard packing box in the barrio. Guatarez's wife, Fletcher knew from their long association, was incapable of holding a job and unable to refuse entreaties for help from her seemingly inexhaustible supply of relatives.

Fletcher liked Guatarez. He liked—unfortunately—all of the native Latino agents who worked for him. You formed a personal relationship with them to get the most out of them. Then they all had a story—became *people* to you— and it was infinitely harder to use them with the proper degree of cynicism.

The waitress brought their drinks and Guatarez kept complaining, and after a while he just looked sad, and fell silent.

"What news from your brother downtown?" Fletcher asked carefully.

"The government has brought in two more units from the highlands. My brother says there is a secret meeting very soon—perhaps even tonight—of the highest officers of the army."

Fletcher sipped his drink with a show of unconcern. "Has he heard of Col. Mariego?"

"Yes. He saw Mariego even this morning."

"Here?"

"At the headquarters."

Fletcher pumped for further information. Guatarez had bits of gossip from here and there, some of it perhaps useful, most of it probably not. Fletcher was patient, and got it all, significant and useless.

Some of the information, of course, he could not evaluate. He would report and let others collate, analyze, conclude.

But when he left the hotel almost an hour later, having given his salesman an "effort bonus" of fifty quetzals, he knew the information about the units from the highlands, in conjunction with an actual sighting of Col. Mariego, was highly significant and must be reported to his superior at the embassy at once.

The information meant, Fletcher thought, that the Junta was moving closer to its attempted coup. For the next few days or weeks there would be little rest for Fletcher or for any of the special case officers who had been sifted in to watch the situation. The guys eager to get back out of here and return to other assignments were out of luck. Nobody was likely to be going anywhere for a while. Apparently— unless they could do something fast—Guatemala was about to explode.

St. Maarten

The man called Sylvester secured both locks on his suite in The Paradise Resort and silently slid the heavy hall table in front of the door before turning to the task of unpacking his two boxes of "books."

He had checked into The Emerald Resort earlier under a new cover identification—"Prof. Peter Coligor," of Boston, Mass., in order to pick up the boxes. Then he had taken the boxes to his car, rented under another name, "H. L. Pekanian," and had driven a mile away to The Paradise Resort, where he registered again, also under the Pekanian name.

Neither name was close to his usual assumed identity, the one under which he was a respected adjunct faculty member at Notre Dame.

Now he felt reasonably secure and ready to proceed with his mission. The "book boxes" were central to his role.

Actually, there were some books—old, outdated texts—in both heavily strapped boxes. Sylvester unpacked most of these first and stacked them on the floor and the coffee table in the sitting room. Then he dug through the Styrofoam chips and began taking out the heavy plastic sacking material and assembling the contents.

Two hours later, he inspected the completed materials: a specially modified Skorpion VZ61 and a 9 mm. pistol of Brazilian manufacture, a Taurus PT99, both equipped with custom silencers; a folding knife of Czech origin with a custom springload opening mechanism; two boxes of ammunition; a tight coil of top-quality piano wire of the type that could be used as a most effective garrote, and a small, flat leather case containing two hypodermic syringes, four small vials of a clear, lethal fluid, a palm-fitting aerosol device and three cartridges to fit it.

Sylvester loaded and unloaded the firearms several times, checking their actions with the precise care of a watchmaker. Finally he was satisfied. The gunsmith who had worked over the weapons had done a first-rate piece of work. Sylvester concealed everything in the false bottom of his large suitcase and slid it back into the corner of the closet.

It had been interesting for Sylvester to sit in the stands at the Hesser school earlier in the day, an anonymous

and unexceptional outsider, and watch Brad Smith play
in the doubles match. Sylvester understood little about
tennis but he had come to understand more about Brad
Smith.

The man was in excellent physical condition and
moved well. His reflexes were still extraordinary. He
appeared intelligent, something Sylvester had already
known. Belgrade had shown it, and Smith's quickness in
recognizing Movlo had been an extraordinary accomp-
lishment.

It was not known how Smith had managed to link
Movlo to the murder of the man named Reilly, or what he
had had in mind in following him away from the party and
out onto the dark golf course. It had been very lucky that
L. K. saw Smith leave, and had pursued. Waylaying Smith
had given Movlo a second chance, and now he was safely in
hiding. Movlo's false identity as "J. F. Mannix" at The
Emerald was no more.

If Sylvester had been here at that time, he would have
killed Smith. Lacking instructions, L. K. had not done so,
and Sylvester's orders were to avoid overt action unless
things started going really sour.

It did not occur to Sylvester to chaff under
these restrictions. He was a professional and he followed orders. But he almost hoped Smith would prove to
be a further nuisance; that would remove the fetters
on Sylvester. He had not forgiven Smith's role in the
escape of the Lechova woman, or the near failure to catch
and kill Dominic Partek. Sylvester had lost some associates in the FBI sweeps that followed examination of the
Partek tape. His professional pride was hurt, and it still
rankled.

Ordinarily Sylvester did his work without emotion. But
Brad Smith was a special case. Sylvester devoutly wanted
him dead.

Jack M. Bickham

Boulder, Colorado

Solution of one of the most difficult problems facing Mannie Hawthorne had fallen into his lap more than a month earlier.

The TSAS-1 subassemblies, with their precious 24864 superconductor wafers already mounted, came to Boulder TechnoSys from Drum Computer Labs in Connecticut. They were delivered, twenty-four at a time, by a technician flying in Drum's business jet. When Hawthorne carefully unpacked the four Styrofoam-dampened cases in September and inventoried the units, he could hardly believe his good luck.

He counted not twenty-four units, but twenty-five.

Telling no one, he checked the shipment further.

The wafer on one board, serial number 0681, was defective, probably the result of accidental static electric shock. Apparently this board had been detected as nonfunctional at Drum, but had been shipped anyway by mistake.

Replacing it was a perfect board numbered 0681R (for replacement), but the shipping manifest showed twenty-four boards and only the number 0681R.

Drum had caught the defect and replaced it, but by some stroke of luck had sent both the defective unit and the good one.

Hawthorne did not report the defective board. It rode home with him in his inside coat pocket. Tests he conducted at home indicated that the board was perfect, except for the precious, top-secret wafer at its heart.

So as a result of a simple mistake he had almost everything demanded of him by the woman who gave him the money to make his monthly payment on his gambling debts. All he needed was a functional wafer. Since that stroke of luck, he had been setting things up to get the wafer; when he could make delivery of a complete

154

subassembly, he would be paid enough to finish out his debt.

Now, with dusk stealing over the Rockies, Mannie Hawthorne was very close to completing the controller portion of his scheme.

Just as he had known it would, the test procedure had finally located the "problem" set up by his secretly skewed computer profiles. All the data pointed to the 24864 wafers. All the units on the assembly and test table in Room 24 had been opened up, and the TSAS-1 subassemblies pulled for isolated testing.

It was late. Despite it being a Sunday, the day crew planned to remain another two hours, running tests on the first few wafers. Richard Perdue was on duty, along with Hawthorne, Virginia Jurgensen, and a man named Heppelmann. They had the subassemblies—small green boards studded with black chips surrounding the central wafer socket—arranged on the far left end of the table for the testing.

Hawthorne's pulse thudded as he stood near the test bench, waiting for his chance. First Jurgensen went to the far end of the room for something, then Perdue. But Heppelmann stayed too close. When Heppelmann finally got occupied with some piece of test equipment, Jurgensen was walking back. Hawthorne needed only a few seconds unobserved, but he was not getting them.

Finally—almost when he had reached the point of screaming in frustration—his opportunity came.

Two of the telephone lines started blinking at once. Heppelmann answered one, Perdue the other.

Virginia Jurgensen was occupied at the far end of the room.

Moving with speed borne of a thousand mental practices, Hawthorne reached into the nearest subassembly and used his chip puller to extract the superconducting wafer. It came out nicely. He slipped it into his coat pocket and, in the same movement, took out the defective wafer he had brought from home. It took three seconds to plug the defective wafer in where he had stolen the good one.

Jurgensen was coming back this way, but there was still time to do what else needed to be done.

Every piece of equipment on the long trestle table was attached with banana plugs or alligator clips to the ceramic work surface, which was in turn always kept at ground potential. Special floor mats grounded all personnel before they could reach the table and risk passing an equipment-fatal static electricity shock to the delicate chips in the TSAS-1s. *Every* precaution had been taken to prevent stray voltages from reaching the units.

Now, with his last precious seconds fleeing, and a good wafer in his pocket, Hawthorne had to make sure the others tested out as defective as the known defective one he had just slipped in as a replacement.

With his left hand, blocked from the view of the others, he unplugged the ground strap from the tabletop. The units on top were now vulnerable to shock. With his right hand, he brought out a plastic box the size of a pack of cigarettes. He pulled a small piece of black rubber tape off a metal stud on one flat side of the plastic box and then pressed the box against the ceramic work surface in such a way that the metal stud made contact with it.

He heard—or imagined he heard—the tiny electrical *ffzzzt!*

His small homemade box contained a network of high-voltage capacitors. He had charged them at home this morning. Current flowing from them would last only for the nanosecond of their discharge, and the amperage would be extremely low. But their voltage potential topped 3,000 volts.

The moment of contact between the box terminal and the work station represented the split second it took for all the voltage to be discharged into the connected—and ungrounded—TSAS-1s. That instant made the secret wafer in each of them just as useless as the one he had substituted.

He reconnected the ground strap in a single motion, and got the capacitor box back into his pocket. Now all the wafers would check out bad. They would be replaced. All he had to do was get back into Computer Processing long enough to alter his test parameters back to the correct settings, and he was home free—ready for final instructions on where and when to deliver the complete, working subassembly . . . and collect his payment.

It was going to be all right, Hawthorne told himself. All the hardest part was over. He was going to get his money and pay off the people in Las Vegas and have a new life. No more of this constant terror, no more bad dreams.

Richard Perdue came over and put a hand on Hawthorne's shoulder. "Ready to start the tests? Hey, Mannie, what's wrong? You're soaked with sweat!"

sixteen

A few thin clouds that had scudded in off the ocean with nightfall had begun to dissipate by the time I crossed the dark fairway that ran behind Al Hesser's villa. Stars and crescent moon bathed the golf course in pale silver. My eyes had adjusted well and I felt like I was walking in a spotlight. Someone in a house nearby was having a small party on their deck and had their outdoor stereo speakers going. Lionel Richie had seldom sounded better, but my heart wasn't in it. After my recent experience out here, I was seeing an attacker in every shadow, and what lay ahead of me was spookier yet.

Security lights flooded the back deck and garden area of Al Hesser's place in vivid amber. One upstairs room had a light in it. I skirted the property, halving the dark distance between his property and the one next door, and came out on Al's curved driveway leading to the parking area. No more interior lights showing in front, and only two yard lights making puddles of white on the expanse of lawn.

Mentally rehearsing my story, I walked up the side of the driveway and onto the expansive front porch. It was not bright here, but anybody could see me. Not hesitating, I pressed the button beside the heavy oak front door. Heard the chimes sound inside. Waited, then pressed the button a second time. Waited again.

Nobody came.

I took the heavy bronze key out of my pocket and tried it in the door lock. The key went in slickly, and when I turned it, the deadbolt slid back with a heavy, audible *chunck!*

The door swung open onto the dim expanse of the two-story foyer, lighted by a common nightlight plugged into a timer in a baseboard outlet. Accustomed to the outside dark, I could see everything: the open, curved glass-and-steel staircase, the vaulted ceiling high over the upstairs railing that bordered walkways to second-story rooms, the rockwork around the little interior fountain where I had had my tête-à-tête with Mia Hesser, the acres of pale ceramic flooring. From the doorway I could see past the end of the rockwork into the big room beyond and all the way out through the back glass wall, where the security lights shone on patio furniture and the dark surface of the pool beyond.

In the huge silence I heard a faint, rapid ticking.

The sound came from somewhere around the corner of the rock wall. I hurried there and found the ash doors of a small cabinet set into the masonry. The doors swung open at my touch to reveal the gray steel face of a security alarm system box. It had a telephone-type touchtone pad mounted on it. Above the pad of numbered buttons two green lights glowed serenely, but a third blinked insistently red in time with the tiny ticking sound I had heard.

Pat, I hope I've guessed right.

I punched in the numbers from the sketch of the floor plan: 6-7-4-7. The red light stopped blinking and went out.

After going back to the front door and using the key again to relock it from inside, I went upstairs. It was huge up here, wide corridors, another big sitting room with a dark TV set that had a screen the size of a moose. Still nobody around anywhere. I hurried.

The room marked on Pat's sketch was on my left, partway down the hall from the airy opening to the steep-curving staircase. The door was shut. I tried it. It swung open. Levolor-type blinds at the windows let in bright splinters off the back security lights, but not enough to do me much good. I pulled out my mini flashlight and sprayed it around.

Office. Dark paneling on the walls and a couple of big splashy contemporary prints. Big desk and chair, loveseat and two overstuffed chairs in a conversation corner, another big-screen TV, worktable between the back windows with impressive-looking computer equipment and telephones on it, two closed doors on my right.

One of the right-hand doors led into a bathroom. The other was a converted closet, but it didn't have clothes in it. On a wide shelf built along the back closet wall I found what looked like a complete amateur radio station: transceiver, microphone, and Morse code keyer, another smaller computer, a glowing blue-green twenty-four-hour clock set to Universal Coordinated Time, other gadgets that were just black boxes to me.

This was interesting, but not what I had come for.

Going to the computer table, I checked things out. Al had a lovely new IBM OS-2 system with a big hard disk in it, a fancy automatic modem to connect the computer to a telephone line, a print buffer device, and two printers, a nice Epson dot matrix job and the other an HP LaserJet+. Beneath the table was a big uninterruptable power source.

I flipped the switch on the power source and a red light blipped on, then off, and a green light came on at the same time the big hard disk in the computer started to whir up to speed. I sat down in the chair, prickles all over my unprotected back, forcing myself to press on. If my guess was right, this would not take long. If I was wrong, that wouldn't take much time either.

The computer's monitor screen came to life with a blinking cursor, and then some white lettering flashed on

160

and off too fast for me to read as the hard disk light flickered, automatically booting programs and getting something ready to run. Then the screen turned pretty blue and a communications program appeared, with a silver block in the middle asking me the predictable question:

>ENTER PASSWORD (RET)

I typed:

FIRSERVE

and pressed the RETURN key.

The hard disk worked a second or two. *I was in.* Up came a menu:

[V]IEW A FILE   [S]END A FILE   [R]ECEIVE A FILE   [O]PTIONS

I moved the cursor to the [V] block and hit RETURN. Another screen:

[S]PECIAL   [H]OLD   [M]ISC

I moved the cursor to the [S] and executed the command. The screen, to my surprise, displayed three names, gold on a black background:

MANNIX, J. F., M/MRS

COLIGOR, PETER

HAWTHORNE, M.

Which made absolutely no sense to me.

All right, dammit. I'm in the house and into the computer and all I've got are three names that don't mean a thing to me. Where have I screwed up? And what am I supposed to do now?

161

Jack M. Bickham

I was beginning to sweat. It had all gone smooth as cream up to this point, but I had no guarantees how long the cruise on the *Tiebreaker* might last, or when someone else might blunder by the house. Pat had thought this was important. Maybe he had died knowing no more than I knew now. But where did I go from here?

Maybe I was in the wrong file.

Hurrying, I used the keyboard to move the cursor to another of the option windows.

At that moment the lights of the room shocked on around me. A voice from the doorway said, "What the hell do you think you're doing in here?"

Cold flooded through me. Somehow I had the presence of mind to turn very slowly in the chair, my hands coming off the keyboard and rising to the level of my shoulders. Before I got turned far enough to see him, memory had identified his voice.

Ricardo, the goon who had come to fetch me to Al's patio breakfast and stock sales pitch only this morning, stood in the office doorway. He was wearing white coveralls and didn't have any shoes or socks on. The revolver in his hand looked about as big as a howitzer, and the muzzle, from my disadvantage point, looked like a tunnel with no light at the end of it.

"Ricardo," I said. "Man, I am really glad you're here."

It surprised him enough to make his Neanderthal features blink. "Huh?"

"Al asked me to come by and see what's been making the computer act up. But I don't know the telephone number to call to get into the information service."

Ricardo thought about it for a few seconds. You could see the physical effort in front of the confused thinking going on inside. Then, however, his eyes narrowed and his heavy lips turned down. "Bullcrap. Mr. Hesser never asked you to come in here. They're on a cruise, and he told me to check the house a couple of times, and he never said—"

"He must have forgotten, Ricardo." Good God, was it possible this was going to *work*? "He gave me a key. It's right here in my pocket—"

My gesture toward my pocket was a mistake. Ricardo jumped like a startled buck. His uncombed hair stood on end. He waved the revolver menacingly. "Don't reach for that!"

"It's just a key. I wanted to prove—"

"Get up, asshole. I don't know how you got in here, but when Mr. Hesser comes home we can figure it all out."

I got up from the chair, slowly.

Again the revolver waggle. "Over here. We're going downstairs."

"Shall I turn the computer off?"

"Do you want one of these hollow-points in your gut? *Move!*"

I walked toward him. If he held me until others arrived, I had had it. I tried to think of something to try. The only thing I had going for me was his stupidity. But people had been elected president with no more advantage than that. *Hell, go for it.*

Ricardo's breath reached halfway across the room. He had had a few snorts. His eyes looked like some marbles I had had as a kid. We had called them Bloodies because of all the neat, curving red lines in them.

"You are really going to be sorry about this, Ricardo," I told him.

He moved. I saw far too late that I had misjudged his condition and underestimated his athletic ability. There was no way to duck entirely under the gun barrel he swung in a tight, vicious arc at my head. The best I managed to do was slide with it, making it hit a glancing blow that sounded a lot worse than it was. Even then, as I made a big production of falling over backward like I had been half killed, real stars spun in my vision and the pain felt like a poker had been drawn across the top of my skull.

I hit the floor hard, bones clunking on wood. I moaned like I was out cold.

His foot exploded into my side with enough force to knock the air out of me. "Get up, asshole!" He pulled his leg back to kick me again.

I rolled over painfully—not having to act at all—and got myself to my hands and knees. A few drops of blood dribbled onto the bare wood floor. I was starting to get really tired of bleeding.

"Get up, or—!"

"Okay, okay!" I staggered erect. Some of my swaying was a put-on, but some of it was genuine.

He stepped back out of the doorway and waggled the revolver again. "Move."

I lurched through the doorway and into the hall. He shoved me in the direction of the staircase, staying belly to back, cramming the revolver into my side with painful pressure.

I changed tactics. "Is this what happened to Pat Reilly?"

For answer, he rammed me harder with the revolver barrel.

We moved across the upstairs landing toward the stairs, the foyer yawning beside us.

"At least let me go turn the computer off!" I said.

"Shut *up!*"

"It's going to blow up back there! Don't you hear it?"

"Huh?"

He slowed a half step. I stepped free of the pressure of the gun in my side. For just a second or two, he almost believed me—half turned his head back toward the office we had left. His revolver lowered a few inches.

If I had had time to think about it, I wouldn't have done it. I am not a very brave person. Risks I don't like. But this was the only chance I had, so I took it, the way you'll kick the accelerator trying to get into a tiny crack in the fast-moving freeway traffic sometimes when it's risky, but you know you may sit here all day if you wait for a better break.

Or like the way you may decide the hell with it and hit your second serve hard on ad-out, set point against you: because, dammit, you do that—you take the chance—or you just sit there and watch yourself go down the toilet anyway.

In the instant Ricardo was slightly distracted by my corny trick, I ducked slightly to the side and stomped the hard heel of my shoe down on the instep of his bare right foot just as hard as I could. I mean, I jumped on it. Staggered, he bellowed like an elk. He started to re-aim the revolver. I hit the floor and kicked his knee straight from the side and something popped and his leg collapsed.

He fell forward and partly to the side, and I got in a desperate shove. He went off the first step and yelled again—higher-pitched, scared this time—and plunged over backward.

He went down that open spiral staircase like a boulder going off a cliff. Head below, legs flying, arms every which way, skull crashing on the steel banister. Then partway down his momentum carried him up onto the side of the railing and he flipped right over it and sailed—for maybe one second—arms and legs splayed out, turning. He hit the top of the rock divider-wall with his skull and flipped on over and crashed to the tile floor.

I went down the steps four at a time, grabbing a chunk of stoneware statuary on the landing. Rushed around the corner of the rockwork ready to brain him with my small stoneware lady.

No need for the stoneware lady.

Ricardo lay half on his side in the sprawled, crumpled attitude of death. An ugly little pool had begun to form on the tiles around his head. He stared at me with egg-white eyes.

Shaking all over, I knelt and checked his carotid, just like the big boys would have done, to be sure. I couldn't find the carotid because there wasn't any pulse in it anymore.

I got back to my feet. Christ, what to do. *Think!*

I was so far out of my depth here I didn't even know

where the bottom might be. I mean, it's all well and good for Travis McGee or Sid Halley to be confronted with a life-or-death situation and think through it in 0.6 seconds. I had just been mildly slugged, kicked, and scared out of my wits, and I was no hero to begin with. *Now* what did I do?

What I did now, I decided, was get the hell out of here.

Fine. But if I cleaned up traces of my visit, maybe they would come back and find Ricardo spread-eagled on the floor, smell booze on him, and decide on the basis of no conflicting evidence that he had started up or down the steps and had had a lethal, drunken accident.

Against all my impulses to run for it like a kid being chased by the schoolground bully, I rushed back up the stairs, back into the office, got out of the computer program, and shut off all the equipment. Carefully pushed the chair back just the way I remembered it having been. Looked around. Knelt to wipe up my droplets of blood from the bare floor, leaked some new ones, wiped those up, too, and stuck the handkerchief on my head to prevent further leakage. Gave the office a last hasty look, turned off the light, and went down the hallway looking for more blood.

Found some at the top and bottom of the stairs, and wiped it up clean.

What else . . . what else. *Christ, hurry up!*

Ricardo's revolver had flown through the air. I found it downstairs and picked it up and stuck it in the back of my belt and went to the front door, which he had left swinging open when he entered.

Nope, nope, forgot something. Wait. Think. Turn the alarm system back on. No. Ricardo would have turned it off when he came in. Sure he would have. And he couldn't have armed it again, could he, dummy, when he had just fallen and killed himself?

His key was still in the door on the outside. I left it there—left the door ajar—and spooked out into the dimness of the hedges. I worked my way around the house half-blind from the sudden outside dark and the aftershocks of what had just happened, but maintained control until I was out beyond the property, halfway across the deserted golf course, sure I was alone and unobserved. Then I sat down against a tree and blew and shook.

After sitting there awhile, it dawned on me that they would look for Ricardo's revolver, and wouldn't find it because I had grabbed it as a souvenir. Brilliant!

I considered taking it back, but only for a microsecond. Too late for that. Whatever happened now, having a gun might even things up for me a little.

Instead of going straight back to the Mary Mary, I checked myself over carefully to make sure I hadn't leaked any telltale bloodstains on myself—which I hadn't—and then knelt at the drainage sluice and used the ruined hankie to clean my head up. Fingertips said it was a very shallow little graze, nothing that would even require a stitch. It had swollen closed and was no longer bleeding. I walked off the golf course and across the road to one of the other small resorts, one called The Great Caribe, where there was some light and canned music in the beachfront bar.

Ducking in the front, I found the men's room before anyone saw me, and checked my appearance in better light. Some of the caked blood showed in my hair, but it wasn't bad at all after I cleaned up. I left the can and went into the bar, where I perched at the counter and ordered a bourbon rocks. I needed it. I could even justify it. *"Anybody see this man last night?" (Showing my picture.) "Sure! He was in here, drinking bourbon rocks."* God. Inspector Clousseau would be proud of me.

After a while, the shakes were entirely under the surface. I left and walked the beach awhile, trying to sort things out.

After an hour or so of that, I felt clearheaded again, and remarkably good for a man who might be excreting pink urine in the morning. Except when I remembered Ricardo's dead eyes, and got the shudders, I amazed myself.

There was an unfamiliar rental car along with mine and the other four I had learned to identify in the parking lot of Mary Mary when I approached through the brush. I left the path and slipped around the rear of the compound, approaching my A-frame from the back.

It was dark and I couldn't see anyone at first. Then, sliding along the low side roof, its asphalt tiles still sun-warm, I saw her standing out front on the beach. There was enough moonlight to identify her in a brief white two-piece swimsuit, high-cut at the hips. Relieved, I hid the revolver under the eave of my house before approaching her.

She jumped when I stepped up from behind her.

"God!" she gasped, a hand going to her throat. "You scared me!"

"Sorry, Beth. What brings you here?"

She looked pale and pretty and flustered in the moonlight. "I—you didn't show up at the training videos, and I got worried. You said you had a nice beach, so I came over to make sure you were all right—I thought maybe we could swim or something—"

I quieted her with a gesture. Otherwise she might have kept on babbling for an hour. I was intensely relieved, and awfully pleased to see her. "I got tied up," I told her. "I'm sorry."

She focused on my face and spotted the caked blood. "You're *hurt!*"

"It's a little cut. But you know how head cuts bleed. I fell down again. Can you believe it?"

"No," she said firmly.

I looked down at her.

"I'm a nosy witch," she said meekly. "I didn't just ask Al Hesser about you, and I didn't just look up that brochure about the diving store on the other side of the island." Her breasts heaved. "I went to town and looked you up. They have a nice little library. It doesn't have everything, by any means, but it has old newspapers on microfiche. I read

168

about . . . Belgrade. And Danisa Lechova. You were working for the CIA."

I didn't reply. She needed to get it all out. I was thinking it was too bad she knew as much as she now did. I was also thinking how beautiful she was.

She went on, "I just want you to know that I'm sorry I meddled in your personal affairs. It was inexcusable. I'll mind my own business from now on. If there's anything I can do, of course I will. You might as well know: I'm an incorrigible liberal Democrat. But I'm not one of those idiots who moan and protest against the CIA because it does mean, ugly things to those sweet, innocent communists."

I grinned at her. "Beth, you're smart enough to know that whatever I might have done once for the Company, I was blown totally and permanently in the Belgrade operation. Sending me out on a job now would be like trying to send a cop undercover wearing his nice blue uniform."

She half turned from me, frowning out at the gentle waves pulsing in onto the sleek dark sand, foaming into tiny constellations of phosphorescence, retreating to be replaced. There were two small boats out in the bay, pairs of white lights, and farther out a bigger craft aglow from end to end with lights of white, green, and red. I wondered if that was the *Tiebreaker.*

Moments passed.

She turned back to frown up at me. "Is your head really all right? Do you need someone to drive you to the doctor?"

"No. It really is just a scratch."

She nodded. "If there's any time you're not busy, and you want to play some tennis or something, let me know. Otherwise, since I've already been such a dunce, the nicest thing I can do for you is leave you alone. I promise that."

"Beth, you're one lovely lady, and I thank you very much."

She started to turn away, then swung back again. "There's one other thing. When I told you my second relationship ended with his dying? That was a lie. I was married once when I was too young and it didn't last and I was crushed—I felt stupid, and a failure—but at least I could say I was a kid. The second time I got married I was twenty-four and I should have been smarter. But I married the same kind of guy again—repeated my same mistake—and *that* ended in divorce, too. It was . . . really bad."

She paused, took a deep breath. When she spoke again, her voice had a flat edge of quiet bitterness. "So I'm a two-time loser and I guess you're lucky you're not free to be interested because I would just screw things up anyway. It's in my script."

"You can change your script."

She smiled. Part amusement, part something else, perhaps sadness. "TA talk?"

"Sure. I've been to a shrink, lots, since Danisa. Transactional Analysis, Gestalt, both. I can talk psychobabble."

"But you're all better now."

"Sure. Perfect."

She looked up at me for what seemed a long time. The faintest breeze came in off the sea, carrying the scents of ocean and night and something like cinnamon. The pale silver of the night sky gleamed over her bare shoulders and arms, sculpting mysterious shadows. Maybe there's something to the stories about danger igniting physical need. My pulse had begun to stir and my mouth was dry. I couldn't believe it, but there it was.

"Well." She turned away. "Good night, Brad."

And the idea of letting her walk away right now was just more than I could handle.

I reached out and caught her arm, tugging her back around to face me. "Wait a minute."

She looked up at me. Our bodies nearly touched.

"Don't go," I said.

She shook her head like a disappointed little girl. "You don't have to be nice to me."

"Beth. Come inside with me."

170

Her lips parted. I felt her breath on my face. I put my hands on the sweet swell of her bare hips, and pulled her closer.

"Really?" she whispered in disbelief.

She was trembling but that was all right because I was too.

Sometime in the night I awoke and she was nestled softly hot against me, her arm over my chest and gently grasping my shoulder. I thought about her, and the past day and part of a night. I was incredulous. It was too much for one day—too much to absorb. *What now?* I decided I would worry about that in the morning.

One of those brief night storms was coming in, and I could see the distant lightning. The wind began to stir and then whip the palms, and the waves slammed in, throwing angry spray. I thought about Danisa and found the sorrow still there, and identified an impulse to feel bad this had happened with Beth because it sort of diminished Danisa—said my grief hadn't been so bad, my loss not so great, or I couldn't be doing this. At least I was smart enough to see that that kind of reasoning was silly, and a dead end.

The storm rolled in. With the first vivid flash of nearby lightning and crash of thunder, Beth startled awake, her eyes showing she didn't know where she was for an instant. I pulled her closer and stroked her back, and then it was all right. At first we only held each other, feeling the warmth and silken smoothness of flesh against flesh. There is nothing to compare with the feeling of another naked body, a loving body, nestled close, touching. I had forgotten.

Then, with murmurs and touches and pairing of tongues and lips and other thoughtless sounds unheard in the pounding of the rain and the thunder against the roof, the deeper stirrings began again and her arms and legs tightened against and around me, and her hair streamed around my face, making a tent, and her mouth was a volcano. And then the things I had dully said earlier to cover

171

the emotional and physical exhaustion of the near-thing at Al Hesser's house—my comments about my being an old gent, and not likely to be very satisfactory—became a joke again, and in the kettledrum pounding of the rain and the brilliant flashes of lightning our own storm became as briefly violent and engulfing as the one outside.

seventeen

Elsewhere

Elsewhere

The Emerald

The last police car had left the resort thirty minutes earlier, during the height of the brief, violent rainstorm. Now, a little past 4 A.M., the sound of rain against the windows of Al Hesser's upstairs home office had abated and the resort was quiet again. But Al Hesser was, if anything, shaking worse than ever.

His office door into the hallway was closed. L. K. Able stood with his back to it, brawny, bare arms folded over his chest. Hesser paced up and down the length of the room, waving his arms, fighting the panic that was on the verge of overwhelming him. Having L. K. nearby was often a comfort. Tonight the presence of the dark, brooding "security consultant" only frightened Hesser more.

"It *could* have been an accident," Hesser insisted desperately. "He could have come in to make a routine check, came upstairs, tripped, went A over T all the way down—"

"The gun," L. K. said, watching him with a brooding expression that did not entirely conceal contempt.

Hesser felt like running across the room and smashing at his "bodyguard's" face. It would have been like attacking a brick wall. "Maybe he didn't *have* his gun, L. K.! Maybe he left it somewhere, goddammit!"

173

"He comes over here to make an unscheduled visit to the house, he comes in and deactivates the alarm system, he starts searching the place?" L. K.'s contempt was no longer even badly concealed. "If he did all that, the only reason he would have was he suspected somebody was in here. So he comes in to check—*and forgets his weapon? Come off it!*"

Hesser faced the man who took orders from him in public and often gave them in private. "So somebody *was* in the house."

"Yes."

"Somebody killed Ricardo. He didn't fall."

"Correct."

"They took his gun."

"Right again."

Hesser could have wept. *"Who?"*

"When my report has been analyzed, suggestions for follow-up will be made. But I have one candidate."

Hesser's gut tightened, making his midsection feel like someone had inserted a tuna hook. "Brad Smith?"

"Who else?"

"Brad might have worked for the CIA once, but he's no professional! He's no *killer!*"

"He was a friend to the other man."

"But Pat Reilly died an accidental death! He—" Hesser stopped, horror dawning as something he had blocked out of conscious consideration suddenly broke through. "Pat *did* die in an accident . . . ? He wasn't—"

"Of course it was an accident." L. K.'s look was hooded. "But Smith was his friend. Suppose he came down here trying to prove otherwise about his friend's death."

"I can't believe that."

"He knew you and Mrs. Hesser were out on your yacht with your friends."

"Yes, but how could he possibly get in? How could he know anything?"

"You have a point. We'll wait for instructions."

Hesser felt the last tatters of his control going. "I don't want to wait for instructions. I don't want any more instructions. I don't want you telling me what to do and not to do. I don't want these goddam resort guests who get special treatment just because their names came in on the computer hookup. I don't want you coming up here in the dead of night and talking to God-knows-who on that radio set in there and—"

"It doesn't matter what you want," L. K. cut in sharply. His face showed dark red splotches of anger for the first time. "If you didn't want to cooperate, you shouldn't have made the original agreement. You shouldn't have taken the money."

"But I want *out!*"

"It's too late for that kind of talk. You know it's too late, especially now. You didn't just come in out of the turnip patch. You knew what you were getting into."

Hesser felt the tears of fear and frustration welling in his eyes. He rushed across the office and grabbed at L. K.'s shirtfront. "I didn't know what I was getting into! I *still* don't know what you people are doing! And I didn't count on any of this! You can tell your people I want out now, I—"

L. K. slapped him across the face so hard he staggered backward, almost fell.

"Be quiet. Get control of yourself."

"I want out! I can't stand this stuff! You've got—"

"Do you want more?" L. K. took a menacing half step toward him, and now the bulky man's hands were balled into fists.

Panic gusted. "No! No! I'll—I'll try to be good—!"

L. K. relaxed his hands, let his shoulders slump. His voice softened. "All we have to do is stay cool. Nobody is in trouble. Nothing more is going to happen. All you have to do is keep on being good old harmless Al Hesser, giving chuckles to the nice folks. Everything else, you leave up to us." L. K. lowered his tone, fixing Hesser with his eyes. "You. Will. Stay. Calm. Understood?"

"Yes . . . yes—"

"Good. Now. There are just a couple of other things you have to remember."

Writhing inside, Al Hesser listened to his instructions. After delivering them, L. K. gave him a fraternal kind of pat on the shoulder and left him alone in the office. The supportive gesture filled Hesser with a new sense of unreality—craziness. He was more afraid of L. K. than he had ever been of anyone in his life.

The sense of entrapment was asphyxiating.

After a few minutes alone, however, Hesser managed to calm himself a bit. He practiced his deep breathing, paced again, opened the casement windows beside the computer station, and went out onto the tiny balcony that ran across the back of the house. The brief storm was past now, no more rain falling, everything glistening wet, the lightning far across the hills, moving out to sea off the far side of the island.

There were no options, Hesser decided. Things were far too advanced. He knew little of what was really going on and he wished he knew even less. L. K. had given him sound advice: run the resort and the tennis school, and follow orders. He had to. He had taken far too much money to allow him to do otherwise. He could never pay it back even if they—whoever "they" were—would have allowed it. Even as things stood, their support was helping him keep his head above water by the narrowest of margins. He *had to* keep going, cooperating, blocking out the questions and fears.

He did more deep breathing of the cool, wet night air.

A little later he went back inside, carefully locking the casement windows. He left the office and padded down the hallway to his bedroom. Opened the door. Found lights ablaze, and the door joining his bedroom with his wife's standing open. And lights full on in Mia's room, too.

"Al?" her voice came angrily from her room. "Is that you?"

"It's me," Hesser said wearily.

Mia strode through the doorway, floor-length white lace negligee billowing open to reveal long, beautiful bare legs. She was pale with rage. "I want you to fire L. K."

"What?" Hesser cried in despair.

"I want you to fire L. K.! It wasn't bad enough that stupid Ricardo fell down our stairs and made that hideous mess in the foyer. L. K. acted like a *thug* when the authorities were here. He was rude to me and Billy, and he embarrassed all of us. I don't like him. I've never liked him. I want him fired, Al. I mean it."

"Mia, please. I can't fire L. K.!"

"Of course you can! Are you afraid? All right, then. I'll do it."

"No!"

"Al, I will not have him lurking around this house!"

"I can't fire him . . . just now, Mia. Please! We don't have enough security. Let me . . . uh . . . give me a few days, all right? Let me check a few things out. I'll . . . do something real soon. I promise."

Mia studied him with narrowed, doubting eyes. "You promise?"

"Yes! I promise!"

She nodded. "I want to go to Miami next weekend. I want five thousand dollars."

"Five thousand—!"

"Yes. I have to go shopping. I don't have anything decent to wear anymore. I'll be conservative, but five thousand is a minimum. If I don't have that much, why even bother to go?"

"Sweetheart," Hesser wheedled miserably, "you know we do have a slight cash flow problem right now—"

She put angry fists on her hips. "Are you saying *no* to me, Al?"

"No! —No, of course not, honey! I—just give me a day or two to transfer some funds—"

"Of course, darling. I'm giving you an entire week's notice, aren't I? I would never do anything to cause problems. You know that, sweetness."

Hesser smiled at her, adoring her and fearing her and thinking how gorgeous and wonderful she was, and thinking at the same time, *Oh, my God, where can I transfer five thousand, when do they give me my next payment, what happened to Ricardo, what am I going to do, what am I going to do?*

"No problem," he choked.

Mia gave him a dazzling smile and a peck on the forehead. "You're a dear." Then she swept out of his bedroom and back into her own. The door closed between them with a soft but definitive thud.

Beth Miles's watch showed a little after 6:30 A.M. when she pulled into the parking lot at The Emerald. She parked and sat in the car a moment, smiling to herself. The sweet scent of hibiscus wafted out of the greenery bordering the lot. The sun peeped over the wall of the resort, turning the raindrops that clung to leaves and branches into brilliant diamonds. The sky looked like an enormous porcelain bowl. And Beth felt like her bloodstream was filled with warm, melted Hershey's chocolate.

My girl, she thought happily, he is one wonderful man. You have been well and truly fucked.

She was so satisfied and pleased with herself that she hadn't gotten further in reacting to any of it.

Leaving her rented car, she cinched the rope belt of her robe around her waist and went through the garden gate to approach The Emerald from the side, intending to use the entrance there. As she had expected, a handful of guests could already be seen strolling around the grounds, or having coffee and Danish at umbrella tables. She felt a twinge of embarrassment despite knowing that any casual observer would just assume she had been off to the beach for an early dip.

To compensate for the twinge, she walked straighter and with more assurance.

As she neared the side entrance, Al Hesser crossed the patio from the far side and waved to her with a wide grin. "Morning, Miss Miles!"

Given no choice, Beth paused. "Good morning!"

Al Hesser held the grin as he ogled her from head to toe. There was a funny element of *weighing* in his examination. "Off for an early swim?"

"Yes, and it was grand."

"Where did you go?"

"Oh . . . just down to the point."

"Yeah." There was some wariness, some curious intensity, behind his expression. He said, "Gee, babe, I hope you didn't go alone. It can be dangerous, swimming out without a buddy alongside."

"Well, I did go with someone."

Al Hesser's grin widened with insinuation. "Hey. I saw you with my old buddy Brad Smith yesterday. Wouldn't have been him, would it?"

Beth hesitated a beat. *She was being pumped. Why?* Then, in the interval of a heartbeat, she remembered Brad's return last night, the little cake of fresh blood in his scalp, what she knew about him. If he was in danger here, if—

"Of course," Al Hesser added chummily, "I shouldn't pry like that! Hey, I apologize! Really!"

"Not at all, Al!" Beth trilled. "As a matter of fact, you're a very observant man. Yes, I was with Brad. He's such a nice man."

"Yeah, he sure is. I like Brad a lot. Helluva tennis player, too. Even if he is over the hill. Of course a lot of us are over the hill. Hey! I mean me, not you! Ha ha. You, uh, might

179

enjoy playing some tennis with him. He's a teaching pro himself, you know."

"Yes," Beth said with a smile. "We talked about that last night."

"Oh ho!" Hesser exclaimed, looking for an instant like Louie on the old *Taxi* show. "You two have really hit it off! That's great!"

"Yes," Beth told him blithely. "We had a lovely evening walk along his beach. I think we were walking when your yacht went out about dusk. We saw the lights and wondered if it was you."

Hesser blinked several times, computing. "You, ah, visited over there at his shack?"

"The sunset was pretty from over there. And those little cabins are so cute! But I must say they're kind of scary in a rainstorm, being so flimsy and close to the water!"

Hesser was thinking a mile a minute. "Yeah," he muttered, preoccupied with his information-processing. "Guess so."

Pleased with herself, Beth provided him with a small, stifled yawn. "See you later in the day, Al!" And hurried in through the side door.

Neatly done, she thought. What Al Hesser or anyone else concluded about her reputation didn't mean a damn to her. Possibly she had just gone through a silly, melodramatic exercise. Or maybe she had been smart. If Brad had needed an alibi to cover any part of the evening, she had just provided him one with a fine show of apparent innocence.

I've probably been reading too many spy novels, she thought with amusement, and walked into the elevator.

Behind her, on the patio, L. K. Able frowned behind his aviator-style sunglasses. He had been close enough to hear every word of it, and as a result most of his theory about Ricardo's death now lay in shards around his feet.

Boulder, Colorado

Mannie Hawthorne got to the lab early Monday morning. Now that the source of the problem with the current batch of TSAS-1 subassemblies had been located, there were not as many early-bird cars in the parking lot.

Hawthorne walked from his car to the building, feet crunching on an inch of new snow, and used his personal key to get in. The security guard at the reception desk checked him through. Carrying his portable NEC, he went directly to the test computer room. No one checked the exact nature of his activity when, as he often had in the past, he plugged in a cable connecting his portable computer's RS232-C port with a data input plug attached to the mainframe.

It took less than a minute for the test program modification data to flow from the NEC into the big computer at 9600 baud.

Hawthorne disconnected and, having fixed the test database so it would no longer report TSAS-1 malfunctions that weren't really there, headed toward Room 24.

On the way he encountered Dr. Pellton, the lab's founding genius. Pellton, wearing red sweats and Air Jordan tennis shoes, bounded up to him like the shoes really did help defy gravity.

"Mannie! Great work you people did, nailing down the problem so fast!"

Hawthorne shrugged modestly. "It was a hassle for a while, there."

"Yes, but we're squared away now. I talked to John Harrington back there at Drum last night, and he thinks those units must have gotten zapped somehow by a static charge in his jet when they were being shipped for assembly. Anyway, he says they've gone onto triple shifts, and we'll have replacement wafers in two to three weeks."

"That sets our delivery schedule far back."

"Well, I know, but at least we know what's been happening. I talked to General Tipland, so everybody knows what the status is. We'll just have to try to make up the time later in the run."

Hawthorne, remembering his latest instructions, figured now was as good a time as any. "With this delay on wafers, it might be a good time for me to go ahead and take off some of the compensatory time I've got built up. Room 24 isn't going to have any pressure until the new wafers arrive."

Pellton nodded agreement. "Sure, if you want to take a few days or even a week, now would be the time to do it."

"Tell you what, then. I'll check out some airline schedules and make a decision in the next day or two."

"Where are you thinking about going, Mannie?"

That was a good question, since Hawthorne hadn't been told yet. "I don't know for sure," he replied. "Somewhere with better weather."

"I wish I could go with you!" Pellton chuckled, and bounded off.

Hawthorne smiled, marveling to himself at how well things went sometimes.

Now all he had to do was wait for the woman's next telephone call, which she had promised would provide him with his travel plans.

eighteen

It was well into Monday afternoon when I drove back around the airport threshold to what locals laughingly called the highway, and returned to The Emerald.

Other than hiding Ricardo's big revolver in a more secure place, I had done nothing constructive earlier in the day. On the assumption someone might be watching, I had spent most of the time sprawled on a beach towel in front of my A-frame, soaking up sunlight possibly rendered lethal by our continued assaults on the ozone layer. (No problem, right? The technology that weakened the barrier to ultraviolet can take care of a little skin cancer, can't it? *Can't* it?)

Besides, I had a lot of reevaluating to do.

Beth had been awake very early. We hadn't talked a lot. It had been gentle, lazy, nice. I had come to with a slight, reflexive tightness in the emotional apparatus, but she had been wonderful. There had been none of the bad things, no *What did it mean?* or *We have to talk* or *How do you feel about it this morning?* or *Are you sorry?* or *I have to share my emotional state with you this morning, please please listen carefully* or *This is too important not to talk about it* or (worst of all when you've reached my state of decrepitude) *Let's do it again.*

She had clung and caressed and murmured, then

183

padded into the arctic shower, from whence she inadvertently issued a few muffled yips and yawps of primal agony, to emerge pink and shivering and grinning like a writer who just sold a book. Then she had toweled off while I took my turn getting shocked awake, and when I came out she was waiting by the door in her swimsuit. I pulled on my trunks and walked the beach with her to the walkway that led to the parking lot, there to watch her slip into a long, shapeless white terrycloth robe, hug, hop into her car.

Again, awareness of some defensive interior puckering. But, from her, there came no *What now?* or *When will I see you?* or *Call me about lunch.*

"See ya." And she drove off.

Clearly, I needed some time to think about this, too.

Walking back to my cabin in the early-morning quiet, I caught my mind doing its trick again, putting Danisa in the A-frame waiting for me, which brought out the sadness again. But the sadness was different: the component of devastation was missing.

When you first lose someone, the wound is so raw that you know it's never going to be any better. You don't even *want* it to get any better, because if it does, your healing diminishes the relationship and the loss. But usually you do heal, and it just happens offstage in your head.

Not that the pain ever goes away, not that one day it gets "all better." The spotlight fades. In the black, deserted theater you look up from the front row, across the empty orchestra pit you can't cross, and there on the vast black stage, each in their own pool of light, stand the people you have lost. They are always there and they always will be, and you will never get over wanting them to come down here with you because it's lonely down here without them, and sometimes scary. But the spotlights that make their features so vivid to you begin to fade. Some of the small things about them—the timber of their voice or the way they make a gesture or how they express a prejudice—are no longer as clear and heartbreaking. You go on. But as you see more go up onto the stage where you can't reach them ever again, the sense of loss may fade a little, but it does not vanish. What you begin to see too is that it's a cast of thousands up there. Finally it will be a cast of everybody.

Danisa was never going to become an easy sentimental memory. While we were together there hadn't been a day when I didn't marvel that it was so. She gave more and was less selfish than anyone I ever knew. Sometimes a little thoughtful word or gesture from her filled me with amazement that anyone could care so much about another human, could be that giving and considerate. I knew how much separation from her parents and her sister in Belgrade hurt her and gnawed at her mind. She mourned the loss of Dominic Partek, the brother whose existence she had never suspected until he was caught in the pursuit that ended his life. She simply didn't brood. She said, "Yes, that's all sad. Now let's get on with things, here."

I had been so proud of her I could bust. And yes, proud of *me* because she loved me. You don't ever wipe feelings of that intensity out of your record book. You just learn, more or less accidentally, that you can cope.

So I watched the sun climb into the lower branches of the palm tree and was careful not to bother the sandcrabs out for their morning stroll, and thought about Beth Miles. She was a beautiful lady and she was now important. What had happened between us was a step in my recovery. She had brought me a step closer back to the human race. Now I needed to consider what my obligations to her were, and how I had to proceed to protect her as best I could.

A lot of the things I thought, standing in front of my cabin smoking cigarettes, were disconnected and associational and a weird mixture of sad and glad. Didn't matter. After a while I got finished with it enough that I could tell myself it was time to concentrate on more practical matters.

That was when I got a heavy plastic bag out of my tiny

store of grocery store supplies and went around the A-frame on the side where the brush came right up to the knee-high eaves and pulled Ricardo's big revolver out of its temporary hiding place. Putting it in the plastic bag, I carried it inside the cabin and into the bathroom. By standing on the dresser I could just reach one of the places near the slanting roof where bolted two-by-eights met four-by-four joists. There were a dozen such junctions, and each made a dusty shelf up there. That was where I stashed the gun. Having hopped off the dresser to stand at floor level, I made sure I couldn't see anything up there. It wasn't very convenient, but I was more interested in hiding it than in a fast draw.

By now, long since, they would have found Ricardo's body and probably missed the gun. And they would be trying to figure some things out. There was no reason why Al Hesser or anyone else should make me suspect number one, but I was sure to be considered and placed on the list somewhere. That made it incumbent on me to cool it for a day or two and make sure everything I did fitted my claim to being here for R & R and nothing more.

Searching Al's place had been melodramatic and amateurish, I thought now. About all I had accomplished on the positive side was proof that Pat Reilly's deposit box materials were all involved with Al. But I had no idea what I was supposed to have found in the computer. All I had were three names remembered from the one file I had retrieved, and they meant nothing.

I leaned toward the theory that Al and The Emerald were involved in a big-league drug operation. A lot of people went through the resort and the tennis school every month. Judging by what I had seen, considerable equipment—from racket stringing machines to computer equipment—came and went. It looked like Al's operation might provide a good cover for clandestine meetings, shipment of dope in mismarked crates, and perhaps even laundering money.

That, however, was totally speculation. Factually my

little foray into life as a second-story man had gotten me zilch.

I could check out the names I had found in Al's computer. I could be alert for new leads. But I was beginning to get a feeling similar to the one I used to get sometimes in a match when I thought I was making the right moves and even hitting a few outstanding shots, but the other guy was already up a service break in the deciding set.

And loafing around in the sun all morning didn't clarify anything for me. It just gave my headache a sliver of doorway to slip back through.

Which was why I was loaded up on Tylenol when I parked in the sun-glittering lot at The Emerald.

If I was looking for any overt signs of what had happened at Al's house last night, I was disappointed. It being Monday, and the start of a new instruction week, the tennis school was in full cry. On far courts, instructors had group and individual lessons going. On one of the near courts, Al stood alone on the expanse of green-coated pavement, cordless microphone in hand, doing one of his funny instructional routines and wowing forty or fifty newcomers scattered around the lower tiers of the bleachers. He looked sort of peaked, but he was in rare form. His stuff about basic groundstrokes was entertaining and was getting the customers in a relaxed frame of mind so they could start drills without the kind of deadly intensity that blocks muscle-learning.

I wandered into the pro shop, where an assistant was using a Tenex stringing machine on a largehead Wilson ceramic.

"Hey, good morning," he said with a friendly grin.

"Hey," I said, figuring everyone might as well sound like Al, "how goes it today?"

"Busy, man."

"Looks like it."

He tied off a string. "Some excitement, huh?"

187

I fed coins into a machine and was rewarded with a Diet Coke. "You mean all the new students? Is this a bigger number than usual?"

"Hell, no, man." He started to go on, but was interrupted by applause from the crowd beyond the door. "Oh, shit. I better hurry. I got three more rackets to string, and they'll be in here screaming for them any minute."

I let it go. The doors of the shop all opened at once and eager folk streamed in, chattering. They were nice-looking people, youthful, pleasantly excited, most of them slim and well dressed in tennis clothes considerably more expensive than anyone needed to play a game. A couple more pro assistants filtered in with them, answering questions and getting down to the serious business of selling equipment.

Seeing no one I knew, I went back outside, where I ran into Al coming my way with a group of five pupils. Under the film of sweat and sunscreen he looked gray and unwell, but he was in form.

"Brad! Hey, good afternoon!" The leer. "You have a big night, baby? Everybody, meet Brad Smith, the great former champion. Brad is spending some time with us this week. Hey, why don't you all go on inside and look around, take a break, we'll start again at two o'clock. Brad, let's stroll up around the garden and have us a confab, what say?"

We left the customers behind and went through one of the gates into the grounds separating the school from the resort.

"We missed you last night," Al told me.

"I was sorry not to make it, Al."

"Yeah, but I ran into your lady early this morning. I guess I see why you figured you had better things to do with yourself."

"My lady?"

"Your lady! Your lady! Beth Miles! I was out and about early, and I caught her just coming in. She said she was out for an early swim. Har de har har. They don't get puffy eyes like that from the sea air, baby. I congratulate you. If I wasn't a happily married man, I might have taken that one for myself. That's class pussy."

I didn't say anything. We had strolled halfway across the garden area and were approaching a large circular fountain with a stone maiden in the middle pouring water out of a pitcher.

A pretty brunette, wearing a rich red blouse and white cotton slacks, approached us. She gave us a brilliant smile. "Hi there!"

"Hi yourself!" Al said warmly. "You sure look nice today."

"Why, thank you!" she trilled, and went on past. From behind, I noticed the extra weight she was carrying belowdecks.

Al noticed too. "Look at that," he said disgustedly. "Will you just look at that? Why don't women ever look at their own ass? She probably gets out of the shower and looks in the mirror and says, 'Hmm, nice tits.' If she ever turned around and looked over her shoulder, she'd see those ten-pound flour sacks she's carrying around on both hips. Jesus Christ. That's a nice-looking woman. That's a *really* nice-looking woman. She acts ready, too. But Jesus Christ. With that ass on her, it would be like sticking it in a Crisco can."

"Al, you really have a way with words sometimes."

"Where were we? Oh, yeah. The stock deal. I need to mention something about that to you, baby."

Again I didn't answer. Better to wait him out.

He was really wired. I wondered if he ever slept. One day, possibly not too far in the future, he was going to get wound just a little tighter, and then there was going to be a spronging noise and you would see springs and sprockets and little gears all over the floor, and no Al Hesser.

"Hey," he said, "have you given any more thought to it? The stock deal, I mean?"

"It's crossed my mind."

"You need to move on it if you want in."

"I'm thinking about it."

"I can set up a meeting for you with one of my lawyers. He can explain it all to you in detail. If there's anything about the operation you think you'd like to check into, like operating reports, financial statements, all that, just let me know and I'll have one of my accountants go over all that with you. I'm not pushing you, Brad, but this is a once-in-a-lifetime opportunity and you're a class act, the kind of person I'd like to have as a stockholder. But it sure isn't going to be available long. I've got people knocking my goddamn door down."

"I'll give it some more thought."

"Okay, great. And listen. I know there are always problems, I mean you've probably got to move some money around and all that. I wouldn't want a technicality like that holding you back. I'll tell you what, I don't want you to miss out on this. You just give me your personal check for five thousand bucks today. I'll tell my people that's a deposit of ten percent, a guarantee you can buy in for fifty thousand worth anytime in the next twenty days. That way you're guaranteed you won't miss out. I'll have my lawyer draw up some kind of legal agreement on it."

"That's generous, Al. I'll certainly take it into consideration."

"Hell, what are friends for, right?" He banged a sweaty hand on my shoulder. "Listen, I better get back, the animals will be getting restless. I just wanted to make sure you heard this down-payment idea personally from me. It's no skin off my ass whether you get in or not, of course. But like I said, if it's just a technical problem with some of your other investments or anything like that, I can fix it so you don't miss out."

"Thanks, Al."

He started back toward the courts, stubby legs churning. "Hang around!" he yelled over his shoulder. "We'll have some courts open later. I already put your name down for one!"

He was all heart, that Al Hesser. I wondered what kind of problem he was facing that an amount as small as $5,000 would help much. Unless, of course, he was giving the same spiel to twenty others.

He hadn't given any sign of last night's burglary and violence, if you didn't count the underlying pallor and a slight shakiness he couldn't very well hide. He was a little deeper than he looked. I needed to remember that.

I walked around for a while, making a very good show of being relaxed and at loose ends. And wishing I could think of something to do that might be constructive. I watched some of the group lessons get under way. Then, while I was concentrating hard on Al's technique with a group of four hacker-class club players below me on the near court, someone sat down beside me on the bleacher plank and I didn't notice her until she spoke.

"We missed you last night."

I turned, mildly startled. Mia Hesser looked smashing in a snug crimson lycra jumpsuit that clung to her arms and legs. Another of her dramatic wide-brimmed straw hats, the brim boldly curled low in front, shaded her face. Her makeup was perfect, of course. She looked ironic and amused. "Do you always jump when someone slips up on you?" she added.

"I guess I was really into Al's lesson down there."

"Yes, he does have a way with his little lessons."

I chose to ignore the cool condescension. "His style is his own. I couldn't teach that way, but I'm learning from him, just sitting up here and taking it in. He's clever."

She sighed. "Are we going to spend the day talking about him, darling?"

"What would you like to talk about?"

"I guess you heard about our sordid excitement last night?"

"No. What?"

She widened her eyes in disbelief. "You *did* sleep late, didn't you."

"I just got here a while ago, Mia, but I talked with Al and he didn't say anything about any excitement."

"Well, one of our security men fell down the stairs in our house and managed to kill himself."

"No!"

"Yes. It was terrible. We found him when we returned from our cruise. Which would have been a *much* more fun cruise if you had been along, incidentally."

"He killed himself, you say?"

"Yes. He was a clumsy moron. Replaceable in a minute. But of course the police had to come, and some other investigator, and a photographer, and it was a mess, just ghastly, all those dirty little people creeping around our home and jabbering in Spanish or Portuguese or whatever it is they speak amongst themselves. And then Ricardo's blood was just all over the floor, and we didn't get someone in to clean that up until this morning. It was disgusting."

"I met Ricardo the first day I was here," I told her. "Sorry he had such a bad accident."

"It's over now, of course, but the whole thing just shattered my nerves. I'm going to fly to Miami at the end of the week for some shopping and relaxation. Believe me, I have it coming anyway. Being nice to all these people all the time, smiling at Al's same old boring jokes and pranks." She paused a beat. "Now what I need to do is find some nice diversions between today and Friday. Do you have any suggestions?"

You had to give the lady credit. When she wanted something, she went after it. Earlier I had thought it might be worth the personal risk to cultivate her, hoping to glean vital information from her without becoming obvious. But she was too sharp for that, and too eager to carry our relationship beyond the point of no return. All I needed right now was the additional complication of a secret relationship with someone like her; she was exciting, beautiful, surely skilled and capable of giving any man the ride of his life. She hadn't gained the ability to fascinate and capture without the other aspects of her kind of personality, however; she was also selfish, manipulative, calculating: a user who seduced men for her own momentary amusement, captivated and emasculated and then discarded them as casually as she would have thrown away anything else in our disposable society.

Perhaps that was the bottom-line fun of this game for women like Mia Hesser: the moment when the man was hers, so addicted or even in love that he would have done anything for her. At that moment she could exercise the ultimate power simply by turning away, having proved again that she was in control and no one—finally—could touch her.

On a more practical level there was also the additional risk factor posed by my stupid mistake in taking Ricardo's revolver. If I had had the presence of mind to leave that behind, his death might have been considered what Mia evidently thought it was: an accident. But *someone*—Al or his bodyguard named L. K. or someone I hadn't identified yet—would have been smart enough to notice the missing weapon and draw the obvious conclusions. That meant I had to be a lot more circumspect; they would be watching for anybody asking impertinent questions now.

I badly wanted to ask Mia or someone about the names I had seen in the computer. They were burned into my memory because they were just about all I had to go on: *Mannix, J. F., M/Mrs; Coligor, Peter; Hawthorne, M.* But I couldn't ask Mia, not now or any other time. I didn't know if there was anyone I might safely ask.

From every standpoint she was off-limits. But how

could I let her down in a way that wouldn't antagonize her? I didn't need her enmity, either.

"My," she murmured with that quiet, ironic amusement of hers. "I didn't realize I asked such a hard question."

I shrugged and took the yellow brick road of apparent stupidity. "It must be impossible for a resident to find much new on the island. I suppose you've shopped and explored every corner of St. Maarten."

"A dozen times! No, I was thinking of something more . . . personal."

"Gosh, I wish I could help you."

Her voice went down half an octave, and only an idiot would have failed to catch the nuance: "I think you could, Brad. I think I've already made that clear to you."

So, back to the wall, stop it now before she's gone even further and made the proposition so evident that any negative response has to be taken as a personal rejection. "I think I do understand, Mia, but I'm sorry. I just don't think that's in the cards."

She was watching the courts, and showed no feeling. "Because my husband is an old friend?"

I was amazed she didn't understand how little I thought of Al. But it was a way out. "That's a large part of it, yes. I just believe in loyalty to friends. We've known each other a long time, Al and I."

"Who said he had to know?"

"He might."

"Darling, I think you worry entirely too much. I can practically guarantee that no one would ever guess anything. I know of places on the French side of the island." She paused, then purred, "I like the French side of things. And who's hurt? No one has to know."

"Who was it," I asked, "who said that even private corruption contributes to the world supply?"

She blocked that, or didn't get it. "It's that blonde, then, isn't it? Beth something? The one with a flat chest?"

I had to grin at that. "Maybe so."

"You'll never know what you're turning down, Brad. You'll always wonder."

"Mia, I'm sure you're right."

She sighed, exasperated. "You disappoint me. You really do."

I didn't respond to that, and in a minute or two she got up and went down the bleacher walk, as elegant, stylish, and fascinating as any model who ever lived, but infinitely more real and obtainable. *You'll always wonder,* she had said.

She was right. A part of my mind followed her like a horny puppy, and another part did wonder, and feel a stab of regret.

Letting the sun soak in, I watched classes for another hour. While my eyes stayed busy oncourt, I tried to hang onto reactions to Mia, thoughts about Beth, analysis of how Al Hesser's Court College got results from its registrants. Because I knew that if I ever let go of these lines of thinking, I would have to come back to what I had been blocking out ever since last night.

But finally, despite my best efforts, my blocking failed and there he was: Ricardo, sprawled at the foot of the staircase, blood, hair, and tissue on the stone wall where his skull had been smashed open against it, the glazed death-whiteness of his unseeing eyes, the growing pool of blood under his head and shoulders, the absolute stillness of the artery in his throat when I felt for it.

He had caught me and wouldn't have hesitated to kill me. If I hadn't gotten extremely lucky, I would in all likelihood be the one who was dead right now. Self-defense, poor and simple. And consider yourself blessed.

That, however, didn't change the reactions deep inside, in the intestines, the lungs, the brainstem. Life is our only truly precious possession, and until you have faced a fatal illness or a gun aimed at the center of your brain, you don't realize how really fragile it is. All of us stand a puff of wind from extinction. We don't think about it, and our advertising for products to relieve the horrors of headache or constipation distracts us from the real problem we all face: the inevitable result of a *serious* malfunction or accident. So we deny that we hang to life by the slender filaments of cobweb delusions, and our funeral homes insulate us from the inevitable reminders, and if we are lucky we find longer-term flights from reality in religious belief. But now there was Ricardo in my mind. I had caused his death and it shook me. There was a guilt and a sickness that superseded "realism." Ricardo's dead voice spoke in my mind. *You too, Smith. Your head will crack just as easily, your carotid will still just as fast; I beat you to the barn, but your day is coming.*

nineteen

The curiosity shop on a dingy side street in Philipsburg was already uncomfortably hot and redolent of cheap incense, leather, and mildew Tuesday morning about 10 when Beth and I went in. I had poked around among the brass bells, wicker baskets, conch shells, and plastic trinkets for about five minutes when she hurried up from the bowels of the place, her expression pink with suppressed excitement.

"Brad, look at this!"

It was a small, fired clay figure, three inches tall, with a crude pinkish glaze: a woman in primitive Indian dress, squatting over a tiny pan.

"She's grinding corn," Beth told me in a conspiratorial whisper. "It's handmade. Do you think it might be valuable?"

"What does the price tag say?"

"Nine dollars! I can't believe it! What do you think?"

I turned the little figure over. Had to hold it just right in the light streaming through the front windows to make out the tiny lettering on the bottom: TAIWAN.

"What does it say?"

I showed her.

197

"Shit," she muttered.

She had come out of the indoor training facility about 3:30 Monday afternoon, finding me still in the stands and still in a funk. I hid the funk from her, and after a few minutes of her happy chatter it was really banished. At 4:20 Al informed me he had an open court, and since I had had the presence of mind to dress appropriately and bring my rackets, and Beth was wearing a tennis dress and shoes from her indoor drills, we went out on Court 22 and faced each other across a net for the first time.

Beth was a better player than she had given herself credit for. Rusty, yes. And struggling with a new service motion Al's instructors had urged upon her. But she had swift, graceful lateral movement, and her forehand had some zip. She sliced all her backhands and said she wanted to develop topspin from that side, but had twice had cortisone injections in the elbow after trying to work on that.

After warming up, we played. I learned she was a fierce competitor. Except for taking a little pace off the ball, and declining a few chances to take the net, I didn't give her much. The few days off the court had rusted me just a little too, and there was the residual minor headache. But she would have made it interesting for me at any time.

We drew a small but interested gallery. If it made Beth nervous, she didn't show it. A lot of our points were long and interesting; she unveiled a talent for a disguised dropshot that proved to be damned irritating. At the end of three sets, both of us were soaked with sweat and my legs had begun to send insistent old-man messages up the spinal cord. The onlookers gave us a friendly round of applause as we left the court.

"Well, what do you think?" Beth asked me as we headed for the showers.

"What do I think? I think you're cute."

"You too, cutey. But I meant about my game."

"Oh. Your game is splendid."

"I'm serious," she insisted, serious.

"You almost killed me out there. If you insist on a postmortem, at least let the elderly gentleman soak muscle spasms in a hot shower first."

She shook her head. "Brad Smith, you are just about as full of it as anyone I ever met. Okay! Showers and changes. Then . . . if you like . . . I'll buy you dinner somewhere."

"Let me ask you this. Is there a place downtown that's disastrously expensive?"

"Yes. There's one out on a pier."

"In that case, I accept."

So. A shower with visions of sugarplums mixing in with bad recent memories and nagging worries about accomplishing anything more in terms of a buddy's death down here, and then a radiant lady awaiting me in an aqua, off-shoulder sundress, beautiful bare legs, and white high heels.

A ride by my place to leave my car, and then a ride on into town in her car, which had air-conditioning. A short wait on the deck of the restaurant, which was all rough timbers and tropical plants and seeming indifference, a table looking out onto the sunset water, a drink, and pompano of the very finest kind, followed by well-chilled melon and at last Courvoisier and coffee under the starlight.

Monday night was almost gone when we parked again in the ratty little lot of the Mary Mary. Beth said, "Suppose you might give me a chance for revenge oncourt tomorrow?"

I reached across and teased a finger through a rebellious blond ringlet. "You make it sound like the evening's over."

Her eyes were large in the dark. "It isn't?"

It wasn't. It went well into Tuesday.

For appearances' sake, or something, she left my A-frame and headed back to The Emerald a little before 3 A.M. By that time a great number of topics had been discussed, thoughts revealed, and pleasant activities indulged in. And she had agreed that, since her next lesson was not scheduled until 1 P.M. on Tuesday, she would be willing to drive into Philipsburg with me again in the morning so I could visit the friendly local doctor and then do some touristy things with her through the lunch hour.

This morning the doctor had not been busy, and had made a quick and relatively painless job of removing my stitches. He examined his work and pronounced it good. My scalp felt better with the tug of the nylon out of there. At which point the lady and I started strolling around the shops.

It was nice. We knew things about each other now that went deeper than conversation. There was a melding that came from the nights. I sensed the intimacy in her even as we strolled along, as casual as could be: the feeling that in some ways we were not now entirely separate individuals, and never would be again. There was a time, after the disaster of my first marriage, when I thought the way to emotional safety was in casual sex. I found out that for me those two words simply don't go together. Even if a liaison with Mia Hesser had been coldly entered into, with calculation of side benefits, I would have inevitably *cared* afterward. The discoveries with Beth ran light-years deeper. She was very, very special. *We* were.

Danisa walked along with us, of course. It occurred to me that she always would. Maybe growing up is learning to live with the ghosts . . .

We left the shop with its authentic local artifacts made in Taiwan and explored some of the many gem shops. When we came to a lingerie store and Beth turned in, I drew the line and said I would meet her across the street at a small cafe.

"Coward," she said.

"No question about it," I told her, and we separated.

I had been looking for a few minutes alone to carry out an idea I had come up with. I hurried along the side of the street opposite the shop Beth had entered and found the florist's on the next corner just where I thought I had spied it earlier.

Inside, a little man with no hair on top gave me a friendly grin. "Yes, sah?"

I told him I had some good friends staying at The Emerald, friends who had done me a kindness. "Can you deliver some flowers to them out there for me?"

"Of course, sah. We deliver every afternoon." He reached for his order pad and pencil. "The name of the people to receive the flowers?"

"Mannix. Em ay en en eye ex. J.F. Mister and Missus."

"And they are at The Emerald Resort? Do you have a room number?"

"No, but I'm sure at the desk—"

"Of course, sah. Now what price range did you have in mind?"

We dealt with all that. I signed a card "*Jack*" and sealed it in the little delivery envelope. Paid in cash. He thanked me and I left just as three more customers entered. They were all Americans and that was good. The more gringos the shopkeeper dealt with today, the less likely he would remember my face.

Beth was just emerging from the lingerie shop when I walked back down the street. She was carrying a small pink plastic sack with the name of the store printed on the side in silver-gray.

"What did you buy?" I asked, taking her arm to enter the cafe.

"Secret," she said wickedly.

"Will you tell me later?"

"I might, if you're very good."

Later, over the salads, she told me, "Actually, I certainly *hope* I get to show you what I purchased. The whole idea, you know, is to keep the gentleman from getting bored with the lady. One way . . . I've been told in the publications of Helen Gurley Brown . . . is little surprises in the boudoir. A little lace, maybe a naughty see-through thing—"

"Let's go see now."

Her eyes danced. "Later. I have a date on Court 16. Eat your salad."

"Damn."

After Beth dropped me off at the Mary Mary, I put on grubbier clothes and used my own oven-temperature rental to drive up the beach road. I expected to accomplish nothing by visiting the spot where Pat's body washed ashore, but you do what you can. I had to eliminate that last shadow of possibility that his death had been accidental . . . if I could.

It was not hard to find the place. When I climbed down the dark rocks to the beach, I found two scuba divers and a couple of snorkel swimmers cruising around the little inlet. I sat on the hot sand near the clutter of their towels and snacks and extra equipment and waited for them.

The snorkelers came out first, two skinny teenage boys wading out with masks and tubes in hand, their big swimfins flopping through the sand. They immediately started pushing each other and horsing around, and then headed off to the west, still acting the fool. I decided they were not likely to be of any help anyway.

A few minutes later, about a hundred yards out, the scuba swimmers popped up, first one and then the other. They bobbed around in the gentle cyan waves and stroked lazily shoreward. At a surprising distance from the shoreline they came up on their feet on shallow bottom and waded the rest of the way in. Before coming all the way out they removed their large transparent fins, then came on up the beach toward me, masks and regulators around their necks, still looking like creatures from outer space in their lime-colored wetsuits, yellow buoyancy compensator jackets and back bottles, hanging black hoses and dive computer gadgets. A young couple, both slender and athletic, both blond. They had underwater camera gear along.

They reached their towels and extra bottles and started peeling out of things. The man saw me watching and gave me a wide grin. "Afternoon!"

I got to my feet and strolled closer. As they came out of their wetsuits, I saw that both of them had a slight case of chattering teeth and goose bumps. "Cold down there?" I asked.

"Feels warm at first. Gets to you after a while."

"Very deep?"

"The rock formations and stuff start shallow, less than twelve feet down, and then it slopes off. Neat stuff."

"*Beautiful* stuff," the girl corrected him, toweling long hair. "I hope some of the pictures come out!"

"I'm Brad Smith."

"David Clarke. My wife Jill."

We shook hands. They seemed like nice kids, from somewhere in the South judging by the softness of their accents.

"You ever dive?" David asked me.

"Just a few lessons. Never anyplace like this."

"You should, man. It's gorgeous down there."

Which gave me the opening I needed. "I don't know," I said dubiously. "I had a good friend who got in a lot of trouble along here somewhere just last week."

Both of them looked at me, concerned. "Bad trouble?" Jill asked.

"The worst. He died."

"Oh, hell!" David said suddenly. "I read about that! He was a friend of yours?"

"Yes. He was a certified instructor. How he could have gotten in trouble if he was diving along here, maybe in only twelve or fourteen feet of water, really bothers me."

"I wondered too," David said, helping his wife pile gear in neat piles. "Maybe faulty equipment. You never know."

"I think he had top-quality stuff. And he was no dummy, as I said. Tell me: are there caves and things down there he might have gotten stuck in?"

David frowned as he continued to towel his hair and face. "Not really. But I thought about it. A lot. I mean, when you plan to dive someplace, and somebody gets killed there, you think!"

"Any theories?"

"Sure. Pulmonary overpressure."

"Come again?"

"Air embolism. On an ascent, you can fail to exhale normally. At depth your lungs are filled with compressed air. If you fail to exhale properly on the way up, your lung volume expands—Boyle's Law—and the pressure gets too great and can damage your lungs, force air into the bloodstream. When the air hits your brain, you're in big trouble."

"Pat was a pro."

"It's possible to have a problem even when you're doing everything just right. Maybe part of a lung doesn't inflate just right on the way up, despite the diver's efforts. Maybe he had a touch of bronchitis or something he didn't even think about. Maybe a lung collapses. Same result."

Some of this was news to me. "And it can kill you?"

"Christ yes. In mild cases, maybe only a headache. Maybe confusion. From there it runs the gamut from convulsions to paralysis to death."

"But surely not," I suggested, "in twelve feet of water."

Jill chimed in, her pretty young face grimly serious. "It takes a hundred millimeters pressure to start possible problems, air forced into the capillaries. You take twenty-five millimeters with every foot you descend."

"Are you telling me it's possible to have a problem at a depth of *four feet?*"

"Damned right," David told me. "There have been cases recorded in training pools."

"Good God," I said with completely honest surprise.

"So," the kid went on, "I figure either he had a malfunction, or he changed depths abruptly and started getting disoriented, and maybe came on up too fast, and lost consciousness, and that was all she wrote. The regulator could have stuck then, emptying his remaining bottle."

"It sounds spooky."

"It can be. That's why we always dive together, the buddy system, and spend half our vacation savings on new, upgraded gear every year."

I shook my head. They started picking up the collected apparatus. I offered to help them carry some of it up to the road, and they said it wasn't necessary, and I helped anyway. Out of the water, most of it was heavy.

"Thanks a lot," David said, shaking hands again beside their car.

"Thank you. For the lesson about lung problems and all."

They got into their Fiesta. He peered back out at me. "Sure sorry about your friend."

"Yes. Me too."

I waved as they drove off.

It was new information that disturbed me. I had assumed from Square One that Pat's death was not accidental. Now I had to face the possibility that his notes to me, and the deposit box, were largely melodrama, his death an accident. For the first time that had to be included on the list of possibilities. But I didn't *think* it had been an accident.

For if Pat had died in a genuine accident, how did you explain the phantom sister—and people like Ricardo and L.K. slinking around?

Jack M. Bickham

By the time I got back to the Mary Mary, I had assimilated the diving information and felt sure again that Pat had been murdered. What I had learned only meant that murdering a scuba diver was even easier than I had thought.

At a few minutes before five o'clock I called the florist in town. He said he was sorry to report that the desk at The Emerald said Mr. and Mrs. Mannix had checked out late last week. I thanked him and told him to send the flowers over to the hospital or something.

When I returned to The Emerald an hour later, the afternoon sessions were just breaking up at Al Hesser's Court College. When I asked for Beth at the desk of the resort, they said she hadn't yet returned to her room from the afternoon lessons. I stood in the lobby, waiting to spot her when she came in, and my friends from Kansas City— the two couples I had met at Al's party—came over. We talked tennis for a while.

"Maybe we could hit a few back and forth tomorrow," Don Abercrombie said hopefully.

"Yeah," his friend Ed Palmer chimed in, nudging his wife Marcie. "Might go over pretty big, walking into the club next weekend and casually mentioning a game we had with Brad Smith."

His wife treated me to a barrage of innocently flirtatious ups-and-downs with her striking gray eyes. "We might take turns being your partner in some mixed doubles."

"If we can get a court," I told them, "no reason why we can't do that one day this week, anyway."

"Has to be tomorrow," Abercrombie said.

"Oh?"

"We leave Thursday morning."

"That's the only bad thing about a place like this," Wanda Abercrombie chimed in. "You just meet new friends, and it's time for either you or them to leave."

"Like your friend at the party the other night," I said. "The man in the white dinner jacket. The gray-haired fellow. I haven't seen him around again."

206

Palmer nodded. "Mannix. He and his wife weren't even scheduled to leave yet, but they just up and vanished on us."

"I guess we weren't the only ones they surprised," Abercrombie added. "When I came through the lobby an hour or two ago to check for messages, there was a flower delivery boy here with this big bouquet for them. All the clerk could tell him was they'd left ahead of schedule. Imagine being a good friend and sending flowers, and they've up and bugged out on you."

I said cautiously, "I knew some people named Mannix once."

"Funny couple," Abercrombie said. "Didn't say where they were from or anything. I sort of figured there was some kind of business failure in the background somewhere, so I didn't push it. He never went on the court more than once or twice, and she spent most of her time up in their room."

"Well," Wanda said, velvet claws unsheathing just a bit, "she *was* about twenty years older than he was, dear."

Abercrombie grinned. "Meow."

"Well, I didn't like *her* at all."

"When did they check out?" I asked.

"Was it Friday night or Saturday night?" Palmer asked.

"It was late the night of Al's big party," Abercrombie said. "Gee, I wonder where they had to go so fast. They didn't tell anybody goodbye."

"Some people," Wanda concluded, "are just *weird*."

I was the one who had been weird. I realized now that I should have chased down the Abercrombies and the Palmers sooner to ask what name my friend with gray hair had been using. It simply hadn't occurred to me that the name he was using might be helpful.

But it was. *Mannix:* the first name of the trio of names in the special file in Al's computer. Which meant the other two names might be just as significant.

Might also be guests.

I knew instantly how I could check this theory out. Turning to walk across the lobby, however, I spotted Al's other "security consultant," the smart one he called L. K., standing near the door of the bar. L. K. looked away fast, but not before it was obvious he was watching me.

I sat down casually in one of the lobby chairs and waited for Beth. When she arrived, I took her out of there. My next move would have to wait awhile.

twenty

Elsewhere

Miami, Florida

Slightly woozy from the two cocktails he had had with his dinner, Mannie Hawthorne returned to his room at the airport Hilton.

Hawthorne locked himself in, tossed his newly purchased magazines onto the wide surface of the bed, and slipped the carrying case strap of his NEC Multispeed portable computer off his shoulder. He placed the case most carefully on the dark mahogany dresser and worked the two zippers. Inside, the ivory-colored computer was undisturbed, apparently in perfect working condition.

Hawthorne zipped the case closed and went to the draped windows of his room. Slightly parting the heavy material, he looked out over amber parking lot lights and the traffic on the highway to a shopping center nearby, and farther away the dark sprawl of Miami International. A big jet was on final approach and he watched its vivid landing lights go lower and lower and then blend into the ocean of ground-level whites and blues that marked taxiways. He let the curtains close again and wished it were morning.

Hawthorne knew there was going to be little sleep.

His flight out of Miami for St. Maarten was scheduled to leave at 10 A.M. He had always been nervously compulsive, so under ordinary circumstances he would have gotten up early, mentally backing off from the departure time. *Departure at 10, so be at the gate by 9, so allow an hour to go the four miles around the airport to the terminal because you never know about traffic, so leave here by 8, so be in the lobby to check out by 7:30 latest, so be in the coffee shop by 6:45, so get up at 5:30, give yourself plenty of time to shower and shave and get things packed and downstairs.* So now it was Tuesday evening, 9 P.M., and he had eight and a half hours until he had to get up—depending on a wakeup call from the desk but setting the travel alarm to be safe—and he ought to go right to sleep, but there was no way in hell he could get calm enough for sleep, even with the two Old Fashioneds under his belt.

When those people moved, he thought, they moved.

Instructions, she had said when she took his call on Monday: Get ready to leave tomorrow afternoon. The arrangements have all been made in your name at the Worldwide agency in that shopping center near your apartment. They'll have your airplane tickets and your reservations ready for pickup anytime after nine in the morning. Your flight leaves at 1:40. Once at your destination, you will be contacted. Your contact will say he or she wants information about data processing. You will say that is not your specialty. He or she will say something with a color in it. You will then follow instructions. Do you have all that?"

"I leave *tomorrow?*"

"Yes. Please repeat the details."

"Pick up tickets down here at Worldwide in the morning. My flight leaves at 1:40. I guess that's Denver Stapleton? My God! I have no time left for anything!"

"The identification procedure," she said, and there was a crisp impatience in her tone.

"They ask about information processing. I say that's not my specialty, they say something with a color in it."

"Yes. Good. Of course you understand you take the special package with you."

"Yes—"

"Good. Have a nice trip, Mannie. Goodbye."

Hawthorne had sat there a moment, listening to the dial tone. *Mannie.* She had used his first name for the first time. As if to establish—finally—some personal note. There was an air of finality to that. He wondered if he would ever hear her voice again. Probably he wouldn't. His final payment, the big one, would come as the others had, cash inserted in the pages of a used book sent parcel post.

Now, some thirty hours after that conversation, here he was in Miami, waiting for a morning connection to St. Maarten, tired and strung out and scared.

So far everything had gone smoothly. No problem with his hasty scheduling of compensatory time from the lab. Much amusement when he revealed what he would be doing during his week *"Mannie, when you sink your teeth into something, you're a bulldog. A tennis camp—wow! Are you trying to become a pro in six months?"* The tickets and reservations had been ready, the flights almost on time. And here he was, with the TSAS-1 subassembly board, including a priceless intact wafer, installed inside the NEC portable in place of that unit's normal board. He had handed it to the X-ray technicians in Denver, asking that they check it manually since the detection machine might damage its electronic innards, and they had glanced at it, handed it back. Security people at airports were getting used to people carrying portable computers onboard.

Tomorrow, once he was past another checkin, he would have the NEC on St. Maarten. Go to the tennis school, check in. Probably have to endure a lot of earnest, sweaty showtime on the court. Wait to be contacted.

He was already making plans ahead to assure himself he would never fall under suspicion. He would continue his tennis workouts once he was back in Boulder. He would talk about tennis a lot. At the lab, he would also be more cooperative with Dr. Perdue and that bitch Jurgensen . . .

Hawthorne nervously paced the room. He was amazed at himself. He had *done* it! He had the subassembly and he had the wafer. Everyone had been fooled. Handing it over would be simple. Then he could fly home again and await arrival of the cash that would buy his freedom from the people in Las Vegas once and for all.

It was going to be so good to be free of them, he thought.

Maybe . . . with any luck . . . he would even have enough money left over for a nice bet on the Broncos a week from Sunday. They were playing the Giants at the Meadow-lands and the spread would be about five, based on home field advantage. That was a good bet. He could double his money, for sure, and then . . .

St. Maarten

Sylvester dawdled over his dinner in the lounge of The Emerald until L. K. Able entered and walked to the bar. It was 9:40 P.M. Able, Sylvester thought, was a man of habit.

Based on his earlier observations, Sylvester knew that the "security consultant" would sit at the far end of the bar, his brooding preoccupation not inviting company; he would have one drink—two ounces of Bombay gin, rocks, with a twist—nurse it for approximately thirty minutes, then stroll among the guests on the deck for an additional twenty minutes or so, and then tour the grounds before re-turning to his room, 308, where he would retire for the night.

Able, Sylvester knew, was a good operative, well trained and disciplined. When the device requiring trans-port arrived tomorrow, Able would handle the contact and transfer carefully, efficiently, and by the book. Under ordinary circumstances, L. K. Able could have been counted on to deal with any unforeseen complications, just as he and Movlo had dealt with Pat Reilly when the American stumbled onto Movlo's true identity despite his cover as a British businessman named Mannix.

Movlo and the woman who had come here posing as his wife were now safely back in New York under other identities. Plans for the transfer of the device tomorrow seemed to be moving smoothly. Sylvester had been keeping an eye on Brad Smith, and had no indication that Smith was anywhere near uncovering anything. As a matter of fact, if Smith had not followed Movlo, alias Mannix, away from the party that night last week, Sylvester would have believed the American knew nothing at all. But Sylvester had to assume on the basis of that single act that Smith was dangerous. Smith had to be watched, the transfer of the device facilitated. If Smith showed signs of tumbling to what was being accomplished, he had to be taken out.

In the meantime, L. K. Able had to be informed.

Sylvester paid his check in cash and walked to the bar, gleaming mirrors and glass along the curving interior wall of the large room. He went to the far end and slid onto the stool next to Able's. Able continued staring into space as if no one had neared him. The bartender came over and Sylvester ordered Pernod.

The drink arrived. Sylvester sipped it. "Lovely evening," he said to Able.

L. K. Able nodded politely, shifting his body weight slightly to turn more away from unwanted conversation.

"I believe it was Dr. Johnson," Sylvester said, "who said the tavern chair is the throne of human felicity."

The "security consultant" stiffened slightly. His glass had been at his lips. He lowered it slowly and turned fractionally back in Sylvester's direction. "Yes. Was it not in *Journey to the Hebrides?*"

"I think not. In Boswell's *Life.*"

The exchange of bona fides was complete. Able's dark eyes bored into Sylvester with X-ray intensity. "I had no notice of a contact."

"I am backup only. Nothing has changed."

Perhaps Able's shoulders sloped an inch, denoting relaxation. "All goes well."

"I know. Two questions only."

"Go ahead."

"With Mannix departed, you plan to complete the shipment yourself?"

"Our contract agent will pick it up at the airport. I will get it that far."

"Thursday?"

"The day after tomorrow. Yes."

"The delivery here is on schedule?"

"Arrival in the morning."

"I'll be close by." Sylvester drained the milky, licorice-flavored liqueur from the cordial glass and turned his stool to leave.

"Your name?" L. K. Able said suddenly.

Sylvester stared at him a moment. "Jones," he said, and walked away.

Able's blurting of the question was an unpardonable breach of procedure, and Sylvester's coldly sarcastic reply had been an obvious rebuke. Able's face darkened with angry humiliation as he lowered his head to stare into the dregs of his gin.

Billy Hesser knocked on the closed door of his father's bedroom. "Dad? Are you in there?"

After a moment's delay, the next door down the hallway swung open and Mia Hesser, wearing a bulky red robe, peered out at him. "Come in, darling."

Billy went to her door and followed her inside. Her huge white bedroom was a mess as usual, clothing tossed on the floor here and there, the big bed rumpled from an earlier nap, cosmetics everywhere on the long vanity. The air was redolent of Mia's heavy perfume.

"I thought he would be back from the video coaching lab by now," Billy told his stepmother.

Mia had been brushing her hair. She glided back to the vanity and sat down again in front of the mirror, crossing her legs as she reached for the brush. The lower half of her loosely belted robe fell open.

She made no effort to cover herself. "I think he's still down there, sweetheart. On Tuesday nights they have all the new-arrival tapes, you know."

Billy stood near the bedroom doorway, staring at her. She seemed unaware, but she was perfectly posed, her high-heeled mules adding sensuality to her beautiful long legs. As she resumed brushing her hair, she glanced toward him. "Is there anything I can do for you, honey?"

"No," he replied. "I wanted to ask about tomorrow's lesson schedule." His voice was hoarse. "I'll . . . check back later."

"Billy," Mia said. "Come here a minute before you go."

As if dragged, Billy crossed the room, a tall, muscular child-man wearing cutoffs, dirty tennis shoes, and a faded blue T-shirt. He reached her side and looked down at her, his expression troubled.

Mia tossed the brush down and reached out and took his hand. "Honey, what's bothering you?"

"Nothing."

"Is it money? Because if it is, I can let you have some."

"No. Nothing like that."

"Are you worried about going back to school after Christmas? You *know* you need an education, and the experience you'll get as a member of a college tennis team will make you grow as a player. You know that, too."

"No," Billy repeated. A facial tic leaped under his left eye. He didn't say anything else. Mia continued to smile up at him, bare legs almost touching him. Everything that was being said was being said aside from the words, and she was enjoying it. A delicious sexual warmth crept through her body.

"I think I know what it is!" she said with a teasing smile. "Have you been having trouble with Molly again?"

"Molly's a pig," Billy said bitterly.

"Why, I thought you liked Molly! My goodness, she's a *beautiful* little girl, and she obviously adores you. Did you have a lovers' quarrel?"

"I don't give a damn about Molly. She isn't who I want. I—I'm going to get out of here."

He tried to pull away. Mia clung to his hand. "You can tell me what's troubling you, darling. Tell me!"

A sharp noise interrupted them, the sound of the door to Al Hesser's adjacent room opening and closing. Mia released Billy's hand. He turned toward the open doorway joining this room with his father's. Al Hesser, a towel over his sweat-soaked head, appeared in the adjoining doorway.

"What's *this* all about?" Hesser demanded, taking in the whole scene.

"I was looking for you," Billy said thickly.

Hesser strode into Mia's bedroom. He gestured angrily at her. "Cover yourself up. Jesus Christ!" His glare turned to his son. "So what is it you thought you could get from me *in here?*"

Billy's throat worked. Smoky frustrated rage colored his eyes. "Nothing," he snapped, and started toward the door.

Hesser caught his arm and swung him half around. "Answer me when I ask you a question, goddammit!"

"Leave me alone!"

"Listen! Stay out of this room, do you understand?"

"Oh, Al," Mia said with weary sarcasm, "does everything have to be a cause célèbre?"

"Shut up!" Hesser yelled. "You know, I'm so sick of you waggling it in front of this kid—"

"Don't talk to her like that!" Billy burst out.

Al Hesser turned to his son with slow, dawning sarcasm. "Are you her protector now?"

Mia said, "Al, don't. Leave him alone."

"Shut up," Hesser repeated, his eyes never leaving Billy's face. "I asked you a question. Is that why you're in my wife's bedroom? To *protect* her? Or—"

Something burst inside Billy. He took a wild roundhouse swing at his father. It wasn't a good swing and his coiled fist bounced off Hesser's shoulder. But it had sufficient force to stagger him sideways.

"Why you little shit! I'll—!"

Mia flew across the room and caught Hesser in midstride. "Al! For God's sake, stop it!"

"Get out of my way!"

Mia struggled with him. One shoulder of her robe was jerked down and it was pulled almost to her waist. *"Stop it!"*

Hesser pushed her away. She struggled with her robe, getting her breasts covered again. Hesser and Billy faced each other for an instant, the squat, hairy older man with spindly bare legs and the boy with the grown-up body. Billy was scared, stunned, ready to lash out at anything or anybody. Hesser's red face and heavy breathing made him look ready for a coronary.

"Both of you stop it!" Mia hissed.

Billy hesitated, then turned suddenly and bolted out of the room.

"I'll talk to you later!" Hesser yelled after him.

"God!" Mia said in disgust.

"What was he doing in here?" Hesser shot at her.

"He told you—"

"What was he *doing* in here?"

"You disgust me," Mia told him, her voice dripping acid.

Hesser's face went blank. "What?"

"You disgust me! The boy came in here looking for *you*. I was talking with him about going back to school—"

"With your robe half off like that?"

"My God, what are you implying? Are you so debauched you think I would consider something with *my own stepson?*"—Is that what you're implying, Al? Is that what you're saying?"

Her shocked tone and expression turned the advantage to her side. Hesser's face suddenly changed—betrayed uncertainty. He looked scared. "Well, Mia," he said, wheedling, "I just didn't like the look of it, that's all. He shouldn't be bothering you, and—"

"If that boy has a problem, Al, it's your fault."

"Me?"

"You! What kind of a role model do you provide for him? How is he supposed to treat girls properly when he sees you pushing me around like a common whore? No wonder he likes to visit with me! I treat him like a grown-up person!"

"Maybe I misstated things," Hesser said miserably. "I didn't mean—"

"Get out, Al. Just—get out."

"But—"

"Please," she said with cold aloofness. "If we have to discuss this further, we can do so tomorrow."

Hesser retreated to his own bedroom. He sank into an easy chair and held his sweaty head in his hands. He had flown off the handle for no reason. He was losing his sanity. Billy hated his guts. Mia was moving farther and farther away. Every goddamned bill collector and process server in the hemisphere was yapping at his heels. He didn't even have the $5,000 to give Mia for Miami in a couple of days. L. K. had said just today that he had no idea when another payment would come from his people.

Everything was going wrong. Everything. Hesser felt

like he would explode—self-destruct. He had to get hold of himself. He didn't know how. His desperation screamed like a crazy animal. What was he going to do? What was he going to *do*?

A small sound made him look up sharply. Mia had closed the door joining their bedrooms.

The key turned in the lock on her side.

Maplewood, Connecticut

It was almost midnight, and ordinarily only the security lights would have been on inside Drum Computer Laboratories. But the windows of the test annex were all aglow when John Harrington, Drum's founder and president, parked his old pickup truck alongside several other vehicles in the paved lot.

Drum Labs had been born in dilapidated buildings which once had housed a small military facility here in rural Connecticut. Its work in artificial intelligence was on the cutting edge and very near a breakthrough likely to change the world forever. In the meantime, research and development of the supercooled superconducting 24864 wafer, heart of the radar guidance system for the B-1B, had kept the company afloat. The failure of an entire batch of TSAS-1 subassemblies, with the wafer at their heart, was a problem that rated somewhere between very serious and potentially catastrophic. Which was why Harrington was checking in so late.

The defective units had been picked up by the Drum jet Monday morning and flown back to Maplewood. Since that time, Harrington's best people had begun the process of disassembling the units, trying to learn how and why they had failed.

Harrington unlocked the front door of the main lab building and went inside. A squat black security robot named Herman promptly hummed into view through a nearby doorway and bleeped its demand for identification. Harrington spoke his ID code and Herman bleeped satisfaction and gave him instructions to sign the roster. Harrington obeyed and went back through the deserted fore section of the lab.

In the test annex he found lights ablaze and three of his people at work. One was a tall, totally bald, and cadaverous man of about forty, bent over an oscilloscope with a complex pattern of waveforms on its face. Another, a young woman with red hair, had test probes inside one of the TSAS-1 units arrayed on a long trestle table makeshifted out of lumber yard doors and sawhorses. Both technicians wore immaculate white lab coats.

The third person was a heavyset man on the wrong side of fifty, wearing clodhopper hightop shoes, a badly frayed straw hat, and bib overalls. He looked up from a small pile of wafers arranged on an antistatic cloth at the far end of the trestle table.

"Evenin', boss," he said with a crooked smile.

Harrington walked over to join him, saw that he was conducting a preliminary test with a signal injector. "Jess, any luck yet?"

Jess Calhoun shook his head. "They're zapped. If I didn't know better, I'd think static electricity."

"That's my theory, too. But how the hell could that have happened?"

Before Jess Calhoun could reply, the door to the adjacent canteen swung open, and a tall, skinny boy of high school age, wearing frayed Levi's and a torn Maplewood sweatshirt, jangled in with a Coke in his hand. He was freckled and redheaded and looked like he was growing too fast for both his clothes and his own skin. "Hi, Dad!"

John Harrington stared in disbelief at this gangling, unlovely kid-genius who was his son. "Rusty, what the *hell* are you doing here at this time of night? You should be home in bed!"

"Aw, Dad, I came by after play practice to watch awhile. I called Mom and she said okay, you could bring me home when you came by on the way in from the airport."

"What if I had gone straight home? Then what?"

Rusty grinned infectiously. "Fat chance. Mom and I both knew that."

Jess Calhoun stirred around in the blown wafers with a grounded ceramic prod. "Rusty's been helping. We wouldn't have all these pulled and sorted by now if he hadn't given me a hand."

"But you haven't found anything yet?"

"Just that they're done busted, just like the people out in Boulder said."

"And," Rusty piped up, "that one funny anomaly."

Jess Calhoun turned to the boy, his homely features intent. "What anomaly is that, boy?"

"I mentioned it to you, Jess, but you didn't answer me."

"I must have been thinking about something else. *What* anomaly are you talking about?"

"The serial numbers," Rusty said.

Each 24864 wafer, given its hand-sculpted final assembly and security status, was assigned an almost microscopic individual serial number laser-scrolled onto its bottom edge.

"You can't read those numbers with your naked eye any more than anyone else can," Harrington told his son.

"Right," Rusty said. "But I figured since we were pulling and piling them up, I might as well run them past the micro-reader and have it make a list. So I did."

Jess Calhoun exchanged thoughtful looks with Harrington. "Not a bad idee," Calhoun drawled. "And what was it you found?"

"Well, all the wafers are in order, starting with serial number 307 and running straight up. Except the one."

"Except the one?" Harrington echoed. "What are you talking about, Rusty?"

"The one has a number out of sequence," Rusty

replied. "it's number 0681. Our shipping manifest shows we sent a replacement, 0681R, for 0311."

"So?"

Rusty's brow wrinkled. "So how come we've got back *both* 0681R and 0311—and we're missing 0326?"

"Let me see that printout," Harrington demanded.

Ten minutes later, the boy's discovery had been verified both on the list and on the chip itself. "Keep after it," Harrington, his face a storm cloud, ordered Calhoun. "Come on, Rusty."

"Home?" Rusty asked, hurrying to keep up with his father as he steamed out of the test annex and toward his own office up front.

"Phone call first," Harrington said, switching on the lights in his office.

Moments later his Drum office machine was up and running. He used his autodialer to search memory for the special, long-unused government security agency number, and dial it.

twenty-one

"This car thing," I said, "is getting complicated."

"I can live with it," Beth said, squeezing my hand.

Tuesday night we had gone back to the Mary Mary in my car, so it was up to me to drive her back to The Emerald Wednesday morning. It was early—the sun was just peeping through some of the palm trees along the road, and you could see footprints and curving ball tracks on the still-wet greens of the golf course—but not early enough. There were already a lot of tennis-type patrons wandering around the resort grounds.

"I guess," I observed, parking, "I should have delivered you back here at four."

Beth slipped her hand out of mine to let me put the gear shifter into Park. "Why?"

"Well, for appearances' sake."

She smiled. "Worried about your reputation?"

"No. Yours. I don't want you to be embarrassed."

"I won't be."

"Are you sure?"

"Very sure," she said softly, and her expression changed.

Actors, especially of the television variety, are highly

223

prized if they have what is called a "wet face." A wet face is one that seems to reflect vividly whatever feeling the character is supposed to be experiencing. A wet face radiates the character's feeling. Such an open, mobile, evocative face—one that tells *everything*—is considered a rare gift in the acting profession.

In real life it's different. Most of us work hard much of the time to hide our feelings in self-defense. We learn suppression so well that often we can't show what we feel even at those times when it might be appropriate, and even safe. Some of us get so good at the concealment game that we no longer know what our feelings may be because we've hidden them even from ourselves.

I was learning that Beth was not so hampered, at least not with me, at least not now. Here, with me, she was a wet face. She had trusted me and the trust had grown and now when we were alone together she was so open and vulnerable it almost scared me.

It's scary, allowing yourself this kind of vulnerability, or letting it develop in someone else. Show your feelings so totally and you are wide open to hurt. Accept such a wet face in someone else, and you constantly face the temptation to pull your punches or lie to protect the defenseless other, and in so doing poison the relationship. It was an act of will for Beth to trust me like this. It made her more special.

She shook herself out of her inward journey and leaned across the seat and quickly kissed me. And dug fingernails into my ribs.

"Ouch. I'm ticklish."

"Ticklish doesn't ouch."

"Maybe I should have said, 'Tickle. I'm ticklish.' "

"Or 'Ouch, I'm ouchish.' "

"Get out of my car, woman, unless thou wishest to be dragged into the back seat where I can use thee for selfish, fiendish delights."

She popped the door. "I wishest, but tennis calleth."

I walked with her to the main building. I felt silly and happier than I had in a long time, and good. This was a very, very neat lady, and the more time I spent with her, the better I liked her.

We reached the lobby and paused.

"Lunch?" I asked.

"You betcha."

"Okay. I'll meet you in the garden."

She nodded. "And we have some discretionary court time this afternoon, so maybe I'll let you play me."

"Will you take it easy on me?"

"I'll blast you into oblivion. Again."

We separated, she to hurry away for a quick clothes-change and appearance at Al's morning group drills/calisthenics. I watched her go into the elevator, then turned down the side corridor that led to the darkened bar and the public restrooms. There were pay and house telephones along the wall. They were well out of sight of the front desk.

I picked up a house phone.

"Yes, sir?" the man at the desk said promptly.

"Mr. Coligor's room, please."

"Sir, he's checked out."

I hung up and got away from the phones. Went out onto the deck and smoked.

So. Mannix, gone. Coligor, also gone. Two of my three names out of Al's computer useless to me.

I would have liked to ask also for *Hawthorne, M.,* but had felt risky enough asking for anybody on the too-brief computer list. These were special people. Knowing what I did about Mannix, they were also dangerous people, at the heart of whatever Pat Reilly had suspected and died because he poked into it. Maybe the desk clerk would not notice a request for one of those special names. Maybe the close juxtaposition of two of them would get his attention . . . motivate a mention of it to Al or someone else . . . start a snowball investigation of the call that could make any further moves on my part potentially suicidal.

If my planned call for *Hawthorne, M.*, didn't turn up anyone or anything later today, I was very near being back to *GO* without my $200, or anything else for that matter. I was fast running out of options. About all I had left was the scheme I had developed reluctantly, as a last attempt. It was better than nothing, but that was about all you could say for it.

The distant sound of a bell signaled time for the opening workouts at Al's school. A number of the guests on the patio got up promptly and headed down through the garden toward the courts, and I joined them. The sun was getting well into the sky now and it was going to be another hot day. At the far end of the courts, dust rose from the spot where trucks were dumping crushed rock to form the drainage base of the grass and clay courts under construction. Students were lining up across several of the courts, waiting for the morning warm-up workouts. I climbed halfway up into the bleachers on the east side and sat comfortably, stretching bare legs out to the sun-warmed row of planks just below me.

Below, the students continued to mill around, finding their assigned places. Instructors with clipboards walked around, helping them get lined up in the proper groups. Up front, Al Hesser conferred with three others of his teaching staff. Then he walked out to start things rolling.

He started his morning monologue and demonstration by explaining why they were going to work on early racket preparation on both the forehand and the backhand, and use those moves in stretching exercises and aerobics. He had his usual big grin and he cracked the jokes and hopped around as he always did, but he was not on his usual game at all. Far from it.

The emptiness was hard to pinpoint. His complexion was grayish, and he didn't bound around or exaggerate his tennis motions quite as grotesquely as usual. His patter, while as fast as normal, lacked his customary comic timing. But the core of the emptiness was somewhere else, lying in something I couldn't quite put my finger on. He was . . . flat. Preoccupied. An imposter, going through Al Hesser motions so well that you shouldn't have wondered, but did wonder: *Where is the real Al Hesser today? Why has he sent out this android?*

The students seemed to notice it, too. They laughed in all the right places, but the usual surprised delight was not there.

When Al got through his demonstrations and the music started, other Court College instructors came out to lead small groups. Al strolled around for a few minutes. Then he looked up into the stands, straight at me, and waved.

I went down and met him beside the high cyclone fencing that ran behind the courts. Up-close he looked worse. I smelled clove on his breath. That much clove usually means an attempt to cover the smell of liquor.

"You give any more thought to the stock deal?" he demanded.

"Yes, Al, I have. But I just don't have the money to put into it right now."

His mouth tightened. "Your funeral, baby." He started to turn away.

"Wait a minute," I said, catching his arm. "I wanted to ask you something."

"Ask," he snapped, "but hurry. I'm a busy man."

So I launched my latest scheme: "Al, you know I do some freelance writing about tennis."

"Yeah, I've seen your sheet in all the mags. So?"

"Well, then, it may not come as any surprise to you when I admit that I haven't been entirely honest with you about my reasons for being down here."

His face froze, and the rat looked out. "Meaning *what?*"

"Al, I wanted to look your operation over."

"Why?"

"I was thinking about doing a major article on Al Hesser's Court College, but I had to assure myself it was the first-class operation I expected, and that I could do a good job on it without my judgment being affected by my friendship with you."

He looked from me to the court to the stands to me again, clearly at a loss as to what he should be feeling. "And so? And so?"

"Al, I sure want to do the piece if you'll let me have a couple of hours of interview time. I think it will make a nice article, and it shouldn't hurt your winter business, either."

He squinted warily up at me. "Maybe *Tennis* magazine?"

"I don't know which one yet. But one of the big ones, yes."

"Well," he muttered, trying to get his feet back under himself, "I guess . . . sure. Hey. It ought to be a dynamite piece for you, and hey, baby, I like to give you guys a break now and then. I—"

"Which," I added, "is why I have to turn down the stock offer, you see?"

He stared at me. I let him work on it a minute.

"Oh," he said finally. The light dawned. "Oh! Shit! Sure! How are they going to accept the article as unbiased if you own a piece of the action, right?"

"That's right, Al."

"Right! Sure!" He brightened before my eyes. "Hey, I haven't been in *Tennis* for a long time. The article can feature me and all my funny stuff, and even mention reservation information, and the tapes and all?"

"I want it complete, Al."

"Okay! Great!" For an instant he was the old Al Hesser. "When do you want to have this interview? I'm real busy all day, but what about after suppertime this evening? Say about eight o'clock. My house. What think?"

"That sounds terrific."

"Okay! I'll be there!" He swaggered back through the fence gate with his old flair, clapping his hands and yelling, "All right, everybody! This is the final set, you can win if you gut it out! Come on, now! The final set at Wimbledon! Gut it! Gut it! Reach down for that something extra!"

I climbed back into the stands and tried to relax. If all else failed, I could really do the article. Al's operation probably deserved one. But of course my intention in setting up the interview was far from journalistic. My chances of figuring things out here were dwindling by the hour. Pat had been on to something. But I felt no nearer to it than when I had gotten off the airplane. The interview with Al would let me poke around, ask seemingly innocent questions that might provide a new lead.

It was a long shot but I had nothing else left.

The drills concluded and small-group practice and instruction began. I spotted Beth far to my right with a group of intermediates. I could tell at a glance that no one in the group could approach her as a player. I wanted to wave. Part of me felt like a schoolboy. I sat and maintained my elderly dignity, and cooked for an hour or two in the intensifying sunlight.

Late in the morning, off to my left, near the training building, two familiar figures came out: the old lady herself, and one of my best pals, Karyn Wechsting. A world-class singles player, the freckled Karyn had been half the team that made it possible for me to get Danisa out of Yugoslavia, and maybe also saved my life.

Billie Jean looked up into the stands, shading her eyes with her hand. It was Karyn who spotted me, waved, and patted the old lady on the back. Billie Jean went back inside and Karyn climbed up to join me. She looked great in tennis whites, with a blue terrycloth hat bagged over her rough-cut, sand-colored hair.

"Hey!" she yelped with a grin as big as Texas and held her arms wide.

I grabbed her and swung her around three times. "Welcome to the land of Oz, Karyn!"

She giggled and looked all around with exaggerated

big eyes. "I sure knew we weren't in Kansas anymore, Toto."

"When did you get in?"

"Just a few minutes ago."

"Has Al given you the grand tour yet?"

Karyn's freckled face twisted in a grimace. "Do I gotta?"

"You gotta, babe. It's required of all tennis celebrities and millionaires."

"How long have you been here?"

"Since last week."

Karyn watched the court goings-on with a frown. "Billie Jean says she gets the impression Al may be having some financial troubles."

"Oh?" I showed nothing, made it a neutral sound.

"Yeah," Karyn said blithely. "He's got her in a little house that backs up to the golf course, and she says the stove is broken, the TV is out of order, the roof leaks, and the plumbing is half-shot. She says she mentioned it several times and Al made jokes about it. Lame jokes. Then she noticed a delivery truck from town backed up to the resort building the other day, and the truck guys were carrying some cooking equipment and stuff out of the hotel kitchen, like it had been repossessed."

"Holy Mackul, Andy," I muttered. "Sounds serious."

"You notice any similar signs?"

"Nope," I lied. "You know Al. He always did spend it faster than he made it."

She frowned but seemed to accept that. She studied my face. "How about you?"

"Me? I ain't broke."

"You know what I mean, buddy."

I accepted her question because it came from honest caring. "I'm better."

"Really?"

"Yep."

"When I talked to you on the phone in July, you sounded like a zombie."

"I'm better, Karyn."

Down below, the lunchtime bell sounded, and instructors tooted whistles. People streamed off the court.

"To what do you attribute your getting better?" Karyn asked. "I'm glad, understand. But . . . is it just time, or what?"

"I loved her a lot, Karyn."

"My God, you dummy, I know that! Remember who was the maid of honor. She adored you, and you walked around with this little dazed grin on your face most of the time, like, 'How could I get this lucky?' And 'How can I be this happy?' I *know* how you loved her. But I can also tell you're better. I'm real glad. I just wondered what turned you around, started getting you out of that terminal funk you were in."

Below us, Beth came offcourt and looked up and spied me with Karyn. Her smile showed she recognized Karyn. Instead of heading for the showers, she hopped nimbly over the pipe railing and skipped up the steps toward us.

Karyn saw the direction of my gaze. "Oh, my. Cancel the question, sir. I see my answer approaching in a pink tennis dress. Oh, Brad. She's *lovely*. Where did you find her?"

The three of us had lunch together. Karyn obviously approved, and kept grinning at us and saying how amazingly well we both looked. Beth blushed and talked tennis and Karyn responded with more sly and innocent innuendos, and I kept quiet. When two women you like very much get together, you stay out of it and pray they'll like each other. Which they did.

At 2:30 there was some court time available, and Karyn enlisted one of Al's pros named Baxter Theiss to form a team to play Beth and me in mixed doubles. We stayed oncourt till past 4:00 and had a great time, especially in the second set when Karyn hit me twice in net exchanges, once in the kneecap and once on the left elbow. They were both nicer with Beth, but with her game she didn't require a lot of kindness.

We might have played even longer, but the heat was fierce by that time, and off the end of the courts there was a bulldozer moving the crushed rock around, smoothing it, making pale clouds of acrid dust, some of which drifted over our far-end court. I spotted Al Hesser down there with the foreman at one point, and judging by their stances and expressions, they were having an argument.

Maybe, I thought, I could sneak up on information about Al's financial plight during tonight's interview. If he was badly overextended and in really deep trouble, his secret involvement in drugs . . . or whatever . . . was explained. With any luck I might even collect a hint or two on how to proceed.

We used the court building showers after the match, then got back together briefly outside the pro shop. I needed other clothes for the evening. Beth watched me for a signal that I wanted her to go back to the Mary Mary with me now, but I didn't give her one. In addition to fresh clothes I needed some alone time to look at my hole card.

We parted with plans to make a quick foray into Philipsburg at 6 o'clock. I cut through the lobby after leaving them and ducked into the hallway with the house telephones.

"Yes, sir?"

"Mr. Hawthorne, please."

There was a brief pause, then: "I'll ring four-fourteen for you."

The room phone rang. Then a soft male voice said nervously, "Hello?"

My pulse was thudding. "Joseph?"

"No. There's no Joseph here."

"Is this six-fourteen?"

"No, this is four-fourteen. Mr. Hawthorne's room."

"Oh, hell, Mr. Hawthorne, I'm sorry. They gave me the wrong extension." I hung up and got out of there.

Back at the Mary Mary I holed up with a fresh can of Lipton iced tea and a cigarette and tried to be smart.

I was excited and frustrated at the same time.

There had been three names in Al Hesser's computer file. The one calling himself Mannix had either killed Pat Reilly or helped dispose of the body, and he was long gone. The one calling himself Coligor had also vanished. M. Hawthorne was the last name on the list—my last lead— and he was in Room 414 at The Emerald.

Now, I could sit around and wait for Hawthorne to vanish too, or I could do something while he was reachable.

The only problem was that I didn't know what the hell to do.

All right, *think:*

The other people on the computer list had been special. Hawthorne was special, too. The others hadn't been here long. Hawthorne probably wouldn't be either. The others had had help. I had almost gotten killed trying to shadow Mannix. If I made a misstep now—got too close to whatever was going on—they were not likely to be satisfied again with discouraging me.

Which made any direct approach to Hawthorne, M., dangerous.

But what course did I have other than a direct approach of some kind?

None.

My confusion, and maybe some creeping cowardice, abetted depression that had started sinking in earlier in the afternoon. The doubles match had been a lot of fun. But in the middle of it I had rubberbanded right back to Danisa.

During some of the points, I glanced at Beth, or anticipated a move *Danisa* would have made, and every time it brought me up short, and hurt.

I hadn't shown it. Had thought the pain was momentary. It was not momentary. Now, away from the others and frustrated as hell with my own stupidity about what to do next, I suddenly found myself off the deep end of the kind of emotional pit I had spent months trying to climb out of.

It was never going to be all better about Danisa, the depression said. I was never going to be quite whole again. I had been an innocent before that airplane hit the mountain, but I would never be an innocent again. And Beth deserved better than a cripple—worse, a man who hid his crippling stuckness in the past, but could never be an innocent again.

In this mood I thought the surprised and growing joy of the past few days had been nothing more than delusion. One bin of bleakness dumped out in my mind, triggering another. I slipped into the kind of downward spiral I had learned to dislike in myself.

You feel bad, the thoughts went. *You should be stronger.* So I felt bad about feeling bad.

My beautiful lady shrink had taught me that I came by my periodic funks honestly. "With your father," she had told me cheerfully, "if you didn't get a bad case of the glums sometimes, I would have to reconsider everything I've ever believed about family scripts."

I don't know if my father was happy. I don't think he did either. The question was simply irrelevant to the way he lived his life. He lived according to the voices he heard in his head, and those were the voices of *his* parents. He was a responsible man. Responsible to his work, first and foremost, because a man was his work, and from his work he derived his value. To your job you gave everything in you: your concentration, your preoccupation, your loyalty, your strength. And I am tempted to add: your soul.

Then, having given everything to work, you give everything again to "improving yourself"—night courses, correspondence study, extra work at the office. You give all of yourself again to your church. You give everything again to teaching your children to adopt your value system and live an unexamined life just as you are living it. You are responsible. If someone should be so [callow] [selfish] [un-American] [irresponsible] [lazy] [self-centered] [unmotivated] [hollow] (pick one or two) as to ask you if you are *happy*, you look at them with astonished disbelief and ask, "What the hell does *that* have to do with anything?"

My father bullied me, terrified me, awed me, manipulated me, saddened me, abandoned me, hurt me, and twisted me, and I despaired of ever measuring up, and hopelessly adored him. He made me in his image. In that he was, like his own father before him, a success. He would not have understood this definition of success because for him it was spelled $ucce$$. But I see it clearly. His grim, gloomy perfectionism is a part of me. He still gets out sometimes. He will not forgive anything he perceives as weakness.

Part of my struggle after Danisa's death was to stop living by the harsh, unforgiving standards he built into me. So, trying to be my own man, I watch vigilantly for him, peeking around the door-corners of my mind and ducking back with rabbit fright because I am scared he will be there, so much larger and more powerful and better than I could ever hope to be. I watch . . . but this evening he had gotten out.

Stop feeling sorry for yourself, he told me coldly, *and do something.*

I smoked a couple more cigarettes and decided his advice was sound, although his gloom was a little melodramatic. I decided I was tired of feeling sorry for myself, told myself to cheer up.

After changing clothes I headed back to The Emerald. It was 5:20 by the lobby clock. Knowing the room number for *Hawthorne, M.,* I dialed it. The same flabby male voice answered. I hung up at once, then dialed Beth's room.

"You're early!" she said brightly.

"Beth, a bit of business has come up. I'm going to have to take a raincheck on the ride to Philipsburg."

"Oh." She sounded disappointed. "Anything I can help with?"

"No. This won't take long. I'll hunt for you later in the evening. In the meantime, no reason why you couldn't show Karyn around. I'm sure she would appreciate it."

"Well, if you don't think she'd rather hang out with her fellow pros . . ."

"Call her and ask her that. And if you come back here later, I'll hunt you up then."

"Okay." There was a moment of silence, then: "Brad?"

"Yes?"

"You'll be careful?"

"Hey, a talk with a man about a new line of rackets?"

Her tone said she didn't believe my lie for a minute: "Bye."

Feeling unduly cloak-and-daggerish, I rode the elevator to the fifth floor and then walked down one. A stroll down the quiet, carpeted corridor located Room 414. I went back down the hall and stood in front of the elevators and watched the door to his room. An elevator came by going up, and I shook my head and indicated I wanted to go down. Later, when people on a down elevator stared at me, I indicated with a smile that I wanted a car going up.

I knew there was a chance I might stand around without results until I had to go meet Al Hesser at eight. But if Hawthorne was coming out for drinks or dinner, there was a good chance he would come out before that time. I walked back and forth a little, and when some people came out of 428 and headed for the elevator, I walked slowly back down the hall like I had just disembarked, then walked back after they had ridden down.

Six o'clock came, and then 6:30. Maybe he wasn't coming out at all tonight.

At 6:35, however, he came out.

He was not a large man. Chunky and unathletic-looking, he wore uncomfortably new linen slacks, a pale green shirt open at the collar, several heavy gold chains around his neck, and white deck shoes just out of the box. His bright red hair needed to be cut and it was unruly. He glanced at me through bifocals that made his eyes look like the bottoms of water glasses, then busily studied the wall beside the elevator doors. He had no tan. When he impatiently punched the elevator call button a second time, his hand shook. A man under pressure and not handling it as well as he might. A man who did not look like your mill-run patron at a tennis resort.

The elevator came. I got on behind him and we rode down. There were four other people in the car, two men and their women. Somebody was wearing too much Brut.

We all got out at the lobby level. Hawthorne peered myopically around, then walked unerringly in the direction of the sign denoting the dining room. I watched him enter, get a table, and start studying the menu. I went into the adjacent bar and sat where I could see him through the joining doorway. I nursed my Manhattan until five minutes before eight, and all I had learned was that Hawthorne ate alone, liked fish, and dropped crumbs in his lap.

Feeling like I had wasted more time, I paid my tab and headed out the back way for my appointment with Al Hesser.

twenty-two

Elsewhere

Boulder, Colorado

The government man who appeared at Boulder TechnoSys Wednesday was of medium height, with thinning sandy hair and a few freckles. He was slightly plump, and wore tweeds and soft Timberland loafers, the kind with a useless leather knot over the instep. The loafers showed his argyle socks. His name was Dyer and he smiled a lot and seemed kind of lazy.

Not to worry, he told Dr. H. I. Pellton and select members of his staff. It was routine to make a visit and ask a few questions off the standard checklist when there was any kind of trouble with equipment or technical components that were on the foreign shipment embargo list. He was apologetic about the red tape.

Dyer was very nice, very low key. He did not mention what he knew about the wafers that had been returned to Drum Labs in Connecticut. Just some questions for the forms, he assured everyone, and he would be out of their hair. No problem. He yawned.

Dr. Pellton and his associates relaxed.

Dyer sort of drifted around, apparently thoroughly disorganized. He wandered all over the place and asked a lot of dumb questions. No one person could have realized

238

that by late afternoon Mr. Dyer knew who worked where, how shipments came in and went out, the way they were processed in-house, what had happened to the TSAS-1 subassemblies, and when, and who had worked on the testing procedures. When told that Dr. Mannie Hawthorne had taken a few days' compensatory leave to go play tennis in the Lesser Antilles, Dyer yawned his biggest and sleepiest yawn of the day.

At 5 P.M. he shook some hands, thanked everybody for their hospitality, apologized again for boring them with the routine visit, and drove away in his gray government Plymouth.

At 5:10 P.M. he made a credit card call from the nearest pay phone booth, one beside a convenience store a mile from the lab. His call went through. He did not sound lazy anymore, and he did not yawn while punching in the top-priority security codes.

"I think we've got a rush order for our friends down the highway," he told his superior when she came on-line. Then he told what he had learned, and what he guessed.

With one soft, frustrated expletive she agreed with him, gave him some new instructions, and hung up.

St. Maarten

L. K. Able glanced up and down the fourth-floor hallway of The Emerald to assure himself no one else was in sight. Then he tapped twice on the door to 414.

The door opened immediately and Mannie Hawthorne, collar askew and sweat filming his forehead, urgently gestured him into the room. He must have been pacing the floor, awaiting the knock, L. K. thought.

"Mr. Hawthorne?" he asked formally.

"Yes. You called me on the house telephone a minute ago?"

"Yes." L. K. was careful. "I've been asked to deliver a

239

message to you. A man told me he wishes to meet with you later tonight."

Hawthorne's eyes snapped nervously. "All right. All right. I have what he wants."

"The package you wish to deliver is small, I believe?"

Hawthorne's small eyes darted around the room. They rested on the dresser a moment too long, then skipped on. "It's—yes. Relatively small. Portable, certainly."

So it was in the portable computer, per instructions. Good. "Mr. Hawthorne, you will receive another call here in your room later in the evening. I am instructed to tell you that a meeting will be arranged at that time."

Hawthorne removed his glasses and mopped at his flushed face with a damp grayish handkerchief. "I've jumped every time that phone rang."

L. K.'s antennae went up, although he showed nothing. "Oh? Have you had so many calls?"

"I guess it's just the casual tropics, right? I mean, it's no big deal. You notice when you're waiting for a call and sort of . . . on edge. Two wrong numbers in the first six hours I was here."

"That's very irritating and unusual, Mr. Hawthorne. I work for The Emerald. I should report this sort of nonsense. Perhaps the desk has not properly updated the telephone clerks on room changes. What did your callers say?"

"The first time, they were looking for somebody named Joseph in six-fourteen. The second time, they hung up."

L. K. nodded. "I'll check it out with the desk. Someone has slipped up somewhere. An occasional wrong number, okay, we're all human. But two in your first afternoon, that's unpardonable."

Hawthorne's grin resembled a skull's hang-jawed grimace. "That's the least of my worries. Let's just get the messages passed and, uh, the merchandise delivered." His Adam's apple went up and down. "And all."

"You'll be contacted, sir. Of course you will follow instructions precisely."

"You better believe it!"

L. K. gave his man a reassuring smile and left the room.

He went immediately down to the lobby and checked the guest listings. No one with a first or last name of "Joseph" was in Room 614. Or in any other room with a fourteen on the end of it, for that matter.

Internal alarms flashing amber, L. K. made another telephone call.

Langley, Virginia

In his cubicle deep inside the big building, Tom Dwight pushed aside a copy of the *Washington Post* carrying big headlines about the imminent collapse of the legally constituted government in Guatemala. It was late and Dwight was not only tired, but harassed.

"It looks like we've had it down there," he told Marshal Exerblein, who stood on the other side of his desk.

"That thing we tried didn't work?"

"Guatemala is down the tubes."

"Sad," Exerblein said without a show of emotion.

"That's not why I called you," Dwight told him.

Exerblein looked at him, waiting.

"You," Dwight said, "are going to St. Maarten."

Exerblein took it like he seemed to take everything, with a maddening yuppie cool. "When?"

"How fast can you get to the airport?"

Was there a twitch of concern in the frost-calm deputy's expression? "Well. Of course I can start filling out the travel requests at once—"

"Marshal, you don't seem to *get* it, dammit. The FBI has figured out that one of those secret wafers in the B-1B

241

system was not returned properly to its fabricator. One of the Colorado lab boys has honked off to that Al Hesser tennis school on St. Maarten."

"The place we were looking into before Guatemala heated up?"

"The same. Now. If that technician has gone down there, and a wafer is missing, then it's safe to assume he took the son of a bitch. You're to get down there *now*, not in the course of due administrative process."

Exerblein frowned. "Very well. I'll go by my house for clothing and what else I'll need."

"There's a car on the way for you. I want you airborne inside an hour."

"Has that fellow Brad Smith been notified of these developments?"

"No," Dwight said with a hint of bitterness. "The decision was to let him twist in the wind, remember? Also he doesn't work for us. Also he hasn't got the qualifications to handle a deal like this." Dwight eyed his associate bleakly. "Also," he added, "we don't know where he is down there."

"Well, is *anyone* else going down there with me?"

"You bet. The national intelligence staff is lending us a man. Also, I have a call in for Collie Davis, if he ever checks in with us today or listens to his home answering machine."

With a sniff, Exerblein examined a fleck of dust on the sleeve of his heavily starched white shirt. With a surgeon's precision he removed the offending molecule. "The last time we worked jointly with NSA—"

"I *know* about that, Marshal," Dwight cut in sharply.

"Also, it should be pointed out that Collie Davis has not operated in a foreign environment for—how long?"

"I suggest you worry about your end of it and let Collie handle his part."

"Still—"

"If you don't stop bitching and get out of here," Dwight exploded, "I'm going to have your balls hanging on the front fence!"

Surprisingly, Exerblein's face curled into a happy smile. It was the smile of an angel, a true innocent. "They make rum on St. Maarten."

"Go!"

Exerblein went. Dwight stared angrily at his telephone, waiting for it to ring. Smith had been right to press on, he thought. *The fucker.* But being right didn't change how snug the fit had become now. If that wafer got out of St. Maarten, some heads were going to roll. And that was the least of it.

St. Maarten

When the man known as Sylvester walked past the desk at his resort a little after 8:30 P.M. and spotted the telephone message envelope in his key box, he knew something had gone wrong. He casually asked the woman behind the desk for messages and carried the small buff envelope to his room before opening it.

M.: *Pekanian, 208*
CALL FOR YOU AT: *1950*
CALLER: *M. Snyder, home office*
MESSAGE: *Contact your sales representative without delay.*

Sylvester slipped the pistol into the back waistband of his slacks beneath his light sportcoat and drove immediately to The Emerald. Parking lot and lobby blazed with light, and a small orchestra played dance music in the dining room, now partly cleared for dancing. The faint sounds of more contemporary music hammered through the walls from the downstairs club.

Sylvester found L. K. Able standing off to the side on the back deck. They made eye contact and Able followed Sylvester around the pool and into the deserted rear garden area.

"What is it?" Sylvester asked.

Able frowned, worried and uncertain. "Our man received two wrong-number telephone calls this afternoon. One wrong number, all right. But two? I thought—"

"You were correct," Sylvester interrupted. "Has the transfer been accomplished?"

"Not yet. I told him he would be contacted later this evening. I felt a need to check with my superior before proceeding, on the chance the telephone calls indicate our man is under surveillance."

"You did the correct thing. Were you given new instructions?"

"I was told you would relay them, and I am to follow your orders without question."

"Where is this Brad Smith at this time?"

"He's with Mr. Hesser. At the house. Conducting an interview." Able paused, then added, "They started a short time ago."

Sylvester made instant decisions. A better chance might not come later. "You will proceed to the house and maintain watch on Smith. If he leaves the house, you will follow him at an assuredly safe distance. His activities are to be monitored and reported to your control. However, unless he takes overtly threatening action, he is not to be interfered with at this time."

"I understand."

"I plan to have a late nightcap in the bar. Perhaps we will accidentally encounter one another there . . . say . . . about one o'clock."

"Yes."

The men separated, Sylvester returning to the lobby.

The confusion was not to Sylvester's liking. Ordinarily his operations ran with the precision of a fine watch. This was too messy, too loose, too uncertain.

Instinct told Sylvester that the wrong numbers had been more than accident, and Able had been correct in reporting them at once. Sylvester also would have bet that the calls had been made by Brad Smith, poking around again in his amateurish way.

Just as he had since arriving, Sylvester wanted to take Smith out. But he could not do that unless Smith became an active interference . . . or until after the shipment was safely out of St. Maarten.

Patience, Sylvester counseled himself. In less than twenty-four hours, the exchange would have been completed at the airport and the object would be safely on its way. *Then* . . . perhaps . . . Brad Smith could be dealt with, and there would be no ongoing operation that might be endangered by news of his "accidental" death.

Meanwhile—now—Smith was off the scene and Sylvester felt the need to move expeditiously. After considering his usual professional desire for the neatest, safest possible operation and balancing it against the added danger that might obtain once Smith had left the interview with Al Hesser, Sylvester decided the best course was to make the best of it and act immediately.

From a lobby house telephone he called 414.

Mannie Hawthorne jumped when the telephone rang. Licking dry lips, he answered. "Hello?"

"Mr. Hawthorne?" A deep male voice, the syllables of his name separated as if every sound were measured.

"Speaking!"

"The transfer of materials is to take place at this time. Please

follow these instructions precisely. Bring your item out of your room and proceed to the rear fire exit on your floor. You will proceed down the fire stairs to the first floor and leave the building by the door you find there. Follow the sidewalk around the back of the garden area and behind the tennis buildings. At the far end of the tennis complex, proceed through the gate and make your way into the construction area for new courts. You will be met there. Do you understand?"

"I go out the back way, around the garden and tennis courts, down into the place where they're moving dirt around for the additional courts?"

"That is correct. You are not likely to see anyone because of the dance in progress. However, if you do meet someone, say you are taking a stroll, and keep moving. Understood?"

"Yes—"

"Proceed as soon as possible. Your contact person is waiting for you." The connection broke.

Hawthorne replaced his telephone, then mopped his face again with his handkerchief. His nerves had been wonderful through everything that had gone before. Surely he was not in as much danger here. But this was unfamiliar territory. He didn't even know if he was to be paid on delivery of the portable computer and its precious cargo, or at a later time. And he could not prevent his mind from speculating about how dreadful it would be, to get this far and then have something go wrong!

The voice on the telephone, however, had sounded reassuringly calm and confident. And even if the caller had sounded like Mickey Mouse, Hawthorne at this point would have had no choice but to obey without question.

Slipping the strap of the NEC's carrying case over his shoulder, Hawthorne made sure he had his room key in his pocket, then left the room with the lights on and the TV still going. He wouldn't be gone long.

The hallway was empty and he made it to the rear exit

without being observed. His heels sounded loud in the hard, echoing environment of the back fire stairs, but again he met no one. Warm moist night air greeted him in the security-lighted paved area behind the building. He could hear music and distant voices and laughter beyond the ten-foot shrubbery bordering the walk.

Breathing shallowly from tension, Hawthorne walked quickly around the garden, down the darkened foot ramp to the tennis complex, around the rear of the pro shop and instruction building. Only a couple of naked sixty-watt bulbs over closed metal doors provided light back here, and the music and voices sounded very far away indeed. Hawthorne shivered, hurrying along, the portable computer thumping against his hip with every other step. It was spooky down here.

By the time he reached the far end of the tennis complex, his eyes had begun to adjust to the darkness, and he was able to locate the battered gate in the cyclone fencing that surrounded the construction area. It squealed on rusty hinges when he pushed it back and went through.

Moonlight showed planks scattered over piles of dirt, and the bulk of a bulldozer hulking in the night like a prehistoric predator. Planks formed a walkway to the level where the earth had been smoothed out, and all the crushed rock dumped as drainage base for the additional courts.

Hawthorne went carefully down to the court level.

As he got down there, a figure stepped out of the shadows of a portable toilet shed, making him jump.

"Hello!" Hawthorne whispered. "You startled me!" He gave a nervous little laugh.

The man stepped closer. He was considerably taller than Hawthorne, and there was a muscular grace about him. He was wearing pale-colored slacks, shirt, and sportcoat. He smelled of cigars. Something about him made a chill wind blow through Hawthorne's heart.

"You have the item?" the man asked. It was the same dark voice that had been on the telephone.

Hawthorne unslung the NEC. "It's in here, just like I was told to fix it. The unit is inside, in place of the motherboard."

The man gestured. "Put it down."

Hawthorne hesitated. "Here, you mean? In the dirt?"

"Yes. I have your payment."

Hawthorne giggled. "I can use that!" He put the NEC on the ground.

The man stepped forward, and for a moment Hawthorne thought he was going to pat him on the shoulder. But then both the man's hands closed around his throat, the thumbs pressing in with shocking pain under the shelf of his jaw. Instantly everything in Hawthorne's vision began to go gray. Then the gray faded and got darker and Hawthorne knew the truth, and panicked, but too late.

Sylvester felt the man's body go entirely limp. Sylvester changed his grip slightly and twisted, and there was a grating sound and then a sharp pop, and the man's head lolled loosely to one side. Sylvester stepped back daintily and let the body fall. It dropped limp and rolled half onto its side.

They were quite close to the spot where Sylvester had already shoveled out a shallow depression in the crushed rock. Moving the portable computer safely out of the way, he rolled the body over four times and it sprawled into the depression. One leg and one arm stuck out. Sylvester arranged them more neatly and then picked up the shovel and quickly covered the body.

The body made the redistributed rock mound a little high. Sylvester raked the area flat again, spreading rock around so everything looked neat and normal. Breathing heavily from his exertion, he made sure nothing had been overlooked. Then he picked up the portable computer, slipped the strap over his shoulder, and climbed the planks out of there.

On the way back to the garden area he lit a cigar. There was nothing like a cigar after work.

twenty-three

"Brad Smith," Al said, trying to sound hearty. "Big as life and twice as! Come in this house, baby, and make me more famous!"

It was a nice try. But when Al himself opened his house door for me, it was immediately apparent that he was not in good shape. The morning's tension had escalated. Tonight he looked more like a man on the edge of a crackup. Something had happened since we talked.

Still wearing his tennis shirt and shorts, he was barefooted, dingy with sweat. Under the superficial sunburn pink and all the black shag hair, his body color resembled pie dough. He had an icy drink in a big tumbler, either bourbon or scotch, the color of coffee. It was half-gone. He looked half-gone, too: twitchy, brimming with phony good cheer that he couldn't quite bring off, the rat looking out of his eyes.

I went in, carrying my portable cassette recorder and notebook. He waved me into the rock-walled den. The air-conditioning was on full blast and a big fire blazed in the fireplace: good old Al; the dramatic fire when it was wholly unnecessary. Some papers that looked like financial statements and bills were scattered over a white, sofa-sized

250

hassock in front of his easy chair.

Al went behind the corner bar and cocked his elbow up on it in a reasonable impersonation of Jackie Gleason's old bartender act. "What'll it be, pal? I gotta do everything myself tonight. Help's got the night off except for Amy, the maid, and she went with Mia into town after some more booze and hair curlers or something." His face twisted. "Just what I need, my man! More stuff charged to my account." He caught himself, made his face look calmer. "So. Bourbon? Gin? Vodka? Scotch? I got no dope. Dope kills. Fucking South Americans getting richer than the Japs, shipping that poison in all the time."

I sat on the couch. "An ounce of that Jack Daniel's would be just fine, Al."

"Done and done." He poured it with a flourish, slopping as much on the countertop as into the glass. He changed bottles to refill his own tumbler: Maker's Mark. He was pretty far gone already, but that didn't entirely account for how badly he was shaking.

He brought me my drink, which I placed on the great masonry coffee table in front of me. He collapsed into the big chair and hiked up hairy legs and bare feet. I flicked the recorder to *on* and leaned back with my notebook.

"How we gonna do this?" he demanded. "Do you ask questions or do I just talk or what?"

"I've got some questions, Al, but however you feel most comfortable is fine."

He took a big swig and shuddered. "Well, lemme tell you thish. Al Hesser's Court College ish going great. Just *great!* We're at sixty percent capacity thish week an' we're off-season. Wait'll the season, baby! You wanna know why we're doing so great? I can launch into an eggspli . . . eggsplanation. You wanna hear that? You got lots of tape? You want me to launch?"

"Launch," I suggested.

He launched. It quickly became apparent that I didn't have to ask anything, at least not yet.

In fact, I probably could not have gotten a word in edgewise if I had tried. Pausing now and then only long enough to take another shuddering drink, he simply dumped his whole spiel: his dreams, growth to date, plans for the future, some of the cash flow problems he was facing, some of the bitterness about his own playing days and the clown role he had had to assume to conceal his rage at discovering less than towering talent inside himself, his salesman bullshit, all of it.

It was an amazing performance. Al Hesser had always been a talker. My visit—combined with the alcohol and whatever had brought on this crisis behavior in him—was the catalyst for a catharsis that quickly became bigger than the idea of an interview. Part of the time—over the next hour or more—it was not apparent that Al even remembered I was in the room.

He got up twice to refill his tumbler again. I passed both times. He paced the big room, gesturing, acting out court moves, dropping in bits of VCR training tape monologues as if he were fuguing into automatic playback. Once or twice he looked at me as if checking to see if I was still with him, and then I inserted a question to show I was tracking the monologue.

He said he was a great tennis coach for two reasons: because he had never had any talent of his own, and because he was a peasant schmuck. Not having any inborn tennis talent, he said, he had had to learn everything, depend on technique. Even as a child he had been aware that his body was not right for tennis, and his ancestry had given him a body better attuned to a hoe or a lathe than a tennis racket. So he knew more about technique than anyone else because that was all he had ever had going for him.

He knew, he said, that people had considered him a joke even early on in life. People had laughed at him—made jokes about his gorilla body and short legs. So they saw a clown? Fine. He would be a clown. People couldn't know who was getting the last laugh that way, he said.

He had thought for a while that technique and being a clown would take him all the way to the top of tennis. It had been another bitter lesson when he learned that the mythology was not true, wanting it and working hard could only take you so far. So he had made the best of what he had, and now look at him, he was famous, Al Hesser's Court College system was second to none.

He talked a long time about his first wife, but he was referring to events I knew nothing about, and much of it didn't make sense. I knew she had been tall and lovely, the daughter of a prominent Boston family, and the marriage had lasted about ten years. The rage and pain that flowed out of him, talking about the marriage, made him almost incoherent.

"*She* thought I was a clown, too. I was always beneath her. A peasant, right? Just a peasant. People said she was a princess. She liked that. She looked like Grace Kelly. They thought I was an ape and she was an angel. She had more affairs in a month than I had in my whole life. She bragged about them. I begged her to love me. She said I was shit. Everybody thought I was shit."

I sat back on the couch and listened, and went with it. Psychic breaks do not happen every day. I had walked into the middle of one. I didn't know if anything he was telling me might be useful, but I had the sense to stay out of the way of this steamroller monologue and see where it might go next.

He was as vulnerable, I thought, as he would ever be in his life. If I could take advantage of that, I would. I felt like a traitor, but there was a core of anger inside me that said being a traitor sometimes—taking advantage—might be the only way to make progress. Al Hesser's hysteria was a bird's nest on the ground; I would accept it with thanks and worry later about my conscience.

After a long, long time, still drinking steadily, he got into stories about how he had gotten control of the small resort on the "wrong," or north, end of Hilton Head island, borrowed to the hilt, and opened his first Court College. Some of the references he made to complex financial maneuvers sounded unethical and probably illegal, and he cackled a lot, reconstructing conversations with partners he said he had screwed. Whatever problems Al had, guilty conscience was not among them.

Pacing again. Waving the hand that didn't have the tumbler in it. "It's like cutting the tennis ball, it's the difference between linear force and kinetic force, see? I mean, fuck, anybody can hit a flat forehand, but when you get into cuts, that's when you separate the players out. That's the basic assumption I make in everything I do. It's behind all the lessons. That, and don't take it so goddam seriously, you can't teach constipated muscles. I did that in all my business dealings. Poke around, find an edge. Bastards! They all laughed at me behind my back. Just like she did. I got to show them all. I got to be bigger than *anybody*. I—"

He stopped suddenly, staggered, almost fell. A look of consternation twisted his eyebrows together and distorted his mouth.

"'Scuse me," he choked, and rushed out of the room.

I replaced my tape and lit a cigarette. From somewhere nearby I heard the ugly sound of his stomach finally rebelling against all the whiskey. Then a toilet flushed and there was silence, and then the sound of water running.

I finished my cigarette. The vast millionaire's room looked down at me in silence. Every item, from the beamed ceiling to the rock walls to the *House Beautiful* contemporary furnishings to the fireplace, its flames now reduced to flickers issuing from broken black remnants of wood, said money; success; fulfillment. I wondered how many rooms like this, in how many parts of the world, sat empty and meaningless, echoing to the sound of puking.

Al came back into the room. His thin, dark hair was wet, pasted to his scalp. He looked like someone just leaving a hospital after a long and serious stay.

"Shit," he muttered, dropping back into his chair. "Where was I?"

"You were talking about—"

"He's gone," Al cut in.

"What?"

"He's gone. The goddammed inconsiderate crummy selfish little fucker is gone. Billy. My kid! Gone! I don't even know where. We've always got some cash in a drawer in my office. Petty cash. Petty! Ha! Over a thousand bucks. He took it. Took off. This afternoon. Told the yard man he had had enough and wasn't coming back, ever."

He stopped and looked for his tumbler, found it on the table beside him, picked it up, thought better of it, suddenly flared with anger and hurled the glass across the room. Booze and the remnants of ice cubes and melt-water spewed into the air, wetting another table and chair and a tall stoneware figurine standing near the far-wall bookshelves. The glass bounced off the rock wall in three or four pieces. I felt like we had suddenly wandered into an old Rod Serling show. Kept quiet.

"Goddamn little bastard! I gave him everything! He started right off, having a better body than I ever had. His mother's genes, right? That's what she used to say. Sneer at me. Pretend it was a joke. 'He has my genes, Al; good genes; not peasant stock.' Bitch. Always thought she was better than me. What did she marry me for if she thought I was such a fucking peasant? I put a racket in his hands when he was three years old. Not some crummy cutoff, I had one built special for him. Nice short length, good balance, a little head-light and flexible to make sure he didn't hurt himself or get bad habits trying to overcome bad equipment. I worked with the little fucker. Didn't push him. Don't want to make mistakes like some people with kids. Just make sure it's fun, show him the right way to do it. And God! He has talent. Always did. More than his peasant old man, right? Right! Give him everything. Don't even pressure him when he fucks off in school, flunks out. Buy the girl an abortion that time. Fix it when he steals that car. Let him come back here, put out the welcome mat. Let him find his own way. Right? Right. What does he do? He shits on me. And then this stuff starts with Mia. I ignore it. What the hell, he's just a horny kid, right? What am I supposed to do when I come in and he's in her bedroom and she's practically bare-assed and you can see his hard-on under his pants halfway across the room? Is that just something else you're supposed to ignore? Are you just supposed to look away and hope your only son doesn't fuck your wife? Isn't there some goddam *limit?* Was I wrong to raise hell?"

He paused, grasping in a breath. But I didn't have to say anything. He wasn't through. He was far from through.

"So," he resumed, giving me a look that scalded with its bitterness, "I guess that makes it all *my* fault, right? That's what she said a little while ago. Where has she gone? I don't know. Is she coming back? I don't know. What am I supposed to tell people when they ask where he is? Where she is? Am I supposed to say, 'Well, my son stole my petty cash and ran off, and my wife got pissed and is trying to find him so she can fuck him'? What am I supposed to say, Smith? You're the writer. You were always the big shot. You tell me. What am I supposed to say, so everybody doesn't know what a schmuck I am?"

He fixed me with burning eyes. It wasn't the rat looking out now, but a kid who simply had had the hell beaten out of him.

"Al," I said, "I don't—"

"Maybe you would just lend me five thousand," he broke in. "I understand if you don't want to buy stock. Jesus Christ, this whole thing is a stack of Tinkertoys that might come down under its own weight any minute. You see that. You're smart enough to see that. Most people don't. I'll get the operating cash. But if I had five thousand, if she comes back, I've got to have that to give her Friday. It's just a little cash flow problem. Actually, everything is going great, no problem."

"Do you think she's coming back?"

He didn't hear me. His mind was careening a hundred miles ahead of any reply I might give. He said, "You've got to help me, Brad. We were sort of pals once. I mean, not close pals, but we got along, right? I never screwed you, right? And you never screwed me. I've got to trust somebody. I am in such deep shit you would not believe it. You've got to help me. Somebody's got to help me."

"Al, if five thousand would—"

"Fuck the five thousand. Forget the five thousand. Forget that. I was just joking about that. Everything is fine. He'll come back when he's out of money. She'll be back. I've got to get out of this deal with L. K. and whoever the fuckers are that are above him. I just can't stand this shit anymore. I'm *scared.* How do I get out of it?"

I had an eerie sense of being alone in the universe with him, as if there were no one in the world beyond these walls. We were suddenly at the precise place I had hoped to approach. Al had broken almost entirely, and he had let me in. The jokes/tricks/lies/pretenses/walls were down. We were at the center.

If I said the wrong thing now, he could snap back into his defenses. I had no time to consider what might be the right thing to say. So I said the first and simplest and most direct words. "Tell me."

Al got up and started pacing again. He wrung his hands. It was impossible to tell now if he was still drunk or in some compartment of his mind that was close to crazy. I held my breath, praying he would stay there long enough to tell me what I needed to know.

"When Pat Reilly got killed," he said, "that was the last straw. I thought it was an accident. It wasn't."

"Who did it?" I asked bluntly.

"I don't know. I don't even know what Pat found out. But L. K. is an enforcer. Then that other guy checked in. Mannix. And Pat died and then Mannix and the old whore he was with—she was his wife about like I'm King Tut— they both vanished. I was—Christ!—Pat was a *buddy* of mine! Was that an accident? I ask you. Was that an accident?"

"I don't think so, Al."

Again he didn't hear me. "No. It wasn't. But did I even so much as ask? Fuck no! Do I want to be next?"

He came back and flopped in the chair, his eyes looking into another dimension. "It's just a cash flow problem, see. When they came to me first, what they presented it as, was they needed a place for making some quiet, secret business deals sometimes. And maybe launder a little money. They didn't say that. I guessed that. Twenty thousand a month. Payable on the first. Cash money. No traces, no taxes. And all I had to do, see, was have a couple of guys on my staff—they pay for these guys—and these guys facilitate meetings and such, no problem. I'm to have an automatic modem on the computer upstairs. Occasionally somebody will call and drop a name into a file. That means this is a special guest, make a reservation, treat him or her nice, ask no questions. All expenses paid extra, on top of the regular twenty thousand. No problem.

"Was that a mistake? I ask you, was that a mistake? Take easy money, solve some of my goddam cash problems? You've *got to* keep growing. Keep up with the technology. Advertise. Expand. Otherwise people think you're failing, and they pull out in droves."

He sprang out of the chair again and went over and poked at the dead fire. "Goddammit, fucking dry wood burns too fast. Don't have any more in here. Let it go." He tossed the poker onto the raised hearth. "I don't know what they're doing. L. K.'s got a radio up there. Every once in a while, late at night usually, he goes in there and puts on headphones and listens. He tunes around, makes some notes sometimes. I was in there once and he had it turned up real high and I could hear through the headphones he was listening to Morse code and taking it down. I don't know who his bosses are. I don't know shit. I want out. I'm scared. Brad! You've got to help me!"

This time he was focused on me. So I asked, "Is L. K. the only one you've got here right now?"

"No. There's a guy named Hawthorne. Just got here. I saw him. He looks like a piece of shit, I don't know what his business is. L. K. will be his contact, like usual. There was another name came in the other day. He checked in, checked back out before anybody got a look at him. What's going on? I don't know. Brad. How can I get out of this thing? I'm afraid of what they'll do if I just tell them to get lost. I'm in so fucking deep. I need the twenty thousand. In a year maybe no, but now I need it. But it isn't the twenty. It's I'm scared *my* ass will be found on some beach if I tell them to get out, I'm through with them. What am I gonna do? You've been around, man. You're a man of the world. Shit, you even did that thing for the CIA. Give me some advice! I'll listen. I'll take it. People think I'm an arrogant asshole that never listens to anything but my own farts, but I'll listen. I'm *scared*."

"Well, Al," I said slowly, "it sounds like a complicated problem. I'd like to give it some thought. Then we can talk again. Maybe in the morning?"

He changed again—his facial expression, his entire demeanor. It was as if another Al Hesser stepped out. Maybe telling it all—pleading for help and getting a splinter of assurance—deactivated something.

He came across the room and put an arm around my shoulder. He stunk of sweat, whiskey, and vomit. "That's great. I'll look forward to that. Maybe first thing, right? Right. Hey, I appreciate it, baby, I really do. But look, keep this to yourself, right?"

"Right, Al."

"And look. You know how I exaggerate. I mean, it isn't as bad as it looks to me right now, maybe, right? And you gotta go now, right? Let me crap out for the night. I don't feel so good."

"Okay, Al."

Still babbling, he watched me gather up my recorder, tapes, and notebook, and then he walked me to the door. Going through the foyer, he suddenly fell silent. At the door I turned to shake hands. Wet furrows glistened on his cheeks. I went out of the house and down the driveway, leaving him standing there, a chubby chief silhouetted against the bright grandeur of the entrance to his villa.

Inside The Emerald, the club musicians in their brightly colored native shirts and straw hats were playing good dance music, and a lot of the patrons were taking advantage of it. I looked around but didn't find Beth. A call to her room got no answer, and I was on the way out when she called my name and hurried across the lobby to catch up with me. She looked bright and happy.

"I thought you had deserted me!" she said, taking my arm. "We had a great time in town. You should have gone along."

"I wish I could have."

She frowned. "What is it? You look like you've seen a ghost."

"I've got some more business I have to take care of, Beth."

"Would you like me to come along now, or will you be back?"

"I'm going to handle this alone, and I'll see you in the morning."

Given the way we had spent time together in recent days and nights, it was not the answer she expected. My impulse was to soften my words, but from this point forward things might be getting considerably more complicated with Al's friends, and I wanted Beth nowhere near. "I'll call you," I added indifferently.

It hit her by surprise and the pain showed for a few seconds: a tightening around her eyes and mouth, and stiffening of her arm where it touched mine. I hated to do this to her.

Then she recovered. "Oh. Well. Okay, Brad."

I disengaged my arm. "Take care. Talk to you tomorrow." I left her standing there, still looking surprised and hurt, as I hurried on outside.

Driving back toward the Mary Mary, I reviewed what had just taken place with Al Hesser and what it meant I had to do next.

Al had overreached himself and grabbed for the nearest visible help, which in this case had turned out to be a piranha. The people standing behind his bodyguard-supervisor, L. K., were not simple businessmen as he had first naively hoped. My suspicions about dope seemed unfounded; he would have known that. Something else was going on here. There were too many people involved and too much technical expertise—the computer system and the radio link—for small potatoes.

Thinking back, I trotted out my army vocabulary as I thought how Collie Davis had wanted me to stay out of this. Evidently *nobody* at Langley thought anything significant was going on here. Not now.

But why? I was convinced Pat Reilly had come here under their auspices, or at least with their blessing. Then when I expressed an interest they had suddenly changed their minds. Since my arrival I had half expected one of them to contact me, suggest that everything was under control, again say I might be happier someplace else, like St.

Kitts. That hadn't happened either. *Nothing* had happened in those terms. Which forced me to the conclusion that I really was all alone down here.

Which, I thought, made them stupid as hell. And made me helpless. If I had been working for them, I would have had a number to call, a way to establish contact. I knew enough now to make a call worthwhile and interesting. It was past the point where I wanted to press on alone. But I had no number, nothing.

I got back to the Mary Mary. Everything was black. The power had failed again. The guests from the far end were having another beach bonfire out in front of their unit, the sounds of voices and a battery-operated tape player tinkling through the night. I skirted them and a few empty A-frames and reached my own, where I groped around and relocated my plastic-wrapped revolver and put it under my mattress. Still trying to figure out what I should do next, I came face to face with the certainty that I really didn't much want to go on with this. Pat had gotten less far than this, and he was dead. My escape from Ricardo had been dumb luck. I couldn't count on luck again. I had no backup.

I felt uncertain, confused, reluctant, scared, and old. I wished heartily I had never come here. Then all I had had were suspicions—suspicions and my adolescent tendency to tilt at windmills. Now I had enough facts to suspect that the windmills had weapons. But, knowing as much as I did now, how did I justify backing off? By saying I didn't know how to proceed? *You never did know how to proceed, Smith. You just blundered along. So don't seize on confusion as an excuse for cutting out.*

Besides. The choices were pretty clear:

(A) Keep on hanging loose and watching, and hope for more good luck.

(B) Go back to The Emerald and grab the man registered as Hawthorne and see what I could shake out of him.

(C) Give it up, hug Beth goodbye, and go home.

I was getting nowhere again. A smart person would

have capitalized on Al Hesser's breakdown. I couldn't see how to do that.

Take the bull by the horns. Make something happen! When the going gets tough, et cetera. What's the matter? Are you scared?

Yes, Pop. I think I am, actually.

I bumbled around in the dark, rigging my string and empty iced tea cans and still thinking about it. Then I heard the furtive footsteps outside.

twenty-four

He was tall and slender in pale slacks and sportcoat, and his eyes got large in the moonlight when he spotted my revolver aimed at his midsection.

"Friend," he croaked.

"Get in here. Slow. Hands on top of your head. *Move,* goddammit!"

He came through the door very carefully. He smelled of aftershave and hair tonic. "What—"

"Stand there in the middle of the floor and keep your hands raised. Face the other way. Away from me." I fumbled behind me for the candle stub and clumsily used my lighter to get it going without having to lower the revolver. The feeble yellow light filled the A-frame. I pulled the front door closed. "Now. You can turn around."

He turned, the flickering light making him appear very pale, his eyes at pinpoints. "You are Brad Smith?"

"Don't lower your hands!"

"Show me your identification," he said.

"I think you've got this mixed up, asshole. You're the intruder and I've got the gun."

He frowned as if irritated by red tape. "My name is Exerblein. We have many mutual friends in Virginia. I'm here with Collie Davis."

"I don't see him."

"He isn't far away." He started to lower his right hand. "I have ID and a note—"

"*Stop.*" I thumbed the hammer back on the big revolver and it made a satisfyingly loud click. He stopped.

"Please understand," I told him. "I'm very nervous, and this thing has a very light trigger pull when the hammer is back like it is now. When you move around like that, I get more agitated."

"Where did you *get* that weapon?" he demanded incredulously. "You can't just bring a gun like that into St. Maarten!"

"I took it off a man I killed. Now what do you want?"

"You *killed*—?"

"What do you want?"

"My name is Exerblein," he repeated. "Collie Davis—"

"Lie down."

"What?"

"Lie down on the floor. Facedown. Arms over your head."

He looked down in distaste. "The floor is filthy. It will stain my clothing."

"My God, where did they *find* you? Get down there!"

Muttering protest, he obeyed. Once he was nicely spread-eagled, I snaked the wallet out of his hip pocket and examined it with quick downward glances. Virginia driver's license, credit cards, bank account ID card.

"In the money compartment," my visitor said.

I saw the edge of a small piece of paper sticking out among the bills. I pulled it out and recognized Collie Davis's hasty scrawl:

Brad—
This guy is OK.

Collie

265

"Okay," I said with intense relief. "You can get up."

He clambered to his feet in a crescendo of brushing and patting. I gave him back his wallet. He stared at me with disbelief. "Did you really kill someone to get that revolver?"

"More or less. I thought saying so would get your attention."

He extended his hand. "I'll take it."

"You'll shit, too. What do you want here?"

He removed a handkerchief from his pants pocket and mopped sweat from his face. "Collie Davis is waiting for us. Will you come with me now in order to expedite a mutual update on this assignment?"

"Assignment? Does that mean somebody is finally taking this seriously?"

"Our manpower shortage," he told me, stiffly offended, "is serious."

"Where is Collie?"

"I saw him less than an hour ago. He asked me to find you while he attended to sending a message. By now, he should be waiting for us in the parking lot across the highway from the airport terminal."

"In that case," I said, "I think we ought to go meet him."

"Are you going to give me the weapon?"

"Hell no." But I lowered the hammer to calm his nerves.

He had a Mexican-made Volkswagen. I climbed into the passenger seat and rested my revolver on my knee.

"You needn't point that at me," he said, mightily offended.

"Hey, I lowered the hammer. Be thankful for what you get."

He drove us out of the dark of the power-out area and back to the highway. There was little traffic, and the occasional intersection lights were on over here. We didn't talk during the short drive to the airport, lights splashing into the night from the terminal building and adjacent freight docks. He turned left into the parking lot and slowed to a crawl, and there near the back stood Collie Davis beside a Ford Fiesta. We parked and got out, meeting Collie between the cars.

"He found you," Collie said. "Good."

"He has a weapon," Exerblein said in the same tone one might use in mentioning halitosis.

Collie's teeth showed in the dim light. "So I see."

I said, "What's going on, Collie?"

"We've got a man down here who probably stole a secret computer component from a research lab. He's staying at that tennis school we talked about. Our job is to find him and get the chip back."

I made a jump. "Is his name Coligor?"

"No. Not unless that's an alias. His real name is Hawthorne."

"Even better."

"Better?" Exerblein repeated. "Explain that."

"He's still at The Emerald. Or at least he was a few hours ago."

Collie nodded with satisfaction. "We've got another man coming in pretty soon. We plan to go out there right away and take friend Hawthorne. What can you tell us about him or anything else you know?"

I told them most of it. I'm afraid my recitation was not super-organized, and it took a while.

"You don't think Hesser really knows what's going on?" Collie asked finally.

"No, I don't. But this guy L. K. does, and I think he's probably very dangerous."

"It figures." Collie thought about it. "Okay. We'll bring the local authorities in on it. While they're nabbing Hesser and this guy L. K., we'll take Hawthorne and get the component back. Is there anything else we ought to know?"

"There was a man named Ricardo, but he fell down some stairs. He's the one I got this gun from. I suppose there could be others."

"Okay." Collie was calm and organized. "We're going to move. I would greatly appreciate it if you would consider lending me the revolver."

I opened the cylinder and handed it over to him. He examined it, rolled the cylinder, closed it again, and stuck it in his pants. "You've done a bunch. Not that any of it was authorized, or that anybody is ever going to thank you for it."

"What do you want me to do now?"

Exerblein told me, "We can take it from this point, Brad." He seemed more relaxed and officious with the gun in Collie's possession. He added, "I'll drop you off back at your resort. You just stay out of the way now where you can't get hurt, and let the professionals handle it."

twenty-five

The Emerald

The orchestra was still playing in the ballroom, but the crowd had begun to thin sharply. It was 1 A.M. Sylvester strolled across the periphery of the large room, but kept going into the adjacent club where he had already noted L. K. Able perched on a stool at the far end of the bar.

Sylvester took the stool beside him and ordered Pernod.

"All is well," he told Able. "The transfer is completed."

"When will you hand it over to me?"

"There has been a change in instructions," Sylvester replied. He explained.

Able nodded. "I will verify the new orders."

"Of course. Now. About our friend."

"I watched Smith leave the villa after a very long interview. He proceeded to his car and from here to his cabin at a place called the Mary Mary. The lights were out. A power failure. They have them frequently in that section due to use of a gasoline generator for the few beach properties abutting the airport property on that side. It appeared he was turning in for the night, and I wanted to be sure to be back to meet you. Therefore I discontinued the surveillance and returned here."

269

"Was the woman with him tonight?"

"No."

"Strange. Is she here?"

"She was at the dance for a while with some of her new friends. Then she retired for the night. I saw her enter her room."

"Now. What about Hesser?"

"He retired for the night after Smith left him. The lights went out in his room almost at once. I feel sure he is sleeping."

"Excellent. You have done well."

Able paused, then asked, "Do you have further instructions for me at this point in time?"

"Your normal routine, I think. You will verify that, also, when you make your telephone call."

"Yes."

Sylvester downed the last of his Pernod. "I bid you goodnight." He slipped off the stool and walked out.

twenty-six

As much as Exerblein's attitude hacked me, I did what I was told. But they hadn't said anything about staying away from The Emerald the next morning. So I got there at 6:55 A.M.

That was not early enough to catch the excitement.

The lobby, usually the haunt of only six or eight sleepy nonplayers this early, echoed with activity. People milled around everywhere, buzzing among themselves. Hotel staff stood around with glazed looks on their faces. At first I didn't see anyone I knew.

Then Mia Hesser, in a white cotton shirt-dress that swept the floor, came swooping out from the counter area and seized my arm. She looked gorgeous as usual, but her eye makeup wasn't on straight. Which told me something really serious had happened.

"Brad!" she whispered urgently. "I have to talk to you!"

I let her tug me back around the counter and through a doorway into a small, windowless office with a desk and two chairs and some computer equipment.

She closed the door and turned to me dramatically. "Al has been arrested."

"No!"

Jack M. Bickham

"They came to our house about three hours ago. In the dead of night, like the Gestapo. I was shocked. They made some kind of search and took Al away with them, and then I called Security and they had arrested L. K., too. I don't know what's going on!"

"Who made the arrests, Mia?"

"The Philipsburg police. But they had a man from Curacao with them, too, a big authority of some kind. They told Al he was being arrested on drug charges."

"What did Al say?"

"He was practically hysterical, of course." Mia's lip curled. "He's such a weakling, under all the bluster."

I was tempted to say how much I envied Al such staunch support from his spouse, but instead I kept quiet and observed her. She was not worried about her husband or L. K., but the police visit had shaken her.

Her next words told me why: "Brad, our attorneys are on the way, but I must ask your advice on something in the meantime. If I go to Philipsburg and try to post bond for Al, do I run a serious risk of losing the money?"

"I don't know the law here, Mia. Maybe there isn't any bail procedure, for all I know. But if there is, and Al doesn't skip the country, it looks to me like your money would be safe."

"It isn't like I'm not *concerned* about him, Brad. But if he's going to prison for ten or twenty years, I have to remember he isn't a young man. He might never come out. I have an investment to protect, here. You understand?"

"Of course," I told her. "But I'm afraid your lawyer is the only one who can give you sound advice right now."

She studied me, and something else moved behind her expression. "Will you help me, Brad? I need a friend. Will you stand by me?" She moved closer, pressing thigh and hip and breast softly against my side.

"Please? Can I count on you, Brad?"

"I'll do what I can."

She moved fractionally away. "Thank you." It was a sincere exhalation of relief. The lady was truly scared.

We talked a few minutes more. She tried to get angry about "Gestapo tactics." She said the publicity was going to hurt the resort badly. She said Billy had changed his mind and come home, and was downtown someplace near his father. She said she was going to cancel her scheduled shopping trip to Miami unless it became apparent that this was going to be drawn-out and messy, and she couldn't do anything here anyway. She sighed a lot, the little nervous gasps people make under extreme emotional duress. I gave her a brotherly hug and she batted wet eyelashes and said it made all the difference in the world to have a friend at your side in times of trouble, and pressed her pelvis against me. Then somebody rapped on the door and it was one of Al's chief assistant tennis pros. He asked about the day's schedule oncourt. Mia turned blankly to me.

I said, "I think you should run the show, Randy, and tell people this is all an unfortunate mixup that will be straightened out soon. Then give the lessons just like Al was here."

Randy glanced at Mia for confirmation. He was a handsome young man, and something in his eyes told me he had had more than private conversations with her in the past. She waved her hand absentmindedly. "Do whatever Brad says, Randy. Go on."

I left her there and went into the lobby again. It wasn't quite as crowded. I saw that the staff had started serving breakfast early on the deck. Somebody was thinking. I looked for Beth out there and didn't see her, and headed back across the lobby when Collie Davis caught up with me. He was still wearing his open-collar shirt and slacks from the night before, and he looked tired.

"Just the man I want to see," he said. "How about a walk?"

We went out into the gardens through a side lobby exit. Hummingbirds worked hibiscus blossoms and bright green-and-yellow birds the size of parakeets scolded us from tangles of bougainvillea. We stopped beside a fountain with the water turned off and some goldfish struggling around in green murk.

"Have you got a cigarette?" Collie asked.

"You quit."

"Give."

We lit up together.

"I hate cigarettes," he said, looking at it, his lip curling in distaste. "Smoking isn't even socially acceptable anymore. I'm going to quit again right away."

"How did things work out?"

"Shitty. We can't find Hawthorne. His room is empty and his bed wasn't slept in. Our information was that he probably had the component hidden in a portable computer he was seen carrying onboard in Miami. We haven't found the computer either."

"What now, then?"

"Well, we're still looking for him. We've got people alerted at the airport and the docks. He must still be around. But he's gone right now and so is the computer, and I get this sick feeling that we aren't ever going to see that component again."

"Collie, if the component is so damned secret, how did somebody ever get so lax that he got this far with it?"

"The way I get it, it's not like it's classified *secret*. It's a component—a wafer chip or something—that anybody could figure out, given enough time. It's like some other computer stuff we have. We might sell it to the Brits or somebody like that, but we just don't want to make it easy for the Russians by selling it to them so they can copy it direct."

"So," I said, "we do the half-ass thing? Fail to classify it, but ask everybody to pretty please be real careful?"

Collie grimaced. "It's not like it was easy for him. It took a fluke on a shipment to give him a chance, apparently, and he must be a computer whiz in his own right to make some tests come out wrong so he could get this thing out as defective."

"And if it really is gone?"

"I don't know. I suppose the Russians get a jump of a year or two on some new radar stuff of their own. And, knowing exactly what our technology is, maybe they can devise some jamming devices that will call for new counter-measures from us on the B-1B, Stealth, who knows what all. Which could royally screw up next month's Summit in Geneva."

"Maybe you'll still find it."

"Maybe." He didn't look like he believed that.

"Al's wife said he went to the clink," I said.

"Yep."

"What charge?"

"Possession of cocaine."

"How the hell did you stick him with *that?*"

Collie tossed his butt into the bushes. "We planted some in his house."

"Did you fix L. K. up the same way?"

"No. We had the locals arrest him, but we've got him now at a safe place outside of town on the French side. A couple of our people are interviewing him."

"With what result?"

"So far, he's told us his name, age, and room number here at the resort. He's tough."

"So what now?"

"We'd still like to find the other guy you described for us—the one you saw with L. K. in the bar. We haven't seen anyone matching the description. That's why I'm here, keeping my eye out. If you see him, find me. I won't be far away. Him, we'd like to talk to."

"Anything else?"

"Can't think of it. Keep your eyes open, that's all."

"Okay, Collie."

He started to walk away.

"Collie?"

He glanced back.

"Want another cigarette?"

"I never use them."

I went back through the lobby and onto the deck, picking up a cup of coffee and a Danish. A couple of the school patrons spotted me and came over. They were all agog over the recent excitement. Evidently Al's arrest was not common knowledge; they didn't mention that part of it. We stood around together and clucked and murmured and speculated about what was going on. The consensus was a drug bust, although a young woman from Omaha thought it might have something mysterious to do with the Bermuda Triangle. I was just heading back for a coffee refill when the outdoor speakers came alive:

"*Mr. Smith. Mr. Brad Smith. Please report to the desk in the lobby, please. Mr. Smith. Mr. Brad Smith . . .*"

I went inside to the desk and identified myself to the young woman behind the counter. "Mr. Smith, you have a telephone call. If you will take it on house telephone number one, please?"

I went to the house phones, picked up the nearest one, and identified myself to the operator. There was a slight delay and then something made a clicking noise on the line.

"Hello?" I said. "Brad Smith speaking."

"*Brad?*" It was Beth's voice. "*Where are you?*"

"I'm in the lobby. Come on down and join me for coffee."

For a moment she didn't speak. When she did, she sounded strained. "*Could we talk up here? In my room?*"

"Is there something wrong, Beth?"

"No! No. Nothing. I just think we ought to talk. Please."

She caught me halfway between irritation and concern. Remembering my intentional abruptness to her last night, I could imagine what she had in mind. So even Beth Miles had the point at which she got emotional, started nearing the brink of panic about a relationship. Why did it have to be a big deal? This morning I could explain most of it. But I would have preferred her to hang in there with me one more time—come down sunny and confident and unthreatened—and have coffee on the deck and let me tell her that I had been rude because I thought things were hitting the fan and I wanted her away from me for the moment and as safe as possible.

On the other hand, my reaction was not all irritation. To have such a lovely lady upset about you was flattering, to say the least. And I had been abrupt as hell.

Remembering Collie's need for an ID on the man I had seen with L. K. in the bar, I told her, "I'll come up, Beth. But I can't stay long."

"I know. I'm probably being silly. But if we could have just a few minutes—"

"I'm on the way." I hung up and turned to see Collie standing there.

"Anything?" he asked.

"I've got to go upstairs and see a lady for a minute."

His expression didn't change. "Ah. A lady."

"That's what I said. A lady. Do you want name, rank, and serial number?"

"Touchy, touchy. Keep it brief, will you? I feel better with you helping me case the lobby for the guy with the nose."

"I'll be back in ten minutes at the most."

He nodded and strolled off. I went to the elevator and rode upstairs.

When I tapped on Beth's door, she opened it immediately. She was wearing pink tennis shorts and top and her

Nikes. Her hair was mussed up and she looked like she had been crying. *Hell,* I thought, *more dramatics than I bargained for.*

She got back out of the way to let me in. I entered the room, moving past her in the closet hallway. "What's the problem, Beth?" I asked.

The door closed firmly behind me. I turned back, but Beth wasn't standing there alone. He had been half hidden in the closet, and now he had stepped out to put one arm around her waist from behind, while the other held a decidedly lethal-looking pistol to the side of her face. Big Nose.

"Be very quiet, please," he said.

I stood quite still, seeing how scared Beth was. She looked on the brink of fainting. I understood the tension in her voice now and saw how I had misinterpreted it. More stupidity on my part. I was using up my quota.

"Mr. Smith," the man said pleasantly, "we are going to take a ride in your car. We are going to go down the back staircase and directly to the lot. If we meet anyone on the way, we will say we are going into Philipsburg to buy the lady a conch shell. Any deviation on your part from my instructions, and Miss Miles dies instantly. Do you understand me?"

"I understand."

He smiled broadly and in a deft movement shoved the automatic into his belt under his shirt. "Please believe me when I tell you this. I can have this weapon in my hand much, much faster than you or Miss Miles can do anything useful against me. I have practiced thousands of hours." His gold tooth gleamed. "Like your western movies, eh? The quick draw. I am a quick draw expert from this position in my belt. A Gary Cooper. A Shane. Oh my yes. Believe me, Mr. Smith. If you test me, the pretty lady dies first, and then you. Do you understand what I am saying?"

"I understand," I repeated, tasting the bitterness.

"Wonderful," he said in a curiously gentle voice. He

278

opened the door to the hall. "Now outside. You will both walk in front of me. Move."

Beth went into the hallway first. She had lost all color and she looked shaky, but she didn't falter. She was scared and she had every right to be. I wanted to touch her and say something reassuring, but Big Nose wouldn't have liked that, and I didn't know what I could say anyway. I kept quiet as we went down the hall to the exit door, then down the interior metal staircase with him close behind us.

"All right," he said pleasantly at the ground level. "Outside, now, and directly across the parking lot to your car, Mr. Smith."

I opened the door to the outside. Humid air washed over us as we stepped out. The day had already gotten warm. Thick, low-lying storm clouds covered most of the sky. The sun peered through, brilliant and steamy, as we walked to my car. *Come on, Collie!* I thought. No Collie.

"Miss Miles in the passenger seat. You will drive, Mr. Smith. Get in."

We obeyed. He opened the back door on the passenger side and climbed in, shoving my rackets across the seat and onto the floor. I hadn't put covers back on the ones Beth and I had used in our doubles game, and they made a hollow clattering noise as they hit the floor.

He leaned against the back of Beth's seat and I saw the automatic in his hand again, the barrel resting on the seatback and tilted upward to aim at the base of her skull. "Now, Mr. Smith, you will drive as I direct you. Please believe me when I say that any unfortunate actions on your part will result in the lady's instant death."

I started the engine. Backed around in the lot. Pulled into the resort driveway. Beth was shaking. I wished to God I had foreseen this, kept her out of it.

"When we reach the highway, please turn north. It isn't

a long way we have to go. The clouds seem to be gathering. These golfers will be unhappy if it rains, eh? Please maintain your present speed, Mr. Smith. It's just right. Thank you."

Traffic on the so-called highway, two-lane asphalt twisting along the high cliffs overlooking the sea, was steady but not too heavy: other rental cars with sightseers in them, light trucks carrying food supplies or builder's equipment, some kids on bicycles puffing up a long, shallow grade in their lowest gear, bent over the handlebars, working hard. Beneath the broken wet clouds, the ocean looked turbulent and unpleasant, with nasty little whitecaps. But there were some sailboats out, distant pocket handkerchiefs on the slate. With the sun out it was hot inside the car. We came to an intersection and Big Nose directed me to take the right fork, turning inland toward the French side. We left the ocean and drove through rough hills, the vegetation wild, scrubby, untended, a mixture of dwarf trees and head-high brush. I saw some goats in a field with a rusty fence around it and a small canyon where a stream tumbled down a hundred feet through fallen red sandstone boulders, turning the water at the bottom the color of blood. A black man sat on the rocks at the bottom of the cascade, holding a fishing pole. The old joke about water in rivers of the American Southwest popped unbidden into my mind: "Too thick to drink, too wet to plow." Why does the mind come up with crazy non sequiturs at times of the worst stress?

There was no traffic on this new road, and after a few miles the broken asphalt turned to red dirt. I had to slow down. The road narrowed. Deep potholes and erosion ruts made the driving harder. A lizard two feet long scuttered off the road ahead of us. A big black carrion-feeding bird flapped away a little farther on, near the crest of a sun-bleached hill. When we got to the bird's former position, there was a dead rabbit in the dirt, blood and intestines dried and sun-blackened, and a swarm of angry flies.

I was trying to think ahead. Part of my mind wanted to believe that the man in the back seat was merely taking us out of action for a while, would hold us, possibly tie us up and dump us somewhere. But the thinking part of me knew that was wishful thinking. A man like him did not go to all the trouble of abducting someone for a few fun and games.

It might have happened like this with Pat, I thought. A minute's failure to be alert, a false sense of security or a miscalculation. Nothing more was needed. Then somebody rapped you on the head or stuck a gun in your face and started making unpleasant, insistent suggestions. You went along because the choice seemed to be instant death, and the instinct for self-preservation always told you there might be a chance later.

There had been no chance later for Pat. Gone now was any tiny, vain hope I had clung to that his death had been an accident. Maybe he had had a ride like this, too. And then they had slugged him and held his head under a bucket of sea water until no more bubbles came up. Then they had driven him to the beach and strapped on his scuba gear and left him to be found. He had never really had a chance.

Big Nose was not going to let us have a chance, either. Which made me think about jerking the steering wheel suddenly, plunging us off the rough dirt road into the deep ditch along the side or into a pile of red rocks. If I did it just right—and he was the slightest bit off-guard—there was the smallest chance that I might get my door open and roll out in one piece while he was picking himself up off the floorboards.

Alone I might have tried it in sheer desperation. Beth, silent and frozen beside me, changed the odds. I knew that the instant I swung the wheel or hit the brakes, he would fire the first shot. The bullet would enter the base of her brain and probably go right on through, tumbling and flattening in such a way that its exit would be a hideous explosion of bone and tissue.

So I drove. Some time ticked off. My mouth tasted like copper and my stomach had felt better when I had the flu.

Big Nose hummed very softly, thoughtlessly. I recognized it with surprise: something from *The Snow Maiden*. I couldn't place the part. Maybe, I thought, I should mentally run through the entire score, and relate it to the performance at Dallas a year or two ago, and try to figure out exactly what scene might be in our man's mind as he pleasantly hummed along and anticipated whatever he had planned for us. I realized I was getting slightly Looney Tunes.

"Ahead less than a mile," he said after a while, "there is a poorly marked roadway to the left. It's below the fallen rock on the right-hand side. You will turn there and go up through the field to the higher ground."

I slowed like a good little boy. The landscape to the right was up-thrusting dirt and rocks, very steep, ugly in the sunlight. On the left were rutted weed fields and then a hundred yards beyond them hills that humped up green-brown, with bigger ones beyond. We were in the middle of the island somewhere now, and it was thirty degrees hotter than along the coast. When I slowed, dust caught up with us from the road behind and swirled around the car, pink and choking thick.

"Here," he said sharply.

The turnoff was not as well marked as some tractor paths back home. A slight depression in the half-burnt prairie grass, a change in the color of the brush. I turned off and we bumped along through the field with weeds and sticks making a hell of a clatter on the underside of the car.

"Not much farther now," he said cheerfully.

"Do you have the computer wafer?" I asked. "Is that why you're doing this? To make sure we're out of the way so you can escape with it?"

"Oh, no," he told me, his voice betraying amusement.

"The assembly is in a portable computer, and the computer is in a small tan suitcase safely stored in a locker at the airport."

"And you take it out later."

"Wrong again, Mr. Smith. Another person already has the locker key. That person will claim the suitcase and be on the flight departing at eleven o'clock this morning—a little more than three hours from now."

"We're insignificant," I said. "Beth doesn't even know what we're talking about. I'm a stooge. Neither of us is a threat, realistically speaking."

"A very good try, Mr. Smith, but no cigar. Ah. Just ahead, there? You see how a side path leaves this one past the big fallen rock? Take that, please. We will climb sharply now. It will be necessary for you to use your low gear selector. Yes. Good." There was a crack of a match, and thick cigar smoke blossomed through the car.

He resumed, "You are the only one who saw me with Mr. Able, I believe. That was one of the reasons I needed to have this trip with you. As to Miss Miles, of course you are correct, she is a true innocent. But I needed her to get you in my control. And now of course she has seen me, also, so . . ." He left it unsaid and puffed the strong cigar.

The Ford labored up the steep grassy knoll, around some rocks, and through a rent in adjacent hills. Then we went still higher. I got a glimpse of surrounding terrain through a break in the rocks, and saw, far off to the left, the ocean far below. We had climbed to some of the highest terrain on the island. Fields lay far below us off to the right.

"You can still let her go," I said. "She has no training and she won't remember significant details."

"I think not, Mr. Smith, but your concern is touching. Please drive slowly past these small trees. Just on the other side we come out onto a promontory . . . there. You see? Yes. You will pull farther out. Farther. You can park along in this area ten feet ahead of us."

We had come out onto a bare dirt-and-rock outcropping that afforded one of the most rugged and frightening views I had ever seen. Slightly higher rocks and brush loomed to our right, while ahead of us and to the left, the world dropped off into a vast, windy vacancy.

It was like a giant had come along with an enormous axe and sliced off the edge of the mountain. The dirt and grass extended out in the form of a tabletop, and then simply—stopped. We could look out across the entire side of the island, the ocean miles away, rolling pastures and weed fields and smaller mountains closer in, a thousand feet or more below the promontory where we stood.

I stopped ten feet from the brink and cut the engine. A high lonely wind sang out of the vast emptiness just beyond the front bumper.

"So," Big Nose said, his reedy voice higher-pitched.

"What makes you think identifying you is such a big deal?" I asked desperately. "Who *are* you?"

"That's the point," he said with a smile in his voice. "I'm no one. I have no identity. To that I owe a long life."

My guts wrenched in agony. I groped for anything to make him talk—buy us more seconds. "They call you something," I said.

"Sometimes, yes, they call me Sylvester."

It hit me with an ugly shock. "*Sylvester?* The same Sylvester they think killed Dominic Partek?"

"The same. Yes."

Beth watched me with an expression of horror and confusion. When he said who he was, I must have showed the impact. She reached out to touch my arm.

"No," Sylvester said very sharply. "You will not make unauthorized movements, Miss Miles. And we have had quite enough of this. You will get out of the car now."

"You did kill Partek?" I asked. My voice didn't sound like me.

He popped his door, then hesitated. I was staring back at him now, and the calm amusement was nowhere on his face. His color had heightened. His lips were tight. His eyes shone with total, malevolent pleasure.

"I killed him," he bit off. He was caught in the moment, too: for the first time his flawless English became harsher, burred by a Eurasian accent. He added, "All your meddling in our internal affairs was for naught, you see, Mr. Smith. You did not get Partek—and in the end you did not have Miss Lechova for very long either, did you. Now get out of the car, slowly. I grow impatient."

Beth managed to get out on her side, unsteadily. She staggered and almost fell. He climbed out of the back seat behind her and moved up to take her arm and prevent her going down. I swung out on my side, and my hand fell right into the narrow channel between the front and back seats, *where he had knocked the rackets.* I shoved my hand farther back and found a handle and pulled my prize ceramic up through the crack as I got to my feet on my side of the car.

He looked across the top of the car at me. His view of the racket at my side was blocked. "Move to the front of the car, Mr. Smith." He shoved Beth in that direction.

The wind pressed up out of the vast emptiness just in front of us, whipping dust and grass, pasting my clothes against me. It was clear what he intended to do now. We would go over the edge, Beth and I, and it would be another unfortunate accident. Perhaps by the time they realized we were missing and could locate our bodies, Sylvester would be thousands of miles away and perfectly safe. The wafer would have preceded him.

But something else he had just said was dinning in my brain, pounding at me, trying to form itself into a meaning so horrible I could not quite admit it to consciousness.

"Move along, Mr. Smith!" His voice was shrilly impatient.

I shuffled to the front of the car, the racket hidden below the fenderline. "What did you mean?"

He pushed Beth toward me so she was halfway between

us, swaying with terror. "No more talk, Mr. Smith. Turn around and step closer to the edge."

"What did you *mean*? About Danisa?"

His eyes widened and he grinned, a tooth gleaming. "You created a great deal of sadness for us. It was my pleasure to even the score."

It began to expand and overwhelm me—the truth. "*Danisa?*"

"Of course. It was no accident. Surely even someone as ignorant as you must have thought of that possibility, Mr. Smith. It is easy to fix an airplane. Adjustments in the hydraulic system—"

I went crazy.

Shall I try to describe the effects? A bursting of pressure inside my head; a graying of the world, and then a dull red coloration over everything, and a roaring in my ears that was louder than any explosion. Every muscle and bit of connective tissue—every *cell*—exploding at the same instant.

Having the racket in my hand provided focus.

I would have gone for him with my bare hands. Nothing else mattered but destroying him.

Beth saw my face and my movement. She turned and tried to grab at his gun. I was flying forward, already swinging the racket, when the gun went off. The explosion half deafened me. Beth cried out and doubled over and started to fall, her outstretched hands clawing at Sylvester's hand and dragging his gun arm down with her. I saw bright blood. My craziness hit another level.

In a slow-motion world, Sylvester finally got his arm free of Beth as she fell. He started to bring the pistol up to bear on me. I swung the racket from up on top with every ounce of energy in my body. It crashed edge-first into the side of his face, shattering bone and gristle. My rage carried me right on through the blow and against him, and blood spewed off his face and the gun hit the dirt at our feet.

I still had the racket. Backhand. Turning the edge as

with a dropshot. Into his throat, knocking him three steps backward. Eyes bulging, he clawed at his Adam's apple. I scrambled for the gun, picked it up. He caught his balance and gauged everything in an instant and turned and ran around the far side of the car, heading beyond it.

I started firing. The gun rocked back hard in my hand. Glass shattered in the car and a piece flew off the roof. I fired again and maybe he staggered, rushing out from behind the car on the far side.

I don't know what he had in mind. But as he came out on the other side of the car, he was within a yard of the edge of the cliff in that area. I was still shooting. I missed and missed and missed and then one hit him *somewhere*—maybe squarely in the back—and he threw his arms up like a minstrel singer and fell sideways like a halfback being driven out of bounds, but there was no sideline marker, only the vast vacancy of the fall. I shot twice more.

He went over, arms grotesquely thrown out to his sides.

And plunged out of sight.

I ran to the edge, crazy, and looked down and couldn't see anything and emptied the gun straight down into the void. I was crying and yelling things, I don't know what.

The gun empty, I hurled it out into space and turned and staggered back to where Beth had fallen.

She lay crumpled, still, face up. There was no movement, no consciousness. And blood—Jesus Christ, *was there this much blood inside one human being?*

I scooped her into my arms and put her in the car and drove like the maniac I was away from the cliff and back down through the fields. I think I was still yelling things.

twenty-seven

I knew it was Sunday because they rang the church bells of Philipsburg on Sunday.

I knew I was in a hospital room because it was small and white, and there was an IV stand beside the bed.

The door opened. A man came in. I recognized him.

"Are we tracking today?" Collie Davis asked, leaning over me.

"Sure," I said. My voice sounded funny. I asked, "Why shouldn't I be tracking?"

He stood up, his forehead like a Levolor blind.

Then I remembered. I sat up with a start. The tube from the IV bottle to my hand pulled tight, and the needle was jerked sharply, making a hot pain. The bottle shook and the stand rocked. Collie jumped to catch it before it fell.

"*Beth!*" I said.

"Take it easy, take it easy. She's all right—alive."

"Where? I want to see her!"

"Sit back, goddammit, or I'll yell for a nurse and they'll put you in restraints again."

That got my attention, and another jumble of mental trash tumbled through my mind. *Pictures:* Collie and the other case officer, Exerblein, standing on the precipice

288

where my shot had dropped Sylvester off the edge, and me screaming at them; the shocked look on the nurse's face when I staggered into the hospital with Beth in my arms; Beth's face, still and bloodless, as if in death; a ride in a car; questions . . . a local police officer and other faces blurred into skulls and gargoyles; a doctor talking to me; fighting somebody—nurses—yelling, them trying to hold me down in the bed—the hot stick of a hypodermic needle in my arm; night; confusion and bad dreams.

I took a few shaky deep breaths. "I've been fucked up."

"You can say that again, brother."

I studied Collie's expression. I felt calm, and suddenly things were in fine sharp focus. "This is Sunday."

"You've got it."

"Beth. I've got to know the truth. He shot her point-blank. I didn't think she could have any blood left in her when I finally got her here."

Collie tilted an eyebrow. "It was a mighty near thing. They said she had zero blood pressure when they got her on the table. The bullet nicked her aorta not far above the heart. They just started pumping whole blood into her while they got ready for surgery."

My heart thumped and lurched around in my chest. "She made it?"

"They got the bleeding under control. What she needs now is a dacron tube to replace the part of the blood vessel that isn't much good anymore. They can't do that kind of work here. It's a miracle there was a retired thoracic surgeon vacationing right here in town, to do as much as was done."

"What now?"

"She was strong enough to be moved this morning and she's been flown back to Miami. They're scheduled to operate on her again in the morning."

"That's tomorrow morning," I said.

"Yes."

"Monday morning, in other words."

"You really are getting your shit back together, aren't you."

I closed my eyes, but when I did that, I got dizzy. So I opened them again. "I remember Sylvester on the cliff. I remember some of the drive to town. Then it's all fragments—crazy stuff."

"You were half nuts. One minute you would seem just fine—badly shaken up, but rational—and then you would start yelling and making no sense again."

"Did I tell you what happened? Did that part make sense?"

"We got that it was Sylvester. *The* Sylvester. He got you and Beth Miles out there on the bluffs, and was going to make you do a swan dive. You tried something—he shot Beth Miles—you clobbered him. He went off the cliff, you said."

"I hit the son of a bitch with my racket. I broke his jaw and maybe the bony socket around the eye. He shot Beth and she fell into him and I got the gun and shot him running away. He did go over."

Collie nodded solemnly. "That's about what we pieced together out of your screaming and cursing."

"Did you make out why I was acting screwy?"

He allowed himself a grim, twisted grin. "You were more than screwy, pal. You were certifiable, scary, violent, totally out of your tree most of the time. The doctors finally had to put you in a strait jacket and shoot you full of morphine or something. I mean they knocked you on your ass. You were out cold for a long time."

"The man who took us to the bluffs, Collie, was the one who killed Dominic Partek."

Collie jerked as if he had been slapped. "He admitted that?"

"Why not? He figured we were as good as dead."

"And that made you crazy?"

"He said," I added, and heard my voice start to shake, "what happened to Danisa . . . wasn't an accident. He said . . . he fixed it. He killed her."

"Oh, no."

"Oh, *yes*. He wanted me to know that. He just had to tell me. He was enjoying it—making me face that pain just before going off the cliff. He was a crazy bastard, Collie. Cool, controlled—but crazy. He enjoyed inflicting that extra pain. Maybe you've got to be, to do that kind of work. Maybe I should have realized that. I didn't understand it in the gut. I didn't see what he was until I stood there and saw how he was enjoying it. He was a monster. He thought I would collapse, and he wanted to see it."

Collie ran his hand through his hair in a gesture of shock. "But when he told you, you went nuts."

"I guess I started to, yes. Pat Reilly was murdered, too. Like I thought. Then, when he shot Beth, and there was all that blood—and I thought he had killed her, too—"

"He probably thought the news about Danisa would put you into numb shock, so he could just shove you off the cliff. I guess he didn't count on your reacting with an attack."

"Collie, if he hadn't run, I think I would have beaten him to a pulp with that racket. I wanted his brains on the ground."

He studied my face, searching me with a solemnity not like him. "Yeah," he said finally. "If he hadn't run, you would have done it, too."

The door of the room opened and a nurse entered with a tray of instruments. She was olive-skinned, dark-haired, not pretty but attractive in her competence. She told Collie, "You will please excuse us for a while, sir."

Collie started for the door.

I told him, "There are a lot more things I need to know."

He nodded. "I've got some things to do, but I'll be back in an hour or two."

Something new occured to me. "What time *is* it?"

* * *

The nurse said it was eleven o'clock. I thanked her. Collie left.

The nurse quietly checked my blood pressure and took my pulse and looked in my eyes and ears with a little flashlight and stuck an electronic thermometer in my mouth while she messed with the flow valve on the IV tube. Then she wrapped tubing around my upper arm and stuck me to take two vials of blood. I made inane remarks during all this, but she ignored me. There was a slight dark coloration under her left eye and I began to suspect with horror that maybe one of the crazy memories in the back of my mind was of me, crazy, hitting her.

She finished up and put things back in her tray. I half expected her to ask for a specimen, but that was when I realized some discomfort down there came from the fact that they had me catherized. For some reason, this realization intensely embarrassed me and I leaned back against my pillow and felt my eyes get hot. I was tracking, all right, but I was still on a raw, naked edge.

I felt torn-up, maudlin, shaky, uncertain, inept, pathetic. Hadn't I screwed up just about everything here? If Beth Miles didn't make it, I would have caused *another* death. Directly or indirectly here I had contributed to Pat's murder, to Ricardo's fatal dive down the stairs, to the savaging of Beth. And now I knew, too, that Danisa's air crash had been revenge by Sylvester and his masters, not an accident. And since I had helped her escape from Belgrade—married her and made her a citizen—I had been an accomplice in the events that led to her murder, too.

I was filled up to here with violence and death. I had gone crazy after hearing Sylvester's boast, and then seeing Beth's blood, and I wasn't ashamed of that. The only thing in my dumpster pile of fragmented memories that made sense—that I clung to with a fierce, exultant hate—was the sight of him going over the cliff. I had done that. *Good!* So while the violence filled me with nausea and sick rage, a part of me reveled in the payback I had exacted.

The nurse left. She said the doctor would be in soon. I noticed the click of the door lock after she closed the door behind her, locking the loony safely in.

I was really tired. It occurred to me that I hadn't even discussed with Collie how things had worked out with the computer thing that had been at the heart of this entire mess. But my mind was continuing to clear, and I remembered now that we had had a conversation about that some time earlier, possibly even before I went batty and tried my Muhammad Ali act on the unsuspecting nurse.

A doctor came in a little before noon, shadowed by another nurse and a hulking male attendant in a white cotton coat that bulged with an embarrassment of muscles. The doctor poked and prodded and looked in my eyes.

"I'm okay now," I told him. "You don't need the bodyguard."

"Where are you?" he asked.

"St. Maarten. I suppose in the hospital in Philipsburg."

"What is your name?"

"Brad Smith."

"Who is the president of the United States?"

"Probably the same jerk who let Guatemala's government fall."

"Would you like another sedative?"

"Hell no."

He removed the catheter, which was a relief, and left with his entourage.

After a while, Collie Davis came back. He sat in the straight chair beside the bed and wiped his face with a soggy handkerchief. "Hot out there."

"Collie, check my memory. You guys got to the airport in time?"

"You mean to head off the transfer of the stuff? Yes.

Exerblein and the guy from Washington went right out there as soon as you told us about it. They watched the locker, and a Bolivian banker named Herrera unlocked it big as life, pulled out the attaché case, and headed straight for the line waiting to board the flight to San Juan. Our guys headed him off and quietly marched him into the men's can, where he got excited and had to be, uh, quieted down by force. They got him outside to a car and stashed. We got the computer assembly back in one piece and it's already gone back to the States. The locals have Señor Herrera, along with your good friend L. K. Able."

"I remembered most of that. You told me most of that."

Collie smiled. "Funny you should remember. I thought you were much too busy climbing the walls at the time to listen to anything."

"Did you get the guy who brought the stuff here, too?"

"Hawthorne? Unfortunately, no. He's vanished."

"He got away?" I asked in dismay.

"Maybe so, maybe not. We've checked passenger manifests and everything else, and if he got out through the airport, he was a magician. So maybe he's still on the island. But he's sure lying low if he is."

"But you got the computer chip or whatever it is."

"Yep. Safe and sound. No problem."

I thought about it. "And Al?"

"Hesser? He's out on bond."

"On the drug charge?"

"Yes."

"Anything else?"

"No."

"Are there going to be other charges?"

"I don't know. That's under review in Washington, I'm told."

I didn't reply, thinking about Al Hesser and his debts, his son, and his expensive wife. Without the money he had been getting from Sylvester's masters, Al might be finished anyway.

Collie said, "I don't know what they can charge him with, actually, and make it stick. I mean, supposing we get him back in the States. Do we charge him with abetting espionage against the United States? Hell. I'm convinced personally that the dumb son of a bitch had no idea what was going on."

"What *was* going on, besides this computer chip deal?"

"As far as we've been able to dig out, the tennis school and resort provided a convenient cover for agents to meet, maybe for some secrets to be passed. L. K. Able took messages from Russian submarines, apparently, on the radio setup of his. It's possible some stuff leaked out of the Coast Guard on sonar technique was passed through here. But it looks to me like this whole operation was just getting started. No telling what kind of clearing house and rendezvous point it might have become. But Al Hesser didn't know any of it. He was a patsy."

"Does he know now what was going on?"

Collie nodded. "Enough. He walks around looking like a man who just puked."

In the middle of the afternoon, Exerblein dropped in. He said without feeling that he was pleased I seemed to be back in contact with reality. He said that frankly he didn't understand what had caused my "psychological break." He said, puzzled, "After all, you were not injured. Your problem was only emotional."

I agreed with him that it was very strange.

About five, since I had been such a good boy, they not only started leaving my room door unlocked; they actually let it stand open to the hall. I showered and shaved, and was sitting in the straight chair in my hospital gown and robe when Karyn Wechsting came about six.

"Oh, my," she murmured regretfully, bounding into the room and hurrying over to hug my shoulders. She was wearing white slacks and a canary blouse and big straw hat and huaraches, and her hair was tied back in a ponytail with a blue ribbon, and she smelled of perfume and sunlight and girl. Then she held me at arm's length. "You look *terrible.*"

"Thanks for the vote of confidence, you turd."

She barked laughter. "You're your same old lovable self, though."

"I'm feeling a lot better."

She perched on the edge of the high bed, swinging long legs. "I came by every day, twice. They wouldn't let me in. They wouldn't tell me much. Your friend Mr. Davis said you were getting good care. Otherwise he was pretty cloak-and-dagger and Rumpole of the Bailey."

"Yeah, well, Collie likes to act like a private eye or something."

"You want to tell me what it's been all about?"

"No."

"*You're* the turd!"

"Guilty."

"Al Hesser is in trouble. He's out, and trying to act normal, but he looks like death warmed over."

"I'm sorry to hear that."

"Everything is going wrong for him, it looks like. The construction crew dumped and smoothed all the dirt and clay and topsoil on the crushed rock for those new courts, but then they walked off. Al says it's a misunderstanding, but the rumor is that they won't do more until they've been paid up-to-date. Do you think he's in that bad financial trouble?"

"Karyn, I have no way of knowing."

"Some of the guests checked out—quite a bunch of them—after all the excitement last Thursday, and Al spending a day in jail and all. And from what I hear, his wife has gone to Miami and it isn't just a visit, she's left him."

"Well, I'm glad to hear all his luck hasn't been bad."

Karyn paused and studied me for a long time. "Are you sure you don't want to tell me what's been going on?"

"Karyn, I've been an innocent bystander."

"Just like you were at the Belgrade International," she said. "Right."

We watched each other warily, and then she grinned and I did too. She changed the subject, telling me about some changes in the Slims tour. It was pleasant to talk about something else.

"When are they letting you out of here?" she asked as she prepared to leave.

"I've got to get out in the morning," I told her. "I have to be on the morning flight for Miami."

She nodded, worried. "Beth's new surgery."

"You know about that?"

"I got it from your G-man friend. My God, I hope she's going to be all right."

"If she isn't—" I began. At which point the hall door swung open a foot or so and we both turned to see who was coming in.

Al Hesser peered in at us. His face was shadowy under the broad brim of a straw hat. He looked tentative, quite unlike him.

"Anybody home?" he asked.

"Al. Come in."

He slipped through the opening without enlarging it. His planter-style hat clashed with his tennis togs, but they clashed with each other, too: bright yellow alligator shirt, vivid red shorts, sweat socks with green and blue bands at the top, just below the knee, and blue-trimmed Pumas. He took off the hat and mopped his hairy forearm over his forehead as he approached the bed.

"Hullo," he said nervously to Karyn. He stared at me. "You're okay."

"Fine," I told him.

Karyn bent to brush her lips over my cheek. "Gotta go."

"I can come back later," Al offered quickly.

"No," she said, giving him a cool smile. "You're the one who told the folks I would give a late seminar on tactics tonight, remember?"

He managed a sickly grin. "Oh, yeah. Guess you better hurry."

Karyn told me, "I'll see you sometime down the tournament trail, pal."

"Thanks, Karyn. I mean it."

She left, closing the door softly behind her. Al stood beside my bed, looking hard at the IV stands and other equipment, and twirling his hat in his pudgy hands.

"You're okay," he repeated finally.

"Doing fine."

"Jesus, man, I didn't know what was going on!"

"I know that, Al."

"I thought it was just a little secret business deal, you know what I mean. Then it all started to hit the fan and I didn't know how to get *out*. Then they came and busted my ass and I heard you'd got hurt, and what's-her-name, your pussy, too, and goddam, I think some of those guys are CIA or something. Is that what they are, CIA?"

"I don't know, Al," I said.

"I'm *sorry*, baby! I really am!"

"Hey, it's over."

"Yeah . . ." The rat came out and stared through his eyes into a corner, as if he would have liked to hide there. He looked infinitely sad and beaten.

"I understand you're out on bond," I told him.

He shook himself back to the present. "Yeah. Right. I got a lawyer. He says they don't have much of a case. I was framed. I dunno who did it. I guess L. K. Shit."

He took a convulsive breath. "Mia's gone. I don't think she's coming back. Billy took off again, too. He started asking lots of questions and giving me a lot of shit and I told him to mind his own beeswax and we had another big fight. I guess maybe . . . there comes a time when you got to stand up to your kids, or you'll get run right over."

"A lot of people have come to the same conclusion, Al."

He sighed again. "I got no more money. The lawyers are going to cost a bundle. If Mia is gone for good, she'll be suing my ass. I had one little emergency account and her name was on it too and she cleaned that out already, got me for three thousand. I called to stop the credit cards but she'd already loaded them up to the max, so I'm in another twelve or so. Do you think there are going to be federal charges against me, if those guys were spies or something? I'm never going to get over this. Never. I'm ruined. I'm a broken man. My heart is broken. I'm bankrupt. I'm screwed. Are they going to charge me with espionage or something, do you think?"

"Al, I have no way of knowing, but I wouldn't think so."

"Right, right," he muttered, eyes darting around the room again. "Mia gone. Billy gone. Drug charges. Bankrupt. My life is kind of fucked up right now, you know?"

"Al—"

"I didn't know about Pat Reilly. I *loved* old Pat! Do you believe me?"

"Yes."

"I'll never get over it," he repeated. "I'm a broken man. My life is over. I'm defeated. I don't have idea one. I'll never be the same. I've had it, I'm whipped."

"A lot of it hasn't come out," I told him. "You'll come back."

"Will I?" he asked, surprised. "You think I will?"

"Sure I do."

"Sure I will!" he said, and suddenly he straightened up, colored. "Hell, baby, they can't keep a good man down, right? I'll get a third mortgage. I can hold a lot of those fuckers off a long time. I can borrow a little more on the Hilton Head operation. It's going great. My videos will be out, and my book, as soon as that asshole that's writing it for me gets on the ball. And hey, Wilson asked me a while back about endorsing some equipment. I can do that. There's money in that. Other than that, all I got to do is come up with, say, a quarter of a million in new investment money, and I'm in business again, bigger than ever. Right? Am I right?"

"You're right, Al," I said.

"Right!" He grinned and did a lumbering little dance step. "I'll be fine, right? They can't beat Al Hesser, right?"

"Right."

"And if they don't like it," he added, the light in his eyes again, "scroom. Just—scroom! Right? Am I right?"

He bounded out a few minutes later, pledging undying brotherhood and an unparalleled opportunity to buy into his operations just as soon as he could contact his lawyers and draw up a new prospectus. The room seemed quiet after he was gone.

God bless the guys like Al Hesser. They never lose because they never quit trying.

The doctor came back early in the evening—proving I must be in a foreign country, if doctors condescended to look in on hospital patients more than once a day—and I told him I wanted out. He didn't think so, he said. I got insistent, being careful not to give him any reason to become alarmed and resort again to the sedatives. Finally he said he would consider it.

At nine or so, Collie came back.

"Don't you have *anything* to do but sit around hospitals?" I asked.

"When I was a kid, they taught me in Catechism that it's a work of mercy," he said, sitting down.

"Collie, I've got to get out of here and get to Miami."

He nodded. "The doctor told me you were making such noises."

"Collie, don't try to keep me back."

He surprised me. "I'm not. You're through here. I've suggested to the doctor that they discharge you at 6 A.M.

tomorrow. If you can get your crap out of the Mary Mary and be ready on time, I've got tickets for both of us on the ten o'clock flight out of here."

"I can be ready," I said.

"I thought you could," he said.

twenty-eight

Red tape and the usual bureaucratic snags delayed our 727 until 10:40 Monday morning. Once we had taxied to the end of the runway, near the weed fields bordering the beach and small resorts, the pilot didn't take long completing whatever checklists he had remaining. With a comforting full blast of power to the rear engines, we rolled. I was on the right-hand side of the cabin and tried to pick out the roofs of the Mary Mary, but I couldn't. We rotated and lifted off, banking sharply to stay away from the mountains, and then we were out over the Atlantic, slowly turning north for home.

Collie Davis pulled his briefcase out from under the seat. "Well, it won't be long now."

"I'm glad we got through to the hospital this morning," I said. "At least we know her condition is the same."

He nodded, cracked the lid of his briefcase, and pulled out some ruled sheets of paper. Using a black, government-issue ballpoint, he started writing some notes in tiny, perfectly formed handwriting.

"Draft report?" I asked.

He shrugged. "Routine crap."

Things had gone on schedule earlier in the morning.

Exerblein was there when the doctor signed my release. They had turned in my rental car and somebody had to drive me back to the Mary Mary. Collie was off somewhere cleaning up some loose ends, and would meet us at the airport.

Exerblein drove. I have endured more boring drives, but only alone, and in Kansas. Exerblein drove as if I wasn't there, and except for a preliminary comment that he was pleased I had *partially* regained my sanity, he volunteered nothing. My experience with ciphers of his magnitude was not extensive, but I had known enough of them to have a policy: if they are merely silent and boring, be grateful. So I didn't press it.

It didn't take long to throw things into my bag at the A-frame. My gold-toothed hostess expressed sadness at my departure, but cheered up when I gave her my Visa card for a final accounting. She was careful to point out to me that I was being charged for another week because she had *reserved* the cabin for me through next Friday, and could not be expected to take a financial loss just because I changed my plans. She said she deeply and sincerely appreciated my patronage and hoped I would come back soon. I thanked her with equal sincerity.

We had time to go past The Emerald, but I didn't ask Exerblein to do that. I knew Al would be there, going through his lesson spiels with desperate gaiety, and Mia would not, and Billy would not, and there would be an abandoned new-court project at the far end of the complex, and a lot of holes in the bleacher crowd where people had canceled as a result of the recent publicity. My business with Al had been concluded last night. I wasn't ready to be handed the new stock prospectus.

How it would turn out for him was anybody's guess. From what Collie had told me—if he was telling the truth—it looked like there wouldn't be any federal charges. I doubted that local authorities could make the planted dope

303

evidence stand up in court. But Al was still left with his vacant house and screaming creditors and mounting debt. Maybe he could scramble out of it. He had always been a great scrambler.

Maybe, I thought, he would keep it together until the tennis magazine published my piece about him and his resorts. I had decided I really would do the piece. Some of his outrageous boasts and colorful stories—before he started getting really drunk or began to crack the other night—had been great stuff. He was not the brightest guy in the world and he had been taken in by some really bad people and he would never be my idea of a roommate. But the interview, regardless of my original intentions in doing it, would make a dandy story and I could use the extra money. If the publicity helped him, too, I wouldn't kill myself.

We flew awhile. The cabin attendants came along with soft drinks and coffee. I took coffee. Collie got orange juice. He closed his briefcase on his draft report while sipping the canned drink.

I asked him, "Are you going to let me read any of that?"

"Are you kidding me?" he asked, offended.

"At least the part about Sylvester," I said.

He sipped his juice. Possibly his facial muscles tightened.

I pursued it: "You and the local police really kept that quiet, didn't you? I looked at the back couple of issues of the paper in my room, and there wasn't so much as a line about his body, burial or transport arrangements, anything."

"You know," Collie said, pointing across me and out the window, "it's really a lovely view out toward St. Kitts from here. I wish to hell sometime I could get a flight over there and look it over. You ever do that?"

"I was on a Puerto Rican airline flight that landed there for twenty minutes once. I *think* it was St. Kitts, anyway.

Really small and desolate, and—" I stopped myself. "Wait a minute, are you changing the subject from Sylvester purposely?"

"Shit," Collie said. "It's done with. Let's forget it."

Things tightened inside me because now I was sure he had been avoiding the subject all along. And I, like a dummy, had merely assumed.

I said, "I'd like to know when you found the body whether it looked like he died from the fall or from my gunshot. Also, did the Soviets have the gall to claim him, or did they send a ringer like they did for Pat's body, or what? And don't I stand to get some kind of a commendation or bonus or *something*? I took out a guy who was a thorn in your side for more than a decade."

He put his empty plastic cup on the pulldown shelf. "You got away with your life. You learned some really bad things about Danisa's death. But *you* got away alive. And Miss Miles will be all right. Let's just let it go at that, okay? Why beat it anymore? It's done with."

"Collie," I said. "Tell me."

"No, forget it."

"Collie."

His chest heaved. "We didn't find the body."

"Didn't find—!"

"We found the place, no question about that. You took us there, whether you remember it or not. We found the blood, the scuffle marks in the dirt, even the spent shellcases." He looked at me, the tight muscles of his face saying he didn't want to go on with this.

"And?" I prodded. I already felt sick.

"We looked for him. First we looked down the gravel slope well below the bluff, and through the brush down there. Then we saw that there's a narrow shelf that runs along under the bluff about thirty feet below the spot where he went off. Reasoning that he hit that shelf, we found a way to climb up to it. We found blood on some rocks and vegetation. Lots of blood. Footprints. No body."

"What are you telling me?" I asked hoarsely.

Splotches of anger appeared on his cheeks. "What does it sound like I'm telling you?"

"It sounds like you're telling me you blew it—I broke his face for him and shot his ass and knocked him off a cliff, and you *professionals* couldn't get out there in time to prevent someone finding his body first and stealing it from under your nose."

"I'd like to think somebody stole his body, Brad."

"Meaning what?"

"Meaning what we're afraid of is that nobody claimed a body up there. What we think happened is that he somehow survived the fall—the gunshot, too, if you really did hit him—and he managed to crawl out of there and find help."

"No," I said. "No. No way. It couldn't happen. I bashed the side of his face in. I know one of my shots hit him. He couldn't survive a fall like that. He couldn't walk away. He's not Superman!"

Collie studied me sadly. "He isn't an ordinary man, either."

"Are you telling me he got away? He's recovering someplace, in hiding, right now?"

"We've got to assume that. No body. No proof. How do we know how many other friends he had on St. Maarten?"

"Why didn't you *tell* me this?"

"Why tell you?"

"Goddamn you! You would have just let me go on, fat and happy, thinking I had gotten revenge—squared the accounts—while he was still living someplace, and maybe even thinking about getting even with *me*?"

"Long term," Collie said stolidly, "I don't know what you would have been told—"

"But short term, you just let me roast in my own stupidity!"

"I just told you, didn't I? I didn't lie about it."

I rocked back in my uncomfortable airline seat and looked out at the ocean. There were some small, medium-level clouds, a chain of tiny brown-green islands off to the east, the long white wake of a toy oceanliner. The shock vibrated inside me. Minutes passed. The attendants came back and collected glasses and cups. I sent the rancid coffee back.

Collie opened his briefcase again. He had his jaw closed tight.

I told him, "I know what he looks like."

He stared at me.

I repeated, "I know what he looks like. Nobody ever had any idea what he looked like. I can sit down with one of your artists and give you a perfect picture of him. If he did survive, you can still have a description and artist's rendition of him, and you can nail his ass."

"We'll definitely want to debrief you on that," he said.

"But?" I demanded.

"I didn't say 'but.'"

"It was there. So say it."

"Fine. I will. If it was Sylvester—"

"It was!"

"Assuming it was Sylvester, and he lives, he's still a very valuable man to them. Worth an additional investment."

I didn't get it. I waited for Collie to say more.

Then my mind turned a page and I thought I did get it after all. And almost wished I hadn't.

Collie guessed my thoughts. "He would have to have reconstructive surgery on one side of his face anyway, from what you've told us. That nose you talked about could be pared down. Maybe add a cleft in his chin, *à la* Michael Jackson. Change his eyebrow line a little, dye his hair a different color—"

"And his appearance is totally different."

"Yeah," Collie said. "Exactly."

"You're *sure* his body isn't out there someplace?"

"We're still searching the area. But no; his body isn't out there. We're just kidding ourselves with more search. He's *gone*. We have to assume he's safe, and he escaped us again."

The disappointment made me feel sick to my stomach. I reached for a cigarette and then remembered that the Calvinist witch-hunters and righteous fascists had decided I couldn't smoke on airplanes anymore. How wonderful it is to have prigs and pricks making my decisions for me in the good old American way, i.e., with a big stick.

The thought occurred to me that Sylvester—if he lived—would have me on his mind again. Sooner or later he would be back to even the score. The mistake he had made on the cliff was probably one of the few he had ever made in his professional life. Next time he would not worry about finding a likely looking accident site. My airplane—like my Danisa's airplane—would simply malfunction and fall out of the sky. Or my car would go out of control and hit a bridge abutment and burn. Or I would seem to die of a coronary, and no one would ever notice the microscopic injection hole where the air embolism had been created in me.

Curiously, fear of such an outcome felt remote. Maybe it was my father's voice again: *When the going gets tough* . . .

My father lived by that code. Then he went out one densely humid summer day to play golf, a game he loved above all things and allowed himself the time to play once a week, for four hours. He had figured it out: those four hours represented less than 3 percent of the week, and he could afford to waste that much time on something that was fun.

DROPSHOT

On the day in question he was on the No. 9 green, waiting to putt, which means he had wasted 50 percent of his allotted 3 percent for the week, assuming his foursome was playing fast enough to let him finish the scheduled eighteen holes in the projected four hours. One of his partners said to him, "I'm in your line; I'll mark." "Okay," my father said, and as his playing companion bent over to mark his ball, he heard my father fall. And that was it.

The funeral is a blur in my mind. The next time I visited my mother was in the fall. She seemed resigned and cheerful enough under, as they say, the circumstances.

On the third or fourth morning of my stay with her, however, I was reading in the living room when she started running the sweeper around me. She was a demon housekeeper, and this was normal.

What was not normal was when the sweeper suddenly shut off.

I looked up and saw her standing bent, her face twisted by the pain.

"I try to be all right," she said. "But sometimes I think, 'What if there just isn't anything after death? What if it's just all a *joke?*'" She started to say something else, but then she broke and wept, standing there, clutching the handle of the sweeper, the pain bursting out of her in ugly, coughing sobs.

I didn't know what to do. There was enough of Pop in me that I wanted desperately to *fix* this, make the pain go away, and there was a small inner rage because I couldn't, and I would have done anything if I could.

I just sat there, numbed and helpless, just the way I was sitting here now on the airplane.

My mother was a lovely, gallant lady. She could be tough as hell. She loved to laugh. The times I liked the very best were at Forest Hills and in LA when we were together, and I was breezing along in the championship bracket, and we had martinis in the bar. She loved her martinis. After two, almost anything was funny to her. I did everything but pratfalls to make her giggle. I still hear her giggle. When the Child in her came out like that, she was just the most wonderful person there ever was.

She did not go quickly like my father did. Toward the very end I went to her hospital room with my sister and she was in the hospital bed with tubes going in and a transparent oxygen mask over her face and she had been turned in the bed so that she faced away from the door, where I stopped. She was so small by then in that antiseptic hospital bed, and her hair was flattened against her head, not brushed and prepared as it always had been. She was so very tiny.

My sister went to her, around the bed, and looked down and reached out with an infinitely gentle hand and pressed her fingers against her brow, and I lacked the courage: I turned and left the room and went down a long hallway to a waiting area with sun-hot windows looking out on bright snow in the parking lot, and the tears just came.

Sitting beside Collie on the airplane, I felt ashamed of being maudlin. The more worldly wise of my friends have sometimes reminded me in the past that our job in life, after all, is to achieve and maintain some kind of sarcastic withdrawal and cynicism. Makes you "mature," don't you know, cultured, sophisticated, and acceptable to the elite of society. At the moment my losses had brought me finally to the point where I simply could not pretend anymore. I felt old. And Sylvester's escape had just robbed me of that rarest feeling—a sense of having evened something out, of having been able for once to strike back and get just a little satisfaction.

I knew one thing, however. If Sylvester ever came after me, he would need to strike first and perfectly. Because, if there was a score to settle, my side of the pad had more names on it than his. And if I ever got lucky enough to have a chance, I was going to go after him just as surely as he would come after me.

Collie scribbled some more. Time passed. I watched the clouds and the ocean. When our engine note first subtly changed, signaling the beginning of our descent, he breathed deeply and put the notepad away again and turned to me as if he had been reading my thoughts.

He said, "If he does survive, he won't look for you."

"Won't he?"

"No. You're not important enough."

"Thank you, Collie. I know I'm not important. But he might show up anyway. It's personal between us now. He might look for me, and I know I'm going to be looking for him."

"Don't be crazy. That's unprofessional."

"I *am* unprofessional. He killed Danisa. He killed her brother before that. Maybe he's killed Beth Miles. Maybe I don't have much of a chance, and I'm not going to spend the rest of my life going around the world carrying a lantern and calling his name. But I'm going to watch. If I get a chance, I'm going to kill him."

"That's crazy talk."

"There's also another guy out there I can spot. He went by Mannix. He killed Pat. I want to tell your artist about him, too. I want to find him, too."

Collie shook his head disgustedly. "Look. You helped save that computer assembly. If you hadn't done what you did—on your own and without help from anyone—it might be behind the Iron Curtain by now. You also brought about the end of one of their cute little spy-contact operations. Be proud of what you accomplished. You did it while the rest of us were sitting on our asses."

"I appreciate that, Collie. But I can't close the book on this. Sorry." I looked at my watch and added, "I can't go back to Richardson and just sit around and feel sorry for myself and make more watchbands and billfolds."

"I know that," he said. "It's just a question of what you

311

choose to do instead. You've got a lot of options now. You're a hundred percent better than you were less than a month ago, do you know that?"

"I know that."

"Then be grateful."

"I am."

"And think about Beth Miles."

"Believe me, I'm doing that."

"Won't you continue that relationship? Didn't you get along?"

"We got along, yes. I think whether it continues will depend on a couple of things. Number one, whether she lives. Number two, if she does live, what *she* thinks about continuing."

He stared hard at me. I felt the force of his friendship even before he reached across and squeezed my forearm like a vise.

He said, "Don't let it poison you."

"I won't."

"That would be as bad as when you were stuck in your grief about Danisa."

"Collie, I'm not going to let it poison me. I *am* different now. I'm better. I'm not going to retreat into self-pity again. But I'm not going to pretend it didn't happen, either."

He continued to look at me with eyes like X rays. Finally he released my arm and shrugged and looked straight to the front, folding his hands over his briefcase. "You always were a stubborn so-and-so."

"Yeah," I said, and grinned at him. And I thought, *We got 'em, Pat. But we're not through yet.*

When we landed in Miami it was raining. We went straight to the hospital. The nurse said Beth was already in surgery, had been for more than an hour.

I asked the nurse (as if she could tell me), "Is she going to be all right?"

The nurse patted my hand. "Sure she is. Why don't you just wait over there in the waiting room, and the doctor will speak to you just as soon as it's over."

I went the way she pointed and found a chair in the designated area. Collie worked on his report some more and rain streamed gray against the windows and I waited to see what next.